# STEAL THE SKY

# STEAL THE SKY

## MARINA MASSINO

ISBN (print): 979-8-9914954-2-4
ISBN (e-book): 979-8-9914954-1-7

# Dedication

This one's for me.

THE FIELDS
THE ENCLOSURES
THE ALCAZAR
DYEUS'S FORCES
THE REALM OF ROGUES
THE WALL
THE SERE
THE PLAINS
NEVOBA
FOOD STORES & AUXILIARY
THE GREAT HALL
SINGLES DWELLINGS
KITCHEN & COMMUNAL
BATHING & WATER STORES

THE RISING SEA
DYEUS
THE FARMLANDS
FAMILY DWELLINGS

# Prologue

When I was young, I didn't know this room was shaped like a womb. I played and laughed as exchanges were made from woman to woman. I taunted the farmhands and fisherman, the only men I saw regularly, who delivered our weekly rations. Their presence made everything seem fuller, bringing with them the deep scent of spice, the fresh snap of green vegetables, and the salt air of the sea on their skin. As I grew, I learned the dragon shifters, the only other men I came in close quarters with, had carved our great hall into this shape for receiving them. They placed the likenesses of the gods in alcoves high on the walls, illuminating each with skylights bored into the ceiling. All to remind us of why we're here — to serve them, so they can serve the gods.

As if it would be easy to forget as I stand here waiting, recalling all the times before the great hall was packed full of bodies. Times when the sound of a mother's ravaged cries echoed as her son was removed from her arms so that he could take his place among the dragons in the sky kingdom.

Today though, the room is silent and stagnant with the press of bodies. Today, we're gathered for the selection. Once a sun cycle, all of us newly eighteen are assessed by the Sar Dyēus, the dragon king, to become a carremai, one honored to bear their children. The old and used are sequestered outside of the hall to greet the hoard's arrival, while the young and virile wait inside, the youngest of us fading into the back of the room. Our duty has always been made clear; they serve the gods, we serve them, and they in turn protect us.

A low vibration passes through my eardrums. A stirring of the wind, the din of feet peppering the ground. A stillness rushes through the crowd as a breeze drifts in from the hall's single opening to the outside. I take that fresh air into my lungs, though most others are frozen, waiting, for what's to come through that opening next.

The cavernous space, alive with laughter and community only hours ago, is muted, the only sound the approach of careful footsteps dulled by the tightly packed room. A group of mothers acting as the hoard's escorts appear first, amid them, my mother, her eyes flitting between me and my sister, her face on the brink of cracking into an earsplitting grin. She's waited for this moment our entire lives. And I've waited my entire life to prove to her that I wasn't a mistake. Behind the mothers, their figures like shadows against the bright opening, come the Sar Dyēus, flanked by his elite hoard, and a half dozen or so eager dragon shifters trailing after.

Locking my jaw tight, I lower my head with everyone else as the Sar Dyēus comes to a halt before us. Beside me, Ninon is still as stone. On her other side, my sister Kalixta bows even lower than most. Mother taught us well. Still, I bend only low enough to conceal my eyes from his view. I will show my strength and worth in my own way. I will do the near impossible and have one of the Sar Dyēus's high ranking elites choose me.

"Rise," comes the commanding rasp of the Sar Dyēus's voice.

In unison we raise our heads, my eyes immediately drawn to his imposing figure. Though he doesn't stand much taller than any of the other shifters, nor is his form particularly broad, his hair is as white as a cloud on a sunny day. His brows are dark as night, skin smooth and pale like the moons, the angles of his face sharp as a star. He appears no older than twenty-five or so mortal years, though I know he's lived many more than that.

The Sar Dyēus's focus is some place over our heads, as if meeting our eyes isn't worth his effort.

"Proceed," he says, his timbre low.

My mother clears her throat. I see her try and fail to keep her gleeful expression contained as she gestures to my sister. "From those who've reached eighteen in the last turn, I am honored to first present Kalixta, sired by Rathon." There's a bite of hesitation as she says our father's name. After mine and Kalixta's marking ceremony as newborns, he never returned, despite my mother's hopeful prayers that he would. We heard no word of him until our fifth year, only to be notified of his death. It didn't matter much to us that he'd died, but it mattered a great deal to her. She was never quite the same after that, and I bore the brunt of her discontent.

My mother goes on with the introductions, taking the responsibility of presenting Ninon, before moving her open hands towards me. I see the tension in the set of her mouth as she prepares to introduce me—the daughter that never should have been, the daughter that ought to have been a son. "Kaisa, sired by Rathon." Her words are quick and clipped, as if my name is hardly worth mentioning.

The two other women alongside us have their mother's present them, taking care to note who sired them. It's an effort not to scowl at the mention of all these sires while our mother's names go unspoken, though today I should be grateful for it. For Ninon. Hearing Myrna's name would crack Ninon's careful facade, despite her mother's unexpected death being four years past. Myrna's passing wasn't the first unexplained death among our people, and it hasn't been the last, but it was the one that hit the three of us closest.

The introductions continue for those who were not selected in previous years' carremai ceremonies, the women returning in hopes of catching the eye of one of the new shifters here to choose a breeding mate.

There are ten of us waiting to be selected and courted by one of the attractive and noble soldiers of the gods. If selected, we'll spend half our time home in the underground caverns of Nevoba and half our time visiting Dyēus, the sky kingdom among the clouds, until we reach the child bearing age of twenty-and-one, when we're permitted to do our duty to help continue their line and ours. In exchange, the dragon shifters offer their protection from the savage rogue dragons that plague our night skies. Together, we act in service for the grace of the gods. All I want out of it is to stay by my sister and Ninon, and prove to my mother that I am not worthless.

I will do what she could not, and all her hate for me will have to fade into the background with the cries of my children upon their birth. Old words she'd sling at me haunt me in this tight packed chamber. "You'd better bear twin sons when your time comes," she would say, condemning me to a life where once my womb was empty, my arms would be too. Fine, then, if that's what it takes.

When the introductions are finalized, the Sar Dyēus steps closer to the line of us waiting to be assessed as a desirable mating partner. Ever since I can remember, I've witnessed these ceremonies take place. Only on a very rare and wild occasion is a woman marked as undesirable, so the worry of that is far in the back of my mind. As I study the horde waiting to choose a mate, all their faces blend together despite their differences. An elite is what I'm after, but as long as I can do what my mother failed to do and produce a son, that will be enough.

I tongue away a sneer forming on my lip and examine my mother's wishful expression. Her attention lingers on those she hopes will choose me or my sister. Then, my eyes snag on a handsome elite with dark skin, a wide face, and close cropped black hair, whose gaze is pinned on my sister.

The intensity of his stare, and the realization that he's the Sar Dyēus's right hand, sets me on edge.

The Sar Dyēus steps forward and hovers an open palm over Kalixta's chest. A dim, yellow light radiates from her sternum, the word "acceptable" barely out of his mouth when the elite who'd been staring at her steps out of line.

"Mine." His voice rolls through the cavernous room like a distant thunder.

The Sar Dyēus pauses, his fingers curling ever so slightly as he pulls his hand back from Kalixta, her eyes wide with shock. The king twists his head, angling it to the side to look at his elite. "Thrace?"

The elite, Thrace, seems to take some effort to hold himself back from moving any closer. His hands squeeze into fists. "Should it please you, Your Highness."

The Sar Dyēus glances back at my sister briefly before returning to his elite. They simply look at one another for a long moment before the Sar Dyēus inclines his head once.

I blink, looking between my sister and the man who claimed her as his with such force, such ease, and without her having any say at all. I know this is how it works. I've witnessed this very thing every year of my life, and yet I didn't truly understand what it would feel like until this moment, seeing it happen to my sister. Watching her get what I always vowed I would.

As the Sar Dyēus moves in front of Ninon, I can't help but watch his face, the subtle change in his expression. He seems... concerned. Or perhaps caught off guard? Of course, it's rare for an elite member of the hoard to choose a carremai. There are so few of them, after all, and many are older and have already mated at least once or twice before, but I can't see how Thrace choosing my sister would be a cause of concern. Perhaps it's required that elites notify the Sar Dyēus of their intention to mate, and Thrace had not? As I puzzle over his expression, the Sar Dyēus's hand pauses above Ninon's chest. He holds it there for a long moment before withdrawing.

"Undesirable."

I snap my head towards Ninon.

No.

We were supposed to do this together. All of us. If Ninon is undesirable, if this hinders her chance at being selected, then she'll be all alone. She has no one but us. I have no one but her. Kalixta has always been favored by our mother. After all, it wasn't Kalixta who shamed her by giving her two daughters. It was me. It wasn't only that; it was our behaviors, too. While Kalixta would obediently affix herself at mother's side, being groomed beyond necessity for her future role as a carremai, I would sneak off and avoid any and all preparation that wasn't required – and when I did, there was always Ninon. Ninon, who strangely was no twin at all, but whose mother adored me as her own.

With my focus snagged on Ninon, I don't notice the Sar Dyēus moving on to me. I don't notice his hovered hand, nor do I lower my head as I ought to. I stand transfixed by Ninon's wide eyed expression. At the relief etched on her face. Never once did I consider she might not want this. And I realize, I never once considered if *I* wanted this. It hadn't occurred to me that not wanting to become a carremai was an option. My mind whirls, dizzying me until unexpected whispers shake my attention, belatedly catching my mother hissing my name, trying to grab my attention.

Blinking, I finally turn to face him. The dragon king's dark gaze bores into me. Heat radiates across my skin as his palm hovers over my lower sternum, over the mark he gave me and has given every one of us women at birth.

I can't leave Ninon. I can't.

I won't.

My sternum burns as hot as steel in a fire. I grit my teeth. His nostrils flare and his chest heaves. The muscle in his jaw flutters and he lowers his hand.

He stares at me for a beat. Then another. The air is muffled with the tension. I don't think a single person is breathing, all of us caught in this electric silence.

Finally, firmly, the Sar Dyēus speaks. "Undesirable."

Without another word, without another look, he moves on, marking everyone else as acceptable while my ears ring with his word and the sound of my mother's weeping.

Ninon's hand slips into mine and she squeezes. I squeeze back, though it trembles violently in her grip. I look from her to my sister, whose gaze is transfixed on the elite who chose her, who will breed her...and who will leave her once she's fulfilled her duty. I wanted what she got. I prayed to the gods and willed it with my entire being and yet...I think this is the only moment of my life where I haven't envied her. A ragged breath leaves my chest.

The dragons choose their carremai, and Ninon and I are not among them.

We are undesirable.

We are unchosen.

I will not bear a son to give the sky kingdom, as I always thought I would.

And I am utterly, unreasonably relieved.

# Chapter One

## Seven Years Later

The smell of birth is not all that different from a fresh kill. That same metallic tang of blood and the deep musk of an animal's hide stains the air. The thought draws more tension to my muscles as I brace Kalixta against me. She rests her cheek on my chest, her breath skittering across my sweat-damp skin, panting, eyes wide like dying saiga I've claimed as mine. I stroke my fingers along her ribs and back, slow and soothing. Her forehead rolls from side to side. Slowly at first, then thrashing. With her teeth bared, she's as wild as the rogue dragons that haunt our night skies. She bears down to push, then stills, in much the same way a creature does in the moments leading up to their final breath. My lips press together tight at how thin that line is between life and death.

The rough-hewn birthing cavern is warm and damp and crowded. The three nursemaids, my mother, Ninon, and myself take up most of the space in the small room. The discordant sounds of Kalixta grunting and breathing through her birth mingle with the quiet reverberations of the nursemaid's melodic voices. I lock eyes with Ninon and mouth, "Blood?" not wanting to add to the cacophony as much as I don't want to alarm my sister.

Ninon's gaze darts down to where Kalixta's knees are pressed wide on the birthing mats. Her eyes narrow a fraction, discerning in the dim lamplight, and my chest tightens with her hesitation. "Fine," she murmurs back.

Fine isn't good enough. Too many mothers have lost this battle before. Not that Dyēus cares once we've bred their offspring. The three nursemaids in attendance mutter prayers to Ervosvis, seeking comfort in the deity who presides over life and death. They murmur their request to have the god's two-sided face be set as life in this moment. I have not spoken to the gods in years, but today I add my silent prayers. Today, I hope they can do more than receive our departed souls from the talons of the dragons of Dyēus.

Kalixta's hands clasp my elbows, her grip firm, but slippery with sweat. "Kaisa," she mumbles my name, twisting her face into my chest as her body coils, readying for another push.

"I'm here." I brace myself for her again. Her forehead slides down until the crown of her head presses under my breasts, where we've been given our marks of protection: a crescent moon upturned like a bowl, rays like the sun streaking out from the curved bottom with one long, vertical line slicing clean through the center of our chest bone. A promise that we are safe from rogues as long as we are underground or within the narrow boundaries of Nevoba. Though often, I'm not.

Kalixta cries out with one final push, and the nursemaids move in tandem, murmurs of encouragement and reverence passing their lips. I hold my breath, waiting, same as I do before the slice of my arrow pierces a rogue dragon's eye.

My mother presses a hand to her mouth. "A boy," she says from behind her fingers, her eyes darting briefly, unconsciously, towards mine before flickering away. Having two daughters is a bad omen, and for me, being the second, it was like having a black mark on my existence. For years, she hardly spoke a word to me after my selection ceremony. At least—until I was chosen after all, without want or warning. Then it was as if the four years she ignored me never happened.

The child is quiet as he enters the world, and my gaze locks on the woman crouched at Kalixta's opening. After a moment, we hear him, the tiny sputters and coughs marking him alive. "He's well," one of the nursemaids says. Kalixta nods, a smile wavering onto her mouth, but this is not the end of her birthing journey. She remains in position on all four of her limbs, leaning heavily against me.

"Remember, your body was made for this," another nursemaid says as I run my hand down the back of Kalixta's head. I bite my tongue against what I want to say, which is to remind her is that this isn't the only thing her body was made for.

"The next will come more easily," the third nursemaid says as she passes the baby, still wet and attached to the cord, to my mother who crouches by Kalixta's knees.

"Can I see him?" my sister asks. I steady her so she can comfortably turn to look upon her son. Her smile puts the light of the sun to shame and I turn from her to look at Ninon. A reassuring nod is all I need to know that things are progressing as they should. I stare down at my new nephew and pray again to the dormant gods that the next is a girl. I pray on silent breaths to their deaf ears that the boy stays quiet and mild before the eyes of the Sar Dyēus, that he won't be a dragon shifter like his father and my sister will get to keep him, at least for a time before he's sent to the fields.

"He's the most beautiful thing I've ever seen," Kalixta says, breath wispy and disbelieving. I hum, agreeing, a smile curling in the corner of my cheek. His complexion favors his sire, slightly darker than the pale tawny brown Kalixta and I share. Our mother looks to the nursemaids and they nod. I help Kalixta support herself back on her heels so she can hold her child for the first time.

I turn away from their tender moment and close my eyes as a fire threatens to choke me from the inside with its fierce smoke, recognizing the feeling for what it is. Destruction. The desire to tear apart those who will likely take that baby boy straight from my sister's arms. To tear apart the men who have turned their gaze from the howling and hollow mothers they take from.

I hear a breath sucked in through clenched teeth and my attention whips back to my sister. Her face is pinching and she hands the baby back to our mother.

"It's time," one of the nursemaids declares, and I take my sister back into my arms. It's not long before the sharp cry of a new child fills the chamber, the sound echoing, loud, and furious.

"A girl," Ninon announces, sighing with relief. I feel like I can breathe again. Even if the boy is a shifter, at least she will get to keep one. At least she will have something.

Kalixta leans her forehead against mine, a few strands of our straight, near black hair twining together. This close, I study her face. It's not an exact copy of mine, but close enough. Heavy hooded lids close to cover the same dark honey brown eyes as mine, my jaw and face a touch wider than hers, her cheeks softer in the hollows where mine dip in, my full upper and lower lip making me look perpetually sullen while hers hold a softer, sensual curve. Our noses are the same, though, except mine is adorned with a gold hoop pierced at my septum. A gift to myself after my eighteenth year selection ceremony.

"You did it," I whisper.

Kalixta smiles, and she opens her eyes to meet my

matching ones. I back away to let the nursemaids do their work and once my sister is arranged and settled on a set of clean mats and collection of lush pillows, the babies are placed in her arms.

I stand back with Ninon, fanning my loose cropped shirt against my sticky skin. The two of us came straight from our patrol, called in as soon as my sister went into labor, only an hour after we left for the evening. I'm still in my riding trousers, loose pants cinched tight at the ankles. My riding wrap I discarded somewhere long ago. My sister smiles down at her two babies, face glowing and serene.

My mother sidles up next to me and places her hand on my shoulder, which I loosen, trying not to bristle at her touch. "I'm so glad she's happy," my mother says.

"She certainly looks so," I say, but I wonder how she truly feels. I could ask her, but I don't want to risk her shutting me out. Not again. Not anymore.

"You will be there next," she says, nodding to where Kalixta lies, holding her children. "I'm sure of it."

I bite my tongue. "Alixor seems content to take his time," I reply, passing a sidelong glance to Ninon that says, *which is fine with me.*

If there were a god of luck, it would be against me. Four years after my presentation at eighteen, Alixor came to select a carremai. He saw me in the crowd, my face aglow post hunting victory and he wanted me. It didn't matter that the Sar Dyēus had marked me as undesirable. Alixor was an elite, and elites get what they want. Even if it goes against the king's decree, it would seem. The Sar Dyēus had only said; "If you wish to fail in your task to breed, then by all means, choose her."

I can still recall the way those words wound around my spine, sealing my fate.

I could have refused, but banishment outside our protected lands, left to the mercy of the rogues, is a terrible way to die.

By the time Alixor chose me, I'd been a huntress for years, bringing game meat home to my people and shooting rogue dragons that slipped past Dyēus's defenses. While I don't enjoy killing, the freedom and seeing the open night sky fills some of the emptiness inside of me. I was content, despite the deep, unending yearning for something...more. So I refused to give up my role as huntress after being chosen, much to my mother's great annoyance.

I slip out from under her hand. "She'll need rest, so we'll be going." I spy my riding wrap on the ground nearby and lean over to grab it up by the tips of my fingers.

"Kaisa," my mother hisses. "You can't really mean to go out. When will all that end? You're chosen now. A cohort of the gods."

The dragons are no gods. The gods are silent and absent. My teeth hurt from how hard I'm clenching them to keep the words from spilling out. Such blasphemous speech has no place in our community. "Yes. And when I've fulfilled my duty as carremai, I will have the hunts to come back to." I will not let them take more from me. And, if I have it my way, I will not have them take anything at all.

"The Sar Dyēus will be here yet. You need rest before Alixor comes with the hoard." I don't miss the displeasure in her tone.

Rest is for the cool quiet of peace and right now my heart is burning and riotous. I need to ride, to feel the wind on my face, but I don't say so. I don't give her that piece of my heart. She doesn't deserve it and she wouldn't understand it in any case. I have hope that maybe one day we can share the love I see other mothers offering their children, given time. For now though, there are wounds between the two of us that have not been tended and my hands are still not yet gentle enough to dig through the weeds without hurting the flowers. I don't offer my mother another word. "Ninon?"

"I'm with you," she says, offering my mother a small

bow as we make our leave.

"Kaisa, wait," my mother calls and I send up a silent thanks to the nursemaid who inadvertently intercepts her from coming after us to give her reassurance on Kalixta's condition. I approach my sister, donning my riding wrap even though I'm still sweltering.

"Leaving so soon?" she asks, a sleepy smile on her face.

"We can stay." I kneel beside her, tucking a strand of hair behind her ear.

"I've kept you underground long enough."

"It hasn't been that long." I don't precisely know how long, but I know I've had longer nights than this out on hunts.

"No, no. Go. I don't want to force you to stay around Mother. Besides, both of you being here will only exhaust me further."

I don't disagree. "I'll be back by the time the hoard comes and I'll stay with you at midday."

"You sleep at midday. Come in the night so I can rest."

I smile and touch my forehead to hers. "As you wish." Pulling back, my gaze falls to the boy. "Will you be well?" I don't have to say more for her to understand my meaning. I let the back of my index finger feather across his soft, round cheek.

"Thrace will care for him. And it won't be the last I see of him, either."

I can't help the worried pinch of my brow, but I do manage to stay silent.

"Ninon," Kalixta says, "my hands are full. Would you help me?"

Ninon huffs a soft laugh and reaches down to smooth the center of my brow with her finger like Kalixta usually does when my face tightens.

I stifle my grin and pull my head away, softening my features before focusing again on my sister. "He might not be a shifter."

"He will be," she says, gazing down at him, tone resolute. Even I can't deny that she's right. I want to say more, to tell her not to expect so much of Thrace, the sire of her children, elite shifter, and, as far as anyone can tell, the Sar Dyēus's closest confidant. I don't want her suffering a broken heart like our mother. I don't want her turning into a husk of a person without his presence. Being with her for the term of her pregnancy helped us heal some of our past wounds of my own making when I'd battled the confusing bout of jealousy I had when she was chosen. I won't lose her again with a set of careless words. Not when, in the end, she will lose Thrace and the boy in her arms, too. I vow to be here for her when it happens.

I press a lingering kiss to her forehead. She tastes of salt, the smell of birth still heavy around her, grounding me.

"Rest," I tell her.

"Run wild," she says in return, bringing the sharp sting of tears to my eyes.

Ninon and I leave the birthing chamber and begin winding our way through the labyrinthine caverns of our home. The network of interconnecting tunnels is a result of an underground river long since dried out. Above us lies a barren, rock-strewn surface that goes on for miles and miles until the sea. Ninon's never seen it, that wide, unending expanse of blue, but when I go to Dyēus, the kingdom in the sky where all the dragon shifters live, I see it. I've stared at the sea for hours and hours until my eyes burn. I want Ninon to see it someday. I want to take her there.

"Where are you?" Ninon asks, breaking my reverie.

I scowl, not wanting to share a wish that I can't give her. "Leaving all this behind," I answer, giving a variation of the truth.

"Would you?" she asks, an uncharacteristic high note seeping through her usual calm monotone.

I frown. Where is there to go? The sea is impossible. According to the fishermen, the boats they use can only go so far before the rough waves destroy the vessels. Attempting to cross the mountains to places unknown is a death sentence unto itself with its impassible jagged peaks. Human men from the lands beyond have made it over to our side, but once they crest over into Dyēus's territory, the dragons take them to the farmlands, so even if there is a path, there's none on ours. The only place left is the Realm, which is no choice at all. Though we've heard quiet rumors of some of our people leaving here to venture into the mists. I'm not certain of the point in that – once you enter, you become the very beasts we slay.

Ninon seems to anticipate what I'm thinking. "That is, if there were a secure way to get to someplace safe."

"Do you know something?" I ask, quirking a brow.

A smirk tips her lips. "I know many things." I laugh, knowing all too well how right she is. "You haven't answered my question, though. Would you?"

A sigh drops my shoulders, and even before the words leave my mouth, my head is shaking. "Kalixta would never leave here, especially now that her son will go to Dyēus. And I can't leave her."

Ninon nods, slow, thoughtful. I drop my head, trying to catch her eye as suspicion creeps up my spine. "Would you?"

She looks to me, her eyes containing a certain desperation that has my heart racing. *Don't leave me*, I want to say. *Where would you go?* She opens her mouth, but then we hear a sob, followed by the low reverberation of voices ahead and we're both on alert.

"Why?" The echo carries to us as more words tumble down the cavern. "Why does this keep happening?" Ninon and I pick up our pace until we round a corner, hearing the next part of the conversation more clearly as they come into view. I recognize them as two of the older carremai who've already completed their duty, their daughters around eight or nine years of age, both their sons admitted into Dyēus as dragon shifters.

"And during a birth," Antir replies, her voice stronger and steadier.

The first speaker, Massa, says, "I wonder if the healers know anything yet."

"With what little help they get, of course not," Antir says with a note of disgust. Massa shushes her, eyes casting around until they land on us. I don't think I imagine her relief that she sees us instead of one of the more outwardly devout carremai. "That's two of us in as many months," Antir goes on without concern.

My heart skips a beat. They're talking of another death—random and unexplained. There's no reason why these women, for the most part healthy and young, should die in their sleep or on their feet, without any warning.

I start toward them, ready to ask questions, but Ninon stays me with a hand to my wrist. "We're running out of time."

She's right. Alixor has waited to call on me, but as much as I hate to admit, it won't be long now. My hand forms a fist as Antir meets my gaze. In her eyes I see the same fire, the same frustration I often see in my own. Ninon tugs me down the hall that leads to the stables, her touch relaxing my fist.

As we near the end of the corridor, the musty odor of the stables greets my nose, the alluring tickle of the open air just beyond that. "We'll make it back in time? Before the hoard comes?"

Ninon enters the open stables and goes to her horse while I tend to mine, a lively and somewhat difficult mare I call Aspa. When I was young, I once asked why the horses simply stayed when there was nothing tethering them in place. Wouldn't they run free, if they could? I knew what I would do. My instructor's response was a simple truth, but something about what she said struck a chord within me. "Why would they leave? They have food. Safety. Comfort.

And, they know as well as we do the dangers that lurk beyond."

Why then did my mare's joy run through my very soul when we were out riding with the open sky above and fresh air filling our lungs? Or, maybe that was my own joy, and my mare was content to stay underground, hidden and safe.

Ninon swings herself onto her saddle. "It doesn't matter." She faces the cavern entrance, the darkness carrying a deep violet that suggests morning will soon arrive. "It has to be tonight."

I mount Aspa, and a vibration courses through my veins. I shake it off, attributing it to my readiness to ride, to feel the wind tear through my hair and pull tears from my eyes. It has nothing to do with Ninon's words, the definitiveness with which she says them. Or that far off look in her eyes that's strange, even for her.

"It will take three days to brew," she goes on, "and I'm not certain Alixor is willing to wait even that long."

I lift my chin and we guide the horses out into the waning night. "We'll get what we need and when Alixor fails to impregnate me, I'll come home and we'll be back together, on these horses, doing as we've always done."

Ninon's fingers tighten on her horse's reigns. Mine tighten on Aspa's and as one, we spur our horses on. Hooves pound the ground underfoot, louder and faster as we gain speed. And together, we fly.

# Chapter Two

The air outside Nevoba's concealed caverns is cool and fresh. The knee-high yellow grass is awash in the blue of night, hissing softly against my horse's powerful legs, the only sound in these final hours before dawn. The twin moons are thick crescents tonight, hanging low and bright, and on the other side of the sky just above Dyēus are two hazy opaque ovals that we call the gods eyes.

Past the plains surrounding our underground home, the barren wastes of the Sere yawn wide ahead, the flatness interrupted by occasional rock arches and monoliths jutting up out of the ground. Far away to the west sit the hazy mountains that blockade us from the world beyond where the common humans reign. To the east, the Sere goes on and on, all the way to the dark coast of the Rising Sea. Above the Sere, along the edge of the coast, floats the islands of

Dyēus, a lush, green paradise with waterfalls that drench the ground below, nourishing the farmlands that feed our people and trickling into the river that serves Nevoba.

Clouds of dust churn behind us as we gallop into the Sere, dodging stones and ruts that we know like the backs of our hands. By day, the Sere is hot, dry and arid, but in this transition between night and day, moisture has managed to manifest itself into the air. I relish the tiny beads of water that cling to my cheeks and thread through my hair. My hands are slick with sweat as I cling to Aspa, pushing her as fast as I dare. Her hoof falls thrum through my muscle and bone and I don't know where my heartbeat ends and the rhythm of her stride begins. Beside me, Ninon looks as free and joyous as I feel, a small, rare smile gracing the corner of her mouth. It almost makes me forget the strangeness I felt from her earlier.

Ninon guides us to the west, giving a wide berth around our hunting outposts to avoid encountering our fellow huntresses. Ninon and I are the only two people who can know what we're attempting to do.

From the outposts, we can barely see the mists that veil the Realm of Rogues. Sometimes at night, we hear the rogues' wild, angry shrieks. When I was a young huntress, it terrified me and haunted my restless daytime sleep. But now, only when they're overhead, close enough that the sound of them is so shrill it can make your ears bleed, do I have any fear. Our hunts rarely end in bloodshed of a rogue—less than twenty in a sun cycle. A testament to how well the dragons of Dyēus do their duty to protect us, I suppose, leaving us free to hunt for game in relative peace.

The sky is growing ever lighter as dawn nears breaking. We edge ourselves towards the mountains and closer to the Realm than either of us has ever been. I wonder if we will see it more clearly as dawn rises or if the mists that shield it from view will appear as thick and impenetrable as ever.

In Ninon's books, the last ingredient we need for my

contraceptive is a small flower that grows in cracks at the base of the mountainside. The flower only blooms as the first morning light skitters across the ground, reaching them deep within the rock that protects them from the harsh elements of the Sere. She's always simply referred to it as "the flower."

"Does this finnicky flower of yours have a name?" I ask as Ninon slows us to a trot once we reach the mountains' base. To the north looms the mists of the Realm of Rogues, their shrieking calls few and far between, but still there, reminding us of the danger.

Ninon hesitates. When she speaks, her voice is a barely above a whisper, as if she were worried the sky itself were listening. "Dracduat. More commonly known as dragonsbane."

My hold on Aspa tightens and she stops in her tracks. If Ninon were the type to crack a joke, I'd think it was one. I've heard of it before—we all have. *Dragon's death.* A fabled herb that's said to poison a dragon so that his blood runs free from his veins and detaches his godly soul from his body. She understands my silence better than any words.

"It's the only way." She's already taking her horse toward the sharp, jagged rocks. "With the petals intact, it's a powerful healing herb. There's no risk to you. I'll make sure of it."

"Ninon," I begin, a warning in my tone. I don't want to die, but that's not why there's a protest on the tip on my tongue. I tie Aspa to the rocks, winding the rope carefully around the jagged edges. Even if I could leave, seeing the mountains so close serves as a reminder that I shouldn't dare attempt to cross them. Each rise looks like a set of sharp teeth waiting to shred trespassers apart. "I shouldn't let you do this. What if the dragons find out you have it?" I shudder to think of what would happen if Alixor discovered I used something like this, but I fear more for Ninon than myself.

She's already tried, on several occasions, to collect the flower, but shorter than me, she's never been able to reach it in time. I accompanied her on her last venture and my reach was long enough, but my timing poor. I grasped it too late, the petals falling from the plant, useless, our time wasted.

"They won't." Her tone is abrupt and resolute. Then she beckons me over to where she's already identified a place where the flowers will bloom. "Can you reach these?"

I stare at her, my mind teetering back and forth on what I should do, but we've come this far, and I don't want to fall pregnant. I lean sideways and stick my left arm into the crevice, my vantage point on the horizon where the sun will rise beyond the mists of the Realm. Above me the stars have all but disappeared, the sky more light than dark now. It's a tight fit, but my fingers brush the soft, velvety leaves and bristled stems. "Yes."

"You'll need to move your body this way or you'll block the light," she says, and I feel her hands on my waist, guiding me back and to one side. I suck in a breath as a jagged rock bites into the skin of my upper arm through my riding wrap, threatening to latch on tight and keep me.

"Are you hurt?" Her face comes into view above me.

"The rock is cutting into me a bit, but," I adjust, making sure I can free my arm when it's time, "it's not as painful as childbirth seems." I crack a smile and Ninon shakes her head.

"Now we wait for—" Her words are cut off by a thunderous screech ripping through the early, silent morning. The glimmer of dawn is still not strong enough to chase away the rogues and we're close to their territory.

My arm still deep in the crevice, I search the skies for a dark figure while I beg the sun to rise. "Come on," I say through gritted teeth, even as my heart leaps in my throat. A moment later, the screech rends the air again, and out of the corner of my eye, I see it.

A dragon. A rogue.

"Ninon."

"I'm on it." I hear her quick footsteps fall away from me, probably heading to her horse to get her bow and arrows. The dragon's form draws nearer. An erratic flight path, a long serpentine body thrashing like a snake in hot sand, wings beating in uneven tempos. A sure sign that this isn't one of Dyēus's dragons. It's so close that I can see the shape of its head and its open maw full of sharp white teeth.

The descending dragon buffets the wind, whipping my hair, sending pebbles skittering and dust billowing. Aspa whinnies and snorts behind me. The very ground shakes as the great beast lands at the base of the mountain, scarcely ten yards away, its long body poised like a viper ready to strike, black scales swallowing the light. It's not blocking where the sun will rise, and it's not within range to land a blow with that attack, so I hold my position and wait for Ninon, heart pounding in my throat.

As the sun's upper crest appears beyond the horizon, Ninon comes into my peripheral. Glimmers of light reach us, glinting off the rogue's scales and the tip of Ninon's pointed arrow. I feel the flower unfurl at my fingertips as the sun enters the crevice and I snatch up the flowers, ripping my arm free and standing tall as the beast lowers his head towards us. In a transformation I've seen countless times before, the beast is enveloped in a churning twist of clouds, though the air surrounding us stays steady with the winds of the Sere. As the vapor clears, the dragon is suddenly in male human form. I step back, snapping my head around to look at Ninon, a question on my lips. Ninon holds her fire, and for good reason. Rogues don't shift. But I don't recognize him as a dragon of Dyēus, either. I analyze his clothes: an open robe, fine in its making, loose and white, and wide-legged pants tied neatly around his waist. Not what the dragons of Dyēus wear. Locks of wavy, midnight black hair shine copper in the rising sun, the ends brushing against his bare chest and across his temples. The sunlight catches on the tanned skin of his high cheekbones, a small, round mark resting just under the outside corner of his left eye. His elongated jaw line squares off at his chin, giving him a regal air. He's so close that I can see the golden color of his eyes—eyes that are locked on mine.

I hold my breath, waiting. He glances down to where my fingers clutch the flowers before returning to my face. A small, crooked grin slides into place, showing the whites of his teeth. Every muscle in my body tenses. He knows what I hold in my hand. He opens his mouth, and I wait for him to say something, to roar at me, curse me, anything, but in the distance another screech fills the air, and he turns his attention to the sky. All the while, Ninon keeps her bow drawn. Her arms must be in agony.

I tighten my hold on the flowers and step forward, intent on demanding answers. "Who—" but before I can get another word out, he transforms back. I startle, but Ninon holds her position, keeping her arrow trained on him. The beast launches himself skyward, swimming gracefully through the air as if he were a fish in water, wings smooth and steady.

"Did I imagine..." I trail off, now unsure of what I saw.

Finally, Ninon lowers her weapon. "No," she says as we watch the dragon fly, not towards Dyēus, but into the Realm of Rogues. "He was flying like a rogue."

We watch the dragon until he disappears into the mists. "He shifted," I murmur, finally looking back at Ninon when the dragon is fully out of view. "A rogue can't shift."

"We've been told many things about the rogues and their Realm." She finally meets my gaze. "We both know that there are always more questions than we have answers."

Unease sends chills down my back. I suddenly have a terrible feeling that I know where Ninon might go if she did leave. I swallow hard and push the thought aside. She wouldn't. The first lesson we learned as children about the outside world is that if we ever entered the Realm, we'd turn into mindless, bloodthirsty creatures. Ninon is the smartest person I know. She would never. Not unless she had a good, logical reason. And as wild as that rogue appeared before the light of the day hit his scales, what came after may have just given her the good, logical reason she'd need.

Another series of trills echoes over the landscape, snagging my attention. "The hoard," I gasp, reality crashing back down on me. "We have to get back."

Ninon moves then, grasping my hand in hers. "Did you get them?"

I nod and open my fingers. A collection of five petaled flowers with squared off ends, pink in the center, fading to purple on the edges, pinned at the base by a thick, round receptacle.

Her shoulders loosen and she nods, dropping her head in relief. "Good. Good." From her waist pack, she procures a rigid box and I place the blossoms inside. "Let's go."

We ride hard and fast back home. I run soothing hands along Aspa's neck as her mouth froths with effort. We make it to the grassy plains, heading for the western stable entrance as we track the hoard descending towards the main entrance on the eastern side of Nevoba. Here the river that hails from one of Dyēus islands ends and streams down into the caverns by the great hall where the fresh water flows down into the lower chambers, filling the bathing room at the lowest sector while channels of aqueducts throughout Nevoba carry the water to the kitchens and washing stations. At the head of the hoard is a brilliant dragon, all white from the tip of his nose to the tuft of fur at the end of his tail, save for a single scale at the center of his chest that glistens as black as night. The Sar Dyēus. I think I spot Alixor's copper figure among them, somewhere in the middle of the hoard, before we disappear into the stables.

The long entrance is lined with carvings inset in the

walls, depicting the two-faced gods on one side and dragons on the other. Though not nearly as ornate as the ones lining the great hall, they are equally detailed in their renderings, the twin faces of each deity staring at us as we enter. Eratex, of time and existence. Erovosvis, of life and death. Erenmaag, of fate and agency. Eriratem, of nature and contrivance. And finally, Erpaceox, of peace and chaos. Each exists within one body like a serpent, the head divided into two faces, looking opposite one another. They each have a set horns like the dragon shifters, but oriented at unnatural angles to signify that which they represent.

We waste no time dismounting our horses, and they break away from us to where their water runs fresh and clear. I consider skipping getting cleaned up and going straight to the great hall, but Ninon is ahead of me and I follow her lead towards our rooms. The bed chambers are empty; all able-bodied women already at the great hall to welcome the hoard.

"I'll meet you out here," I say, barreling through the beaded curtains into my chamber.

"No," Ninon says, following me inside and grabbing my brush. "I need to get started on your tincture. I'll help you get ready."

I'm already stripping my clothing and don't bother stopping. "Ninon, no. You'll get in trouble." I leave my clothes where they lay on the ground.

Ninon's attention remains pinned on my discarded pants, shirt, and jacket for a long moment. "No one will notice me gone."

"I will notice," I argue, dipping a cloth into a bowl of water to wipe the dust from my face and neck. She's right, though. Aside from me, it's only Kalixta and my mother who would care. Ninon's mother died many years ago, one of the first who'd died without warning or reason. Even before her mother died, Ninon was unusual. Quiet and often on her own, reading tomes she found or organizing collections of stones and herbs she decided were of importance to her. After her mother passed, the few women who had given her the time of day suddenly stopped. I'd hear rumors, the fear of sudden death simply by association. It angered me as much then as it does now. Ninon is a treasure and anyone who doesn't see that is a complete fool.

I grab a set of gauzy finery from my shelves and Ninon intercepts me to swipe a bit of kohl under my eyes and across my lashes, forcing me still. "It's better that they don't notice I'm gone, so try not to make it too obvious I'm not affixed to your side."

"Who will be there to glare at Alixor when I have to pretend to adore him?" I ask, shaking out my skirt when she moves to start on the other eye. When she finishes that, I tie the skirt around my waist, the fabric light and airy across my bare legs, high slits on both sides of my thighs.

"Kalixta does a fine job of that," she says as she smudges some rouge onto my lips and cheeks. I loop my top around my neck and across my breasts in the simplest, yet securest way, leaving my mark almost completely exposed. Ninon pushes me down to a sitting position, quickly untying the cord wrapped around my hair and gently running a brush through my tangled strands. "Better. We don't have time for more than that. Now go."

As I rise, I place a kiss high on her cheek. "I'll come find you after."

I'm leaving the room when her hand wraps around my wrist. "Whatever you do, don't let him take you today. We've worked too hard to get this point. We need three days," she reminds me.

"We'll have three days," I promise, squeezing her hand over top of my wrist, but it's a long moment before she finally lets go.

As I race down the halls, I wonder if there was something else she wanted to say.

# Chapter Three

I slide into the back of the great hall, the space packed full of nearly three hundred women, adults and children alike. Skimming along the worn, smooth wall, I make my way towards the front where my mother, Kalixta, and her babies are already meeting the hoard. Sunlight trickles in from irregular natural openings in the ceiling, each one sealed shut with glass, the color casting a pale purple glow like twilight. High along the wall, metal sconces lit with fire mimic the setting sun. It's as if the great hall is attempting to replicate every color the sky has to offer, and though beautiful, it fails to bring the same feeling as seeing the real thing.

The quiet anticipation is heavy. The women along the edge of the gathering allow me through. Some offer light touches to my shoulder in encouragement, while others look away with disdain. My mother isn't the only one who disapproves of me continuing the hunts now that I'm a car-remai. Each movement I make creates a ripple through the crowd and any chance I had at going unnoticed is lost. I feel the eyes of every member of the Sar Dyēus's elite hoard on me as I make my way towards the center. When I'm near enough, I place my hand on Kalixta's elbow and she wordlessly moves to make space for me to stand at her side. The tension of the crowd presses on me, but still I lean in to place a kiss high on her cheek, my fingers lightly grasping my nephew's toes as he sleeps in my sister's arms. On her other side, my mother holds my niece. Only after I greet my sister do I turn to the hoard.

Standing in a V formation near the sloped opening to the caverns are thirteen men, each beautiful and ethereal, all unique in their own ways. However, it's the Sar Dyēus, front and center, who never fails to steal my breath. His hair is the color of a solitary cloud on a clear blue day. His skin is as pale as the polished alabaster walls lining the underground fortress we call home. His dark eyes, the color unreadable in this low light, are pinned to me, his dark brows and stoic expression giving no insight to what he may be thinking or feeling. He doesn't look a day older than he did on my eighteenth year presentation. He and all shifters, are granted with long life and ever-lasting youth, with skin smooth and unmarred by time. Even the oldest among the hoard appears no older than forty years. I finally offer a bow in acknowledgement of his presence, my eyes staying trained on him until the very last moment. Even then, my gaze stays on his hands, watching them flex before relaxing at his side. After a moment I rise, his stare holding mine for less than a shallow breath's time before focusing on Kalixta and my nephew.

Silence permeates the air. Beside me, Kalixta remains completely still. Her eyes are trained on Thrace, the sire to her children, to the immediate left of the Sar Dyēus. Her expression is strained, her skin pale and dewy. She shouldn't be on her feet like this mere hours after giving birth. This is the way it has always been though, for as long as I can remember. A woman gives birth. The hoard comes. The Sar Dyēus marks the girl and takes the boy. Flames fan in my chest so fast and swift I want to scream.

Thrace is the picture of a perfect breeding partner. His eyes hold tenderness. Love, even. I've always enjoyed the interactions I've had with him during my visits to Dyēus, but that's natural. All shifters are pleasant and amicable. The longer I stare, though, the more I notice. There's an underlying emotion on his face, a tension. Worry? I look back and forth between him and my sister, and finally see Kalixta's lips are pulled tight in a thin line.

I clench my jaw and put my arm around her waist and after a beat her weight sags against me, a sigh escaping her lips. My mother shoots me a look, brows drawn tight together, but smooths when she sees the paleness of my sister's face. Thrace seems to relax a little.

Standing to the right of the Sar Dyēus is Alixor's father, Selnor, an almost untraceable sneer raising his lip at the display. I wish I could slap that expression from his face. The Sar Dyēus doesn't comment though, so the hoard remains silent. Behind Selnor stands Alixor, who offers me a wry smile that I don't return, since I'm certain that baring my teeth at him wouldn't do anything except satisfy my anger.

The soft thrum of the Sar Dyēus's voice breaks the silence. "What are we to claim and defend?"

My mother clears her throat and I'm grateful for her speaking on Kalixta's behalf. "A daughter—" she says, then proudly, beaming, as if having her daughter give up her child is nothing, "and a son, Your Highness."

"A female to continue hosting our mighty bloodlines and a male, who we hope will be granted with the gift," Selnor announces, loud enough for the whole gathering to hear. Even though his words are meant to honor us, they sound hollow in my ears, bland and bleak.

The Sar Dyēus doesn't comment. He simply holds out his hands. "The female."

My mother takes a step forward, and Thrace meets her, taking his daughter into his arms for the first time. For most of the dragons, it's the only time they hold their daughters. Some come again, visiting during the postpartum period. But after a few weeks, even that stops. Thrace gazes down at his daughter, a fond smile gracing his lips. His face was meant for smiling. His broad mouth and lines by his eyes brighten everything about him. For all of my grievances against the way things are, I'm glad he chose my sister. I sense he will be one of the ones who comes again. Perhaps for another brood, as is sometimes—though very rarely— the case.

Thrace places the baby in the Sar Dyēus's arms, grasping his forearm once the child is settled. There's a quick exchange as they meet each other's eyes, fleeting, but tense. I cast a glance around to see if anyone else noticed. Everyone seems as usual, somewhere between serene acceptance and strain at what's to come next, except Antir, who outwardly frowns.

Then, Thrace steps back while the Sar Dyēus works. The king handles her delicately, but without affection. He's done this hundreds of times in his long life and will continue to do so long after I'm gone. His voice is a soothing drone through the chamber. "Daughter of the hunters, females of the earth, as your sovereign king of the sky and all that lies beneath and above, you shall be blessed with protection from the rogues, and all that threaten your lands, hence forth from this day." Adjusting her so that she lies flat against his forearm, head cradled in his palm, he presses the pointer finger of his other hand to the bottom of her chest bone. My niece wails a short, sharp cry, and it's over. The Sar Dyēus gives her back to Thrace. He takes his time soothing her, shushing her, and startlingly, placing a kiss to the top of her head. Her cries are quieter now, and he carefully hands her back to my mother, her small fluttering chest now marked with the sigil.

"Now the male," the Sar Dyēus says, his focus solely on Kalixta.

I feel her clutch the boy to her, and I tighten my hold on her in response. What would happen if she said no? A part of me wants her to. A part of me wants to rear up and defend her choice to my last breath. My mother murmurs something to her so soft I can't hear the words, and my sister gives a faint shake of her head. Thrace's face is drawn tight. He's probably hoping she won't be indecorous. I catch Selnor narrow his eyes. After a moment, Thrace approaches Kalixta, and her body softens in my arms at his approach. I let her go as she straightens to move toward him. Before she can even take a step, he's there in front of her.

"Kali," he whispers as he tucks a strand of hair behind her ear.

Silence is required in the hoard's presence, but the air shifts as the women around us take in sharp breaths, the sound of women holding their tongues. Such displays of affection outside of our visits to Dyēus are uncommon.

Kalixta's lips tremble, her eyes glassy as she looks at him. They hold each other's gaze for so long I wonder if the Sar Dyēus will say something, but when I look to him, his attention is on me. I lift my chin, daring him to stop this moment. Daring him to rush my sister into giving up her child when he will get to keep him for his own use for centuries. Movement at my side finally breaks my concentration, the feel of Kalixta leaning on me again. Thrace brings my nephew to the Sar Dyēus, and he's so intent on Thrace and the child, that I wonder for a moment if I imagined our entire exchange.

The Sar Dyēus holds my nephew's head in the palm of his hand, the rest of his small body stretched lengthwise down his forearm, tiny feet pressing lightly into the tailored white jacket covering his bicep. The Sar Dyēus places a hand over the baby's chest, illuminating the truth lying in my nephew's bones. My chest is wound tight, waiting for the words that will either take him to Dyēus as a shifter, or send him to the farm fields when he turns five.

"He is strong, this one, but—" he pauses, the quiet so thin you could hear the fall of a feather. Then a faint tick at the corner of the Sar Dyēus's mouth. A smile? "He is strong-willed, too. We welcome this new shifter into our midst." The Sar Dyēus turns, placing the child in Thrace's arms. By the grand smile gracing Thrace's strong, handsome face, he's thrilled. Of course he is—he's proved to the hoard he's capable of producing one of their own. Whatever status he has will only grow stronger from here. In my arms, Kalixta begins to shake, her hands balled into fists, pressing into her chest.

"Peace and security has been granted to these new lives," Selnor announces. "Now, to the skies."

My sister blinks, looking from where Thrace holds her child, back to the Sar Dyēus. In a flash her face changes, panic swelling. "No. No—please. Not yet."

"Be still, Kalixta," my mother hushes, tugging her back by the shoulder.

The Sar Dyēus looks at my sister with a soft expression. "You have done well. As is custom, you'll visit him when Thrace calls for you."

"Only until he's three," I hiss. The quiet words leave me so fast that I don't have time to think to stop them. Kalixta hears me and her fingers find my wrist. My mother hears me and snaps her head to me, aghast. And the whole elite hoard hears me, too.

Alixor's tan face pales. The Sar Dyēus tilts his head, a piece of his perfectly swept-back hair falling to the side with the motion. "Indeed. By then he will have had his first shift. Any distractions would be dire for him, and those around him. You would not wish harm to befall your nephew? Your sister? Now would you..." he pauses, his mouth forming a word, and for a moment, I think he's going to say my name, as if he knows it, but then he turns his head vaguely in Alixor's direction. "What is her name?"

"Kaisa," Alixor provides, but his voice comes out clipped. Tense.

"Kaisa," the Sar Dyēus sighs. I have to physically force myself not to shiver at the sound of my name on his lips. "Above all, it is my duty to keep your people safe. I will not let harm befall your sister. See that you behave yourself." Beside me, Kalixta tenses, and my eyes brim hot with anger. He straightens his head, once again becoming the great, unruffled leader, his attention finally drifting from me to his hoard. "Let us depart."

Together the hoard stamps their left foot, then their right, looking for the world like tantruming children. As one, the hoard turns, exiting the great hall and marching up the ramp that leads outside. Kalixta watches Thrace leave with her son, chest rising and falling quickly as if she ran across the whole of the Sere. My mother whispers to her, lifting the girl child towards her arms, trying to remind her of the living, breathing thing before her.

Many women follow to bear witness to the new shifter child ascend to the sky kingdom. The mother is traditionally encouraged to stay inside while the hoard departs with the male. I suspect it's so they don't have to hear her heartbreak. I press a hard kiss to Kalixta's temple, once, twice, and follow the hoard out. Perhaps it makes me a coward, too, but I cannot stand to watch her suffering right now. I will return for her, but now—now there is nothing to do except witness her child being taken. The realization will set in for her later, and when she rages, when she cries, when she's broken and struggling to pick up the pieces—that's when I'll be there.

Either way, I don't have a choice in the matter. I go because I am carremai to one of the hoard. I fall into step beside Alixor, doing my duty to accompany him as he makes his leave. He takes me by the arm. I close my eyes, tamping down the rage roiling in my chest.

Outside, the day is clear and bright, filled with the song of a soft wind. Alixor leans in and places a chaste kiss on my cheek. "Was that you I saw riding back at the break of dawn?" he asks.

My heart slows. This dance with him I can handle. It is familiar and methodic and predictable. Controllable. "Well, you know me," I offer. He doesn't, of course. Only the parts I've allowed him to know. He preens with pride.

"Who was with you?"

Having grown up with my mother, I know displeasure in a tone when I hear it, so I assume his question comes from a place of curiosity. He's not shown me anything but respect, admiration, and certainly desire. If I was a woman who wanted to breed with one of the shifters of Dyēus, I'd be happy to have a dragon such as Alixor choose me as his carremai. Unfortunately, I'm not. And, unfortunately for Alixor, he's made the wrong choice in me.

"One of the other huntresses," I say offhand, not wanting to speak with him about my closest friend. "We had a good opportunity and couldn't pass it up."

"You succeeded then?"

I twist my mouth to the side, attempting to hide my pleasure. "It's a start to a good thing."

"Well. They'll have to continue on their own," he says, stopping to cup my cheeks in his palms. "I think it's time for you to come and stay for a while."

I was expecting this, but I still feel a shock radiate through me. I hold myself still, fighting the urge to pull out of his grasp. "Today?"

"It certainly is as good a time as any."

"But my sister," I start to say as his hands trail down my face to my neck, his thumbs resting on my collar bones. "She needs me."

"Then I shall come for you tomorrow."

I shake my head, resisting the desire to step back. "I'll need a week, I think."

He leans in, whispering against my ear as his thumbs run delicate lines along my throat. "Surely you won't have me wait quite that long? Seeing you with your sister's children has me wanting."

My heartbeat threatens to choke me, and I hate the small feeling of physical desire unfurl inside of me at his hands and his words. He is attractive, and he's been kind. We've done physically intimate things I've enjoyed, but I need those three days before anything further can happen consistently. Despite everything I know about my cycle and when I'm most likely to conceive, once I'm in Dyēus for breeding, I won't be able to deny him. I need the three days. I need the contraceptive ready before I go anywhere. I take in a shuddering breath.

"I know you're nervous, but seeing how well your sister did, I cannot wait a moment longer." He stares into my eyes, and I bide my time, letting him hang on to the anticipation, letting him feel like he's won something when I finally speak.

"Three days," I say, my voice quiet. Meek. Then I add, "Please."

He scans my face, gaze hot and hungry. "I can grant that, but I won't much like the wait."

I lean in, to him and to the physical desire, a feeling I've worked to my advantage to make sure he doesn't suspect anything. "I'll make it worth your while."

"I trust that you will," he murmurs in my ear.

I instinctively raise my shoulder to shrug off his closeness, but turn it into a coy gesture, looking away and over my shoulder. The Sar Dyēus is watching us—me. Again. I curse my bold actions earlier in the great hall. The last thing I need is the king of the skies giving me his notice.

"Three days," Alixor says, drawing my eyes back to him. "Then I will come for you." It is a promise and a sentence to a life I have no choice in living. He kisses my cheek once more, lips lingering against my skin before he moves away to join his father.

I find Thrace a little way past the others, and he nods at me to join him. He places the boy in my arms, and I hold him tight to me, a thought of darting away into the underground fortress coming and going within a blink.

"He's safe with me," Thrace assures.

"Kalixta seems to think so," I say, placing my nose against the child's head, inhaling in his newborn scent.

Thrace's expression is soft as he watches me. "She's a smart woman."

"She is more than that," I say, my tone a warning. I don't welcome his vapid description of my sister to placate my feelings or hers, should he think I'll run to tell her what he's said.

"I know. For me, she is everything."

I frown, looking for the lie in his face but find only sincerity. Then the hoard begins shifting around us in a maelstrom of swirling vapor. Men's bodies settle into serpentine beasts with colorful manes and sharp claws and brutal teeth, the fans of their wings tucked tightly to their sides. Thrace runs his thumb down his son's cheek once more. "Take care of her while you can," he says, gaze flickering to somewhere over my shoulder. "But I think I'll be seeing you soon." He steps back before he shifts, too. In his dragon form, sitting back on his haunches, I come up to his shoulder, his height about twenty hands tall.

Another woman comes to Thrace, securing a linen cradle around his neck and shoulders like a harness so that the child will rest against his heart, the soft fabric protecting the baby's delicate skin from the stone-hard scales. When that's done, she gestures for me to place the child inside. After a beat, I carefully tuck him in, adjusting the cloth over his small frame. Thrace holds one of his large taloned hands over the babe, creating a cage with his claws for additional security. The sight does not soothe me. It enrages me more and more until I cannot breathe.

Without warning, or after some silent command among them, the hoard bursts skyward, their bodies twisting and twirling towards Dyēus. As I watch, the only thought in my head is how desperately I want to pull back arrow after arrow and shoot each one of them down to the ground.

# Chapter Four

My sister does not rage. She does not weep. She does not do much of anything at all, but eat when told, and nurse when the girl child cries. Kalixta supported me in sending my mother away, letting me be the one to help during this time while I can. Truthfully, my mother could have stayed. There's room enough. But I wanted Kalixta and my niece all to myself. I don't know how long I'll be gone and I want to help while I can. So, I sleep while Kalixta and the baby do. I wake when the girl cries, stroking her back as she latches on to her mother's breast. When that does not soothe her, I change her wet napkins, and when that's settled and still she cries, I rock her and cry with her out in the cavernous halls where her howls won't reach my sister's ears, giving her the rest she desperately needs. While my sister sleeps and the baby is quiet, I whisper words of strength and resilience to them both. Hope and love.

It is not until the early morning hours on the day before Alixor is to come, while both Kalixta and the baby are deep in sleep that I seek out Ninon. I carry a candle with me through the darkened halls, the lamplight dim along the smooth, worn walls. Her room is quiet and dark, a sharp smell lingering in the air. I pick up a folded parchment on her bed, and thumb it open, reading the words: *Meet me there*. I don't have to wonder what it means. I pocket the note in my trousers as I leave her room.

Nevoba is a network of interconnected caverns and caves divided into sectors. The eastern end holds the sleeping chambers for mothers with children, while women over selecting age are given their own private sleeping chambers on the western edges. In the center we have spaces for cooking and gathering. The great hall is used for the rare occurrence of receiving the Sar Dyēus's hoard, often for letting the children run and play freely, and weekly for deliveries from the farmhands. The upper section on the western side is storage for food, weapons, the stables, and nightly rooming for the farmhands following a delivery. The huntresses spend most of our time here, and once a week we take advantage of the presence of men from the farms.

The delivery won't come until the afternoon, leaving this area quiet, the hunters out on watch or taking their hard earned break elsewhere. I pass the empty rooms and make my way through the storage area and take the small opening that leads out to the path where we burn our waste. The acrid stench always lingers on the air out here and Ninon and I learned early on in our youth that this was the perfect place to disappear. Other children find this area, too, of course. Like Ninon and I, they discover and claim little crevices or nooks as their own, but no one has ever found ours.

The dark is thick, my candle stub long since burned out, but my feet know the way over each rise and fall of the ground. Soon the familiar scent of burned waste leaves my nose and I smell something else that has me recoiling.

"Gods, Ninon," I say as I lower myself down into a small gap between the rocks along the base of the mountain that frame in Nevoba's caverns. "Are you alive down here?"

I crouch to crawl through a smooth rock tunnel that opens into a bigger chamber, glowing with the light of a fire. The smoke and scent rises, leaving through fissures in the hard stone earth above. The sunlight seeps in through the cracks, casting shadows and further illuminating the smooth rock walls of our secret hideout.

Ninon sits on her heels, a cloth of fabric wrapped around her nose and mouth and I bring up my shirt to cover my own.

"The text warned of a strong odor."

"A scent this strong calls for more than mere warning," I say, squinting.

Ninon grunts her agreement.

"How's it coming along?" I blink the tears from my eyes.

"Everything is going as it should," she says. She occasionally stirs the mixture in a pot over the flames. "It's almost boiled down to the right consistency. During the day it will rest and steep off the flame. Then I'll run the mixture through cloth, then leave it to rest until tomorrow evening when it's ready for consumption. Do you understand?"

I look from the pot, back to her. "I do, but why should I need to?"

She shrugs. "In case you ever need to concoct it yourself."

My brows furrow. "How long will this last?"

"You only need a single drop under the tongue daily for it to work. This amount will last a year, I should think."

"It's more than enough, then." The idea of being trapped in Dyēus, away from Ninon and my sister, ties my stomach into knots.

"We'll see how persistent Alixor is," she muses, stirring the mixture slowly again.

"I'm sure I'll be allowed to return for visits, and it's not like you won't be here to make another batch." I watch her face, waiting.

The pot bubbles and hisses. "You never know."

My breath hitches in my chest and I look away from her. "I hate when you say things like that."

She's quiet for a moment. "I know."

I snap back to her. "No. You don't. Just because your mother—" I stop myself, pressing my lips together tight. We've had this argument countless times before. The words *other women* and *the children from our youth* burrow deep, despite Ninon's strength of heart. And mine.

Her eyes look into mine for a beat, then to the pointed tip of my ear, then beyond, over my shoulder. "How's Kal?"

Forgoing covering my nose with my shirt, I rub my face with my hands, digging my heels into my eyes. "Exhausted."

She lowers her mask and scratches her nose. "Is she alone?"

"My mother will be with her soon."

"You should go. Be with her while you can. There's nothing for you to do here."

I frown. Ninon enjoys time alone. I, on the other hand, hardly know the meaning of the word. And in moments where I do happen to be by myself, I feel lost. Empty.

Always in the days leading up to when I leave for Dyēus, Ninon does this. She pulls away, turning into herself. I hate leaving her. The pain of knowing I won't see her for an indeterminate amount of time stings like a popping ember landing on my skin.

"Have you been eating?" I ask her.

A wry smile curls her lips. "The food stores are near. I'm eating."

I huff a laugh. "I'll check on you again tomorrow night."

"Stay with your sister."

"I won't leave you," I say, scoffing at how ridiculous her request is. But she doesn't look at me. She only folds her hands in front of her. "You're doing this for me. If anyone ever found out, you'd be—"

"I know. But you have to. She needs you."

I know that, too. "You'll be all right?"

She looks back to me then, resolution settling into the subtle change of her eyes and set of her mouth. I've seen that look before, in moments before she looses an arrow to kill. "I will. Don't worry about me."

"Impossible."

There's a tightness growing in my chest. I know I could be gone for months, maybe longer, while Alixor tries to impregnate me, but ever since that morning we rode out to collect the dragonsbane, I've felt like this is the end of something. What if something does happen to Ninon while I'm gone? "Why do I feel like you think you're never going to see me again?"

"We don't know what the future holds for us, what Erenmaag has predetermined."

"Or what they've left for us to will," I say, offering a counter to her invocation of the god of fate and agency.

"In the end, we can only wait and see which will prevail."

"I will always take matters into my own hands. Nothing will happen to you, Ninon, and I will see you again."

Ninon looks at me, brows pinched before they soften into something akin to understanding. "I believe that."

I smirk, rising to make my way out. "You'd better."

I stay with my sister for the rest of the day, but that

evening, I need to hunt. A delivery from the farmhands came in the afternoon, and the northern sector is alive with noise as I enter, shouts rising in greeting. I smile, waving and ducking around mingling bodies as I make my way towards the stables, joining the women who are gearing up for the night.

"What are you doing here?" asks Haven, another huntress, as she finishes attaching her pack to her mare.

"The dust storms are weeks away. You need me to help stock the provisions."

Haven blows air out from between her lips. "Sounds like an excuse to me."

"I got restless," I relent, running a hand down Aspa before loading her up, too.

"Get your restlessness out with one of them." She nods to the crowd of men sharing drink with the women or attempting to ply them with small pots of honey. As if any of us need encouragement. They're as handsome as their dragon shifter fathers, though none hold the ability to shift. Their ears are gently pointed like ours, unlike our human counterparts in the world beyond the mountains. Sometimes, a group of men with their softly rounded ears from beyond attempt to pass over the mountains, seeking to serve the gods. They're all taken in and given work in the fields, marked as all of us are who dwell below the safety of Dyēus. They're not permitted to leave the fields to make deliveries, so I've never seen one myself, but the farmhands love to tell stories. When I say nothing, Haven raises a brow. "Or a few of them?"

I laugh and shake my head. "Not tonight."

"I guess you are going to get plenty of that sort of entertainment in Dyēus," she comments with a smirk and I roll my eyes skyward. "Where's Ninon?"

Her and I rarely go on hunts without one another. That, and Ninon usually volunteers on the nights of the farm delivery since she has no interest in partaking in relations with men. Usually I'm the one that stays behind on this night if I can help it.

I know exactly where she is, but of course I can't say. "I took her place tonight. She has her nose stuck in a book somewhere."

"She wasn't on last night either," the other young huntress with us, Dashka, says.

"She was with me and Kalixta," I answer calmly, though my body prickles with sweat. "She'll be here tomorrow night, I'm sure."

Haven huffs out a laugh. "She'd better. With you gone we'll need all the hands we can get. We're all praying you get pregnant soon so you can get back to the hunts quickly."

Dashka's mouth pops open, head swiveling to me. "Will you hunt while pregnant?"

I shrug a shoulder. "Why not?"

Haven laughs again. "When your belly is swollen with children you won't want to get anywhere near a horse."

I snicker. "In the beginning it won't be a problem, but by the second or third term, well, you might be right." My heart swells with affection. They don't judge me for continuing on with them even though I've been made a carre-mai. We all understand what it's like. We all crave the unnamable feeling of being under the open sky, of riding fast, of providing for our people with the animals we hunt and bring home. When I look at these women: strong, capable, intelligent, I wonder what it was about us, about them, that made the Sar Dyēus deem us undesirable?

Whether he knew it or not, he released me from a fate I didn't want, at least for a few years, and doomed me to suffer my mother's undying disappointment.

Swinging up onto our horses, we set out into the Sere as the sun lowers. In the coming weeks, torrential winds will carry dust in large swaths that will coat the land and drive our hunters home. Our people will feel hunger in these times. I remember when I saw a storm come in from the comfort of Dyēus's islands in the sky. Anger that I wasn't home to help, where I ought to be, rolled through me as swift as the storm. It was the moment that I'd become well and truly disillusioned from any enchantment the sky kingdom had ensnared me in those first few months after Alixor chose me.

Across the desert there are several outposts and blinds we use to hunt for game. Others are closer to the Realm and for the sole purpose of keeping an eye out for wayward rogues that slip past the sky kingdom's defenses. With the guard's encampments constantly on the move in anticipation of weak points around the Realm, it's rare that we encounter a rogue, but we've all noticed that it's been happening more often than usual.

At twilight, I fell a saiga. I'm not ready to go back yet, so another huntress offers to return home to dress it. And, I suspect, to enjoy the evening with the farmhands.

Haven shakes her head, scoffing. "Lucky."

"You could have volunteered," I say.

"Nah. I'm fertile. Not worth the risk."

It's not strictly against any rules to have children with the farmhands, but they abide by the same conduct as children of Dyēus do, and typically a woman will only have one child instead of twins. It works out sometimes, like with Ninon, but often the pregnancies ultimately fail.

"Oh I don't know," I say, scanning the dark horizon now that twilight has wheeled into night. "Hands and mouths can provide plenty of pleasure if you ask me. You don't need to take it that far if you don't wish to."

She sighs. "I can't help myself."

I grin. "Insatiable."

"Pot calling the kettle black, I think."

I toss my head back and laugh. "I think you may be right."

"I'm still jealous of you getting that kind of attention

consistently when you're in Dyēus." Haven, several years older than me, told me when I became a carremai that she desperately wanted to be chosen, to see the sky kingdom, to feel like someone wanted her. Her mother, a lot like mine, had a less than favorable reaction to the undesirable distinction placed upon her.

My attention is pulled to where the islands float in the sky. "I'm trying not to think about it."

Haven puts a hand on mine, giving it a squeeze. "Sorry. I know you don't really want to do this. I was only attempting to point out some good you'll have of it."

I place my free hand on top of hers. "I know. Shall we head to the outposts? I have a feeling tonight."

"Yeah?" Haven asks, brow raised. "At your leisure, then."

That tugs a smile from me. My pace is never leisurely. I'm pleased when Dashka matches my speed, both her and Haven flanking my lead on either side. My heart thunders and pulls, remembering my ride with Ninon two mornings ago and the dark-haired rogue staring at me as if he could see my very soul. The farther we get from Nevoba, the more desolate the Sere becomes. Twisted, leafless trees with bark as dark as coal and pale, scrubby brush collect in the crevices of the rock monuments that rise up, powerful and imposing, like waves in the ocean. Vegetation is scarce, but brings the saiga and the hare. We hunt both, but we're here for neither now as the darkness of deep night takes hold. In short order we make it to our outpost, relieving the earlier crew. Once they're gone, our horses replace theirs in a deep rock outcropping that conceals them.

Next to the outcropping is a low, wide arch of rock, the white stone cast blue in the growing light of the twin moons, and the three of us hunker down into it. I position myself facing the Realm of Rogues with Dyēus's sky kingdom to my right. Haven sits next to me, facing the opposite direction while a few short yards away, Dashka faces the mountains, poking her head into the dugouts for us to shoot arrows from.

"You said one would come tonight," Have begins. "Want to place a wager?"

"You have nothing I want."

Haven scoffs. "I've seen the way you look at my mare."

Sure enough, Haven's mare is swift, but I would never give up Aspa. "What use do I have for two horses?"

"For when one gets tired and yet you have not?"

I laugh. "Fair point—it's a deal then." I won't actually take her horse, and she knows it.

"It's a deal."

After that, we're quiet. The nights at the outposts are not for words or idle gossip. The night here is for listening. The night here is for blending. I've been shooting and taking down rogues since I was eighteen, on the hunt since I was twelve, and wielding the bow since I was six. The tip of my arrow gleams in the moonlight, ready to cut into the flesh of rogue serpents of the night—ones who betrayed the gods, their curse a punishment for their crimes, or those of us turned by the curse upon entering their Realm. So we're warned. Ninon seems to believe it though, and for the most part, I believe what she does.

There's tension in the air. Lean muscles coiled, sharp eyes trained, delicately pointed ears perked—one of our only gifts from our fathers. Gifts that we take and use against our enemies.

When I continued coming on hunts after Alixor claimed me, my mother and others tried to have me tend to the other mechanisms of running our community instead, as was commonly the duty of the carremai. But I was too accurate, too useful here in the Sere when I wasn't visiting the opulent sky kingdom, and so the arguments to keep me confined soon ebbed. I would have kept coming regardless, would have found a way even if they tied me to the stone walls each night, even if I had to chew through bindings or cut through stone.

Movement to my left catches my attention and a dark streak slices through the sky, stars winking out for a bare moment before returning to their glory. I signal with a hand to Haven and she drags her fingers through the fine layer of rock and debris, the sound a message to Dashka. *Look to the sky.*

We hear the shift of wind first. Then the zip of an arrow is loosed, sprinting through the night. A tumult of air beats against the rock arch, sending tiny pebbles skittering. The arch is deep enough that claws cannot reach inside, and thick enough that it can't be crushed, though it's riddled with claw marks that show it's not for lack of effort. I watch Dashka loose another arrow.

"Missed again!"

"Get out of there," I hiss at her. She's revealed her location twice now. When the dragon comes back around it will know exactly where to strike.

"No, I've got it, it's turning back around."

I curse and scramble away from my position, throwing my body into her dugout. I have to climb several feet to reach her.

"Wait—" she pauses. "Where'd it go?"

My skin prickles with sweat, my ears straining to hear. "Get out, get out, get out," I repeat quickly, grabbing hold of her ankles. With a single hard tug I pull her back as the mouth of the dragon collides with the opening.

Dashka screams. Rubble crumbles down on our heads, sticking in our hair, coating our mouth. Now she's scrambling back, our bodies awkward and tangled as I wiggle out of the channel. The dragon strikes with his claws again and again, sending a storm of rock and debris into our faces.

Haven grabs my legs and pulls us out as the dugout collapses in on itself. The dragon's high pitch scream pierces my ears.

"Haven, to the right," I shout. "I've got the left."

Haven goes wordlessly, and at my back Dashka pleads, "I'm sorry!"

"Stay here," I reply, snatching up my bow and arrows.

Out in the open air, I see the dragon swoop low, shoulder dropping, wings loping on the air. The beast gets so close I catch the cloudiness of its eyes in the moonlight. My arrow is already drawn and I let it fly. The rogue's head kicks back, a pained keening ripping from the beast. The creature lands hard, thrashing and tangling itself in its wings. I watch, even as tears pinch my eyes. I watch, even though everything in me screams at the wrongness of it. Every time. It's like this for me every single time.

Haven is breathing hard at my side as the rogue's limbs stop moving, its mighty wings drooping.

"Well. I guess I owe you a mare."

"You pulled me out from being buried alive. Let's call it even."

After another moment, vapor rises to envelop the beast, slow and sluggish as the dragon at long last, turns back into a human. I once thought death was the only way a rogue could shift back into its human body. A rogue, we're told, is a rogue because it couldn't shift into a human again. An abomination to their kind when they turned against the gods. After what Ninon and I witnessed two mornings ago though, I'm not so sure. I try and fail to recall if the dragon Ninon and I met had clouded eyes, like this one, before it shifted.

Dashka's at our side as we approach the rogue. A male—not one of our women. I'm not surprised. It never is. Women used to disappear all the time when my mother was young apparently. Now, it doesn't happen. If there are any Nevobans in the Realm of Rogues that were cursed to turn into beasts, they've never made it out again.

"Wow," Dashka breathes, swiping a tear from her face with the back of her hand.

"Your first rogue slaying?" Haven asks.

"Yeah," she murmurs, nodding.

I want to tell her that the feeling never gets better. Instead I say, "When we get back, send word with a raven to Dyēus. One of the collectors will take care of this. I'm done for tonight." Then I turn, go back to my horse, and head for home.

# Chapter Five

Ninon is not in our meeting place when I come home. The space has been cleaned out, save for the lingering stench creating the tincture left behind. There's a sinking feeling in my stomach. I can't explain it, but something inside is screaming at me to find Ninon.

I scramble out of our hiding spot, the sun lighting the horizon, chasing away the cold, dark night. The northern sector is a mess from the gathering with the farmers that night, snores and soft, sensual sounds emanating from their rooms. They'll be up soon, preparing for the long journey back to the farms below Dyēus.

I race through the halls, trying to stay silent on my feet as I enter the corridor of sleeping chambers. I walk into her room, telling myself I'll see her wrapped in blankets on her bed, book in hand. "Ninon?" I whisper into the darkness.

All the sleeping chambers have a cutout in the ceiling to let in light, but the hunters usually cover it to sleep during the day. I reach up to the center of the room, fingers grasping the fabric she'd tacked up to cover the opening, and rip it down. My heart stops in my chest at the sight of her empty bed. Her room is clean, as usual, but it's missing things. Clothes. A few books. Her satchel. All gone.

My chest rises and falls, trying to catch the breath that keeps escaping my mouth, too hot and too fast. I turn in a slow circle. She must be somewhere else in the compound. *No, she's not.* Maybe she went to get food. *No, she didn't.* Maybe she—

My eyes catch on a book, pulled a little out of place from the ones left behind. It's not like Ninon to leave her books anything less than perfectly aligned. I reach for it, and pull it all the way out. Behind it is a bottle the length of my palm and two fingers wide with liquid inside, a golden hair stick, and a note.

I grab the note and ignore the rest.

*Kaisa,*

*Dab one drop of tincture under your tongue daily. Rinse with mint water directly after to neutralize the odor.*

*The hair stick is a gift, and like you, it is beautiful, but deadly. Wear it.*

*I won't say goodbye. You know where to find me.*

*-N*

My ribcage billows as I try to catch my breath. I knew something was off with her. I knew and still I did nothing. I curse, taking the hair stick in my hands, the part that goes into my hair sharpened to a point. The gold ornament was fashioned to resemble one of the leaves that float on the wind to us when the weather is cooler, the shape like a fan. Ninon collected them when we were younger, pressing leaves between the pages of her books. I hold the ornament end in my fist, the point threading nicely between my fingers. I suppose if lodged in the correct spot, it could kill.

She doesn't trust the men of Dyēus, despite their good nature. We both agreed on that. Still, I can't imagine killing any one of them, and this weapon is not for hunts. I carefully slip it in my ponytail for now.

My fingers shake as I take the tincture from her shelf. The liquid is thick, like oil, and dark green in color. I won't open it until I take my first dose tonight since I'm not sure if or how the air might affect it. My hands suddenly feel heavy and my arms drop down to my sides, but I hold on tight to Ninon's gifts. She's gone. She's really gone and I know where she went, but I can't do anything about it. I squeeze my eyes shut and let my head fall back, the dawn's morning light filtering over my face. I can't help but wonder if I pushed this on her, that I asked too much in having her make the contraceptive. If she worried for her safety and fled to keep herself out of harm's way, I'd hate myself. I don't understand why she would think the Realm of Rogues was any safer than here, despite what we witnessed with the rogue the other morning. What did she know that she didn't tell me?

"Why?" I whisper, my voice cracking. Why didn't she tell me? Why did she leave me? But I was leaving her first, wasn't I? By going to Dyēus, not knowing when I'd return. Who else does Ninon have but me? Kalixta has her child now. And Ninon, she has no one and nothing here. Not really. She only had me. And I wasn't enough to get her to stay. I curse and wipe my cheeks with the back of my hand. I pocket the note and the tincture and walk out of her room, but I'm pretty sure my heart stays there as I leave.

When I enter Kalixta's room, her eyes widen seeing me and she opens her mouth, but Mother is in there too and I give my sister a subtle shake of my head. Her mouth closes.

"Kaisa, there you are, where have you been?" our mother chastises. "Look at the mess you are. Go get cleaned up; Alixor will surely be here soon to collect you."

"The message he sent said mid-morning," I murmur,

recalling the missive I'd received from Dyēus yesterday afternoon.

Mother clicks her tongue. "You'll need nearly that much time to prepare."

"Mother," Kalixta says, interrupting her. "I think I need some more balm. Would you mind going to get it?"

Our mother looks between the two of us and sighs. "Give her some advice on how to behave while in Dyēus, hm?" she says before striding out of the room.

I listen as her footfalls disappear down the hall.

"What is it?" Kalixta whispers, grasping my arm with her free hand as I sink down to sit beside her.

I open my mouth and no sound comes out. How can I say the words? How can I speak the truth when I don't want to believe it? "She's gone."

Kalixta searches my face, fingers going to her mouth. "Ninon?"

"Oh, she's alive," I assure her, realizing she might think Ninon dead. I suck in a breath. "Or at least, I hope she is. She left, Kal."

"Where would she..." Kalixta shakes her head, brows furrowing, then she mouths her guess. "To the Realm?"

My lips are pulled tight as I nod.

The girl in her arms squirms and Kalixta rocks her gently from side to side. "I see." I'm a little surprised when she doesn't have more to say on it that. I get a needling feeling that she knows something that I don't, but I don't want to cause her undue stress, so I keep my questions to myself. She watches me carefully, and I hate the look of agony on her face. "Are you still going to Dyēus?"

I huff out sigh, trying to dissolve the sobs stuck in my throat. "It's not like I have a choice. I can't run away." I run the back of my hand down her cheek. "And I can't leave you."

"You could you know," she says, searching my gaze. "You could leave now. Before he comes."

"Kal," I sigh, pulling my hands away. "You know it's not possible. He'd search the Sere for me and then what? Be put to death for trying to avoid this?"

She leans in close. "Isn't that what you're trying to do anyway?" I don't answer her. The less she knows the safer she'll be. "At least if you went there they couldn't touch you."

"And I'd turn into a monster and never be able to see you again. Or watch my niece grow up." *Or be myself*, I think, which feels like a struggle enough as it is.

"You don't know that."

"We don't know anything for certain about the Realm and I don't intend to find out." I close my eyes for a moment, trying to keep the images of Ninon turning into a monster at bay. "I have a plan."

"I suspected as much." She chews her lip. "What did she do for you?"

"You don't need to know."

Kalixta gives me a long, hard stare. She's intelligent and quick. I'm sure she knows even without my saying.

"Enough," I say. "I'll take care of myself."

She sighs, quiet for a time. "Yes, you will. You always have."

I let my fingers drift over the top of the fine, dark hair on my niece's head. I don't want to talk about me or Ninon anymore. "The naming ceremony will happen while I'm gone."

Kalixta doesn't miss a beat. "Anila," she says.

I look her straight in the eye. "You're supposed to keep the name in your heart until the ceremony. It's bad luck to share it before then."

She stares at me earnestly, brows raised. "You are my heart. I'm not sharing if it's something that's already mine."

My eyes burn with the threat of unshed tears. But if I start, I know she will too, so I hold them back. "It's a beautiful name."

She gazes down at her child. "I wonder what Thrace will name him."

"Probably after the king."

Kalixta's mouth jumps into a grin, brief and fleeting, before her expression sobers. "He wouldn't."

"Thrace seems like the strong, traditional type." I shrug, as if that's answer enough to what he'd name the child, among other things.

"He's more than that."

I remember then what Thrace said to me before he stole her son to the sky.

"I'm sure the name he chooses will be as good as the one you chose for your daughter."

She's quiet for a moment before she says, "I'll miss you."

"I'll miss you, too." I wrap her up in my arms and press a hard kiss to her head.

"Go, before mother returns and starts on you again. I'll be there for your departure."

I give her a final parting kiss, leave her room, and prepare for Alixor to take me.

Alixor arrives gleaming and resplendent against the clear blue sky outside the entrance to the great hall. And even though I expected everything, down to the final draft of air that his body pushes towards me, blood rushes through my veins and dread coats my tongue. My sister squeezes my hand, slick with sweat, even though I've bathed and the day is relatively cool despite the Sere's usual heat.

My mother places a heavy hand on my shoulder. "Do your duty and you'll be fine."

I hate her hand on my shoulder and I hate that fine's not good enough for me.

Alixor lands gracefully, his shift seamless as his clawed

foot changes into a booted human one, swaying the pale yellow grass, the dust of our dry land billowing around him. As he approaches, he looks me up and down, a warm smile on his face. He's given me this look before, and I would be lying if it didn't make me feel wanted. But that's not enough, either. There's something inside me, calling for more.

"Absolutely radiant—as bright as a thousand suns," he says, reaching for me. I give Kalixta's hand one final squeeze before releasing her and stepping forward, placing my hands in his. "You have grown even more beautiful since I chose you."

I tip my chin up, demanding his gaze meet my eyes, away from the loose, sheer, waist-high skirt that barely conceals my legs, away from the sleeveless, high-neck cropped top that covers my marking, but leaves my midriff bare. I don't have a bag, since I'm given clothes to wear in the sky kingdom, so my tincture is tucked between my breasts, Ninon's pin tucked into a simple bun at the top of my head. "And what else is there?"

"And what else is there," he says in agreement, as if I didn't ask a question, but had simply stated, *But what more could there possibly be in the person he chose to bear his offspring?*

My breath halts in my chest, every instinct telling me to turn and run. Maybe Kalixta was right this morning. Maybe I should have fled.

Alixor's hands run down the length of my bare forearm, a frown pulling at his face. "What's this?" He lifts my arms, revealing the scrapes I'd earned when I pulled Dashka out of the archery nook. Clicking his tongue, Alixor drags the palm of his hand across the abrasion, and heat radiates from him, more than what skin alone can deliver. When he removes his hand, he reveals my skin, healed but not without scars. There are some things even dragons can't control.

Seemingly satisfied, Alixor touches my cheek with the hand that healed me. "Let's not delay this any further. I was eager three days ago and that feeling has only grown since." He tugs me to him, and my legs, always so strong riding Aspa across the Sere, feel weak and untrustworthy as they follow his lead.

I turn my head, watching my mother clutch Kalixta, the cries of my niece stolen by the wind. Alixor takes a step back from me to shift. I catch my mother's eye and see the relief etched in the fall of her shoulders, the softness with which she strokes her granddaughter's cheek. It's what all the mothers want for us, and how can I blame her? This is all we've ever been told to want.

Alixor, now transformed once again into a large, pale bellied beast with bronze scales and soft yellow mane—the sun incarnate—lowers for me. I've done this countless times before. Foot atop his leg, I hike myself up over his body just as I would mounting Aspa. But I'm unsteady. I feel as if I'm watching my body move from afar.

The moment I settle, I hear the cries from my people. I hear their well wishes, the prayers for fertility, the praise for my service, but it's as if I'm hearing them with my head submerged under water. What if the contraceptive doesn't work? What if it works and Alixor keeps me in Dyēus for years. My hands start to shake. I can't do this. I can't. It's then that my body and mind realign, words on my lips, the urge to shout *stop* cloying in my throat. In that same moment, Alixor shoots us into the sky, and my heart and its protests drop into my stomach. The ground is far below and where there was once dread, there's a tremendous relief. It's done. There's no turning back now. I've made my choice. Now it's time to live with it.

The sky is dotted with puffy, low hanging clouds and Alixor delights me by following the curves of each one that lies in our path. The hot sun sets his bronze scales aflame, and like every moment I've spent in the sky upon his back,

I feel that restlessness inside my skin sink down, content for now. Once, in the early days of visiting Dyēus with him, that sensation had nearly lulled me into thinking that being with Alixor was the right thing to do. But every time my feet touch the ground, the feeling dissipates, and I know it has nothing to do with him.

All too soon, the raw, deep brown rocky underearth of the sky kingdom comes into view. The closer we get, the more I can see gnarled roots and hanging vines clinging to every crack and crevasse. I don't want to land. I'd be content in the sky all day, soaking in the sun, breathing in the crisp air, aimless, save for the pursuit of flying through the air. But that's not why I'm here, and it beats my heart down every time I remember it.

When we crest Dyēus's horizon, my breath escapes me. It's terrible and beautiful. Mounds of rolling green hills, sprawling fruit trees, and sky-reaching buildings span across the islands. The touch of dew soothes my dry skin and brings the sweet scent of vegetation to my nose. It's everything Nevoba isn't. As magnificent as it is, it reminds me of how we would struggle to survive if the dragons of Dyēus were to suddenly to pull our weekly rations from us. Not that they ever would. They need us, just as much as we need them.

Alixor rises higher and beyond the white stone abodes dotting the mountainsides of the smaller islands, past the flowing rivers cascading down to drench the arid Sere below, the Sar Dyēus's castle looms, vast and mighty. Home to him and all the elites in his personal hoard, the fortress is a towering white structure at the northern tip of the largest island, spanning nearly the entire width. High towers with pointed spires pierce the blue above and endless rows of wide peaked arches of open colonnades alongside open air walkways allow the dragons to come and go at their leisure. In the distance, dragons crisscross the sky, their bodies moving in languid, serpentine waves through the air. The constant temperature is ideal, not too hot, not too cool, allowing for all the structures to be open to the outside world. No scorpions scuttle along the ground, burrowing into nooks as they do in Nevoba. No pestering flies. Nothing but total and complete paradise for the shifters of Dyēus.

It is, of course, one of the benefits of being chosen to breed. Once during each of the four seasons of the year, the carremai visit, and we have access to this beauty and bounty, this sheer luxury of living as we acclimate to their ways and rituals, as we strengthen our relationships to ensure a successful coupling. In the beginning I relished it. Felt entitled to it, even. But now it feels like a trap—the palace spires look less like the mountains they were meant to embody and more like teeth.

I grip Alixor's mane, and feel the rumble of his approval beneath me. I'll let him continue to think this is what I want. And when I don't give him what he desires, he'll return me home and choose another. I'll let him think I'm at comfort and ease around him. I'll take him to his bed, allow him access to my body, revel in my access to his, and then I'll return to the hunt and be on with the rest of my life.

Alixor takes us towards the castle's central promenade, flying above the dwellings nestled in the lower valleys among the hills that house the faction of dragons called the merchants. Their duties include crafting and trading coveted dragon glass for fabrics or food or spices from places over the mountains. The smaller outer islands are home to the collectors who perform the grim work of collecting the bodies of rogues that have been slain and the souls of the mortals who've passed in the land beyond. It's then the duty of the Sar Dyēus's elite hoard to deliver those souls to the gods.

Alixor lands in one of the palace's vast atriums, allowing me to disembark before he shifts into his human form. I wonder what would happen if he shifted while I was still

astride him, but something about that feels far more intimate than I'd like. I shake my head, dispelling the thought
and the heat rising to my face.

"Are you all right?" Alixor asks, noting my distress.
He cups his hands around my cheeks, surveying my expression. "Are you feeling ill? Did the ride not sit well?"

Feeling entirely uncomfortable, I gently remove his
hands on the pretense of holding them instead. "I'm well.
I love flying, always. I'm just getting used to the idea that I
might be here longer than a few weeks this time."

He smiles. "Well, hopefully not too much longer than
that."

*One can hope*, I think to myself.

"Not that I mind taking my time with you," he whispers in my ear, low and suggestive.

His words cause a resounding pulse deep in my core.
Now that suggestion I wouldn't mind. "I should hope so."

"I meant to tell you the other day that I can't stop
thinking about the last time you were here. All the places
we explored. The way you made me feel."

I warm all over again, recalling that final day before
he took me back to Nevoba. The little-used corridor and
corner we'd found after dinner, the heat of our tongues on
one another, our hands dipping between our bodies, fingers
curling and tugging at our most aching parts. The way he'd
turned me around and pressed himself against me while his
fingers worked me above my clothes.

"I remember quite well," I say, breathless. Despite having no desire to produce children at this point in my life—
my desire in the act it takes to make such a thing happen is
particularly strong.

He inhales deeply, scenting my arousal with a feral
smile. His mouth catches my bottom lip between his teeth,
giving me a playful nip. "We could start where we left off."

"As enjoyable as that sounds, don't we have somewhere to be?"

I know how this day goes—I've attended banquets for breeding ceremonies before and heard enough talk to know what to expect. Though, much of the conversation I've heard was of what to expect the night following the feast and celebration, which is something I'm already well acquainted with.

"Don't go ruining all of my surprises," he says, thumb running along my lower lip.

"It's no surprise when I'm groomed to know what to expect."

His mouth twists up into a smile. "Then humor me."

I clench my teeth as I return his smile, knowing that's all I do anyway. Humor him, pretend to like him, make him like me, all to make this process as harmless as it can be until the moment he releases me. I refuse to be another womb, another mother with her heart split in two.

"The banquet won't be for a few hours yet," he says. "You should get ready, though. I'll escort you to your rooms."

Alixor moves to grab my hand, but I hesitate, making him frown. "My nephew," I say. "Can I see him first? My sister asked and I won't be able to concentrate on us until I see him." She didn't ask, but I need to see him with my own eyes to make sure he's alive and as well as he can be without his mother.

"Ah," he says, understanding smoothing his features. "I see."

"Please," I beg, letting my lashes flutter.

He searches my face, a small smile playing on his lips before he sighs, deep and resigned. Sometimes I can't believe how easy he is to manipulate. "I can't go with you. Access is restricted, and strictly speaking only sires and nursemaids are allowed, but I think it would be good for you to see him."

I try not to appear too eager as I ask, "Where is he?"

He hesitates. "The west wing."

His words take me by surprise, my head swimming.

"Oh." I've explored this castle from every angle I could, except the west wing. I never knew that's where the nursery was. Why should it be? The west wing was the Sar Dyēus's personal suite.

"It's fine," he reassures. "The nurses will be there, they won't mind, but don't enter if you see any of the males and whatever you do, don't go past the nursery's entrance. The Sar Dyēus has wards to his personal suites—dangerous ones. I don't want anything happening to you, so be careful."

A nervous energy vibrates through my limbs. I nod, and Alixor pulls me so my cheek is pressed to his chest.

"Thank you," I say, returning his embrace.

His hand slips up to cup the back of my neck, tilting my head back. "I expect a more intimate thank you later." His mouth lands on mine and I sink into the feeling of his lips. We're both only doing what we need to. I try not to blame him for the situation he's put me in.

"I'm sure I can think of something," I say as I pull back and leave him, making my way around the castle to the west wing.

# Chapter Six

In all of my visits to Dyēus over the years, I've never had any desire to go to the west wing. The moment I learned that's where the Sar Dyēus most often kept himself, I steered clear. I've already raised enough flags for him; first with being undesirable and second by being chosen by Alixor, anyway. Who's to say what might happen to me if I caused any more trouble for him than I already had.

The hall leading into the west wing is wide and quiet. From the smooth floors to the sharp detailing adorning the tops of the columns, to the sloped concave arches of the ceilings, everything is a pristine white, like glistening round clouds on a sun filled day. But as beautiful as it is, it feels empty, desolate. Entering the hall, I hear the babble of little mouths, the cries and screams of babes. It's the only thing that feels alive in this space and I hurry down the halls towards it, not another soul in sight.

I peek around the doors to the nursery and see a tall figure standing by the windows on the opposite side of the room. I duck away before I can tell who it is, hoping I wasn't seen. Of course a nursemaid would be here. Someone had to watch over the children after all. I only hope she'll let me see my nephew.

Slowly this time, I step into the opening and stop in my tracks, motionless as a stone column. Not a nursemaid after all, but the Sar Dyēus, looking over a small bundle in one of the cots. I take a step back, sure he didn't see me, hoping he didn't hear my approach, when his voice—deep, melodic, pleasant—floats over to me. "Come to see what's in store for you?" He lifts his head, my gaze captured by a pair of dark eyes.

Every hair along my spine and the back of my neck stands at attention. My voice is trapped in my chest, but I swallow and decide to go for the truth. "My sister's child."

"He's lovely," he says, turning back to the baby.

My breath stills. *My sister's baby. He's looking at my sister's baby.* I have the sudden urge to bare my teeth. "That's him?"

A strong, smooth pale hand raises, silently beckoning me over. I hesitate, but I want to see my nephew, and it's not as if I can deny the Sar Dyēus in any case. So I step inside the nursery and stand across the cot from our great ruler. My nephew sleeps soundly, his cheeks rosy and round. My body relaxes as I stare at him for a long while, momentarily forgetting the Sar Dyēus's presence until he speaks again. "You know Alixor has tried before."

I tense, hoping he doesn't notice. I didn't know that, nor does it matter. Not to me. I lift my head and find him staring at me, his black eyes not exactly black, but a deep, deep green. I've never been this close to him before to have noticed. Even during my selection ceremony, there was more distance, more darkness between us. His hair, longer on top than it is on the sides and at the nape of his neck, is starting to lose hold of its usual slicked back look. I don't dare respond.

"Perhaps it was the woman. Perhaps it was him," he goes on.

Still I don't speak. His lips, full and wide, tremble—annoyed, amused, or about to say more, I'm not sure.

"He won't like to fail again."

I was never supposed to be chosen. I was marked as undesirable. So, why would Alixor choose me if failure to produce offspring wasn't an option for him again? Anger rises in me, swift and hot. "Perhaps he should have taken that into consideration when he chose an undesirable breeding partner," I seethe, and the next words slip off my tongue unbidden. "Someone must have made a mistake." His hand flexes at my insinuation and bile churns my gut.

His eyes narrow, then he walks around the cradle only to pause at my shoulder. His scent reminds me of the wind when it comes from the sea in spring mixed with something earthy, like well-worn leather. He leans down, close to my ear. "Dragons have a keen sense of smell, you know. We can scent a great number of things. When you're fertile, and when you're not, for instance. When your body is ready and willing."

My pulse is a flutter in my veins at his words, his nearness. The vial sits uncomfortably between my breasts. He doesn't know. He *can't* know.

"So I've heard," I say, my voice coming out breathless.

"See that you remember." As he straightens, the backs of his fingers ghost against mine. My eyes flick down, catching him pull away and flex his hand. Slowly, I twist my head to look up to his face, but he stares ahead. "The nursemaids will return soon. Be sure that you're gone by the time they do," he says, then walks from the room.

When he disappears, I cast my eyes around, finally taking in the nursery. Babies lay asleep or sitting up awake in their cots. More empty beds line the far walls on both sides, and another opening reveals a gaggle of carefree toddlers corralled in a large enclosed space with low climbing structures and wooden toys. A woman rushes by, chasing one of the toddlers, but she doesn't notice me. I place a hand on my nephew, to make sure he's real, because what just happened felt an awful lot like a dream. Or a nightmare. I puzzle over the Sar Dyēus's words, what he meant about Alixor and what it means for me. I think about the vial tucked between my breasts and the scent of the contraceptive while it was being made—could he smell it on me? Doom twists my insides into knots. I may have made a great and terrible mistake.

Heeding the Sar Dyēus's words, I don't linger in the nursery. The banquet for Alixor's and my breeding ceremony will begin in the late afternoon and lead into the evening. I don't do much to get ready except allow the attendant who showed up to apply cosmetics to my face. I tell her to leave my hair, which she argues against, and tries to help me dress, which I also don't allow. Once she's gone, I undress and hide the tincture under the pillow on the bed. I know I'm close to fertility and I'll need to take a dose before Alixor does anything tonight, but it's still too early to use it.

The floor-length dress left for me crisscrosses at my chest around my neck, much like my shirt did, but leaves my back and sides fully exposed. The front is arranged in such a way that it covers my marking, though there is a strip of my low belly showing before the skirt begins, flaring out from my hips with slits along both legs starting at the top of my thigh. The fine material, silky and shimmering, is the perfect match to Alixor's bronze dragon scales. I'm frowning at my reflection in the mirror when there's a knock on my door before it opens.

Alixor's eyes rove my figure.

"You didn't wait. What if I was naked?" I ask.

"Well then all the better." He smirks, coming up behind me to wrap his arms around my abdomen and place a kiss against my neck. "However, you are breathtaking like this, as well."

"Thank you."

"And what about me?" he asks, pulling away and backing up with his arms out so I can look him over. Truly, not much is different except his clothes have a little more ornamentation than usual. His suit is dark blue silk with ornate stitching along the arms and sides of the legs, his tailored jacket open to the crisp short-collared shirt beneath. His hair, the same bronze of his scales, is a carefully swept back look that plays well off the angles of his face.

"You look fit for a banquet that precedes you bedding your carremai," I answer honestly.

As I expect, his head jolts back in a hearty laugh. "Your directness is a delight as always. Are you ready?" I nod and he guides me by my lower back out the door into the hall, his gaze drinking me in all the while.

I set a pleasant smile on my face. I'm beginning to wonder if I can handle his attention for more than a few weeks.

Alixor leads us down the open-air colonnade and the soft breeze carries the rich, green smell of Dyēus's lush gardens and trees. I inhale deeply and detect the barest hint of the dry, earthy Sere, reminding me of home. I hope it won't be long before I see it again. We reach the end of the colonnade and we enter the dining hall. The early evening air sifts through the high arched openings along the back and sides of the room, making the sheer cream and white drapes dance against the columns. The polished white floors glitter gold against the sinking sun. The blue of the sky glistens as it passes through the dragon glass windows set in circular panes of the vaulted ceiling above. I take in a fortifying breath, tasting the salt of the sea on the white puffy clouds sliding against the edge of the balcony. The clouds rarely travel into the Sere, stopping here instead to drop every ounce of precious rain on Dyēus.

In the center of the room, there's a long table, around which about thirty guests are seated. The pale wood table never ceases to amaze me. There's no tree around Nevoba to have created it. I try and fail to imagine how large and grand it must have been, alive and full with leaves or fruit. Currently, the table overflows with dragon glass vases brimming with white and orange-gold flowers, gauzy citrine runners and bowls of fruit, while goblets of water and wine catch the light. At the head of the table sits the Sar Dyēus. There's quite a bit of space separating him from the rest of the hoard, but seated on his left is Selnor, and on his right, Thrace, with two empty seats next to him meant for myself and Alixor. The rest of the seats are filled with the remaining elites and their carremai, or a guest of choice. I've heard banquets like these for the lower ranking dragons and collectors are more casual, and located on whatever island they call home. Being a carremai of an elite though, these banquets are more of a formal production, and the only kind I've ever witnessed.

Our presence is announced and all except the Sar Dyēus rise at our entrance. Praise is given to our coupling, and prayers are spoken to Erovosvis to honor our mating and bless my womb, to Eretex to protect our future brood, to Eriratem so that they are well in nature and in their creation. I let the words float past my ears as Alixor and I stand there. I keep my chin high, my eyes on the circular opening to the sky above the Sar Dyēus's head. Once the prayers have been read, we are lead to our seats and stringed instruments begin to softly play. I cast my gaze back towards the entrance, and see women tucked against the only solid wall in the room, playing the soothing tunes.

Alixor reaches to pull out my seat for me, but Thrace is swifter, standing to offer me the seat beside him. Clearly he wants me there for a reason, and I have no reason to object. Alixor's smile is tight as he moves to push me in, then takes the seat beside me. The elites to his right immediately engage him in conversation. I do my best to avoid looking in the Sar Dyēus's direction. I can feel Thrace's eyes on me, like he wants to say something. Touching the tines of my fork with the tip of my finger, I push hard, feeling the bite of pressure against my skin. "Kalixta and the girl are well, in case you care."

His shoulders relax a fraction, betraying the tension they held. "It's good to hear that."

I wait for him to say more, because it looks like he wants to, but out of the corner of my eye I see the Sar Dyēus's attention is on us. On me.

My heart skitters like a rock across the ground, but dwelling on him and his presence takes away from this opportunity to speak with Thrace while Alixor is occupied.

Before I can even begin, Thrace leans in and whispers into my ear so quietly that there's no way the shifters around us hear a thing, since I'm hardly able to make him out. "I am glad she's healing, but if I know Kalixta, she's not well. How is she really?"

Does he know her? Maybe he does understand my sister better than I do—he's spent more time with her than I have these many years. I release the fork, running my thumb over the indentations in my finger as our first course is presented. A thin broth, light in flavor, with tiny droplets of spiced oil glistening on top. "She's wondering why you haven't sent word." If I wasn't watching him, I'd miss his expression, as if I punched him in the gut rather than spoke the truth.

"I've tried, but I'm being kept on a tight leash."

My gaze flits over to the Sar Dyēus. He's no longer looking at us, but I keep my voice low. "What have you done?"

Thrace huffs out a laugh. "A great many things. Some that I hope are never discovered, not the least of which being actually falling in love with your sister."

My breath halts. *Liar.* Dragons don't love. Not really. They wouldn't steal our children, then abandon us, leaving us heartbroken if that were true. I scan the room, quick and thorough, but no one pays us any mind. "I don't know why you feel the need to pander to my emotions."

"I don't know why you feel the need to dismiss mine."

I stare at him, open mouthed. "If you had any emotions beyond your instincts, I would."

Thrace sighs. "Your sister said you'd be difficult."

I rear back at the offense. "What are you talking about?"

"Kalixta knew if she tried to tell you we're in love, you'd think it was one-sided. I told her I would persuade you that wasn't the case. Still, she had her reservations, and now I see why."

I don't believe him and I don't know why it matters. "So why bother telling me at all?"

"We think it's important that you know. *I* think it's important that you know."

"But why?" I urge.

"Because she's going to live here, Kaisa. With me. With our children."

My hand goes to my stomach, my heart plummeting there from my chest. The stringed instruments increase in tempo. "She's...what?"

"I'm sorry to tell you this now," he says, face earnest. "I wasn't sure when we'd have another opportunity to speak."

"Why wouldn't she just tell me herself?"

"She didn't think you would believe her. That it would actually happen."

I can't argue with him there, as much as I'd like to. My heart is pounding so hard that I can feel it in my ears. Was this why Kalixta wanted me to run away? Because she was never going to be there for me in the first place? "When is she coming?"

"I'm hoping to retrieve her soon. Things here are... tense."

I scan the room again, but I don't notice anything out of the ordinary. Same banquet. Same elites and their quiet, obedient carremai at their side.

"Kaisa," Alixor says with a chuckle, interrupting my thoughts. "Why do you look as if you're out on a hunt?"

I bite my tongue and try to control my breathing. "It's nothing, I only—" I stop short when I hear Selnor scoff.

My body's coiled too tightly and I can't stop myself from lashing out. "My sincere apologies, Lord Selnor, but is there something wrong with me performing my duty for our people?"

"Your *duty*," Selnor sneers, "is to provide offspring to our kingdom. That's what the carremai are for, and it's a disgrace that you've continued to hunt."

"I'm good at it," I snap, thrumming with the need to exert my full bite. Alixor opens his mouth as if he's about to interject, but his father is quicker.

"Let's hope you're good for more than that and that your mouth serves you better in the bedroom than it does here."

I burn with the need to leap from my chair, sprint across the table, and tear his head from his neck. My anger is becoming unbridled. It's so close and visceral I don't know if I can hold it inside any longer—I don't know how I'm going to get through the rest of—

"Leave." The command is low and dangerous, but resounds through the room. Conversation halts and the string instruments fall silent. For a moment, I'm not sure to whom the Sar Dyēus spoke, but Selnor slowly turns his ire from me, to the dragon king.

"Zhoric," Selnov hisses, using the king's true name, a warning in his tone. Alixor presses a hand on my thigh, staying me. I didn't even realize I'd started to rise, and lower back down into my seat.

"Do not make me repeat myself," the Sar Dyēus says, his focus solely on his meal.

Selnor's face twists into a silent snarl, but after a moment he rises from the table and leaves the room. Silence permeates, cloying and uncomfortable. The Sar Dyēus offers no further words or explanation. As soon as he moves to pick up his glass, the musicians resume their playing.

After another two courses of food are served, a male attendant comes to the Sar Dyēus's side and whispers something into his ear. His eyes rise from his meal to scan the sky outside. When the messenger backs away, the Sar Dyēus rises, and we all stop what we're doing and rise with him.

"A matter needs my attention. The banquet is over."

"Your Highness, you've yet to give your blessing," Alixor says. Traditionally, the Sar Dyēus closes these ceremonies and sends the couple to their mating room, but that doesn't appear to be happening.

"We will attempt this again tomorrow."

"If you could only—" Alixor tries.

The Sar Dyēus doesn't offer him another glance and raises his hand. "Tomorrow."

"This is absurd," Alixor says through his teeth. As the Sar Dyēus leaves, the guests return to their seats, their eyes straying to us as they occupy their mouths with the rest of their meals and soft murmurs.

I cast a glance back to Thrace, but he's gone, already following the Sar Dyēus out the door. Alixor moves to follow them when another elite reaches out a hand to stop him. "Alixor, I wouldn't."

Alixor snarls in his face. "I wouldn't attempt to stop me. First he dismisses my father and now he insults me by not giving his blessing at my own banquet? I won't stand for it."

My blood rushes, adrenaline spiking hard in my chest. This is not the calm and poised Alixor I'm accustomed to. This is a child, crying at what he cannot have. While a child may hang upon its mother's legs in hopes of getting what they want, I can't understand why Alixor believes he can do so with the Sar Dyēus.

"Alixor, maybe we shouldn't," I hedge softly.

"No," he snaps. "This is an offense that will not stand. I'm done waiting. I will have you tonight." Snatching me by the arm, he leads us out of the banquet hall to the main corridor we came through, before leading us towards the west wing.

I can either placate him, doing my best to calm him, or let this scene play out. If he confronts the Sar Dyēus, perhaps the king will exert his power and punish Alixor. I can't know what that would look like, but if there's a chance he'd revoke Alixor's privilege of producing offspring, it might free me of this, so I keep my mouth closed.

We don't get far when Alixor stops at the end of a short hall where we see the Sar Dyēus, Thrace, and another man standing with them. My skin prickles and I grip my skirt in my fist.

I recognize that frame. His wavy, chest-length hair. I know that golden gaze as it looks down the hall at me, and that sharp, crooked grin rising the beauty mark at the top of his cheek by his left eye. That face has seared itself into my memory since the moment I saw it days ago with Ninon. The rogue that does not behave the way a rogue should. My fists are clenched so hard my palms sting with the sharp bite of my nails.

"Who is that?" I ask, the question passing my lips before I have a chance to stop it.

Thrace stiffens as he notices us, but the Sar Dyēus doesn't even look our way. His intensity is directed at the mysterious stranger.

Alixor curses, but it seems even the presence of this stranger won't deter him. He releases me and marches towards the three men. He doesn't make it far. The Sar Dyēus's hand shoots out, and without even touching him, Alixor stops in his tracks, his body rendered immobile. I see strain and tension in the tendons of Alixor's hand as he fights against whatever magic the Sar Dyēus has put upon him.

The Sar Dyēus doesn't looked away from the stranger, but the force of his power keeps Alixor pinned in place. "Leave, Alixor. Before you make me do something you will regret."

The stranger angles his head, his crooked grin unchanging as he slides his hand into the pocket of his pants. "I wonder, do you have that kind of power?"

My brows furrow. The Sar Dyēus has depthless power granted to him by the gods themselves. So why did this rogue question it? And why was the Sar Dyēus meeting with a rogue at all?

Alixor spits a strangled warning from between his teeth. "You do not want to do this to me."

That seems to get the Sar Dyēus's attention and he slowly turns his head to look at Alixor. He inhales. Slowly. Deeply.

My heart aches with how fiercely it pounds, my soul begging him to release me, to tell Alixor that he cannot have me.

The Sar Dyēus doesn't look my way, almost pointedly ignoring my presence. "Take my blessing and leave." The words are strained, as if he doesn't truly wish to say them. He holds Alixor in his thrall for another moment before releasing him.

Alixor opens and closes his hands and straightens his jacket before turning on his heel. It wasn't a public blessing, nor was it in the proper phrasing, but Alixor accepts it all the same. "Come, Kaisa. It looks as if I'll bed you tonight after all."

I close my eyes and allow the sudden hollowness in my chest consume me wholly, and then open them again. The Sar Dyēus, Thrace, and the stranger are all looking at me, and I can't help but wonder if they care at all what happens to a woman like me.

# Chapter Seven

My thoughts run faster than Aspa across the Sere as Alixor drags me away. "Who was that?" I ask again.

"It's no concern of yours," Alixor snaps, leading us back to my room.

I need to let it go. I won't get anywhere with Alixor. At least not this way. But the taste of freedom was on my tongue when I'd convinced myself that the Sar Dyēus would remove me as Alixor's carremai and all that's left is a deep ache in my chest. Kalixta will come here. Ninon is gone. And I don't know where I belong anymore.

The sun is sinking low now, casting everything in golden yellow that will soon fade to shades of orange and red, before deepening to the shadowy purple and blue of night. I wonder about that mysterious shifter and how he flew to the Realm that day. Perhaps our eyes deceived us. Maybe he's he's a high ranking soldier defending us against the worst of the Realm. I wonder if Ninon is there now, morphed forever into a dragon's body. I wonder, a little, what that would feel like.

In my room, Alixor's brow is drawn, his mouth pulled down in a frown. It doesn't matter where I belong, because right now, I'm here. Right now, I have to figure out a way to get Alixor out of my room so I can take a dose of the contraceptive, because whether I want it or not, whether I like it or not, Alixor will have me.

"The Sar Dyēus gave his blessing, yet you're still upset," I hedge.

Alixor shoots me a dark look. "Very astute, Kaisa."

I haven't the strength rein in my expression, so I turn to hide my face.

He sighs, then slips back into the softer skin I know well. "I am upset. I do not mean to take it out on you."

"Perhaps you should seek out your father," I say, turning back towards him. "Find comfort and wisdom in him."

"What about you?" he asks, rubbing his hands up and down the bare skin of my arms. Bumps erupt along my flesh at his touch and he easily accepts it as anticipation.

"I'll be here and ready for when you return," I say, working hard to give a suggestive slant to my voice.

Alixor leans in and tracks his nose across my cheek to my ear. "You are phenomenal. What did I do to deserve such a match?" *Absolutely nothing*, I think as he leans back. "Perhaps I don't need to see my father. Perhaps I only need you."

I silently curse myself. I either took it too far in my coquetry or he is simply that eager. "Perhaps some medical attention, as well," I deflect. "The Sar Dyēus's power was intense. I didn't know he could render a man motionless." His eyes flash with annoyance. "And he dismissed your father from your banquet. I wonder what Lord Selnor would think of the way the Sar Dyēus treated you after."

Alixor's hands tighten on my arms. "You are right. I'll consult my father. Then, I shall return for you."

"Take all the time you need." I give him a congenial smile, thinking of my niece and nephew to make sure he believes it.

Alixor takes his leave swiftly and as soon as the door shuts behind him I rush to the bed and feel around for the vial. A sound escapes me when my fingers don't immediately close around it, but another swipe of my hand and I feel it against the tips of my fingers. I pry out the cork and the scent immediately assaults my nose. A curse flies from my mouth and I press the top back on. Waving the air, I stride to the window and push it open to clear the room. I open the vial again, stopper it with my index finger, and tip it. The cork goes back and the droplet catches the light of the sun. Just as I'm bringing my finger to my mouth, the door opens. I go as still as Alixor did when the Sar Dyēus ensnared him with his magic.

"Kaisa?" Alixor's voice is a terrifying combination of curious and calm. "What do you have there?"

Lie. I need to lie. But what can I say when my heart is beating so frantically I know he can hear it? I press the tip of my finger under my tongue, giving myself time to think. Holding the vial tightly in my fist, I remove my finger and have to swallow a few times around the taste before I can speak. A mild numbing sensation buzzes along the edge of my tongue.

"It's something to help calm me," I say, going for some modicum of the truth. "I need to finish freshening up—I didn't expect you back so soon."

Alixor shuts the door behind him, the sound of the latch echoing as he crosses the room. His movements are a slow, steady prowl, eyes locked on my hand clutching the vial. "I was informed my father is delivering souls to the gods. I didn't wish to disturb him in the skies."

Blood rushes through my veins, heating my skin. He's in front of me now, gently caressing the back of my hand, then twisting my fingers until I release the vial.

Alixor leans in close, his other hand coming up behind my neck to jerk me to his mouth, crushing his lips against mine, forcing me to open for him with his tongue and teeth. If I wasn't trying to hide something, a kiss like this would be thrilling—wanted. I'm hoping beyond hope that he doesn't know the taste on my tongue and what it means.

Then, he yanks me back hard, putting such little space between us that his hot breath burns my lips. "I have *tried* being gentle with you, Kaisa. I have tried being patient with you, making you feel *calm* and *comfortable* and ready to take my seed, and you return my gestures, my affection, with this." I flinch at the sound of the vial shattering into pieces. "Did you truly think I wouldn't know the taste and smell of dragonsbane? I will not have yet another female undermine me and forgo her duty." He snares me around the waist, hands rough, fingers digging into my back.

He crushes his mouth against mine again, hate and pain radiating through the contact, then he drags his cheek across mine, all the way to my ear. "I should kill you for what you've done." He breathes in, deep and ragged, then sighs. "But you have so much potential in you. I can feel it." He nuzzles his nose forcefully against my jaw. "And I will use it for my brood, even if I have to make you, and then...then, maybe I'll kill you."

With another rough jerk, he throws me to the ground. I spin and catch myself with my hands, turning so that I'm crouched in a low fighting stance. He swaggers towards me, laughing, shaking his head. Seeing me take up my position must be wildly amusing for him. I'll let him think whatever he wants. It will only serve me better. I'm shaking my head, too, my disbelief at war with something Ninon and I always believed. The dragons of Dyēus shouldn't be trusted. I shouldn't be surprised at this turn in him, but I am, and my heart is wounded all the same. For me, and for all the women who came before me. Who else has this happened to, if it's happening to me?

"You may be skilled in taking a dragon out of the sky, but you stand no chance in defeating one in a real fight. Relent, Kaisa. Do your duty. Bend to me easily and I will let you go home and live your life. This will not end well otherwise."

His words only serve to boil my churning blood, making me dangerous and volatile. I bow my head and relax my body as I stand, keeping my arms loose at my sides. I look up at him from beneath my lashes. What other option do I have?

He smirks. "Excellent choice. Now, I would much prefer to do this in an enjoyable manner, for the both of us, but if you fight, I won't keep any promises. I am getting my offspring from you, Kaisa, one way or another."

A scream builds in my throat, threatening to erupt in his face. A warning. A promise. Instead, I say nothing. Do nothing. I let him come, bracing myself. Alixor approaches slowly, savoring the moment, drawing it out. He circles me once and I stay still and silent.

"Bear my offspring and return home, Kaisa," Alixor says again, whispering in my ear, soft and sweet like a lover. "You were made for this."

It's in that moment I know. When he touches me, I will kill him. I let him think what he will, because I intend to show him exactly what I was made for.

Then he's in front of me, his hands on either side of my face, pulling me to him again in a kiss that once might have set me aflame in the best possible way. This kiss makes me want to turn everything to ash. I meet him, throwing years of pent up rage and disappointment into the kiss.

I dive my hands into his hair, gripping and pulling him closer to me. He growls his approval, relenting a step, relaxing his body. My hands fall to his cheeks as his lower to my collar before falling on my breast, the other lowering to cup my backside. I undo the upper stays keeping his jacket in place, the buttons of his undershirt, and expose his bare chest while his arms remain trapped in the binds of his sleeves. He breaks the kiss and pulls back a fraction. "That's more like the Kaisa I know," he purrs. "Let me ease your nerves. Let me forgive you."

He knows nothing and forgiveness is not what I seek. I answer by pressing my mouth against his again and drag my hands back up over his shoulders, fingers digging into his jaw, his neck, before reaching behind me as if to pull loose the tie holding my dress in place. He smiles against my mouth. I smile too as my fingers grasp the pin in my hair. I slip it out. My hair cascades down my back. His smile widens, hands coming behind me to twine into the loose waves. I take a wide step back, the motion tugging against his hold on me, and as he moves to follow, I thrust forward back into his space, into his momentum, and drive my pin straight up into his heart.

Alixor roars, and throws me with such force I slam into the wall across the room. "You, *bitch*," he snarls, looking down at the pin sticking out of his ribcage. A wispy line of blood trails from the entry point.

He yanks it out, throwing it to the ground, the clatter of it still in my ears as he's on me. His first strike is a slap straight across the face that fills my mouth with the sharp taste of iron. His next shot is a gut kick that steals my breath and has me sliding down the wall, curling into myself, clutching my stomach. He grasps my ankles and yanks me until I'm flat on my back. He rips my skirt aside. I scream and kick, but I'm dizzied by his blows and he's strong, unbearably strong and he pins my arms above my head, and traps my thighs to the floor with his shins. Blood leaks from his chest onto mine. Still I scream. I scream and scream until he hits me across the face again, my vision darkening as I see him undo his trousers. My body is uncooperative as I try to pry my arms and legs from his hold. He moves his legs off mine, but before my body can react to the freedom, he grabs me under the knees and pulls, positioning himself between my legs. He's panting, hands fumbling, his body swaying slightly as my vision blurs.

"You bitch," he spits again, his voice climbing an octave. "You've ruined everything."

My struggle is weak as his body lumbers over me, so I scream again, rage pouring out, tearing my throat apart. His grip on my wrist falters and I pull a hand free and reach up, fingernails clawing, trying with everything I have to distract him. My fury comes out in grunts and screeches. He looms above me, grimacing, his gums bleeding. The whites of his eyes are consumed by the thin red lines that expand wider and wider until blood leaks from the inner corners. Crimson drips from one nostril, then the other. His next breath is a shudder and more blood falls from his mouth, landing on my cheek, the corner of my lips. My surprise turns into a smile, remembering Ninon's words; *Like you, it's beautiful, but deadly.*

"Dragonsbane," I whisper, the word hoarse and filled with rage, "you *son of a bitch.*" His eyes widen, teeth clenching before he coughs and more blood speckles my face. His hand comes around my throat and though he's dying, it does nothing to quell his brute strength as he squeezes.

Alixor's face blurs and I hate the sight of him. I hate that he's the last thing I'll see before I die, and I wish I could see anything else before my heart beats its last. Then, as if my ravings were prayers, I do. I see another face over his shoulder. For a moment, relief floods me. Someone heard. Someone has come to stop this. Then, I realize who the face belongs to.

The rogue.

"I was going to kill you, anyway," I hear him say.

Fear rears its terrible head again as more blood sprays

over me, and a hot, unbearable pressure drops on my chest. The hold on my throat loosens and I suck in desperate gulps of air. Then Alixor's head disappears and, with a wet thump, the pressure is gone. The rogue is outside my line of vision, but I hear him curse. I need to get up. I need to move.

I shake away enough of the dizziness in my head to push myself up on my elbows and see the rogue standing before me. I follow the line of his arm down to his large, strong hand. He holds a mop of orange-gold hair, attached to which is a head. I catch the slope of a familiar nose, the curve of lips that kissed me, threatened me, lied to me, all the way to the gore trailing from Alixor's neck. The room is cast in red from the sinking sun, drenched in smears of scarlet. Halfway across the room, his body is flayed open from the back, a bloody mass cast to the other side—his spine. Saliva coats my tongue as bile rises to my throat. That could have easily been me.

I manifest the strength to keep myself upright. The stranger tosses Alixor's head to join the rest of his body and when I avert my eyes, I see my pin on the ground. I lunge for it, closing it in my fist, but the rogue takes hold of my hand and I'm brought to my knees before him. "It's mine," I growl, baring my teeth as I try to wrestle my grip out of his.

"Now, now. Don't think I'm going to let you blame this on me."

"As if I have the strength to rip out a man's spine," I spit as I tug on my hand, trying to pry it from his.

The rogue smirks. "I think you and I both know this little trinket was laced with dragonsbane. I did see you collecting it the other morning, after all."

"Then I'll dispose of it and all that's left will be what you've done."

"The room reeks of dragonsbane. Even if they don't know about this, they'll know you tried to defy your suitor.

And isn't that an offense all its own?"

My chest heaves. He's right. Of course he's right. We breed with them and they protect us. I didn't intend to hold up my end of the bargain and so Alixor had no reason to uphold his. And because I wouldn't relent, I'm walking down the path to certain death. "If you didn't want blame then why do this?"

"I don't like men who take what's not theirs," he answers.

I pointedly jerk my hand back and I stumble onto my backside when he lets go, pin still in my hand. I look from it, back to him. "Who are you?"

His gaze flickers to the glowing red sky beyond. "Someone whose company you won't much enjoy unless I leave now."

My eyes follow to where he's looking. I remember him wild and terrifying in his dragon form until the moment the daylight hit his scales. "Night...you only shift at night?" I question. That can't be true though, I've seen and slayed rogues in the day as well as the night.

"Such is the curse of the Realm."

My eyes widen a fraction. "So you *are* a rogue."

"Some say I'm *the* rogue. Ozias," he says with a mock bow. He looks around the room as if the carnage is nothing. "They'll put you to death for this."

"Not if I blame you. I can clean up my mess and simply leave yours."

I stare at him, pure adrenaline keeping me upright despite the ache splitting my head. He's right, though. They *might* find out I killed Alixor, but they will *know* what I was trying to do if I can't clean up the contraceptive well enough. The Sar Dyēus's words linger in my ears: *we dragons have a keen sense of smell.* Then there's the fact that I wasn't exactly quiet, and it's likely someone else might even know I refused him. As much as this rogue's time is running short, so is mine. Then my heart stops. Kalixta is coming to live here, if what Thrace said was true. What will happen to her if I stay? If she has to watch me die? Will they punish her in some way, too? I killed an elite. I defied him by trying to become impregnable. I curse, looking around, avoiding what once was Alixor. I work my jaw and finally meet Ozias's eyes again. "They'll blame us both. Whether you delivered a killing blow or not, you destroyed his body. They won't stand for that."

He smiles again. "Clever little creature. Lucky for me, they can't get to me where I'm going." Then, his gaze flicks to the skies. "Speaking of, it's time for me to go. Good luck, Kaisa."

The words fly from my mouth before I can think to stop them. "Take me with you."

He raises a brow, but his expression remains unsurprised. Somehow, I know I'm playing into his hands, but I don't have another option. Not if I want to live. "You know what happens in the Realm, don't you?"

"I'm beginning to think I don't," I answer. "You're no monster."

"Not yet."

"And the others in the Realm? Do they remain human, too?"

"They all do by day. The night is another story. And here beyond the Realm, well, we're practically savage." He pointedly looks to the darkening sky.

My mouth dries at that revelation. I want to ask after Ninon, but our time is running out and I'm afraid of the answer. Afraid that if I don't hear she's there and well, I'll let my grief decide for me. Instead I ask, "Can the dragons of Dyēus truly not enter? Will I be safe from them?"

"Yes. But are you ready to live with the rest that goes along with it?"

I lift my chin. "I'm not ready to die. You see evidence enough of that here." My body shudders with the effort it takes to breathe. Ninon might not be there, but hope and what he's told me has to be enough for now. Is this the right choice? Do I even *have* a choice? The risk of leaving is great, but the one of remaining is certain.

"Will you take me?"

Ozias says nothing and silence settles between us. I have nothing to give. Nothing to offer. Then, he shrugs and struts towards me. "Who am I to deny a damsel in distress?" His eyes rove down my form, then he snatches me around the waist, drawing me up against him. I hiss at both the pain Alixor inflicted and an unexpected feeling that ignites with his touch, filling me, making me feel powerful in his embrace. I struggle to breathe, my head suddenly dizzy. Ozias leans back and peers down at me, humming. "Interesting." My brows knit together, watching his eyes track over my face. "Stay still and quiet," he warns before scooping me up from behind the knees to hold me against his chest.

The atrium outside my door has access to wide openings for dragons to come and go at their leisure. Ozias doesn't make it very far when I hear a familiar voice behind us.

"Ozias?" Thrace says.

"Play dead," Ozias whispers to me. I hesitate and he gives me a firm squeeze. I relent, my face going slack, my body heavy in his arms.

"Are you going to stop me?" Ozias asks, angling his body towards the sound of Thrace's voice.

"You know that's not possible," Thrace replies, and I wonder at that. Surely he could alert the Sar Dyēus. "But I hope you will stop. *Think*, Ozias."

"I am thinking. I'm doing an awful lot of thinking right now and I like what I'm thinking." Could Thrace help with the mess I've made? Even if only for the sake of my sister? My mind spins in sluggish circles, trying to find another way out.

"She killed Alixor with dragonsbane. The others are

coming, are they not?" I know the answer when Thrace remains quiet. Even if he would help, there's not enough time for it. Ozias goes on. "When they find out what she's done, they'll call for her death. Tell me, how will you explain *that* to her sister?"

Thrace's answering growl is threaded with menace. "What are you planning?"

"You and Zhoric have your designs, and I have mine."

"Ozias, that's not fucking fair and you know it."

Ozias laughs, the sound vibrating from his chest into my muscles. "Fair would be if my people could shift at will. Fair would be if we could change form at night outside of the Realm. Fair hasn't exactly been the name of this game, but perhaps *this* is the beginning of fairness around here," he says, hefting me up higher and I try not to squirm at his firm, unrelenting hold.

Ozias's words grate against my mind. I don't know what he means. I don't know what any of this exchange means and I'm wondering if I've made yet another grave mistake in asking him to take me. But I can't stay here. Here, there is only death for me now.

"Don't get her killed," Thrace says.

Ozias huffs a laugh. "I intend to give her a life worth living." Then Ozias is walking again, my mind swaying with his easy movements. The air around me is cool with the rapidly approaching night. Ozias's hand tightens where he holds me, then he's shifting, my body held close to his. I tumble down into the cradle of his claws, tucked against his chest, much like my little nephew was only days ago in Thrace's. There's the telltale moment where I feel weightless, and I know we're in the sky. I open my eyes, catching sight of the sun, a tiny ember dipping below the horizon. Panic grips me. *Savage.* That's the word he used if he was caught outside the Realm at night. He's not going to make it. The night will turn him into a bloodthirsty beast. He's going to kill me and I have no one to blame but myself. I should have relented to Alixor when I had the chance. Even the very thought churns my stomach in protest.

I hold onto consciousness, though I feel it slipping from me as my injuries settle and my adrenaline fades. I'm not sure how much time has passed when the ground meets us, solid and jarring. Ozias transforms and I'm in his human arms once more. The swift cadence of his steps pounds in time with the ache in my skull. I hear what sounds like a hundred voices. I pry open my eyes and the shadow of Dyēus looms in the distance, outside the boundary of the Realm. Too many people clamor around for me to make out much of my surroundings, to hear anything beyond their buzzing words, but I see iron. Pale brown stones. Creeping vines in a color only found in Dyēus—*green*. Ozias twists one way, then another, perhaps seeking someone out, but the action blurs my vision and nauseates me, so I close my eyes to shut it out.

"Chain her. Now," Ozias orders. I feel myself passed off to other hands. I want to scream. I want people to *stop touching me*. I'm desperate to fight the hands that grip me, but my movements only dizzy me. I'm moved again and I think I hear Ninon call my name. *Ninon. Ninon is here.* Relief floods me. Perhaps this reckless decision was worth it. I think I hear Ozias tell her to be quiet; I'm sure I hear her when she tells him to fuck off.

I want to call out to her, but all I can do is sob with the reassurance of knowing she's alive. That she's here. The hands lay me down on my stomach, carefully adjusting my head. A net of cold, heavy weights are cast over my prone form, and I'm suddenly back in my room in Dyēus, trapped under Alixor.

*No.* I blink my eyes open.

"No. No, stop. Please," I beg, my voice scratchy and pathetic.

"It's for your own good," Ozias says, kneeling up by my head.

My pulse flutters frantically and I feel the moment night settles in. My vision sharpens and my eyes feel like a dagger slices clean through each orb. "No, take me back," I whine, my breaths coming in short, painful pants. I can't become this thing I've killed most of my life. I have a fleeting moment where I realize Ozias was telling the truth. Hands, human hands, handle me. This place isn't full of monsters. Ninon isn't a monster. The rogue, Ozias, isn't an outlier. Horror cuts through me. Just what have I done by shooting those creatures out of the sky all this time?

Pain like I've never felt before lances through my core, like I'm ripping at the seams. It's so sudden the terror of it grips me and refuses to loosen its hold.

"Don't fight it," Ozias says.

I don't listen. I scream as the transformation tears like a wind across the grassy plains, swift and unforgiving and powerful. I push against it as hard as I can, trying to hold onto my frail human frame. Try as I might, teeth grinding hard, I contort and reshape.

My bones crack and bend.

My skin twists and splits as scales and soft fur replace my flesh.

My jaw unhinges, opening wide, accommodating my elongating teeth. The razor sharp edges slice my lips.

My fingers splinter, talons curving from the nail bed, my hands unrecognizable as they slide into the ground, as if it were the ripe silt of a riverbed instead of solid rock.

My back arches, muscles bunching, and my wings unfurl, but I'm held tight by the chains. It is torture. It is agony to be given these wings and not unleash them into the sky. I gnash my great teeth. I rear my mighty head. I scream and screech and bellow from the depths of my massive chest.

My eyes wheel upwards, towards the newly star speckled night, searching for the familiar away from the chains that bind me and my body that betrays me.

I roar and rage and rage. My heart pumps wildly. And

finally my mind spins inward towards a deep unknown inside myself, and then I feel nothing else but the desire to
destroy. The world goes dark, and my soul goes with it.

84

# Chapter Eight

My body feels painfully small back inside my human skin. I should be glad; it means Ozias was telling the truth, and yet, a small part of me is aching to expand into that beast once more. Then, I think of the transformation, the pain and revulsion of it seared into my mind. The rest of the night comes back to me in fragments and shards of multicolored glass, like gazing through a sunbeam. A slash of white, gritting teeth. Silent screams from a wide open mouth. A black so deep it has no end. A sky littered with stars fading into nothingness. Chains slipping against scale covered muscles, a tangled mane tugging and tearing on links, wings heavy and grounded, tongue dripping with blood. My body is a bruised fruit, my blood like sticky juice leaking from its broken skin.

Twisting my head, my cheek grazes the grit on the cool

compact dirt floor. From between the heavy chain link net, Ozias stares at me. He's sitting, leaned against an expansive brown stone wall, forearm draped over one raised knee while his other leg stretches out long in front of him. His open robe is held together by a single band across his ribs, showing off his clean cut abs and chiseled chest. In contrast, I'm panting, sweat dripping down my temples. My dress torn and tattered. Exhaustion and the blows I suffered have swollen my eyes, making them difficult to keep open. I press my mouth shut and squeeze my eyes closed.

When I open them again, Ozias is still there. The sun must have risen some time ago since it's bright, even in the pits of what I've made out to be some kind of holding chamber. From my position pinned to the ground, I can't make out how high the walls are. I press myself up, but only get so far with the heavy chains holding me down. I shake first from the effort, and then from some deep-seated, innate response to confinement. My airways constrict.

"Get. Me. *Out*," I snarl. My throat is torn to shreds and I hardly recognize my voice. A violent tremor rocks my body.

Ozias tilts his head to the side. "I won't be the one to do the honors, but someone is coming."

"No," I pant, my muscles coiled tight. "I need to get out now. I can't." I suck in a deep breath.

"You can. Breathe. Someone is coming." His calm demeanor only enrages me.

I huff out a harsh exhale. My body is beyond sore and holding myself up beneath the chains is doing nothing to regain my strength, but at least it makes me feel like I'm doing something. "Get Ninon. I don't want anyone else."

"I can't do that."

I bare my teeth. "Horseshit. As *the* rogue isn't this is your Realm? You can do anything."

His eyes narrow a fraction. "How I wish that were true." He studies me, watching my chest billow. "She doesn't want to see you. Not yet, at least."

I bark a laugh, which spirals into wild hysterics. The fight in my bones leaves me and I wilt down onto the cold, hard ground, letting my cheek rest in the fine scattering of dirt. "That's the weakest lie I've ever heard."

"It's no lie," he says, as gentle as a breeze. "She doesn't wish to see you now; she will see you when she's ready."

A sob teeters on my breath, and any remaining strength I thought I could muster goes with it. Perhaps I imagined Ninon last night. Conjured her in my mind, and this man is torturing me, manipulating me to bide his time like I did with Alixor. "I'm tired. Go get her and be done with this."

When he doesn't reply, I tilt my head to see him better. Rising from his resting place, he comes to me and leans in close so I can see his face more clearly. As handsome as I remember, but I liked it a little better last night when he helped me than I do now. "I'm sorry that you came to be here without fully knowing what you were getting into, but I'm glad that you are." I can only narrow my eyes at him, though with my swollen eyes, I'm certain the effect is lost.

We both turn our attention towards the walkway, hearing the sound of approaching footsteps at the same time. My hearing has never been as good as a dragon's and suddenly my mouth dries as panic sets in. "Your help is here." He rises and steps away.

"No. Wait."

He keeps moving, his voice echoing back to me, "We'll speak soon."

I don't know who's coming. I don't know where I am or what I'm doing here. I hazily recall the words he left Thrace with, his intention to give me a life worth living. If only I believed words spoken with dragon breath. "Send Ninon," I scream after him. When there's no response, I shout again, my voice cracking on the words, "Send her!"

I don't have long to suffer. As promised, someone comes. I maneuver enough to see up to their hips, but nothing beyond that. They bend down into view on my far right. A Nevoban. A woman. Her brown hair falls in wide, loose curls around her beautiful face, her skin a touch lighter than mine. The chainmail net jangles and there's a click as the mechanism unlocks. A few moments later, the weight lifts from my head and shoulders, and after the chains are removed from my lower half, I'm gripped firmly but gently under the arms and pulled up into a kneeling position. My body feels like it's floating from the lack of restraints, and I press my fingertips into the ground. The woman kneels in front of me. Her soft amber brown eyes rove over my face, flitting to every point of pain marring my skin. Her lips press together firmly as she tucks my hair behind my ears. "Their true colors are not so beautiful, are they?"

I draw a sharp inhale through my nose. "They are what they are."

"They are not all like that. *We* are not all like that," she assures.

"We?"

She only smiles. "I'm Atlanta."

I wait for her to explain. When she doesn't, I offer her my name. "Kaisa."

Atlanta nods. "Your friend Ninon has spoken of you much since her arrival."

The world tilts and I allow my hands to take more of my weight. "Is she well?"

"The transformation is an adjustment for all, but she's handling the shifts well enough now. Even still, the mornings are needed for recovery in these early stages. Can you stand?"

I nod, but she braces me by the elbows all the same, ensuring I'm stable on my feet before guiding us out of the enclosure, a simple three walled square with no ceiling. We walk down a long, open-air corridor. The wall Ozias had been leaning against stretches long in either direction, its top thick with vines and leaves. A space wide enough for a dragon to pass separates that wall and running parallel to it is row after row of sectioned off enclosures butted up against another wall at the back. The rooms are open to the walkway, but at the center of each is the same chain net that held me down last night, affixed to the ground by iron rings that no doubt sink deep into the earth so that a dragon's strength cannot break it. The enclosures count nearly a dozen, but most look unused: dried leaves and twigs collect in corners, the chain netting covered in fine layers of dust and grit. I have no doubt that Ninon didn't know what was in store for her. There's no way she'd ever willfully chain herself—she's too much like me in that way.

"Ozias said Ninon doesn't want to see me."

"She didn't expect you here. At least not this soon. She will see you after you speak with Ozias, I'm sure."

There's a kindness to Atlanta that I choose to accept, at least for now. And, if she won't bring me to Ninon after I speak with Ozias, I will find her myself. By any means necessary.

Once we're out of the hall of stark chains and hollow walls, the full glory of the Realm of Rogues stretches out before me. Where Dyēus is all crisp white stone and carefully cultivated trees, the Realm is a wild aggregation of roots, trees, and foliage twisted into buildings and fortresses, like the earth grew a city from its soil and the sun gave it life. The morning light streams through the leaves of the canopy, birds singing from one branch to the other, their melodies sweet and peaceful. Tears spring to my eyes. Ninon has never been close to such greenery and I wonder how she felt seeing it for the first time. It's incredible, how something like this could grow in the midst of our desert plains. Seeing this place and Dyēus are the only things that make me believe the gods truly exist. The mild, misty breeze lifts my sweat soaked hair. Some dragon here must have magic akin to that of the Sar Dyēus. That power calls to me and the desire to follow where it goes pains me.

More astonishing than the greenery is the people. So many people. Mostly younger looking, though I note a few of my mother's age, even less a bit older than that. Children run and weave through the roots and pathways, both boys and girls shirtless in the warm sun. Not a single mark mars the girls' chests. And there's women, so many women. The people we pass don't say a word to me, but their gazes linger. The hair along my body begins to rise, anticipation churning under my skin, though I sense no danger.

I'm led through well-manicured paths, up steps made from roots, and along wide swaying bridges trussed between the trees. Below, mounds made of earth and stone hunker down between trunks. People come and go from them, and when I look closer, I realize they have doors and windows. Among the trees, branches reach out long and hold aloft more structures that encircle the trees in part or in whole like mushrooms I've seen before on the trees in Dyēus, stacked upon one another and connected by platforms and twisting stairs. Dwellings, I guess, from the cooking workspaces and cozy seating I see as we pass the windows.

We walk onto a large bridge, arched and stationary, positioned above an open central square. The stonework and dragon glass inlaid into the square's ground sparkle against the light of the sun sneaking in between the leaves. A faint, happy tune playing on a wind instrument reaches my ears, and my footsteps falter.

"Not quite what you envisioned?" Atlanta remarks.

"No," I murmur, shutting my eyes, tamping down the tide of emotion threatening to overwhelm me. I've killed these people. I've taken family members, ruined lives, all because of a lie. We were told savage creatures prowled these lands. That a fate worse than death awaited us if we dared enter this place. What fools we are. "Does everyone here transform?"

Atlanta studies me before answering. "Every one of

us." There's a weight to her words. There's more she wants to say. There's more that I need to hear, and I'm not certain I'll like it. "This way," she says, leading us over the crest of the bridge and my eyes widen at what creeps into view before me. It's the grandest tree I've ever seen, its breadth spanning the width of two dragons side-by-side with their wings spread. More of the same semi-circular structures climb the tree, deep into the boughs, and at the very top, a massive edifice exists between the branches, rising above the canopy. At the end of the bridge, we reach a set of stairs, steep and worn smooth. Atlanta begins the ascent, and I follow.

"This is the Alcazar, where some of us live and where we meet to discuss our...predicament."

When she doesn't continue, I prompt, "Which is?"

Atlanta inclines her head to all that's around us. "Once you adjust to the shifts at night, you'll see. We are not savage here inside the Realm. It's only if we leave this place do we fall prey to the curse that makes us feral. All of us are trapped, and we've been trying, for many, many years, to free ourselves."

My nostrils flare as I struggle to get air into my lungs. I've jumped headfirst out of one trap, straight into another. The question I have now is, who set this one?

"I'm not sure I understand what I see or what to believe anymore." Did Ninon know it would be like this before she came? Is she even here? I thought I heard her last night, though now I'm not certain. Both Ozias and Atlanta said her name, but only after I revealed it. They could be manipulating me.

"You might not have sought out these questions you didn't know existed, but you'll get the answer to them all the same."

With each step growing heavier than the last, we continue to climb, on and on. A thought swirls around in the back of my mind that I can't comprehend or name. It comes to me as a broad question: How? How was anything here possible? Finally, we reach a landing where there's a circular arched entrance. Atlanta leads me in, and it's bigger inside than I thought possible. Open and grand and quiet, the inner atrium immediately makes me think of Ninon. Sunlight drives in from all angles, catching dust motes that shimmer like stars against the dark backdrop of bark and creeping vines. Tomes and trinkets line walls of shelves that appear grown from the limbs themselves. Halls divaricate from the round chamber at odd angles and levels, all of which are connected by more carved steps.

I'm led down one of the halls to a door and Atlanta opens it, revealing a bedroom. The wood floors are worn soft and smooth and even. To the right, another door leads to a small bathing chamber, and on the left hand wall there's a dressing table with a wardrobe beside that. Against the far back wall is a bed covered in soft blankets and pillows in shades of green, amber, and gold.

"You can clean up." She nods to the bathing room. "A change of clothes is on the bed."

"You're not afraid I'll run away?"

Her eyes move across my face, head tilting. "Where would you go?"

My limbs fall heavy at my sides. It doesn't matter where I am, it seems. I was trapped in Nevoba. Trapped in Dyēus. And now I'm trapped here, too.

After Atlanta leaves, it's a long while before I finally look down at myself. My dress is stiff with Alixor's blood, the edges frayed, the once luscious silk covered in snares. Blood flakes and falls to the ground as I peel the fabric from my skin. Alixor was not the man he pretended to be. That much I know is true. Dyēus has dealings with the Realm, which I never knew, but saw with my own eyes. The Realm...the Realm is not what Dyēus claimed it was. How deep does the deceit go? And where is the truth?

Catching my gaze in the reflecting glass above the

dressing table, I freeze. "My mark."

I ghost my fingers along my sternum. The symbol has faded, the lines once dark and vivid, appear washed out. My brows cinch tight as I touch the image and feel something deep within me rumble in response. I pull my fingers away and turn, inspecting my back over my shoulder. The thought comes swift and fierce, the image of wings springing from my spine, my skin sliding into scales. My skin tingles. When I face my visage again in the mirror, my pupils dilate.

"Kaisa? Are you all right?" Atlanta calls.

I whip my head toward the door, hands trembling. "Yes," I call out, rolling my shoulders and shaking my hands until the feeling is gone. "Yes, I'll be out in a moment."

Once I'm cleaned and dressed in the clothes Atlanta left for me—dark brown high-waisted trousers and a high-neck cropped shirt—I leave the room and Atlanta is right outside the door. Without a word, she lifts her hand near my face and I flinch back. Her movements slow, but she doesn't drop her hand. "May I?"

Gaze flicking to her hand, then back to her face, I nod. As her fingers land on my cheek where Alixor struck me, a heat spreads and the throbbing pain lessens as if she were pulling it out of my skin. I blink, my mouth opening. "How?"

Savage beasts, that's what we were told the Realm holds. Mindless, flesh-eating creatures that slip out at night to feast on us. But this...this is as if...

"Did you think you would reclaim this form and not have the powers it comes with?"

I capture her wrist in my hand, blood rushing to my ears. "The dragons of Dyēus have this power, *they* have the power. You, you shouldn't."

"Kaisa," Atlanta whispers softly, a placating tone on her tongue.

I shake my head. "What you're saying...it sounds as if..." My chest heaves, and I am choking, drowning in the words she's yet to say.

"You know what I'm saying, Kaisa." She lays her cool hand on my cheek. "Even if your mind can't yet comprehend it."

I shove her away with more force than I knew I had. She gracefully steps back, as if she allowed me to push her that far. "Stop." I press a forefinger and thumb against my hot, stinging eyes. "No. This can't be. They take our children; you cannot mean..." I cover my mouth to press in the sob clawing at my throat, to keep myself from uttering the words. Ridiculous, impossible words. She quiets me with a gentle shush as she wraps both my hands in hers. I want so desperately to deny it.

"I don't expect you to believe me," she says. "Most women who come here, like Ninon, discovered the truth—that we are dragons, as much as they are—or at least suspected it enough to try to find the answers. You and me though? We were not so fortunate in the manner in which we came here." She holds my hands tighter, bringing them close to her chest.

Dragon. There it is. That's the truth I couldn't bear to hear. That she is...that *I* am, a dragon. My hands shake in hers, my shoulders rattling. Something inside me stirs. Atlanta stands a little taller than me, and though I don't tilt my head to look at her, I'm watching her face from beneath my lashes. There's a wariness as she stares back at me, like she's waiting for something to happen. Even though she looks my age, there's a depth to her eyes that I've seen in Thrace's gaze, in the Sar Dyēus's, and even Ozias's, that speaks to years lived longer. "How old are you?"

"Dragons don't keep track of the years. But I was born shortly after Zhoric took power. The tactics to get dissidents to breed back then were not as...conniving, as they are now. Ozias saved me, when the rumors of this place were worse than they are now, and I've been here ever since."

My mind flashes with images of Alixor forcing himself upon me, demanding me, attempting to take from me. Atlanta must recognize what she sees in my expression, because she's nodding. "Ozias told me what happened to you in Dyēus." Her fingertips flutter against my hand, like she wants to let go, but she keeps hold. "You should know that, even without the contraceptive, you wouldn't have fallen pregnant."

My head shakes lightly. "I don't understand. How?"

"Your body was already set on rejecting it. It cannot happen unless you are willing for it to be so, even with part of yourself locked away." Her gaze flits down to my mark. "The men didn't understand the power we have over ourselves. They didn't learn the art of manipulation and seduction until later, well after me and women like me were subjected to far different methods. Much like what Alixor attempted with you."

Hot tears brim my eyes and burn my throat. "That's what happened to you."

Her jaw flexes. "It's in the past."

"It still happened."

"Yes," she says, eyes glazed with tears of her own. "It did."

I only nod. There are no words of comfort I can offer that time has not already tried.

She presses the fingertips of one hand against my fading mark. "What has been stolen from you, you've taken back." Understanding dawns, bright and hot. *They* didn't take my ability to transform into the great and powerful creatures I've envied my whole life. *He* did. The Sar Dyēus stole it. From all of us. From *me*. "This mark will continue to fade as you change and discover that full potential living inside of you." Atlanta holds my gaze. Fierce. Strong. Protective. Her hands continue to hold mine. My lungs no longer feel like they're contracting, the muscles of my neck soften. I loose a shaky breath from my lips, the whole time keeping my eyes on hers. Then she nods and tows me along with her as we leave the hall. "There's much more to learn, and my story is only a small part of it. Now come. Ozias is waiting to speak with you, and patience is not a virtue of his." And without further conversation, we go up.

# Chapter Nine

Atlanta takes us up a final rise of stairs to the top of the Alcazar. It's another wide open space, much like the room below, but with hardly any walls. It reminds me of the colonnades back in Dyēus. The openings, wide enough for a dragon to pass through, are formed by branches that drip down and weave back into the floor. A canopy of green leaves overhead casts dappled light across the floor. I pick up a yellow leaf that's fallen to the floor and spin it in my fingers. It looks precisely like the hair stick Ninon gifted me, like the ones she used to collect. This high, I can see the clear, open sky meeting the Sere that stretches on for miles to the sea. There are no mists that shroud the view to the outside world. My eyes teem with unshed tears. What agony it must be to see this, to turn into those creatures, but not reach what lies beyond. And I realize that agony is mine, now too.

"You're looking better."

I spin on my heel. Ozias stands by the single wall in the room, made up completely of the same branches that melt down and sink into the floor. I'm sure he wasn't there when Atlanta and I first entered.

"Different is the word you're looking for, I think," I answer, dropping the leaf. His gaze moves to Atlanta, then back to me.

"And do you feel different?"

There's a thrumming beneath my skin. I feel too small and too large all at once. I don't know who I am, or what this place is. I press my fingers into my mark as I shake my head, not at his question, but at what I know. "I can't live like this," I whisper, the words firm, my shoulders heaving towards my ears. "I can't have this thing inside me and yet do nothing with it. It was one thing when I thought I wouldn't remember. When I thought I'd become this beast, this savage thing at night and I would remain here, unable to hurt anyone, but to believe..." I cast my gaze to Atlanta, before returning to him. I swallow hard. "To believe that this is what I'm meant to be and still not be free? It's torture."

Ozias's gaze travels down the length of my body and back up and I flush under his attention. It feels different from when Alixor would look at me. It feels curious. Intrigued. Like he wants something from me, but only if I willingly give it. After a long moment he addresses Atlanta. "Check the border stations for new developments. I'll be in touch when I'm done here."

Atlanta lowers her eyes, dips her head, and clears her throat. "Of course."

Ozias watches as she leaves, and when she's gone, he turns and starts walking towards the wall. "Follow me."

I'm so deep in my head, I feel like I might combust. The very air around me is too thin to take in. I'm teetering on the edge of panic and I start naming things I see.

*Smooth bark. A falling leaf. A twisted root.* Ninon does this when she gets overwhelmed, and I calm myself enough to move my legs. It appears as though he intends to walk straight into the wall, but at the last second he turns by a narrow margin and walks through a concealed opening. If I'd blinked, I would have thought he disappeared. I quicken my pace and exit from the same spot, to see him climbing yet another set of steps that leads into another chamber built between the highest boughs of the tree.

"Why is the wall like this?" I ask.

"I got tired of making doors," he responds as he waves a hand around. "There were so many to craft."

His answer confirms one thing—he built this place, or at least the Alcazar. "And I see you didn't tire of crafting stairs?"

He looks over his shoulder at me with a wry grin. "Steps lead me to where I want to go. Doors have only ever stood in my way."

The stairs open up to a more enclosed room. A large table stands in the center, strewn with papers, and a full scale model of our lands, complete with a replica of Dyēus floating above. The scene is illuminated, mimicking the sunlight exactly as it is right now. I have the urge to stare at it to see if it will brighten as the morning morphs into afternoon. Beyond, a small desk sits to the left, and to the right, a set of low plush settees overlook a wide open-air window. Between them is a glass table with a two decanters and two glasses sitting on top. I notice a wall of the same making as the one we came through behind the couches. He offers me a seat, and I lean over, attempting a glimpse beyond the wall.

"If you're interested in seeing my bed, I'll gladly show you," he offers, his voice low and inviting. My belly coils in response, and I note the interest in his eyes. He's not simply teasing, but there's something else there, too. A test. What happened last night with Alixor has left its mark, but

I won't let it take from me. I allow myself to feel as my gaze travels over him in consideration. I let myself take interest and grin in appreciation.

"Perhaps another time," I say. His eyes widen in amusement as I firmly take a seat. "Though I'm certain you have no shortage of female companionship, given that there are so many here."

"We've been taking in women from Nevoba for a long time, one way or another."

I hum, wondering at all the ways my people have found their way here. How is it that we haven't all discovered this secret and come flocking here to free ourselves? Except, I'm not free, and then, I think of my mother. Completely devoted to the dragons of Dyēus; most women in our community exactly like her. I remember women whom my mother and others shunned when I was a child. I remember when they disappeared, never to return. We were told they were chosen to work in Dyēus. I wonder if some of them really ended up here.

Ozias leans forward, the wide sleeves of his robe rising to expose forearms corded with muscle and laced with scars. He looks me up and down, eyes staying on the center of my torso. "Fascinating."

I look down at my breasts, then glance back up to him. "Perhaps you don't see much female companionship after all."

Ozias chuckles at my lightly crude joke. "Your mark, Kaisa. It's already fading."

My mind clangs against the word already. So, this isn't unique to me. Though something about it is. "What's fascinating about it?"

Ozias leans forward to have a closer look. "It usually takes longer to fade to this degree."

"Will it disappear entirely?"

"Hopefully."

I trace the mark again, suddenly upset about the loss,

then drop my hands into my lap. "Atlanta said it was placed to keep us from transforming."

"Yes. It kept you in your human form and severed you from your celestial self, or your draconem, as we traditionally call ourselves."

I scan his chest, my gaze lingering before meeting his eyes. "You don't have one."

"The curse Zhoric placed on me is not the same as yours."

*Curse.* The don't know the word in this context, but there's a stirring in my veins that feels familiar. "What does that mean? What did he do to you?"

"A curse is the use of magic to hinder or oppress. Over a century ago, Zhoric stole the power of a god for himself. Those who opposed him, like myself, were cursed by his newly claimed magic to remain in our dragon forms at night with our minds turned into brutal beasts that craved violence and desolation. By day, we were trapped in our human forms. There was a battle. As you might imagine, dragons who cannot organize themselves or transform by day didn't fare well against those who sided with Zhoric. It took only one night and one day for us to realize we needed a place that could protect us—and keep others safe from us—so I created the Realm."

Ozias is claiming the Sar Dyēus has the power of the gods themselves. What could he do against that? "How?"

"I have a unique power that allows me to replicate magic. I took the curse that was cast on us and molded it into a barrier. Anyone who entered would fall prey to the same fate we had."

My brows draw together as I try to make sense of everything I've heard, everything I've seen. "Why did the Sar Dyēus do this?" I ask, not brave enough to use his name. "I imagine he had his reasons for placing such horrendous curses on us all."

"Not all the events that followed his coming to power were entirely in his plans, but it doesn't matter. It happened, it's still happening, and Zhoric got to keep what he wanted."

"And what was that?"

"Control. Power."

I lift my chin. "You realize you're expecting me to believe that you're the victims and the dragons of Dyēus are the enemy? They've protected us from you for years." I say the words, but I find that I don't really feel them. My transformation last night has awakened something in me and it's hungry for more.

"No, not from us." Ozias picks up the glass decanter filled with amber liquid, unstops it, and pours himself two fingers worth.

"Oh no? Need I remind you that I transformed last night and went completely out of my mind with violence? That you nearly bit my head off yourself the first time we met?"

Ozias raises a brow at me while lifting the bottle. The smell hits my nose and it's familiar enough that I understand what it is. I lift a finger. He pours me a smaller portion.

"You needn't remind me of anything," he says, passing it to me. Our fingers touch and our gazes meet. He doesn't let go of the glass. "The power your transformation revealed was felt by all of us here. I wouldn't be surprised if Zhoric and the strongest in Dyēus sensed it. If the very gods themselves did." He lets go of my glass and takes up his own. "But no, the creatures you kill are something else. We don't leave the Realm at night, and most of us don't leave during the day, not unless we want to tussle with a dragon of Dyēus when we can't even shift at will."

There's more to know about the dragons I've killed, who they are, but my chief concern right now is him. "You left," I remind him.

He smirks around the glass raised to his lips. "I'm special," he says before taking a sip.

I give him a placating smile, and he must know it because he chuckles. I twist my glass in my hands, watching a thin layer of liquid cling to the sides. "What do you mean by the power my transformation revealed?" I recall all the long looks I got while walking here. I assumed that all new faces were met with the same reaction, but perhaps not.

"You tell me." He takes a long sip. "Why don't you tell me your story to see if we can figure out how this all adds up?"

I take a drink, then wet my lips after swallowing down the burn. "I don't know if I want to help you figure out anything at all, at least until I see Ninon. I don't even know if she's really here." Aside from my own life and my sister's, right now, she's the only thing that matters to me. Everything he's saying could be a lie. Everything Atlanta said could be a lie. I can't deny what I'm feeling inside my body, though. It's as if that missing piece I've felt my whole life has finally been placed in the palm of my hand; I only need to twist it until it fits right.

Ozias snorts. "You were wrecked when we arrived, but not deafened. You didn't hear her screaming for you? She'd been so quiet up until then. Certainly didn't expect that level of profanity from her."

She had told him to fuck off. I draw my lips into my mouth, stifling my smile, considering what I should do. Our eyes meet, his golden gaze blazing with hunger. Desire. And while I know that look all too well, he has good reasons for wanting to know about me, and I don't pretend it's anything otherwise. Still, I'm here, for better or worse, and I can't leave without risking my life, or someone else's. And there's a large part of me that wants to know more about this, whether it's a lie or not. Even with the violence and loss of control last night, I've never felt more powerful, more myself. "Where should I begin?"

Ozias tilts his head, loose hair falling from the knot

at his crown. "Let's start at your selection ceremony, shall we?"

And I so tell him how the Sar Dyēus deemed Ninon and me undesirable, the heat I felt in my chest when he did. I tell him of the first time I saw Alixor, and how he wanted me immediately.

"The Sar Dyēus reminded him I was marked as undesirable. Alixor's father, Selnor, even protested the selection at first." I shrug. "Alixor was adamant though, and so he got to have me. By the time I went to Dyēus, Alixor's father didn't seem at all concerned."

Ozias hums. "I know Selnor's elahi," he begins, but elaborates at my curious expression. "Elahi is a unique power that only some have, which makes us stronger than others; or as Dyēus call themselves, *elite*—but Alixor was born only fifty years ago. I never found out what his was. He must have sensed your power with whatever elahi he had. My suspicion is Zhoric placed a concealment on you during your selection ceremony; otherwise others would have wanted to breed with you, too."

My eyes widen as I remember Alixor's words. "Last night, before Alixor attacked me, he said something in that vein. About my potential?"

Ozias smirks, his head shaking as a low chuckle rises from deep in his chest.

"What?" I place my empty glass down on the table next to us. When I lean in, he does, too.

"I think the Sar Dyēus is about shitting himself right now. The question is, will he try to get you back, or is he going to let this thing play out here?"

I straighten in my seat, pulse pounding in my ears. "He can't do that. You said I'd be safe here."

"Oh, you're safe here," he says, but then he shakes his head. "That doesn't mean there aren't other ways for him to get to you." Ozias taps his knuckles against his mouth, then stands and paces a little in front of me. "The Sar Dyēus wants no other in the world to have more power than him, and I think you might end up being his match. Which is exactly what we need."

My fingers curl around the arms of the chair as I watch him pace, figuring things out at breakneck speed while I rush to catch up. "Did you know this? Before you took me?"

He leans down close enough that if I surged upwards, our mouths would meet. "You mean before you begged me to take you?"

"If that's how you remember it," I say, not backing down.

His mouth is a pretty smile. "I think you should ask me what my elahi is."

I tilt my head. "Why would I think you have one?"

"I told you I was special."

My mouth twists into its own little smirk. "What's your elahi, Ozias?"

He pins me with his amber eyes, glittering and alive. "I do believe that's the first time you've said my name. It sounds lovely coming from your lips."

I lift a brow and wait. He's as smooth as one of the farmhands on delivery day.

His mouth twitches in and out of a smile. "Aside from replicating magic, I can see potential bonds between draconem pairs."

I close my eyes and draw in a deep, slow breath, then open them again. "What, exactly, is a bond?"

Ozias grins. "I'm so glad you asked." He draws away and pours himself another finger's worth of liquor, then motions that I'm welcome to help myself to more. I don't.

"Bonds are sacred, cherished among our kind."

I tuck my hair behind my ears in an attempt to ignore the rippling under my skin at hearing his words. Ozias gives me a sidelong glance, pausing long enough that I take in a few controlled breaths to calm myself. He sets down the decanter and looks out to the open sky.

"Dyēus doesn't allow bonding, but draconem here will—though we can't make use of its true purpose. The bond is what keeps us whole, for lack of a better word, when we collect souls. For every soul a draconem collects, their partner is supposed to cleanse." He picks up a decanter of water and pours it into the glass of amber liquid until it runs clear, spilling over onto the table, down to the floor. "But, if the second half of the pair isn't there…" He fills up the glass again, this time with the alcohol until the liquid turns the clean water brown, the smell overpowering, the cup running over the edge.

"And because Dyēus doesn't allow bonding, the draconem out there collecting souls are turning savage and dying. Without a bonded partner to purge the impurity they take from a soul before it can be granted to the gods, they're consumed by it."

"Are all souls filled with such malaise?"

"Most have a little, some are teeming with it, and a very rare few have nearly none. Without cleansing from a bonded partner, it stays in our bodies. The dragons you've slain, the ones you thought were rogues, are those diseased dragons—the ravaged, we call them. They, as much as you, didn't have a choice in what happened to them. They are the boys they've forced you to surrender. The ones they've stolen from us. They are the draconem they've deemed less than." With every word he says, I wrap my arms tighter and tighter around my middle, my fingers digging into my ribs. I don't want to believe it, but how can I not? I've witnessed them take and take and take and seen the meager rations we get in return and have been out in the Sere to cut down the creatures they supposedly protect us against. I don't want to hear anymore, but Ozias doesn't stop. "And when one of them dies, another draconem, or someone who was meant to be, dies too. Someone they had potential to bond with."

It takes a moment for me to register his meaning. If all of us in Nevoba are supposed to be draconem then…my mouth falls open. "The deaths in Nevoba." Ninon's mother. All the others.

He nods, his expression grim. "Here, too. And in Dyēus we imagine."

I cannot undo what I've done. I know that, and yet I recall every dragon I've taken from the sky. I squeeze my eyes shut for a moment. "Can they be saved?"

"We've never had access to one to find out. What we do know is that the deaths are happening among our weakest shifters. Among those who don't have an elahi. You will be safe, as far as we can tell based on what we'e seen from your energy output, but…I cannot say the same for your friend. She's taken a long while to acclimate to the transition, and none of us feel an elahi within her."

I hang my head and press the heels of my hands against my eyes so tight that colors dance behind my closed lids. Ninon's always worried that her fate would match her mother's. And now…she might actually be right. My ears buzz and my head swims.

Ozias's hand lands on my shoulder near my neck. "We can't change what's happened. We can, however, change what will be."

I shake my head, and when he moves to pull his hand away, I grab his wrist, clutching him tight. I lift my head, heavy and reluctant until I meet his eye. "How? You've been stuck here for over a century. What change can happen now that hasn't already been tried?"

Ozias kneels down so that we're eye to eye. "I told you I can see potential bonds. And now, because you're here, there's something new we can try. Something that has never been done before. Something only you can do."

My heartbeat thrums. "What I can do?" Is he telling me he saw a bond between us? That his elahi and whatever mine is can accomplish something together? Or perhaps my elahi on its own can help.

He keeps his gaze locked with mine, making sure I hear him, making sure I understand. "You can bond with the Sar Dyēus."

My ears ring and I'm suddenly dizzy. I suck a deep breath through my nose. I couldn't have heard him right. "What?"

"I saw it yesterday, Kaisa, clear as day, when the two of you were in the same space. I saw the line connecting you."

I can't fathom a reason he would lie about this. I curse Erenmaag, the god of fate and agency, to have laid this burden upon me. I press my lips into a thin line. "Is there no one else?"

"Not in all these years have I seen a bond going to or from the Sar Dyēus. Not until yesterday. Not until you."

"What would bonding with him accomplish, exactly?" I snatch my hand from his wrist, and he sits back on his heels, giving me some space.

"When you bond, you share power. What's yours is his, and what's his, is yours. Once bonded, you'll be able to remove the god power he stole. When it's returned to the gods, the balance of our world should restore as well."

"No more sudden deaths."

He shakes his head slowly. "No more."

I chew on the edge of my thumbnail. If it will save Ninon, there's no question, none whatsoever, on whether I'd do it. And yet, a thought churns in the back of my head. This unshakable sense of self-preservation that my mother always called selfishness. And perhaps it is. "Will I have to stay bonded to him? Once I've removed the god power?" I cannot tie myself to that man for my life. I'd kill him before I endured that fate.

"A bond can be broken at will."

I nod, squeezing my hands together. "How is it done?"

"As with most things, it's easier said than done. And

there's much we'll need to do before we get to that."

"The deaths in Nevoba have become more frequent." What I really mean to say is, do we have the time to do what is necessary? Before it's too late?

"It's been the same here." His gaze strays to look out the windows surrounding us before focusing back on me. I feel like I can't get enough air into my lungs. Ninon is at risk and every day that passes could be her last. I realize he's waiting for me to say something. He's waiting for my answer.

I look him in the eye. "I'll do it. I'll do whatever it takes." And I will do it quickly, because I don't have another choice.

# Chapter Ten

The sun is settling into late afternoon by the time Ozias leads me out of the Alcazar. Most people we pass smile at him. Occasionally, they acknowledge him with a wave or a cursory nod, but most go on with their daily tasks. No one pauses in what they're doing to bow before his presence. No one stops and remains silent as he passes. He is no king here, but there is an admirable amount of respect. The farther we walk from what appears to be the Realm's main hub of activity, the thinner the trees and the fewer number of people there are. The land begins to look more and more like the Sere I'm familiar with. Scrubby trees replace the lush. Dry, cracked earth replaces the rich brown soil. Eventually the rise of the mountains appear as we reach an open swath of ground. A small gathering of people clusters around a group of children. My steps falter at the vaporous cloud emanating from the center of the cluster; a succession of others follow.

"They're...shifting," I realize out loud.

Ozias smiles. "Come and see what's possible."

As we draw nearer, a familiar figure stands out from the crowd. Her spine is as straight as her long auburn hair tied at the nape of her neck. I'd know her anywhere. I wanted her to be here. I thought she was here, but seeing her in the flesh makes everything that's happened until now feel unreal; she is the only thing that makes sense. The figure turns and my heart lurches as a half dozen small dragons lift into the air behind her.

"Ninon," I whisper, taking a half step before dashing toward her.

Ninon meets me with sure, fast steps and she doesn't stop until she has me in her arms. I pull her to me and grip her tight. Her hold is steady and familiar. I don't stand a chance of holding it together. I crack, my face crumpling, an aching sob heaving out of my chest.

"You left me," I wheeze, the words warbled and horrible. I want to take them back into me. I don't want to blame her or make her feel like she's done wrong.

"I'm sorry," she whispers, holding me tighter. "I had to."

I'm nodding, over and over again. I know it as well as I know I couldn't bear a child for Alixor, but there's still so much I don't understand.

Ninon pulls back and glances over my shoulder. I follow her gaze to where Ozias is walking away. A dragon flies low overhead, banks around him, then flies back to the center of the ring where they transform into small child, no older than seven years. She shakes out her hair, spinning on her toes and smiling. I suck in a breath. A girl. She bears no mark on her torso, though I suppose if she was born here, away from the Sar Dyēus, there'd be no reason why she would. The other dragons transform back into their human forms, a mix of all ages and genders. Ninon links her arm through mine and pulls me a little farther from where the people are gathered.

I turn my attention back to her and a sudden rush of anger heats my blood. Did she know this about the Realm? That the savagery was a lie? That children, young girls like we once were, could transform into these horrible, magnificent creatures. "Why didn't you tell me?"

"By the time I knew enough about this place and knew I would leave home, Kalixta was pregnant. I didn't want to make you choose." She pauses, her shoulders tensing beside mine. "I didn't want you to try to make me stay."

My anger spits hot like grease. I bite my tongue and hum my understanding. I fear what I'll say if I open my mouth.

Ninon waits, watching as the girl speaks animatedly, arms and hands flying around. "This upsets you."

"Of course it does," I snap, but pin her arm against me to keep her from pulling away. "You didn't give me the option to decide because you didn't tell me."

Ninon unwinds her arm to stand in front of me and places her forehead against mine. "I know. I thought...I believed I was doing the right thing. But then you ended up here anyway, and Ozias told me what happened to you." She leans back to look in my eyes, her hands gripping my upper arms. "I caused you more trouble in the end."

Sighing, I bring my hands up to cup her elbows. "You gave me what I needed to stop Alixor. You couldn't have known it would have ended up like that, but I'm glad you thought it was a possibility." I heave another sigh, trying to diminish the fire raging inside, and pull her in for another embrace. We stand there for a time, simply holding one another. In many ways my life has been wrought with disappointment and change and choices that weren't my own, and through it all, Ninon has remained my only constant. Until now. It feels like something has cracked between us. Not unmendable, but certainly changed.

Finally I release her and wipe my eyes and face with my palms. "How did you find out about all this?"

"I didn't know everything. Not until I got here. That was the other reasoning I gave myself when I decided not to pull you into this." Ninon nods and we walk closer to the group gathered to watch the children shift. As first, it happens slowly. Not at all like the swift, rapid change I'm accustomed to seeing from the dragons of Dyēus. As I watch, it appears as though they're vibrating, like the beating of a bee's wings, but their bodies remain absolutely still. It reminds me of waiting in the Sere to be relieved by another hunting group, feeling the ground tremble under us, dust and pebbles dancing at their approach. I feel an echo of that now beneath my own skin. The air becomes thicker as a subtle glow emanates from their bodies, and what looks like steam rises from their skin before clouding their forms from view as their transition takes hold. Over a dozen small dragons now stand where the children once were, craning their heads, stretching their wings, shaking their manes as if to say *watch this, look what I can do*. I turn back to Ninon and find her staring at me, her gaze discerning.

What I'm witnessing is impossible in the face of everything I know. And completely incredible if I deny what I thought I knew for even a moment. "If you didn't know for sure what you'd find, what was it that made you decide to come?"

She looks away from me towards the mountains. "You know of the passages in certain texts I have that seem to suggest we shouldn't believe everything the sky kingdom tells us. And my mother's notes in the margins of others."

We pored over those lines together as children. It gave us the confidence to feel what we did when it came to Dyēus, even if we never spoke about it to anyone but each other.

"I've thought of those lines often, but it wasn't until we started to look for a way to create the contraceptive that I learned more. Then, one of the first times I tried to retrieve the dracduat, I found a binding of parchment tucked into the crevice among the flowers."

That was well over a year ago. "What was it?"

"A letter from the women here in the Realm, telling of our truth and encouraging us to claim it. Hundreds of names were signed."

"How did you know to believe it?"

Ninon shakes her head, almost imperceptibly as she watches the dragons ground themselves and return to their human forms. "My aunt's name was on it. It was enough for me."

I straighten and just manage to keep from craning my neck around like a wild creature. "Is she here?"

"No." Ninon smiles sadly. "She passed. Like my mother."

My emotions feel as dark and tumultuous as a raging storm above the Rising Sea. That's two people close to Ninon who've now succumbed to the sudden deaths. It's beginning to feel less a question of if it will happen to her, and more like when. Bile stings my throat with the urge to throw up what little liquid sloshes around my stomach. "Ninon…"

She shrugs, and turns back to me. "More than wanting to find her, I wanted to believe this place was real, that what I'd read was true. Enough to find out for sure myself, but not enough that I wanted to put you at risk. You had a life back at home. And I couldn't continue being a huntress even if I'd stayed."

Ninon only became a huntress alongside me because we'd vowed in our youth to do everything together. While I was content enough in that space, glad of the distractions from the farmhands when they came and the camaraderie of the other hunters, Ninon was always learning something new. Trying something else, as if searching for her own place. Once she'd learned that the women here weren't entirely mindless monsters, there was absolutely no way she'd remain a huntress. None of us would.

"So, now what do we do?"

Ninon presses her shoulder against mine. "We watch. And we learn."

So we do. For the next hour or so, we watch the children shift back and forth between their two forms. I can't keep my eyes off the girls and the pure joy on their faces; how freely they slip from skin to scales.

"Only the children and some of the more powerful dragons can shift at will during the day," Ninon explains. "From my understanding, everyone, Ozias included, turns savage outside the borders of the Realm after nightfall. For us, I'm told we'll feel savage for the first few nights as our dragons are released, but then we'll settle into the change. After that, we can try to shift back into our human forms at nightfall inside the Realm if we wish."

An odd sensation washes through me. Relief mingled with disappointment? "What do most people do?"

Ninon shrugs. "I'm not sure yet. I haven't yet kept my mind from going savage. They tell me it can last a few days to a few weeks."

"And until then, you'll be stuck as a..." I pause, wondering about the correct way to phrase it. "In your dragon form?"

Ninon nods to the group that's starting to break up. "Until we're strong enough to shift, that's the case."

I draw my bottom lip in between my teeth. One of the things that bothers me most about turning into a dragon at night is the lack of control I have over it. The sooner I can figure it out, the better sense I can get of this place. Ninon came in knowing what to expect, like Atlanta said. I don't do well with showing up unprepared.

"I trust you've had a happy reunion?" Ozias asks from behind us, breaking me from my thoughts. "With the figment of your imagination, of course."

Ninon raises her brows.

"I wasn't sure you were actually here," I explain. "I believe he's attempting to tease me, and failing."

"Oh, I wouldn't go so far as to say that. You look fairly riled to me." He smiles, showing all his teeth. I twist my head away from him. I enjoy his smile entirely too much. It's threatening to raise my spirits. "Now let's eat before the night makes you both a lot less fun, but far more interesting."

Ninon gets hung up on his words, her lips pursing, but I crack a smile. "He's teasing. And failing. Again."

"You sure know how to take a stab at a man's confidence."

"And his chest," Ninon responds, and I squeeze her arm in surprise, my eyes widening.

Ozias's face brightens even more. "A woman of many talents."

I shake my head, drawing Ninon to my side to follow after him. "I believe that joke was too soon, Ninon."

"Alixor's death should have been sooner, considering he chose someone who wasn't even presenting herself for breeding, then proceeded to force himself on her."

I can't argue with her there.

Not until the smell of food hits my nostrils does my stomach twist to remind me how long it's been since I've eaten. The air is thick with the aroma of spices and the promise of nourishment. The food is laid out similarly to how meals are served at home with a long table hosting an array of options from stewed vegetables, dried and fresh fruits, and roasted meats and fish. We help ourselves to a stoneware platter and fill up with what we like. Ninon has already filled her plate and settled at one of the communal tables with Atlanta, who beckoned her over. I fill my plate lightly, unsure of how much is available and who still needs to eat.

"This is your first meal since last night," Ozias observes, adding a serving of roasted venison to his plate.

"I wasn't aware you were tracking my eating habits." I keep my eyes on the food, choosing lightly, but wisely.

"You need energy, Kaisa," he says as he adds more meat to my plate. "We have plenty for everyone."

I know how much work preparing and providing food takes. In fact, it makes up the majority of our days back home. It would be one thing if I were contributing to this meal and then taking what I want, knowing I can and will procure more.

"When we're able to shift at will, our need for sustenance is less. It took me a while to learn how to eat what I needed with so much time spent in my human form."

"A dragon doesn't eat?" I'd never really thought of it—I assumed they did.

"Our dragons are our celestial forms, and as such, don't require anything. Not food…" He pauses, lifting a small, round fruit, the color a deep purple. I recognize it as one I've eaten before in Dyēus, but never saw in Nevoba. "Nor any other physical desire, for that matter. Unlike these human forms of ours, which desire for much and ache with all our wanting." He lowers the fruit in front of my mouth, his liquid gold eyes watching me. For a moment, I think he might try to feed it to me. Instead, I take it from him with my fingers and pop it into my mouth. The sweet juice bursts across my tongue as I bite down. I hold his gaze as I swallow.

"And if I decided to stay as a dragon forever? When I learn to shift?"

"Your human self would feel a vast loneliness that your dragon wouldn't be able to ignore. Life is about balance, Kaisa, not about being one way or another. You can have both." I don't have to ask him to explain. I know it, I know the feeling because it's what I felt all my life, living without this other piece of me.

I follow him to the table to sit with Ninon and Atlanta. The small bite I had reminds me again of my hunger and

I waste no time digging in. The food is familiar and tastes of home. I wonder if Thrace has retrieved Kalixta yet. I wonder what the Sar Dyēus thinks of my crime. I imagine Selnor's rage at losing his son. I chew hard and swallow harder. It feels wrong to feel sorry for him, for either of them. I shouldn't feel for his pain when I don't regret what I've done. It makes me wonder what kind of person I am, and what killing Alixor has unleashed within me.

We're halfway through our meal when a woman with long pale, dust colored hair that's shaved close to her head on her right side and light, sun-kissed skin comes to Ozias's side. "Dyēus's units are on the move."

"That's sooner than usual," he says, which sounds like it ought to be alarming, but he goes on eating as if the news were nothing to concern himself over.

"We suspect they're changing their pattern."

"Are their movements consistent with ours?"

"Too early yet to tell."

"We'll get some keen eyes on it tonight so we can map their movements."

The woman nods, her eyes locking on me for a moment before sliding over to Ninon and lingering. "I'll gather volunteers."

"I'll join you." Ozias stands, taking his plate with him. "Atlanta, will you make sure they get settled in the enclosures tonight? Then meet me at the wall."

"Of course," she says, wiping her hands.

"What wall?" I ask when Ozias and the woman walk off.

"We have a boundary wall that surrounds the Realm all the way to the mountains. It's another line of protection against Dyēus and a clear boundry of the barrier for us here." She nods at their departing forms. "Issa handles most of the day to day, but there are occurrences when Ozias and I need to assist."

Dyēus's main base on the ground is at the edge of Nevoba's hunting area. They keep soldiers there as the first line of defense in any rogue escape or attack. Though I have a mounting suspicion that may not actually be the truth.

"You told me no one tries to get out. So what are they there for?"

Atlanta rises and Ninon and I follow suit, carrying our soiled dishes to a collection bin where people take them away for washing. "No one's trying to escape, but we do have needs to fulfill that require us going outside the Realm. Hunts, for example. But, as you know, hunting during the day is rather unsuccessful. Anyone who can shift by daylight will often go out to sea to fish."

Food. They leave to feed their people. And Dyēus has a hoard waiting at the walls, not to protect us as they've claimed, but to stop the rogues and take them to use as collectors. Dread coils around my spine, uncomfortable and threatening. I want to scream at myself for all the lies I've believed all my life.

"So, going out to sea, that's something you and Ozias do?" Ninon asks, unaware of my inner turmoil. She must have learned some this information already.

"Probably one of our more important tasks, yes."

Desperation to repair the damage I've done grips me by the throat. "Is there anything we can do to help?"

Atlanta shakes head, her curls lively with the action. "You'll both have plenty to do once you've settled into your forms."

"I'd like to see how fishing is done," I say. I enjoy the process of hunting, and I've always wondered about fishing, too.

"I'm sure Ozias would take you if you asked," Atlanta says.

I huff out a breath. "Why would he?"

"I think he'd do just about anything you asked," she says candidly, her flat intonation giving nothing away, which feels a bit like she's trying to hide something.

"That seems rather reckless."

Atlanta lowers her head to catch my eye. "Your unique position has given us a new opportunity. You are going to do us a great service, Kaisa. You deserve to know the answers to any question you have, even if it's as simple as how we fish." She finishes with a smile that melts away the lingering strangeness I sensed from her. "I hope you'll give our people the opportunity to see anything they wish to see for themselves one day."

"Right. No pressure, though," I say flippantly, as if the fate of hundreds of people isn't sitting upon my shoulders.

Atlanta tucks her curls behind her shoulders and scrunches her brows, shaking her head. "No, no pressure."

"What's this about?" Ninon asks, gaze flitting between the two of us.

"I can explain, as long as you're comfortable with that, Kaisa?"

For a moment, I think of Ninon withholding her information about the Realm and wonder what it would feel like to keep something from her. The fleeting thought tells me I'm still hurt and I brush aside the feral thought. "Ninon can know anything about me," I say.

"We do plan to keep this information to only a few of us. It's too early yet to know if it will work, or if it's even possible, and false hope can incite discontent."

"Ninon can keep a secret," I assure, and though I didn't mean for it to sound critisizing, Ninon casts her gaze down to the ground. I take a steadying breath and soften my words. "I trust her with my life. Always. She won't say anything."

I half listen as Atlanta tells Ninon about my potential to bond with the Sar Dyēus, though she, like Ozias, calls him by his true name. I sense more than see Ninon try to catch my eye as Atlanta tells her more about my strength, and the elahi that they suspect I have. Dusk is settling swiftly, and people move more quickly, finishing up the washing, turning to their dwellings or the Alcazar, others heading to the open field where we watched the children shift.

While I don't mind Atlanta telling Ninon about what they hope I can accomplish, I still haven't had much time to think on it myself. It's almost easier to pretend that this is something temporary; not my reality. Akin to how I felt whenever I visited Dyēus. If I fail in the task Ozias has asked of me, or worse, if I can't even begin it, my hands are proverbially tied to the fate of living here as this creature, contained and restricted, and Ninon may not live to experience much of this new life at all. The very idea tightens my chest.

"So it's true not everyone will shift at nightfall?" I ask once she's finished explaining to Ninon, attempting to distract my mind from the tension in my body.

Atlanta shakes her head. "Some will. The fact remains we don't have a lot of space for us all to transform comfortably at once. We often take turns shifting and spreading our wings. But Ozias and I, and others who've been able to master shifting at will during the daylight hours typically leave the night for those who cannot."

"What stops so many from being able to shift at will during the day?" Ninon asks. Her twilight blue eyes meet my darker ones. I wonder if Ninon suspects the same answer I do.

"Those who have an elahi eventually learn to shift at will. Something about having a unique ability beyond our usual draconem powers makes it easier to shore up the energy it requires. And for others, like myself, it's through sheer willpower and hard work. It took me a long time to master it, but…it was something I knew I had to do. For myself."

"You must feel incredibly proud to have accomplished it," I remark, impressed.

She hums a little in agreement, smiling to herself. "It's been worth the effort."

When we arrive back at the enclosures, sharp panic needles my skin at the idea of being confined again.

"I'll go first," I offer. Seeing Ninon restrained would ruin my resolve and I don't want another embarrassing display of my discomfort like this morning. I try not to think of it. From my transformation last night, I know this is completely necessary.

We stop before the enclosure I woke up in this morning, empty and waiting. I go inside, and lie down willingly, noting the marks gouged into the ground beneath me. Sweat breaks out along my skin as Atlanta secures the chains across my body, so heavy, yet with ample give. Enough space that when I transform I'll be confined, but not fully restricted. It's as humane an enclosure for a dangerous beast could be, I suppose.

The sky is purple with the impending night by the time she has me fully secured. My panting breath flares my ribcage, pressing against my confinement.

"I'll be back for you at first light," Atlanta says.

Ninon kneels at my side. "Remember to breathe. Envision the shifts you saw today. It makes the transition easier."

"Yeah?" I ask, the word strained. I can already feel a crawling sensation under my skin.

"Yes." She grips my hand through the net, solid and warm and real. "I'll see you in the morning." Then they go, leaving me alone. I hear the scrape of chains in the enclosure next to mine. The sound of locks clicking into place. Lying there, unable to move easily, I remember the pain of the transformation last night, the wrongness of my mind disappearing from me.

I don't have a chance to do as Ninon advised. Night falls and I hear the high-pitched scream of a dragon. My skin feels hot and itchy and I squirm and breathe hard, fighting against what's coming. A roar shakes the walls, so close it rumbles through my core. *Ninon—that was Ninon.*

I know it with every fiber of my being. Then, my own body betrays me. Twisting and breaking and cracking, the beast bursts its way out of my skin, my mind slipping, slipping, until it's nothing but fear and terror. I know only snippets of images—hands digging into the ground, shifting from talons back into hands, over and over, the long column of a pale throat, head tossed back. Clouds by day and stars by night, and endless rows of scales and teeth and claws. I have a deep, pressing need to exert this power, this strength, but no way to do it, no real goal. Only anger. Only sheer, undiluted outrage. So much power, taken from me. This thing that is somehow impossibly me, taken and reclaimed, but not what it should be. Not at all.

Then, oblivion.

The next morning follows the pattern of my first, except instead of taking me to Ozias when Atlanta releases us, we're led to some rooms in the Alcazar to rest. By afternoon when we wake, we watch the children shift, trying to figure out how to do something we should have naturally done in our own youths. A precious, glorious time of our lives, stolen from us. I learn nothing new about the Realm or Dyēus. I eat with everyone, but only speak to Ninon, and on occasion, Atlanta. I do not see Ozias. I wonder what he's doing, where he is, if he's in the Realm or out beyond it.

That night, the transformation takes hold again. I turn bloodthirsty. Savage. Desperate. And the next night it happens again.

And again.

And again.

# Chapter Eleven

The night I shift into my scales without pain, my mind stays sane and I no longer feel the savage pull of the curse placed on the Realm.

I look with my dragon eyes and see the material of the world in shining dots and shifting colors. With it comes a keen sense of knowing. Of everything that has been. Of everything that ever will be. The sensation is vaguely familiar, like some long-distant dream I'm only now remembering. The sensation is too grand, too great. A part of me, the part I know most, tucked into the cavity of this great beast who knows so much, trembles and shies away. She cannot look upon this knowing without her heart racing. She cannot look upon this with acceptance and because her will is strongest still, even in this skin, I too have a sense of feeling unsettled. So, I don't dwell there. Instead, I crane my neck up, looking at this new world right in front of me to discover. Dragons drift lazily overhead, like clouds on a hot day, or else tear across the sky as fast as a shooting star. The color of their scales bring new brilliance to the night sky, the gleam of their teeth and talons like clusters of stars. Night is but a concept in this form. I hear change in the air with every twist and turn of a wing, and see the energy their passage leaves behind. It's as if I've seen the world with gauze tied over my eyes, and now it's lifted. The human in me is terrified. This gift is crushing and if she were not already accustomed to staring out at the endless Sere, the vastness with which the draconem can experience would crush her. How can she exist now in this great knowing of the world, when there is so much she didn't know before? This does not sit well with her. She is angry.

I shake my head hard and fast, mane swaying and sliding across my neck. My dragon is thinking of me, separate from myself—or maybe I'm thinking of myself as separate from this creature. I sigh, coming out as a huff from my nostrils.

I've tried to deny what I've seen and felt and experienced here in the Realm. Every time I work to convince my mind that the Realm is trying to deceive me and turn me against everything I've ever known, I remember the dragons of Dyēus who claim to be our protectors in the name of stealing our children. Here, though, I've only seen kindness. I've seen their children transform freely, with ease and patience. Each time I remind myself that Ozias wants something of me, I remember that the dragons of Dyēus demanded much more. Every time I try to deny that my skin is as much a dragon as it is a woman, this unnamable thing within me cries and screams and thrashes their head, unwilling to be silenced. Like ignoring my instinct on a hunt in the Sere, which has only led to missed marks and empty stomachs.

Deny as I will, I've watched the symbol on my abdomen fade. Deny as I will, I've witnessed young girls here transform into dragons at will during the day, safe and unchanged in the place they were born. I see them, and I know, I know, this is what I always should have been. Until the Sar Dyēus stole it from us. From me. I close my eyes and breathe, but my heart does not rage out of control like it does in my human form when I think of him—his bone white hair, his pale skin and high cheekbones and full lips, his eyes a green so dark they register black. I studied his face every moment I was in his presence when others cast their eyes down, a small defiance even when I didn't know the truth.

In the halls of Dyēus I'd watch him from the corner of my eye. He never looked my way, nor did I ever expect him to. My talons dig into the ground as I imagine Dyēus, rich with splendor and food, while we Nevobans get whatever is left. I imagine its grand fortresses and tall spires. Its winding halls and windows so vast you sometimes feel like you're standing on a cloud. I'm imagining it so well, I venture down the halls that led me to the nursery on that fateful day I found the Sar Dyēus staring at my nephew. The nursery is dark, though it was daylight in my memory. Faint coos and cries emanate from one bassinet or another. Two nursemaids flutter about the room, tending to them all. I blink, as if I'm watching in real time, then turn away, facing a hall I've never traversed—the one Alixor warned me against.

As I stare, I realize the hall is not as long as I would have thought, considering it leads to the Sar Dyēus's personal chambers. Smooth, solid white walls. No windows. Nothing open for a dragon to fly freely in and out of. I move past the nursery into the darkened hall. There's a shift in the air, a breeze from behind, like an encouraging hand at my back beckoning me forward. I slip through an archway at the end of the hall and stop before dark wood double doors, intricately carved with a scene of the sky—billowing clouds and pairs of dragons, sun rays streaking across. The lower half of the doors depict the ground, peppered with trees and rivers and people—a place I've never seen. I move to touch it and watch as my human hand passes through the wood. I jerk my hand back and stare at the solid material my fingers dipped into as easily if it were water. Holding my breath, trepidation wracks my body as I reach out again with my fingertips, only for my hand to move through the solid wood as before. Slowly, I let my hand drift through, then my arm. No pain, no change in sensation at all. With a mighty inhale I lean forward until my head passes through into an open room. My feet follow without my mind fully deciding to do so.

Inside it's dark, like it was in the hall. I can hear the faint, distant cries of the children. An intense sadness envelops me and I press a hand over my heart. It thumps against my palm, fast and deep. This dream is strange and I wonder how my mind has conjured an image of a place I've never seen. Venturing further in, I pass an undisturbed bed. Across the wide room from the great wood door I passed through is a circular balcony surrounded by a low railing made of smooth marble stone. The space is hardly bigger than the width of four horses standing side by side and it juts out into the open air from the rest of the room. From here, I can't see any buildings. No light. The gods eyes, the very gates to the heavenly realm, are perfectly framed between a set of columns on either side, and the depthless sky and stars beyond.

Sitting in the center of the balcony, is the Sar Dyēus.

I enter the circular colonnade, and cast my gaze up to the open night sky. Directly above where he sits, the gods eyes stare. The horizontally stacked ovals take the shape of clouds, but are too perfect in their curves to be natural. From between the two ovals, a kaleidoscope of colors pulse as if the sun or some distant star sits within the clouded center. Tonight, the light is dim, flickering frantically, but faintly. I step slowly, cautiously around the perimeter of the balcony until I'm standing in front of him. The Sar Dyēus's face is pulled tight with tension, teeth clenched. His head is tipped back, exposing the long white column of his throat. My heart seizes and I have to grip one of the columns to keep myself from falling over. I've seen this before. In images that pass by my eyes every night I've transformed, I've seen bits and pieces of this.

Of *him.*

His eyes are shut tight, though they work furiously back and forth behind his eyelids. He looks so young and so old, all at once. He looks pained. My fingers twitch, itching to smooth over his face, to stop whatever is happening. If he's in pain, I should let him suffer for all he's done. Gritting my teeth, I curl my hand into a fist. A question forms on the tip of my tongue, tumbling out of my mind hot and sharp.

*What are you doing?*

His body bows forward violently, as if he took a punch to the gut, then his head snaps up, his eyes opening and zeroing in on mine. I startle back a step, my spine pressed hard against the balcony railings.

"Get. *Out.*" His snarl pulls his lip, showing the straight white lines of his teeth. Impossibly, I stumble back another step, through the railings. I fall over the edge. A scream lodges in my throat, but instead of falling, I'm hauled away by an unseen force at unfathomable speed. Everything I saw getting here reverses direction until I slam back into myself, the night still too dark for my eyes, my pulse pounding in my ears, the weight of the chains draped over my body.

My human body. The dawn is near, but it hasn't broken yet. I should still be a dragon. My breaths come and go in short, frantic bursts as I try to sort out what happened, why I'm like this. Something's wrong.

A swift wind buffets the air and I shut my eyes tight against the dust churning around me. There's a resounding thump of a dragon's landing and I sense the billowing vapor of a shift.

"Kaisa?" The voice is breathless, as if he sprinted here on his feet instead of flying on wings.

I blink open my eyes. "Ozias?" He's kneeling at my side, adjusting the chains to see my eyes. "What happened?"

"You shifted."

"Yes, I gathered as much. But why?"

"I'm unsure," he says, his hands moving to undo the locks.

"Wait, what are you doing?"

"I know it's early, but I'm beginning to think our questions for one another have rather obvious answers."

"Ozias," I chide. "It *is* early. Aren't I at risk of...shifting back?"

"Even if you did, you passed the stage of savagery. You're no threat to anyone now." He throws the chains off my back. I press up to my hands and knees, and Ozias grabs one of my arms to help me stand, holding me steady. "Well, strictly speaking. What I meant is, you're not going to tear anyone apart without intending to at this point."

I sigh, long and steady, trying to quiet the image of me shifting into a feral, bloodthirsty creature and tearing apart anyone within range, him and Ninon included. In the next enclosure over, I hear the disquieted caws and frustrated grunts of Ninon's dragon form, the clanking and clattering of her chains as she moves her body to free herself. I frown, wishing I could see through the wall to her. She's been here far longer, yet she's still not settled into her dragon.

Ozias takes my chin between his fingers, guiding my attention back to him. Once he has it, he removes his hand and I realize how cold my skin is absent of his touch. "What happened?" he asks gently.

I catch my lower lip between my teeth. Instinctively, I don't want to share that I dreamed of the Sar Dyēus. It felt realer than any dream I ever remember having. Ozias wants me to help him take down the Sar Dyēus and telling him

I'm dreaming of our common enemy could be a conflict. I decide to go with a variation of the truth.

"I had a bad dream."

Ozias stares at me, his eyes moving across my face before he nods. "Come with me." He doesn't wait for my reply. He wraps my hand, cold and clammy, in his warm and dry one, and leads me out of the enclosure. I cast a glance behind me to Ninon. She left me to come here, so why does it now feel as if I'm the one leaving her behind?

Through the dark corridors and walkways, my eyes struggle to adjust. It's the time of day that turns everything blue and shadowy, and I wonder what my dragon eyes would pick up if I were wearing them instead.

Ozias leads me all the way to his private rooms at the top of the Alcazar. He'd been silent the entire way and now he turns to regard me with a keen look.

I fidget under his attentions. Does he know I'm lying? If he waits another moment to speak, I'll fold. I'll tell him everything and beg to keep my place here. "What's all this about?"

"Your energy," he says. "I can't figure it out. It's unlike anything I've ever felt."

My chin falls towards my chest as I loose a breath before looking up at him. "Is that a good thing?"

His head tilts as he considers. "It must be a good thing."

"Said with all the confidence in the world," I quip.

His smile is slow and lazy. "It has something to do with your elahi, which is a good thing. We just need to figure out what it is."

Turning from me, Ozias gestures over his shoulder for me to follow him. "I want to show you something."

We move to the center of the room and the table where the model sits, along with scattered parchments and maps. Instead of addressing it though, he catches my gaze with his stunning amber eyes.

"I've asked you to help us bring down Zhoric by bonding with him," he says and I tense at the sound of the Sar Dyēus's name so soon on the heels of dreaming of him. Instead of asking me about my reaction, though, Ozias's next words are aimed to ease my tension on what he assumes is my discomfort. "The power you emit is evidence that you can do it." He gestures to the mess with widespread hands. "This is our plan to make everything that comes after seamless."

I pull my lips into my mouth, then open with a pop. "Looks simple enough."

He laughs, moving closer to me, his arm pressed against my shoulder as he points to a thick manuscript sitting at the center of the table. "There we've compiled all the possibilities of what could go wrong when Zhoric falls from power, and our plan for dealing with the fallout."

The moment he mentions the possibility things could go wrong, my shoulders pull taught. I agreed so easily before, when I thought I would take the Sar Dyēus down and everything would be set right. Nothing is ever so simple and I flush with shame that I didn't consider all that could happen otherwise. I was so desperate to help make things right. To give my people back this incredible thing that's been stolen from us. And now I really think of my people, of having everything they've ever known suddenly ripped from them.

"All the Nevobans know is the rule of Dyēus," I say, shaking my head. "Most like the way things are and those that don't are not suffering in a way that is unbearable." Even as I say the words, I think of the wailing mothers and tired girls. I think of restless huntresses. I think of shoving my dragon back down into myself, never connecting with it again, and my stomach clenches. But my people don't know that feeling. Changing their whole world, their entire way of living for something they never knew? I don't know if that's saving them at all. "How can liberating them from a life they understand to one they don't cause anything but cause chaos? It's all they know."

"We will prepare them." He casts his hand across the table. "There are a thousand steps in this plan, and we will do everything in our power to help your people transition. But none of it, *none of it*, can happen until you are ready. The path we were on before you was long and toilsome. One we recognize may have never had an end. It was a dream. A wish. With you, we have a real chance. Not everyone will change easily, but change they will. It is inevitable. Without it, the deaths of both our peoples will continue. It will grow worse by the day. It already is. Being draconem is their right. It's part of who they are. Whether they are aware of it or not, whether they ever accept it or not.

"There's a lot of history that you don't know of yet, Kaisa." Ozias's tone is low, meant to soothe. I straighten my spine. "There's much that happened before you, and more that will happen yet. I want us to have a true partnership. One built on mutual trust and respect."

I bristle at the word trust, my shoulders drawing up towards my ears.

"Ask any question, and I will answer it. Spend time here with anyone from whom you wish to seek answers. We are not your enemy, and we want the same thing."

I find myself falling into his eyes as he looks at me with such hope. Such intensity. "I believe you," I say, the words hushed and precious. How can I not when tonight I felt what I did inside a dragon's skin? In my *own* skin. There's no sense in denying that, at least. What these two warring parties want with power and control means nothing to me. Giving my people possibility is everything. Saving Ninon from her impending fate is vital.

Ozias's features grow soft and he lowers his head, as if he's about to say more. Then, he looks over my shoulder and a second later, I hear it, too. Hurried footsteps drawing nearer and louder.

A woman walks in without announcing herself, Atlanta right on her heels. I recognize her as the woman who came to Ozias the other day to talk about Dyēus's dragons at their border.

"Issa? What is it?"

Issa looks from me to Ozias. She doesn't speak.

"Anything you need to say can be said in front of Kaisa," he assures her, all the while looking at me with such an earnest expression I've never before witnessed in a man. A wave of affection slinks along my skin.

Issa casts a look to Atlanta, who inclines her head. This appears to be enough for Issa as she strides further into the room, her long legs reaching us in five steps. "Another unforeseen death tonight."

Ozias's hands tense on the table. My throat constricts and I have to swallow a few times to ease the sensation.

"That's the second this week," he says, and I suspect does so for my benefit.

Issa nods. "The frequency has risen in the past month."

"Continue tracking them. We're continuing to include the Nevoban deaths in these numbers?"

"The ones we get information on, yes."

My eyes widen and I snap my attention to Ozias.

"Very good. Is that all?" he asks, as if he's expecting more.

"For now. You know there's always something else," Issa responds, shaking her head, a weariness taking its toll on her harsh features.

"You'll have the care packages sent to the families?"

"Already on the way," Atlanta interjects.

Ozias nods. "I'll visit when I can."

"Soon," Issa says, catching him in a hard stare.

He gives her a gentle smile. "Soon," he promises.

Issa dips her head, spins on her heels, and leaves. Atlanta ventures further into the room and settles beside us at the table.

"How are you getting that information? From Nevoba?" I ask, casting a glance at them.

Ozias shrugs, his brow quirking knowingly. "Your huntresses aren't the only ones who interact with the farmhands of Dyēus."

A shiver works its way down my spine. It doesn't take me long to figure out how the farmhands get the information they do. Flashes of memories of me lying with one farmhand or the other come to my mind, their whispered words and questions as I drifted off in a sated state. "How do they get that information to you?"

"The Sere is full of useful nooks and crannies. Any one of them might be hiding secrets," he says.

I hadn't really wondered until now how Ninon came across the information she found buried with the dragonsbane. In our youth, we found all sorts of things hidden among the rocks of the Sere, placed there by time or wind or hands that came before ours. I'm beginning to wonder if any more Nevobans back home know about this. If they're waiting for a way to get here, or if they decided against it, for one reason or another.

"Do you not account for deaths in Dyēus?" I inquire.

Atlanta sighs, pulling her mess of curls back from her face and up into a bun. "They don't have any."

"We don't know that," Ozias retorts.

Atlanta almost rolls her eyes. "If they did, they would be as frantic as we are."

Ozias shakes his head, but addresses me. "Bonds are secondarily meant for reproduction. As Dyēus only has male draconem, the deaths they might experience would be lower than what we're seeing on the ground. A few deaths of their own means nothing to them."

"They take our people any opportunity they get, the majority of which are women. We know they seal them into their dragons forms and force them to collect."

My mouth drops open in horror. Of course they would do that, though. If they sealed the women of Nevoba in our human forms, I'm certain they would do the opposite if it served them.

"It's still not enough," Ozias argues.

"And still we're not seeing enough deaths to reflect those turned ravaged."

He presses his fists into the hard wood of the table. "Of which, we should be grateful, not questioning."

I get the sense this isn't the first time they've had this discussion and I'm proven right when Atlanta says, "We'll continue to disagree on that."

My interest piqued, I tuck my hair behind the points of my ears and turn my attention to her. "You have a theory?"

Atlanta's gaze flits to Ozias. Annoyance surges within me and I realize it's because I don't like that she looks to him, as if she needs permission to speak. I straighten and cross my arms. "I don't really care what Ozias thinks," I tell her. "I'm asking you."

"I'm wounded," he complains, placing his palm over his heart.

"You'll heal," I shoot back without taking my eyes off Atlanta.

She holds my attention with hers and I see the moment she decides to speak candidly, her spine straightening. "I've been tracking the numbers of the soul collectors and when they turn ravaged. Many disappear shortly after turning," she explains. "I think Dyēus is harboring them."

I can only imagine what Dyēus might do with a ravaged horad. "For what purpose?"

"It's no secret we're trying to escape our fate here. I think they're keeping them so that when they need it, they have a ravaged hoard ready to unleash on us."

My pulse pounds in my throat and I can't stop myself from spinning towards Ozias. "Tell me you're taking her seriously."

"Disappearing ravaged could happen for a number of reasons. The human lands are not in a state of peace and the draconem aren't honored and accepted as we once were, and it would stand to reason that just as many are lost in the world beyond the mountains. What's further, Dyēus let the ravaged roam over Nevoba so that they can believe in the lie they've crafted to keep them in check. They wouldn't risk cracking that façade by hoarding them. Letting them be dwindles our numbers as surely as hoarding them and releasing them upon us would."

"But it dwindles Nevoba's, too," I offer. "Many of us are discontent that Dyēus isn't doing anything against the plight. Could this be them doing something?"

Atlanta gives Ozias a pointed look. "An excellent point."

"It is. And if their goal is to keep the Nevobans placated, which it *is*, they would never unleash them on us."

Atlanta pinches the bridge of her nose, then drops her hand, giving Ozias a stern look. "They would when the time comes. Don't tell me they wouldn't be willing to unleash on us that which would decimate us two-fold."

"There is no proof, Atlanta, and even if these theories were true, we have no recourse." He pins her with an unyielding stare.

Atlanta flicks her gaze to me, then back to Ozias, her jaw flexing tight. Then, she twists away, as if she can't stand to look at us. "You're not hearing me."

"I *am* hearing you," he continues, each word like a stake impaled in the ground. "You just don't like my response."

She stands rigid for a moment, then storms from the room without another word. Ozias's eyes hold smoke from a long simmering rage as he watches her go.

I massage my brow, trying to wrap my head around their arguments. Threat of a ravaged hoard or no, all of this depends on me and my success to move it forward. It depends on me to ensure Ninon can have a life in this world she's claimed as her own. As for my people, as long as they are prepared, I can do this for them. I will do this. Another mother doesn't need to have a child needlessly torn from her breast. The huntresses will no longer wonder why they feel a deep, unending ache when the wind caresses their face. We won't be sequestered underground any longer. We will take what is ours. I will steal the sky, and give it back to them.

"I hope Atlanta is wrong," I finally say, then point to the large manuscript Ozias said held all the possibilities of what could happen after the fall of Dyēus. "But in the event she's right and we do have a ravaged hoard on our hands, I'll have to strike when they don't expect it. I'll have to take down the Sar Dyēus discreetly. Quietly." The pressure is already a hefty weight on my shoulders, but I hold my head high. They won't trust me if I fold now.

Ozias sighs, laying a hand on the book. "You will do what you can, and we'll make it be enough. You're not alone in this."

I regard him for a long while, then finally ask the question I'd been wanting to know the answer to for days. "That morning by the base of the mountain. What were you doing?"

Ozias holds my gaze, his face full of hope. "Finding you."

# Chapter Twelve

"Lay back and relax," Ozias's voice soothes. "We'll go easy this first time."

I do as he says, keeping my eyes trained on his form standing over me until I'm on my back, knees raised, hands resting on my stomach. We're on the terrace off of his private room, much of it covered overhead with a thick canopy of vines and those curling leaves in the shape of fans. They sway in the gentle mid-morning breeze, a soothing rustle drawing my notice, even if my brain is a maelstrom of thoughts, my emotions a thunderous riot beneath my skin. Being still when I feel like I ought to move, to do something, is its own sort of torture.

"Find comfort in your body."

I'm about as comfortable as a dying saiga in the midday sun with a vulture wheeling overhead. With Ozias slowly pacing around my form, I'm sure we resemble pre-cisely that. My fingers twitch as my head ticks from side to side and up and down, trying to find a comfortable spot to rest the back of my skull.

"Find *stillness*."

Air whooshes out of my nostrils as I lock down my muscles. I manage to keep myself immobile for a few more moments before rolling back my shoulders. As it turns out, remaining motionless is no easy feat for me. Have I always been this way? Being in my own head while riding Aspa or skulking around the corridors of home is one thing, but to keep my body still while trying to clear my mind feels a bit like slicing the pad of my thumb with a knife. On purpose. Repeatedly. I breathe deep and attempt to empty my head of thought. My delicately pointed ears pick up the sound of his pacing, footsteps landing beside my hips, torso, my shoulder, drawing closer and closer to my head.

"Perhaps comfort would come more easily," I grind out, "if you weren't within a hair's breadth from stepping on me."

"Distraction is a facet of shifting you'll always con-tend with. Noticing your distractions and learning to keep them at bay will get you one step closer to transforming at will." He lands a step close to the side of my head, nearly scraping my ear, sending a wave of anxiety through me so fierce I react blindly. My hand darts up, clasping onto his ankle as I kick up. One leg swings around his front to put force against his hip while I use the thigh of my other leg to trip him behind the knee. Using the force I generated on the upswing, I drive him down while grabbing his wrist with my free hand. As he falls to the ground, he lands with a loud groan, and the momentum and my hold on his wrist propels me upwards so that I'm hovering over his form, our limbs tangled.

Under my control, he jerks his head up off the ground and bares his teeth. "*What* was that?"

"Taking out the distraction," I hiss, lunging further into his space. "Step that close to me again and I'll choke you out."

A salacious smile slips across his face. "Don't make promises you don't intend to keep."

"Don't make the mistake of convincing yourself I don't keep my promises. It might not work out so well for you," I shoot back.

His smile stays plastered to his face, his eyes lighting with mirth. "Fair, but it was still a dirty shot."

I lean back a little, but don't let go. "Dirty or not, perhaps if you were good at multitasking, you could have stopped me."

"Who says I couldn't have stopped you?"

My mouth opens to protest, but remembering how fast and strong Alixor was and what *he* did to Alixor., Of course Ozias could have stopped me if he wanted.

"And," he adds, raising up on his elbows, putting us closer again, "I'll gladly show you exactly how good I am at multitasking if you're set on convincing yourself I don't know what I'm doing."

The dark look in his eyes, his attention fully focused on me, on my mouth, has my mind imagining roving hands and lips, tongue and teeth, all working in tandem across my body. This close to his face, I notice the mark near his left eye is a near perfect circle. His smile broadens and I can only huff out a laugh as I push away from him, sitting back onto my haunches so that he's no longer nestled between my legs. My eyes sweep down the long line of his body and back up to see a lazy, crooked smile and a raised brow.

"Ah. Another distraction," I say, smoothing back my hair. I scoot away from him and lie back down, trying to get comfortable. I breathe out again, and close my eyes. "Very clever."

The rustle of his clothes alerts me to his movement, then his hot breath caresses the soft shell of my ear. "This wasn't the sort of distraction I had in mind for today, but it works just as well. And, it's more enjoyable." His voice is a sultry murmur and I squirm at the sound. "However, seeing as it is causing you some distress, I'll try to keep my distance."

My body awakens, tingling bumps raising up along my arm, across my chest, as if reaching for him. Traitorous body. I breathe out. "See that you do."

"I think I can manage as long as your legs don't wrap around me again." This time his words are farther away.

I hum out a laugh and crack an eye open to see him standing above me. "Then it's probably best not to give me a good reason to."

He says nothing for a moment, face now serious. "Yes, that's probably for the best." I open my eyes completely to watch him continue circling me, this time staying a little farther from my body, but not by much. He's silent again, allowing the room to settle after my outburst.

"Once you can relax into yourself, you'll find that you can reach out to your dragon. Or perhaps you already feel her call?" His voice surrounds me as he continues his stride and I close my eyes, attempting to shut out the draw I feel towards him.

I do as he says, reaching down within me to find my inner dragon, but she's quiet. It feels like she's…resting. My mind turns to those moments when the sun fades and the moon rises, when I feel the beast awaken and crawl to the surface of my skin, bursting out along my seams. I recall feeling myself holding onto my human form, this comparatively frail body and complicated mind. I know I'm afraid in the moments right before I change. Afraid of those teeth, those scales, the spikes along my spine, and the sharp claws of my hands. After years of killing this thing I've become, I am both afraid to face what I've done, and what I must now live with. I spent years jealous of what these creatures could do but I could not. Years fearing them. Years hating, what turns out, is myself.

Venom, hot and cloying, rushes through my veins thinking of the Sar Dyēus and what he's done to me. To my people. Ozias says I can take him down. Bond with him. Steal his power. Break the curse. Then I'll be free. My people will be free. I can take to the skies and never look back. I can—

"Your mind is wandering." Ozias's words break me from my musings. Sucking in a steady flow of air, I draw my mind back to my body.

"Feel yourself on the ground, sinking into the earth. Notice what you hear, what you smell. Take stock of your physical presence in the world. How you fill up the space. Imagine taking up more and more space, becoming more and greater still."

I do as he says, and I stay with myself for a time. I envision the dragon inside me taking up space, though I sense she remains asleep. When she doesn't tangibly do what my mind conjures, my thoughts wander again, drifting to what will happen next. I begin to question; if taking down the Sar Dyēus is the right thing for my people, if the Realm dragons are in fact the enemy I've always known them to be, and Alixor was just one man, one dragon, who couldn't keep his promise among many that did. But a promise to keep us safe from something that was never really a threat is no promise at all. My mind swarms, wondering what will happen if this works. Wondering what will happen if it doesn't.

"Doubt has no home here," Ozias murmurs, soft and low.

"Do you have the power to read minds too, then?" I ask, snapping my eyes open and rising up on my elbows.

There's a long pause, then a restrained laugh, held deep in his chest. "As curious as I am to see the inner workings of your brain, no. You're very expressive. It doesn't take much to figure out what you're thinking."

I purse my lips towards my nose, septum piercing moving along with the motion as I relax back down and close my eyes. I fooled Alixor, my mother, and countless others by having control over my expression. I don't think it's simply that. I try again to relax my features, but my mind spins towards the curse that forces the rogues to change at night, the one that, if they're outside the Realm, turns them savage. I think of my mark, slowly fading. It forced me to stay in my human body all these years. Any silence I found drifts away, these questions taking the full force of my focus.

"What's the difference?" I ask, and I hear the soft shuffle of Ozias's steps pause. "Between those who come here and the children? Why can they shift at will, but many of the others can't?"

There's movement from him again. I open my eyes as he sits down near my shoulder, legs crossed, bare forearms draped casually over each knee with his golden eyes focused on the mark below my breastbone. "The children who are born here don't trigger the curse. As long as they don't cross the barrier I've cast over the Realm, they continue to have the ability to shift at will."

I turn on my side, propping up my head with my hand. "That doesn't explain how those who enter from the outside can overcome being savage. Or how you or any of the original draconem here were able to do that, for that matter." In part, I'm looking for a lie. Some gap between what he's already told me and what he's telling me now to uncover any deceit. I want him to trust me, but I *need* to trust him.

Ozias casts his gaze down. There's a heaviness to the air as I wait for his reply. "There's another barrier I cast over the Realm. One that happened days after I made the first. Those days...they were so dark. We found any way we could to restrain ourselves, to keep ourselves in the Realm. To keep us from attacking one another. Then, there was someone Zhoric reversed the curse on."

My blood stills in my veins. "He reversed the curse on someone? Why would he do that?"

"The question you should ask is for *whom* he would do that."

I wait a beat for the answer, my mind spinning. A bond perhaps? "And?"

"It was his sister."

I suck in a sharp breath. "She wasn't on his side?" A pang in my chest hits me hard, remembering when Kalixta and I were at odds after her selection and all the ways we did and didn't support each other during those times.

"Their relationship was complicated, but they loved each other. He couldn't stand to see her like that, so he lifted the curse from her. When she made it here, I replicated it as well as I could. But I couldn't replicate on every individual, over and over. I was only strong enough to expand the magic across the Realm like a net and give the draconem who trigger the curse the ability to find the opening to the light beyond the savagery."

Scanning his face, an idea bubbles in my mind.

"I don't understand. If Zhoric has a god's power, couldn't he have stopped you? Then? Now?" I don't have the courage to say the word *kill*.

"That was his intention, once." A shadow settles across his face and I suddenly have the sense that I'm looking at the real man behind the swaggering front I'm accustomed to.

I lay my hand over his, my thumb pressing the inside of his wrist. "What happened?"

The muscles along the side of Ozias's neck tighten and I slowly run the pad of my thumb against his pulse point. "His sister was killed by someone close to him soon after he took power. Following that, he wasn't much inclined to eradicate us lest he ever needed to use us against the draconem who follow him."

My mouth tightens at the notion. Things must have gone according to the Sar Dyēus's plans if he didn't go forward with that. Although, the fact Ozias could meet with him safely suggests the Sar Dyēus is still keeping the rogues in his back pocket.

"Then the draconem who followed him found us more useful alive than dead by using us to influence the Nevobans, so they no longer called for our deaths. To the Sar Dyēus, that meant everything was under his control."

I work my teeth over my lower lip. "How did we end up like this? What happened to the women back when the Sar Dyēus took control? Why didn't we fight back?"

Ozias sighs, his shoulders sagging. "Anyone who defied Zhoric and his followers in that first divide of our people was cursed, one way or another. His power was like a dust storm; wholly consuming and unstoppable. Everyone who followed him, or didn't choose a side at all, fell to his whims. The women who were lucky, if you could call it that, fled here. The others who weren't so lucky had the mark placed upon them, suppressing their dragons. That first generation of your people were cursed so they couldn't speak of the past and what you are. So when the second generation came and stories were passed down, truths were told as well as they could through fables and legends, but even those changed with time. We became the monsters, and eventually the dragons of Dyēus donned the shepherd's skin to make you feel safe and secure for nearly a century."

My throat is thick as I swallow. A hundred years seems like both an eternity and no time at all for such a significant shift, but Ozias lived through it. Atlanta experienced an early phase of that new world. A deep valley of sorrow carves its way across my heart. So much lost. So many women who came before me living abbreviated lives. The ones who knew what they were supposed to be, silenced, their wings clipped from ever reaching the full extent of who they were again. That valley in my chest fills with heat and hate.

I clench my teeth so tight they could crack. "I want him dead," I say, so low that I wonder if Ozias hears me, but of course he does. His next words stun me.

"We can take his power. We can reverse the curse and mend things back to the way they ought to be, but he needs to live, at least for a while yet. He has too many threads of magic woven into the world. We don't know what would happen if he were to depart from this plane too soon. He has much left to do before he can pass. Things he needs to answer for." Ozias's words hold a tenderness, but his face is severe, leaving not an ounce of space for argument.

So I don't. I also won't let his words control my ultimate decision when it comes time to do what he asks me to do. I vow to myself that the last dragon I kill will be the Sar Dyēus. I search his expression, seeing something familiar. Protective. I pull my hand from his wrist and press my fingers to my lips, then tuck them under my chin. "He's your friend," I guess, as if that both settles the matter and accuses him of something. "Or once was."

Ozias doesn't dispute my claim, causing me to wonder over their relationship. His face has turned cold and distant, his mind elsewhere. "I said I would answer your questions. The answer to that is…it doesn't matter what he once was. He's the enemy, now." He juts out his chin. "Back on the floor. We'll do these exercises every day until you can focus for at least an hour."

I lie back down and try to settle into my skin that feels like it could burst at any moment. "And when I master this? How will I get close to the Sar Dyēus to enact the bond?" I tilt my head back to see him.

Ozias holds my gaze, but I feel as if he's watching me through fogged glass. "I'm still working on that."

My jaw clenches, nerves firing along my bones. "I'm continually inspired by your confidence," I say, hoping to bring back some levity.

His mouth quirks into an easy smile, some of the

clouds disappearing from his expression. "One step at a time. With how slowly this is going, though, we'll have plenty of time together to come up with an inspiring idea."

The longer this takes, the riskier it is for Ninon and all the others. What if Kalixta doesn't have an elahi? My mother? Who else is at risk that I know? I adjust my septum piercing and shake my hands, trying not to linger on his words. "Your selfless dedication might outshine your confidence."

He picks up where he left off pacing my form. "I do what I have to."

I think that's the sincerest statement I've heard from him yet, and I'd do well to remember it.

When Ozias releases me, I rest in the room I've been given until it's early evening, the dusk near enough I can smell it on the air—a cool moisture, a shifting wind bringing in the salt from the distant sea. The Alcazar is quiet. By now, most people have gathered for supper or else are off preparing for the night. I'm passing the staircase that leads up to Alcazar's highest rooms when I hear low conversation travel down the steps. I slow as I recognize the voices. I press against a wall and make myself small as I hear my name on Ozias's lips.

"Have you spoken with Kaisa?"

"No, she was still resting. I didn't want to disturb her before it was absolutely necessary," Atlanta answers.

Ozias hums and silence follows. I dare not breathe. I'm not foolish enough to believe I'm not spoken of when my presence is absent. Still, it sets me on edge to hear it all the same.

"I'm worried, Ozias," Atlanta says. Their words are soft now, at complete odds with how they spoke with one another when I last saw them together.

"Why am I not surprised," Ozias replies, a tease in his tone.

"You said yourself, their bond potential is powerful. I worry, especially with her inexperience, that it might be easy for her to be...swayed by it."

"She won't."

I don't blame Atlanta for worrying, but it's unfounded. I'm only glad Ozias believes in me.

"You can't know that," Atlanta shoots back.

"She already despises him. There's no getting around that after she's learned all that he's done to her and her people."

"Zhoric isn't only what he's done. She has a good heart, Ozias. She will see that."

I tense and cast my gaze up the stairs, even though I know I can't see anything. What more can there be to the man they claim has done such horrors to my people?

"I'm aware," he says, voice deepening.

An inhale, soft and steady. Atlanta's, I think. "It's too much of a risk to have that happen."

"I realize that," Ozias retorts.

"Has there been any indication she's seen him?"

A pause, then, "No."

"Ozias." His name comes out terse and knowing.

"She mentioned a bad dream."

My heart skips a beat and I bite the side of my cheek.

"Did you ask her about it?"

"I didn't want to pry."

"Pry. If she's mind walking, we have to know. We can always go back to the original plan."

"There is always that," Ozias says, but it's clear from the weariness in his words he doesn't like the idea.

Atlanta doesn't immediately reply and when she does, her own tone takes on an edge of annoyance. "You're certain she's strong enough to force the bond?"

"Of that much I'm certain."

"A bond so powerful will only lead to her heartbreak."

My frown deepens and I ache at the thread of grief in Atlanta's words. As though the idea is close to her heart.

"I know how incredible their potential is, Atlanta. Even though you may think so, I've not forgotten the allure of a strong bond." His pause feels poignant. "But she is strong. She will do what we need of her."

I hear a long, frustrated sigh and I imagine Atlanta's face turning away from his, her curls bouncing. I wish I could see their expressions. "And after?"

"And after, her ties will remain firm here. She will be cared for," he says, reassuring, then his voice pitches low and my ears strain to make out the words. "I'll make sure of it."

A quiet longing fills Atlanta's single-worded plea. "Ozias..."

Leaning my body past the threshold, I strain to hear. Atlanta hesitates in whatever she was going to say, or else she says it so low I cannot hear it.

"Unless there's a reason I shouldn't?" he asks. I hear the scuff of movement. "Tell me. Even if it's to tell me of your distaste for it."

I bite the knuckle of my thumb. *Distaste? Distaste for what?*

"And if I did tell you?"

This time, Ozias's answer comes immediately. "Then I will find another way. Tell me, and I will find another way."

There's another lengthy pause. I put my hand over my mouth as I exhale slowly, waiting for Atlanta to speak, trying to decipher precisely what they mean.

"You like her." It's a statement, spoken so plainly I cannot begin to guess what she thinks.

There's another pause. "I do. She's strong and beautiful. Interesting and bold. And...you *know* why." My heart swells a bit hearing his words, even as my steady pulse trips over the mystery of what he could be referring to.

When Atlanta says nothing, a deep, suffering sigh escapes from Ozias. It sounds like the way I feel when I come up empty handed after a long hunt.

"You're certain, then?" he asks, soft, and tender. There's a long pause, then, harsher, I hear him say, "I won't ask again." Again, there's nothing for a long, long while. Finally, Ozias speaks. "Then there's nothing more to discuss on this."

"No. No, I suppose there's not." She sounds…frustrated. Tired. "I should retrieve her."

I don't wait to hear more. I turn back the way I came, going quickly and silently until I reach the room and let myself back in. For Ninon, I've put my trust in Atlanta and Ozias. For myself, I'm working with them to connect with my dragon. And for my people, I've agreed to attempt the impossible task they've given me. I've been agreeable, at least to an extent, to everything, and yet overhearing them bothers me. Do they think I'll return to Dyēus and reveal their plans in hopes the Sar Dyēus will reverse the curse on me? Although, I suppose that is an option. I could reunite with my sister, reclaim my old life. But, is that even what I want, after all I know? After having experienced the full extent of who and what I am? What would it be like, to deny being a draconem, to push myself back down into the depths of my consciousness once more? I imagine it and feel the crushing weight sink low in my stomach. Hidden and hurting, wanting to claw its way back of out me.

I don't register the approaching footsteps and I gasp at the tentative knock on the door. I swallow and let out a long, steadying breath. "Come in."

The door opens and Atlanta glances around, a puzzled expression crossing her face. "I wasn't sure you'd be in here."

I pull my hair over my shoulder as my pulse picks up speed. "Why wouldn't I be?"

"I didn't...never mind."

"You didn't what?" I implore, feeling the need to gain information I can after overhearing her and Ozias.

She shakes her head and enters the room. "This will sound strange, but I didn't sense you. Since your first night here, your energy has been very clear. Right before I knocked though, I couldn't feel you."

"Oh," I blink, then stand. "And do you now?"

"As clear as ever." Atlanta shrugs. "I was a little in my own head before I knocked. I'm sure that's why I didn't sense you. There's nothing to concern ourselves over."

I give her a pleasant smile, despite how distraught I am. "If you think so."

"Right, well, unfortunately it's that time," she says, gesturing to the fading light beyond the window.

I make my way towards her, determined to do as I'm told, to make them trust me. After what I overheard, I can't let them know my dream about the Sar Dyēus. We don't have that kind of time to waste. Not with the increasing deaths. Not with how weak Ninon seems. "Ozias said I passed the stage of savagery. Am I still to be chained?"

"Oh, sorry, no." Atlanta shakes her head and comes to me. "I didn't mean to imply that. I simply meant you will shift. And well," she looks around, "this space isn't particularly conducive for that."

Following her gaze, it's obvious of course that the room wasn't built for dragon forms. "Ah, right. So then where will I go?"

Atlanta pushes her hair off her shoulder. "Where would you like to go?" she asks as we make our way to the atrium and down out of the Alcazar. "We have the field. That's where most of us go, but there are other more secluded spots around the Realm."

I didn't realize I'd have a choice in the matter. Working my lower lip with my teeth I ask, "Where will Ninon be?"

Atlanta's mouth purses. "She's still working past the savagery. She'll be chained again."

"I want to be near her."

"Back at the enclosures?"

I nod, then suppress a shudder that works its way down my spine. "Not chained, but I don't want to leave her alone."

Atlanta sighs, thinking it over. "I wouldn't recommend showing yourself to her. It would only distress her."

"I'll keep myself in the enclosure next to hers."

Silence settles between us, the only sound our footsteps and the distant murmur of energy I've grown used to over these days.

"Your loyalty to your friend is inspiring. Are you certain you don't want to go to the fields? Fly?"

My brow draws tight. Of course I want those things. And I'll get there one day with her at my side. Besides, if Ozias and Atlanta believe that the Sar Dyēus could pull me deeper into this bond than I'm willing to go, that I'd be willing to risk Ninon, I'll show them where my heart lies. Always. "Where she goes, I go."

# *Chapter Thirteen*

I'm not unused to Ninon and I learning at different paces. While horse riding came naturally to me, Ninon floundered. Reading the stars and navigating across the wide open Sere was something Ninon picked up easily, as if she'd been doing so her whole life, whereas I would get turned around in the dark. Where I could move silently and swiftly, she lumbered. Where she could sit for hours reading texts, I lost interest the moment there were no illustrations or diagrams.

It's no surprise that shifting is the same. Still, I was hoping my presence would keep Ninon from turning savage, but as night spills across the sky, I hear her grunts and huffs, the clattering of her chains as she thrashes.

Last night, I was overwhelmed by all the things my dragon eyes could see and my senses could experience. Tonight though, I flex my wings, stretching them tall behind me, testing how far they fan out in the confined space of the enclosure. I examine myself, this body that's suddenly mine. My scales are the color of the underbelly of a fat cloud over the Rising Sea, a silver gray with the promise of rain. I flick my long tail to coil around my body, the tuft of hair on the end a mossy green. I watch, mesmerized by the tendrils as I flick my tail up and down, over and over.

Incredible as this body is, relishing in the feeling of it being mine and my own means of reaching the sky, I grow bored. I lay my head down. As my eyes drift closed, I remember seeing the Sar Dyēus and they snap back open. I don't want to see him again. Last night I was thinking deeply of him. Perhaps if I don't think of him at all, I won't dream of him again.

Instead, I think of Ninon, wondering when she'll overcome this stage of her transformation. I think of home, the women we left behind. I wonder if my mother knows, if anyone has bothered to tell her, that I'm not in Dyēus with Alixor – that he's dead. Maybe they told her I'm dead. My eyes close as I wonder if Kalixta is in Dyēus with Thrace, reunited with her boy child, like he said she would be—she would know then. Would she send word to our mother? Would the Sar Dyēus allow it? I can just imagine his steely expression, the sardonic twist of his mouth, his perfectly placed hair falling out of place, like the way he spoke to me the morning he took Kalixta's son to the sky. My heart trips on a beat.

I catch my thoughts too late. I look down and my feet are on the smooth polished floors of the castle. I look up and I'm in his rooms once again. I didn't even realize I'd fallen asleep. *Wake up*, I urge myself, but nothing happens.

The room is empty. I try to wake myself up again, when I feel a pull; something like a thread tied around my middle, guiding me to the doors that lead to the halls. They open and the Sar Dyēus walks in.

He pauses, eyes on me for a moment, so intense and

unyielding that I'm certain he must see me, but then they drift by, glancing around the rest of the room before he ventures all the way in, passing through me like a hand through smoke. I watch, eyes wide like a saiga stuck in my sights as he moves about the room. He loosens the cuffs at his wrists and neck, setting the links down inside a set of drawers near the bathing chamber. He rolls up his sleeves and moves to the other side of the room, passing me, so close that his shoulder should knock into mine, except it slips through as if I were made of mist. It's all so mundane; the strangest dream I've ever had. It's almost as if I walked in on him, a spirit watching from another world. My thoughts bounce from this realization to what I overheard earlier in the night. What word did Atlanta say? Something walking? Is this a dream, or is it something more? I know draconem have powers, most I don't understand. I have to wake up.

I grasp for the thread I sensed earlier, only now it's gone. "No," I whisper, twisting around, hoping to feel it again. I press my fingertips into my temples. "No, no, wake up, wake *up*. This isn't real. This isn't happening. It's all a dream."

The Sar Dyēus pours water into a kettle and sets it over a flame. He stands there, hands braced on the table, shoulders hunched, his back to me. He stays still as a stone, but I feel I'm flickering like a flame, my form all heat and no substance.

Cautiously, I take a step toward him. His fingers curl deeper into the table. I take another step and he rises to his full height, turning to look out at the night sky.

I approach slowly, angling my body so I can see his face. I swore when he walked in he looked directly at me. Last night in my dream, he told me to get out. That seemed more dreamlike than whatever this is. In fact, if this is a dream, I'm not certain how my thoughts are so clear.

When I draw up to his side, I study the smooth angles of his face for a moment, before I whisper, "Can you see me?" I don't know how I'm expecting a dream to respond.

He inhales deeply, then turns back to the table and spoons dried tea leaves into a pot.

Anytime I wanted something when I was here in Dyēus, one of the attendants would do it for me. I look around again. No servants; no one but him and me.

His hand moves with ease, pouring the now steaming water over the leaves to let them steep. He arranges the pot and a cup on a wooden tray, lifts it from the table, and takes it over to the open balcony where I saw him last night. He sets the tray on the smooth stone floor before folding himself down next to it. Then he simply sits there, staring out into the dark night, lit only by the stars, the twin moons, and the gods eyes in the sky, the area between the ovals glittering bright like a hazy, sun-bleached rainbow.

I slowly pace the room, hoping the mundane nature of this dream will wake me or move me to another, but no matter how I try, I always end up facing him. I twist away, grunting in frustration. Trying another tactic, I go to his drawers to rifle through the contents to see what my mind might conjure, but my hands pass uselessly through everything I touch. Out of the corner of my eye, I catch sight of the door. I walk towards it with purpose, but stop hard about a centimeter away, as if I ran into a wall.

"What?" I raise my hand and it crosses through, but when I try to make another step forward, it's as if a rope is tied around my middle, stopping me from going any further. I spin around to face him, and he's still sitting there, sipping his tea.

"This is ridiculous." I try the handle again, but every effort only proves how stuck I am. With a huff, I drop my hands heavy against my thighs, a loud clap echoing through the room. The Sar Dyēus pauses in his motion, the cup in his hand hovering over the tray on the ground before he places it back down. Had he heard me? I stride across the room, stopping mere inches behind him. He doesn't turn.

Doesn't say a word. I lean down next to his ear, looking him sidelong in the eye. "Blink if you hear me."

He glances down, picks up his cup, and takes a noisy sip.

I furrow my brow. "What an annoying dream."

His hand tightens around his cup, his eyes locked on the gods eyes above us. I follow his gaze. The ovals shimmer, iridescent in the darkness, steady and far brighter than last night. Otherwise the sky looks unchanged, no cause for the tension I'm sensing from him.

With nothing else to do, and nowhere to go, I sit beside him. And since he cannot see me, I stare at him. Elbow on my knee, chin resting on my hand, I leisurely run my eyes across his face, appreciating the slope of his nose, the bow of his lips, the stern set of his brow. It's a shame he's done such horrible things for as beautiful as he is.

With the room silent, and my head empty of thoughts as I gaze at him, I hear muffled sounds of crying babies in the nursery. I look towards the noise. A small baby wails, the sound pained. When I turn back to him, the muscles around his eyes are tight. Then his eyes close, almost as though he can't help himself.

"How strange," I murmur. Why would he endure sounds like this when he can silence them? A memory charges through me, fast and furious. Once, when I was young, a mother giving up her son refused to remain silent. The girl she'd born didn't survive and when they took the boy, she wailed and screamed while others held her back. Even with the great hall densely packed with all of us to witness, the sound of her shrieks still echoed in the caves, splitting my ears. I remember not being able to breathe. I remember Ninon putting her hands over her ears. I'd pulled at her, trying to leave, but she wouldn't. Then the sound stopped. The mother's mouth was still open, throat corded, eyes bulging as tears streamed down her cheeks, but there was no sound. The Sar Dyēus's hand was raised in a fist, and I knew, right then, that he'd taken the sound of her despair, or covered it so it could no longer be heard. Ninon left with me after that. I cried that day, praying that I wouldn't have to endure what that woman did.

My chest rises and falls in a violent wave. Finally I look away from him, my jaw tight. I stare at the gods eyes for so long my vision blurs. Then, I squeeze my eyes shut, put my hands over my ears, and scream. I scream and scream into the endless darkness, knowing I'm the only one who can hear it and the release of it builds until it's something else, until it's no longer despair, but rage. Rage at what he stole. Rage at what he has done. I whip my hands from my ears and whirl around in front of this man who has taken everything from so many. From *me*. His face is set in that same neutral mask it always is, his gaze somewhere off in the sky. Fast as a viper, I wrap my hands hard around his neck. I expect them to pass through, but I meet resistance at the contact. My eyes widen and I thrill as I squeeze until my knuckles turn white, but his skin doesn't depress at my touch. My teeth bared, gritting tight, a snarl ripping from my throat, I squeeze harder, delighting in the feel of my fingers wrapped around his throat. When I glance up, he's looking at me. I know he doesn't see me there. He doesn't even know what's happening. He doesn't know my rage. He doesn't know anything about me. The thought sweeps through me so fiercely, I can't stand to look at him any longer. I let my head drop, thumping against his chest, hands still wrapped around his throat. I breathe hard until the anger withers away once again into despair.

"*Why?* Why *you?*" My words stumble on a sob. The fates could bind me to anyone, and yet they chose him.

I give one last lingering squeeze before I finally let my hands slip away and I wilt back, sitting heavy on my heels in front of him until my body curls into itself like a seed. I put my face in my hands, and weep.

Dawn is near when I wake, and I feel that no time at all has passed since I laid my face in my hands and cried before the Sar Dyēus, to opening them now. I'm in the enclosure once again, only this time, I'm still a dragon. The only sounds are the soft rustle of leaves and the distant flap of wings in their last flight before morning. I twist my neck to the wall next to me where, in the next enclosure over, Ninon should be. I hear no grunting or scuffing of claws. I hear nothing at all.

Panic grips me and squeezes tight. *Ninon?*

I'm not expecting an answer, and so after a beat, when there is one, I jolt upright.

*Kaisa?*

As if I've had this body my entire life, my motions are graceful as I glide out of the enclosure, around the corner, and come face to face with Ninon. Still covered by chains, but gorgeous and awe-inspiring in her dragon form. Her scales are like the twilight sky, a purple so deep you could see the first few winks of the stars within it. Her mane is inky black, her antlers a lightning strike against the dark. I sense, more than hear her gasp.

*You're beautiful*, she tells me.

*So are you*, I tell her.

Then, somewhere we cannot see, the sun crests the horizon and in a soft mist we melt into our humanity. Ninon crouches on her hands and knees beneath the netted chains and I pull the keys hanging from the wall and rush to release her. Flinging the chains off her back, I pull her to me and hold her. I hold her and I cry.

"What happened?" she asks, a trickle of alarm in her voice.

My arms tremble as I clutch her to me. I want to tell her I don't think I can do this. I hold her tighter instead of letting the words slip from my lips. She squeezes me back, compressing my ribs against my lungs.

"Are you all right?" I ask, finally pulling back.

Her smile is as bright as the dawn of the new day. "I did it."

"Yes, you did." The rush of new tears sting my eyes. I imagine never seeing this face again. I imagine being too late for her to spread her wings in flight. I won't let that happen. The sooner the cycle is stopped, the safer she'll be.

So wrapped up as I am in Ninon, I don't even hear Atlanta's approach. "Oh good," she says. "You got her out."

I clear my throat and release Ninon. "She broke out of the savagery, sometime early this morning."

"Is that so?" Atlanta asks, a smile broadening her face. "Well then, congratulations. You both will have an exciting night tonight." She shifts her attention to me. "And you? How was last night? Any more bad dreams?"

Even if I hadn't overheard them last night, it's clear what she means—what Ozias knows, she knows. Instead of putting me off though, I respect her candor. Which is more than I can say for myself. I'm suddenly met with an overwhelming sense of shame. I open my mouth and the words won't come. A creeping sensation works its way up my spine, curling around my throat. I've felt this before, any time I thought of falling pregnant with Alixor's brood. Like being trapped. I can't be pulled from this task simply because my mind likes to conjure an image of the dragon king. I will keep Ninon safe. I will keep my distance from the Sar Dyēus at all costs. I will do what I must.

"No." The lie tumbles from my mouth. "No dreams."

Atlanta regards me for a passing moment, then nods. "Good. Let me know if they return. I'm somewhat of an expert in...bad dreams."

"Of course."

Satisfied, Atlanta nods again. "I'd like to show you both something before you rest, if you're interested."

Ninon and I exchange a quick glance and nod our approval.

Atlanta leads us through the Realm, but instead of bisecting the main square to the Alcazar, she takes us westward. Here the trees are dense for a good kilometer before they thin out again and we're met by a towering rockface wall that looks as if it was pulled from the ground and flattened at the top. Every few meters there are arched openings to the Sere beyond. Along the edge of the wall is a steep staircase that looks as if it leads to a structure perched atop the high wall.

"What's the point of a wall if you're going to have so many openings?" I ask.

"The openings allow us to send our people out to hunt and for Nevobans to enter" Atlanta explains as she begins her way up the steps. "Plus, it has an added benefit of providing vantage points around the Realm to keep an eye on what goes on beyond this place." I suppose that makes sense. It's not like a wall would keep out a hoard of dragons anyway.

As we climb, Ninon's breathing becomes heavy.

"You all right?"

"Yes," she sighs. "I'm tired after last night, but I'm fine."

Ahead of me, I see Atlanta looking back at Ninon, her face taut, but she doesn't suggest stopping. "I think what you're about to see will be of particular interest to you, Ninon."

The promise of intrigue perks Ninon up and she keeps up better after that.

Wind sweeps our hair back as we reach the top, the Sere awash in gold as the sun rises from its resting place. Long shadows of the rock monuments and large wooden structures I've never seen before rake the ground.

"Those are Dyēus's battlements," Atlanta informs us.

"The ones closest to Nevoban's hunting grounds are

not nearly as large as those," Ninon says and we exchange a glance.

"Have you ever seen these from Dyēus?" Ninon asks me. I shake my head.

"You wouldn't have," Atlanta informs us. "Like our concealment to keep them from seeing our fortress, they use an additional concealment barrier to shield us and their encampments from view so the Nevobans can't witness who we truly are and what they do to us. The small bases you see make it seem like Dyēus is so powerful it needs little to control such an impressive enemy."

I huff my annoyance at the effectiveness.

Atlanta continues. "They move their units in erratic patterns, typically during the day, attempting to keep up with the exits Ozias creates in the barrier around the Realm. They use any chance they have to ambush us."

"Exits?" Ninon questions before I get the chance.

"We need the draconem who can shift during the day to go out and procure meat and fish. If they pass through the barrier, they'll trigger the curse, so in order to let them continue shifting at will, Ozias erects specific entry and exit points. Lately though, Dyēus has gotten more aggressive in their movements, and too many of our people have been trapped out there."

Understanding dawns on me swiftly. "For Dyēus to take and turn into soul collectors."

Atlanta nods. Then, another thought occurs to me. "Why didn't Ozias open the barrier when he brought me here?" If I didn't trigger the curse when I entered, then wouldn't I be able to come and go as freely as those who hunt?

"You needed to cross the barrier to destroy the mark and release your dragon. Even if you hadn't wanted it released, Ozias was doing too much when he brought you in for that to have been an option. It was a race against time, and his magic was already working as a shield to keep you both safe from Dyēus's ground forces."

"That's a lot of trouble to go through to bring me here," I muse.

"He's putting a lot of faith in your success." Atlanta must see the anxiety on my face because she throws me a quick wink. "But no pressure, right?"

"Right," I agree with a shaky laugh. My head swims with all the information I've learned since remaining conscious in my dragon form these past two days. This curse that forces the nightly transformation of the rogues must be stronger than the one the Sar Dyēus places on us Nevobans if it can unleash our dragons, and I can't help wondering why that is. Especially if Dyēus knows that the Nevobans escape here from time to time, which they must if they've crafted such lies to keep us away from here.

Atlanta leans over me to address Ninon. "Getting our people out and in safely is why I wanted to bring you here. We believe Dyēus works in a pattern, or a variation of patterns. You told us that you enjoy working out puzzles and so we were hoping to have you here a few days to see if a fresh pair of eyes would help us catch anything we've missed."

Ninon scans the horizon intently. I know she's already mapping the lay of the land, the way the shadows fall on this morning, on this day. I know she'll remember it a year from now when this day returns. Her ability to see detail is unparalleled. Ninon's chest rises and her mouth widens a fraction in her small, contained smile, that familiar look she gets when she's on the edge of something new and exciting. "Are you giving me a job?"

Atlanta shrugs, her eyes alight at Ninon's expression. "On a trial basis. If you like it. If you're any good."

Ninon turns to her. "You mentioned a team already working on this."

"Would you like to meet them?"

"More than anything."

Pride and affection fills me to see Ninon so hopeful and eager. I didn't realize until now how dim her light has been at home. How much she'd turned into her shell against the coming change of us growing older, and realizing there was nothing more for us. Not unless we bore the children of Dyēus.

We follow Atlanta along the parapet, wind whipping our clothes as we walk. She leads us into the building we saw from below; a long, enclosed space with a window spanning its length on either side, looking out over the Sere to one side, and to the Realm to the other.

Sitting around a low rectangular table on pillows, steaming cups in front of them, are three people I don't recognize, along with Ozias and Issa.

Ozias looks between Ninon and me before landing back on Ninon. "A successful night, then?"

She inclines her head.

Ozias smiles, his teeth gleaming with pride. He has this effect, I think, on anyone he meets. You feel warm and welcome, whether you want to or not. He holds out his hand to the remaining seats and makes introductions to those around the table as we sit and cups of tea are passed to us.

"We've just finished discussing last night's movements," Ozias explains.

Issa scoffs, twisting her cup by the rim. I go to lift mine, but it's too hot to hold comfortably for long.

"They've placed themselves near the opening Ozias created last night. Again," Issa gripes.

"Have you closed it, yet?" Atlanta asks, alarm straightening her spine.

Ozias sucks on his teeth. "I have. But supplies are low. We need to get a team out tomorrow, or at the very latest the following day."

My brow pinches, remembering what he said to me the first meal I had here in the Realm. "You told me there was plenty to go around."

Issa blows a sarcastic laugh from her lips.

Ozias knocks his knuckles twice on the table. "I needed you to eat."

I narrow my eyes and bite the inside of my cheek. Ozias waves his hand over a collection of papers on the table in front of him. "Somehow they're figuring out where we're planning to be. Our assumption is they have a draconem who has an elahi that can sense minute changes in energy signatures."

"If they do, I think they've sensed a rather large shift here as of late that's making them pay extra close attention to us," Issa says, her pale eyes trained on me.

I raise my brows but say nothing.

"We're working on getting that under control," Ozias answers.

Ninon tilts her head. "Why not use it?"

All eyes at the table turn to her. Atlanta raises her finger and points it at her before pinching it to her thumb again. "That's...actually a very clever idea."

"Explain," Issa demands, leaning her weight on her forearm against the table, her focus intense on Ninon.

"Plant Kaisa somewhere near the wall to draw Dyēus to her energy, then have Ozias create the openings elsewhere. Use her to wash out the energy he's using."

"They'll eventually figure it out and just ignore whatever she's doing in favor of the energy level they know is you," Issa says to Ozias.

"True. To be most effective, she'd have to match the energy expenditure I'm using to create the opening, which takes incredible control," says Ozias.

"Kaisa can do it," Ninon says.

"Ninon," I warn in a low voice, then say louder to the rest, "I'm humbled by her confidence, but people's lives are at stake here. Is now really the time to try something new?"

"In times of desperation, sometimes the extreme is the only way to survive." Ozias's voice is a quiet rumble, his gaze fixed on me, and I know what he's trying to convey. Did I not do the same when I took Alixor's life while trying to save my own? Are we not doing the same in trying to take down the Sar Dyēus? "Would you be willing to try?"

"Of course I'll try." I move to pick up my tea to give my hands something to do, but snatch it back when the heat registers on my fingertips. "Is it even possible for me to match energy?"

Issa eyes me up and down, then leans back and crosses her arms over her chest. "Yeah, it's possible, but you'd have to be pretty delusional to believe you could do it any time soon."

With my visions of the Sar Dyēus, I think delusions are not too far outside of my capabilities. I clear my throat and look her straight in the eyes. "Then I suppose we're going to see how delusional I can be."

# Chapter Fourteen

After our briefing on the wall, Ninon and I rest for a few hours before returning. As soon as we reach the top, Ozias leads me right back down.

"You couldn't have met me down here?" I ask once we touch ground.

"I could have, but then I wouldn't have a tangible example to explain my lesson. That, and I'm enjoying seeing how far I can push you before you show your teeth," he says with a winsome grin.

"How old did you say you were again? I thought practical jokes were for children."

"You're never too old for a bit of fun."

"Your lesson?" I remind him.

His smile doesn't diminish as he explains. "I imagine right now your heart rate is elevated from the climb up and back down. And possibly from your annoyance with me."

I snort and crack a smile. I answer for both. "Of course." No matter how strong or practiced, exertion will cause a heart rate to rise. That, and whatever it is he's doing to toy with me.

"Our magical energy is a bit like that. You can feel it happening when you exert it, but it's a little difficult to maintain at an even level or at a level you wish it to remain." Ozias and I walk along the base of the wall, the air cool despite the heat I know must be emanating from the Sere at this time of day. "If I had you climb and descend another time, you would find it difficult to maintain your current heart rate." I nod my understanding and he continues. "Besides physical efforts, your heart rate can change with your emotions. The same is true for magic."

"Emotions can affect magic?"

"Many things affect magic, but in its basest form, emotion is tied to our magical energies. It's why the meditations we've been practicing are so important. The more you can control your emotions, the more you can purposefully control your magic. Emotions make our magic volatile, difficult to wield, and unpredictable. A poor combination when faced with collecting souls during human wars. But we are what we are—a combination of the gods and the humans. Our emotions, our magic, our very essence are inextricably bound. Everything we are, is balance. Between worlds, between our two halves, between the mortal and the mystical."

"Complicated," I say.

"Complete, I like to think."

I smile at that, looking down at our feet while we walk and when I look back at him, he's studying me intensely. "You've essentially told me that what we discussed this morning is impossible for me to accomplish. At least with how much I know now."

Ozias inclines his head and we veer off to a darker,

more secluded place along the wall. "Due to the delicate nature of maintaining an energy signature, and our urgent need for supplies, we thought perhaps we'd try something that would surprise Dyēus's forces, to try to get what we need as soon as possible."

"What did you have in mind?"

"A large energy output to conceal what I'm doing on the barrier. We think it may work in our favor this once. Twice if we're lucky. But it will give us time to get what we need before I can teach you the nuisance of your magic."

I frown. I've only been in my dragon form twice since I passed the initial stages of savagery, and in both instances I've been calm. Content, even. I can't imagine feeling anything other than that. Even coming back from my dream about the Sar Dyëus, I felt calm in that body. Then I remember when I first turned. My anger, the complete sense of wanting to destroy the world. I suppress a shudder. "How will I do that?"

Ozias pauses and I stop alongside him. He turns to me and I face him, the wall at my back. He takes a step closer and my breath hitches at his nearness. "Two of our greatest emotions are anger and love—a close adjacent of which being lust."

I fill my lungs with a deep inhale. I'm not unfamiliar with that emotion. It's rather close to the surface now as the heat from his body radiates against mine, with his attention on me, his gaze searing me from the inside.

"I could probably make you feel anger, but I must admit, I'd rather if I could make you feel something else. Do you think that's possible, Kaisa? That I could make you feel wanted?" The intensity of his stare sears me, his eyes like liquid fire. His hand lifts, fingers beneath my chin, his thumb lightly pressing against my bottom lip.

Heat pools in my core. It's been so long and my body responds ravenously to his touch, to my own needs I've ignored for too long. For months, I've been tending to Kalixta and preparing for the moment Alixor would take me away. I've had no time for much else. My desire flutters and he smiles knowingly.

"So that's what we'll do? We'll fuck and my lust will send energy out into the world?"

His laugh is a deep rumble in his chest. "All we need is to bring your lust to the surface. You can do it on your own, if you like." I frown, disappointed, and his smiles grows as he goes on, "Or, I'll help you, if you'll allow it." His thumb lazily strokes across my bottom lip, spiking my desire once again before he drops his hand.

I miss the contact immediately. "And if it doesn't work?"

Ozias leans in close, his breath coasting along the shell of my ear. "I'm fairly certain it will."

I shudder, my body responding by tightening everywhere I imagine him touching.

"And if by chance it doesn't, we'll find another way. We always do."

"We'll try tonight?" I ask.

"Tonight," he promises.

That evening as the sun prepares to sink below the horizon, I meet Ozias along the wall, somewhere to the south. It's quiet and dark, the cold stones leeched of the lingering heat of the day. I've thought of our meeting all afternoon—I haven't been able to help myself—the anticipation keeping my mind preoccupied, brimming with the lust he said would aid my energy output. I imagine it's exactly what he intended when he propositioned me earlier.

"This is a bit strange," I admit, twisting my fingers.

Ozias hesitates a beat, then asks, as if the thought only now occurred to him, "Have you been intimate before?"

"Oh," I breathe out in surprise. "Of course. Many times."

He nods. "Somehow that doesn't soothe me as much as I'd hoped it would."

I smirk, pleased, but not fooled. "Trying to make me feel special?"

"You are." His answer is quick. Earnest.

My skin flushes. I've always enjoyed this aspect ahead of being intimate with someone. The feeling of being wanted. It eases some tension within me, and even if the respite is only brief, it stills a part of me that always feel like it's running.

Ozias draws nearer and runs his fingertips up my bare forearm, along my shoulder and collarbone, the side of my neck, sending static through my veins. He locks his eyes with mine.

"When you transform, think of me. Think of all the things you wish I'd do to you, the things you wish to do to me. Hold them in your mind and let them rush through your dragon. She will emit that energy out into the world, desperate to put it somewhere. When you transform, it will no longer feel sexual, but it will be powerful all the same. Hold onto that power for as long as you can to give me time to open the barrier."

All while he explains, his hands rove my body, skipping every possible place I want them to rest, and my mind struggles to hear him properly. I'm thrumming with need and I see him as a means to an end. A very attractive, alluring means to an end.

"Kaisa," Ozias says into my ear, his voice so inviting. His thumb presses under my chin, tipping my head back. "Did you hear me?"

I hum, leaning into his touch. "I don't think I could let go of this feeling right now if I tried." I love physical contact. Crave it, desperately sometimes. His fingers coil into my hair. Then his other hand is on my wrist, fingers on my pulse. He tugs me closer to him, then guides me until my back is against the rough stone, the contrast of the cool surface and the molten heat of his body delicious.

He cups my jaw with his palm. His thumb sweeps across my bottom lip. "Can I kiss you, Kaisa?" His voice is breathless, his eyes intent.

The question surprises me, given that we've already agreed to this, but it warms something in me that I can't name. I press myself closer to him and manage a shallow nod.

His smile unfurls just before he fits it over mine. The kiss is soft at first, tentative, like an apology he's not sure he can give. Then his teeth flash against my bottom lip and I open my mouth, tongue meeting his. He groans as I sigh and he uses the moment to dive deeper into me, and my insides feel like the beginning of a rockslide—trembling and inevitable. He tips his forehead against mine until our mouths part.

"And if I wanted to touch you, what would you say?"

My voice is a rasp. "Where did you have in mind?"

He hums, the hand on my jaw trailing down my neck to hover over my breasts. "Here." The hand that had clasped my waist travels lower, fingers dancing dangerously close to the curve of my backside. "And here. For starters."

My breath is coming fast and loose. "I would say yes."

Without another question, his strong hand descends on my breast, a firm press of his palm, fingers tightening and loosening, brushing across my peaked nipple. His other hand cups my bottom, pulling us closer together, bodies flush, and I can feel the full extent of his arousal pressing against me. I slip my hands up his arms, hard and tense with corded muscle, until my fingers curl around his neck, bringing his mouth to mine again. Our tongues dive and dance together, teeth nipping and biting. His hand leaves my breast to dive into my hair, where he tugs, gently, angling my head back more, giving him better access.

"Kaisa," he breathes against my mouth, my name a plea upon his tongue.

Ozias fully molds his body to mine, trapping me against the wall. I press my hips forward and feel him, hard and full of desire, like a brand against my hip. He trails a hand down my mark, my stomach, all the way to the band of my pants.

I suck in air through my teeth. "Ozias. *Please.*"

"I know what you want, I can smell it," he growls, gripping the waistband tight against my skin. "So instead, tell me what you need."

I arch my back, pressing my hips closer to his, rolling them against the all too light touch he has on my trousers. He grinds himself into me and I gasp. "This? This is what you need?"

It is. I'm over stressed and over aroused. I want him and I'm not going to stop myself from riding that feeling. I nod.

"Tell me." His finger slides side to side inside my pants, tantalizing my skin, his mouth skimming mine.

I whimper with anticipation, my breath running ragged with need, but I'm more impatient than I am demure and I can't keep quiet under his teasing touch. "Get your hands on me and make me come undone."

A groan slips past his lips, then he delves beneath the waist of my pants. His hands are steady and sure, his fingers hot as he slides one, then another along my center, slipping easily. He shudders, gritting his teeth, then he thrusts them inside me. It isn't as slow and tedious as the rest of this process has been, but fast and merciless. He bows over me, teeth and tongue scraping my neck and ear, a growl tearing at his throat. I open my legs wider and press against his palm, pumping myself on his fingers.

I'm so wet that my inner thighs are coated with myself. *I need, I need, I need.* I feel the moment I start to tip, and he pulls his hand away. I cry out in protest, but the moment doesn't last. So fast I hardly register, he moves down, taking my trousers with him, exposing me to the oncoming night, lifting my leg up and out to open me wide again, and then his mouth is there, taking me in, drinking me, winding me back up.

He groans against me, the vibration sending pebbles along my skin. I toss my head back, giving into the sensation. He drags his mouth away to lap up what's spilled onto my inner thighs, teeth biting hard enough that I buck in response.

His fingers dip back inside me, tongue against my center for a few blissful moments, taking me close to the edge again. Then he's standing, claiming my mouth, giving me a taste of myself. A taste filled with want and need, the demand and promise for more. His fingers work me back to that precipice as he holds my waist with his other hand so I have purchase to grind into him harder, faster, deeper, my rhythm stroking my thigh against his erection.

Somewhere beyond, I hear the calls and shouts, warning of the oncoming night. Somewhere within me, I know that means I'm about to change, but I can't do anything but this. I'm so close, and right as I am about to fall over the edge, as I am about to give into the ferocity of this moment and the blinding pleasure, his hand pulls away again and I hiss in frustration, teeth bared.

Only this time he doesn't fall to his knees, and when I buck my hips forward to make contact, to take those last few motions that would give me release, he backs up, his smile all teeth, his pupils blown wide with desire as he keeps me pinned upright against the wall so I don't collapse.

But I desperately need this release, so I remove one hand from his bicep where I'd braced myself and place it between my legs. He grabs both my hands and secures them above my head, and I snarl, snarl at him, while my hips lift toward him, seeking to fulfill the swell of my desire.

"You need to stay here. *Right here.* Keep this feeling with you," he says into my ear, the sound of his gravelly voice hardening my nipples painfully.

Tears prick my eyes. "You're terrible." When I agreed

to this, I didn't think I'd be teased to the edge of insanity.

Ozias only takes my mouth again, the kiss messy and wanting. "No one said I wasn't."

My gut clenches and I know the sun has set and any moment now, I'll turn. I haven't yet, but I know it's coming.

Ozias's eyes narrow a fraction. "You need to shift now, Kaisa. Fall into her, stoke this energy, and keep your mind there."

My body is on fire and I don't know if I can leave it here like this. I shake my head. "I don't—"

"You will. And if you enjoyed yourself as much as I did, perhaps we can continue this some other time."

The promise of it is enough to settle me, enough that my transformation drags me under hard and fast, like a flash of lightning.

In my dragon form, the need for sex shifts. My energy is a presence, large and expansive. I feel like I'm vibrating, like I could move the very earth with my will alone.

I bare my elongated teeth at Ozias as he stares up at me, still human, still beautiful, his eyes wide.

"Stunning," he whispers.

I blow out a breath, mist clouding his image for a moment. When it clears, he's transformed, too. He presses his forehead to mine for a long moment.

*Stay here. Keep this feeling as long as you can,* he tells me, mind to mind, just like Ninon spoke to me the other night. Then, he's racing away.

I do as he says, holding onto the feeling for as long as I can. Unlike anger, lust fades quickly when the object of your desire is out of reach and even more so when this form doesn't register sexual desire the same way. It's turned into a need I cannot name, but feels similar to that restlessness I get when it's been too long since I've hunted. A sensation that I ought to be doing something, even if I don't know precisely what that something is. I sense the moment the intensity falters, and somewhere else nearby, I feel a pulse of energy. Ozias. I know it's him, as sure as I know my name. I think of him, of everything he was giving me, and it fills me back up. Far away, I feel energy surge again. Not Ozias. I draw that to me, too. It feels like I'm swallowing mouthfuls of water after being without on a long, hot day, and I drink and drink and drink and there's no one to stop me, no one to tell me to slow down.

There's a loud smash and I jolt towards the sound. *The wall.* I think something on the outside smashed into the wall. The energy I'd been swimming in dries up and I'm left with the remnants of what my lust created, a low simmering instinct I'm unused to.

By now the sky is dark, coated in stars. Another slam and I step back, toss my head around and bare my teeth.

To my left, a large form swoops in at my side, wings tucking tight. I know without her telling me it's Atlanta.

*What's happening?* I ask, hoping that speaking the question in my mind will reach her.

Atlanta answers immediately. *It worked. Dyēus is testing the barrier here to gain access.*

Through one of the arched openings, we can see men on the other side, and a few in their dragon forms sending energy into the barrier, testing to see whether it's impermeable.

I stand there, transfixed, as they try again and again, until finally they move back, looking as if they're discussing what to do or where to go.

*I've never felt anything like that before,* Atlanta says.

I turn away from the scene. *What did they do?*

*No, not them.* You.

Unease trickles down my spine. Aside from holding onto the energy just now, this is the first emotion I've felt in this body that has me unsettled.

*Ozias and I...*

*No. I know. I meant after. Ozias was creating an opening and then suddenly, his power faltered. Right when yours rose.*

*What does that mean?*

Atlanta shakes her head. *We can figure that out later. All that matters right now is it worked. You did it, Kaisa. And we're all grateful. I'm grateful.*

She says the last part like it needs to be said, but I get the feeling there's something else she wishes she could say, too. I think back to the conversation between her and Ozias.

*Is there anything else you'd like to tell me? Anything else that you think I could do to help?* I ask.

Atlanta blinks, as if clearing her mind of something. *No, Kaisa. You're doing enough. Now go rest. Or fly. Whatever you wish.*

*Where's Ninon?*

*Resting, too, back at the enclosures. The first few nights she'll be tired, but after a while she'll venture out, I'm sure.*

I grunt, sidling up beside Atlanta as she gracefully walks along the perimeter. Dyēus's units are finally moving, directly alongside us on the other side of the barrier—I'm not sure which of us began walking first.

*What will you do?* I ask.

*Follow them. Alert Ozias if they get too close to the openings.*

I stop. Atlanta stops. And so do the units. Atlanta looks from them, to me. *Walk back a few steps, would you?*

I do as she says and Dyēus's men move with me.

She hums, her eyes calculating. *Perhaps it's best if you stayed here tonight. If you don't mind?*

I can see what's happening as well as she. For whatever reason, the dragons of Dyēus can still sense my energy and are following it. I don't want to risk accidentally guiding them to where Ozias made openings in the barrier. I briefly think of Ninon, but if she's resting, my presence might disturb her anyway. *Of course.*

Atlanta gently bumps the side of her head with mine,

and I instinctively grumble approvingly at the action. It feels like camaraderie. Something more than the tight community of women in Nevoba, but less overpowering than being in the Sar Dyēus's presence, or even in Ozias's. And I find myself wondering at all the ways living beings can connect and all that I've missed because of what has been done to me.

# Chapter Fifteen

The Sar Dyēus is there again when I close my eyes.

I hate him for it. This time though, he lies in his bed, asleep. The babies are wailing. I don't know how he can sleep through their screams. At least in the twists and turns of the caverns back home in Nevoba, the sounds are muffled enough to fade into the background.

I pace the room like a caged creature. This is no dream. I understand that much now, but I don't know in what capacity. I don't know what I'm doing that's bringing me here. It's clear I can't talk to Ozias and Atlanta, but I need to know more about it. Somehow.

The Sar Dyēus shifts slightly in his overly large bed and even that action sets my teeth on edge.

No. It does no good to stay here. I need to leave. My eyes travel about the room and lock onto the balcony that looks out over the Sere, towards the mountains.

Tilting my head, I step outside and my hands gliding over the smooth stone railing, solid beneath my touch. I frown at that. The previous two nights, the only things my hands have been able to feel with any solidity was him. I look out over the edge. Above, the gods eyes are an ever watchful presence in the sky. Below, I can see only the mist of the clouds, and the deep, unending blackness of night.

Hoisting myself onto the balcony's railing, I swing my legs over and slide down until my toes reach the landing on the other side. Holding onto the ledge behind me, I peer down, the height taking my breath. If I jump, maybe I can jolt myself awake. I fill my lungs with air and lean further out. My fingers cling to the stone. All I have to do is let go.

As my fingertips set to release, an unexpected voice reaches my ears.

"Don't." Zhoric's baritone is soft in its depth, but the command rings harsh through the night air.

My blood turns cold. I slowly pivot my head towards his bed. He's sitting up now, propped on one muscled arm, the other reached out towards me. The smooth planes of his bare chest and lines of his abdominal muscles catch the silvery light from the twin moons outside his window. A tear-dropped shaped hole in the center of his chest swallows all the light, and I recognize immediately, intrinsically, for what it is. The god power is a large, solitary dragon scale. I know I'm staring, but I can't seem to tear my eyes away. He has no scars, save for a few faint lines above his heart. So different from the many scars I've seen on Ozias's skin, on Atlanta's, and Issa's and all the other dragon shifters I've ever seen in close detail. Though, beyond his flawless skin, which rubs me the wrong way, he has always been a terrifying, beautiful anomaly. Completely inaccessible. Until now.

My gaze slips back to his face, but his hasn't moved from mine. "Did you just speak to me?"

Getting up from his bed, he ignores my question. He wears only loose, low-slung pants, his bare feet silent as he approaches me with careful steps, his gaze purposely elsewhere, examining every inch of space around me, but never landing on me. "Anything you do here will reflect back on your physical self."

My eyes widen and I reel myself in until my lower back hits the railing. I glance back down. I'm not desperate enough to leave this dream to find out whether he's telling the truth.

"Why tell me?" I say over my shoulder. "I would think that after killing one of your elites you'd be happy to be rid of me."

If he's surprised by my admission, he doesn't let on. "I've been known to suffer from bouts of insanity. Continue, if you are intent on death after all."

Turning my body so I'm facing the room again, I hold on tight and lean back, glancing behind me to the drop below. He watches me, eyes tense.

"So this isn't a dream? If I let go, I die?"

He waits a beat. He doesn't answer my first question. "You wouldn't awaken on the other side."

*The other side.* He must mean where I am in my dragon form in the Realm. "Why?"

His slow steps take him to a column where the balcony meets the outside wall. It takes me a minute to notice that he's inspecting a spider web tucked into the high corner of the column. "Mind walking is like that web." My fingers tighten on the railing. Atlanta said those words. *Mind walking.* "It's an intricate, delicate thing that works wonderfully for its intended purpose. But," he runs his fingers through it, the tendrils breaking and drifting the breeze, "any careless hand, any greater act, can loose the threads to the wind."

I pull myself in and climb over. On solid ground, I lean back against the railing and cross my arms. Though this form isn't physical, I can sense the rapid beat of my heart. "And what is the intended purpose? Of mind walking?" The words feel at once strange and familiar on my tongue.

Finally, he looks me directly in the eye. The moment our gazes meet, a tide rises in me, swift and boundless, terrifying and thrilling. "Connection."

I swallow hard past the tension in my throat. "And what's connecting me to you?"

Almost as if he can't stop himself, his eyes travel across my body, and even though my form isn't real, it burns all the same. What is happening? I must tense up enough that he notices, and, like a startled hare, his focus returns to my face before skittering away. I catch the longing in his expression before he wipes it clean, devoid of all feeling, all life. His brows lower. "Nothing that I have not already destroyed."

"So then why am I here?"

"I do not know. Nor do I wish to."

"You may not want to, but I do. You claim to have destroyed something, and yet here I am. Does that make the all-powerful Sar Dyēus a failure or a fraud?" I immediately bite my tongue, his words about my bodily safety coming back to me swift and sure. Then I remember my hands wrapped around his throat. How he didn't struggle for air, how his skin didn't depress beneath my touch. Throwing myself off the balcony may harm me, but we can't seem to physically affect one another here.

His eyes stay on me now, like he's daring me to say more. When I don't, a long blink and turn of his head is enough to tell me he's shutting me out. "Leave, Kaisa. You have found your freedom."

A shiver wracks my body at the sound of my name from his lips. I cannot tell if it's a pleasant one or not. "I'm free am I?" My voice raises. "Stuck in the Realm? Knowing my sister, my mother, my *people* are the way they are because of you?"

The silence rings louder than my words, pounding in my ears.

"It's all I can allow."

I sneer. "You're a monster."

"Then do not make the mistake of chaining yourself to me by continuing to come here. Stay away, Kaisa. Find a way to live a life you are proud of."

I laugh, harsh and sharp. "That advice coming from someone like you is an insult. I should kill you for all the things you're proud of."

His mouth opens, then slowly closes, the muscles in his jaw jumping. One brow glides up his forehead, mouth tight against his teeth as he says, "Get *out*."

I step up to him, so close that if we could touch, he would feel the heat of my words on his skin. "Make me."

He glares at me, eyes narrowed. Then he moves past me and plants himself down on the ground. "I have better uses for my energy than to force you out," he answers.

I walk around and sit in front of him. "But you could. You did before."

He doesn't answer me.

"Right?" I prompt.

Again, his answer is silence.

"You're ignoring me." I pause, then say as realization sets in, "Again."

"I should be glad you aren't a complete fool."

The flare of my nostrils is the only answer I give him, but he doesn't see because his eyes are closed. Then, I feel the surge of his power, sense a fluctuation of energy behind me. I turn and look, but all I see is the dark night sky and the gods eyes. And, I'm still here.

"What are you doing here?" I ask, gesturing around the balcony. The first time I came to him, he was doing exactly this. Is it some kind of meditation, like Ozias has been guiding me through?

"I think the better question is what are you doing

here?" He opens his eyes again, and because I'm sitting directly in front of him, they lock with mine immediately and my breath lodges in my throat.

I let my head fall back against the balcony railing. "Despite my best efforts, I can't seem to stop myself from coming. I turn into a dragon, I fall asleep, and then I'm here."

"You haven't alerted any of the Realm's inhabitants you see me? Ozias perhaps?"

I keep my mouth firmly shut and I think I see the ghost of a smile play across his lips.

"So you do see the uselessness in asking your enemy questions."

"You were once my king. A man who sealed me with a vow of protection," I counter.

"And now you know the truth of it."

"You won't deny it? Even in the slightest?" He doesn't answer. "Would answering me reveal some great secret I could use against you?"

"Perhaps."

At the same time, we hear a child cry out. We both tense, and he winces before his face hardens a fraction. My curiosity piques again and it feels dangerous, treacherous. He's not at all like what I expected him to be. Then again, I never expected to get close enough to know him.

"Why?" I ask.

Again, I'm met with silence.

"The babies? The crying? Why do you allow yourself to…" I open my hands and twirl them around in the air, looking for the right way to phrase what I mean.

"Hear it?"

"Yes."

"What would you have me do?"

"Silence them?" I offer.

"That's rather bleak, even for me."

A surprised laugh bubbles out of me. It's *not* a funny thing to joke about. However, I've been known to use macabre humor during difficult times and hearing it from him catches me entirely off guard. He grimaces, but I think it's a kind of smile. I think he's amused.

I clear my throat and set my brow, sobering a bit. "It wouldn't be the first time I've seen you use your power to keep someone quiet."

His gaze goes distant. "Hearing them serves as a reminder."

"A reminder of what?"

"Of everything I've done."

Now I'm the one who's silent. He sounds like a man full of remorse. Is that what Atlanta was telling Ozias the other night? The thing that could connect me deeper to Zhoric, that could overpower my hate? The potential that he possibly regrets the thing he's done is painful, but what's worse, he's done nothing at all to alter the course. He continues to brand our girl children and steal their ability to shift. He takes our boys to the skies and keeps ailing mothers at a distance. He can regret all he wants, but if he isn't doing anything to change any of it, the remorse, the regret, it doesn't matter at all.

"That has to be the most vile thing you could have said," I hiss at him while getting to my feet.

I walk away and put my face in my hands. I don't know what to think or make of this. Ozias has tasked me with bonding to this man to take his power. A task that, once I'm strong enough as a draconem, I should be able to force upon him. All I want to do now is end his existence, end all that he began. I wish now that Zhoric had said nothing to me at all. I barely register my thoughts used his proper name when he speaks again.

"Does it disturb you that I may still have my humanity after all I've done?"

I spin on my heel, eyes wide with rage. "What disturbs me is you seem to know you've done wrong and yet you do nothing to change it."

"Exactly. My humanity is intact, and yet things will not change. It will stay this way, on and on forever. Because of what I've done."

I study his features. After years of being Ninon's friend, I can see when someone's face is saying more than their words. And there's a great number of things he's not saying. His expression is veiled in a cool mask of apathy, but below, I see sorrow. I see…desire. "Irredeemable."

"Pardon?"

"You want to be irredeemable."

A fire flickers in his gaze, a spark. A challenge. "You know nothing of what I want."

"A person who regrets and chooses to do nothing? You're living in a place where redemption cannot exist."

"And if I've tried and failed? If I've made every move I could and still nothing changes? If I make a move and something worse happens?"

The thrum of my blood through my veins feels so real in this moment, if I cut myself, I would bet everything I have that I would bleed. "Have you?"

Zhoric gives me a look you'd give to a child who thinks they've finally figured everything out, when you know they have a long way to go before they understand the truth of the world. "Do not look for something that isn't there. I've done nothing but allow what I've created to grow beyond me."

I stand straighter and lift my chin. "I'm not so naïve. I understand your life led you to the choices you made. I know that now more than ever after what I've done. There's always something more."

"Your empathy will get you taken advantage of. Or killed," he warns.

"I'd rather bleed with my heart on my sleeve than live a lonely life like this."

His shoulders tense. "You sound like Thrace," he murmurs under his breath.

My throat constricts at the sound of his name. My sister. Gods above, am I putting my sister in danger by speaking to him this way? "Please." The word comes out like a whisper.

Zhoric's eyes narrow. "What do you have to beg for?"

"My sister. Please don't...please don't harm her because of me."

His chest rises as he inhales deeply and he pins his mouth closed. His hand forms a fist. "No harm will come to your sister."

I don't know how I can believe him.

"It's time you leave."

"I *can't*," I grind out.

His eyes hold mine, the depth of them speaking of a hurt I cannot begin to understand. "Then allow me to help you." With a flick of his wrist, I'm hurtling back through space, the stars streaks of light above me before I slam back into myself.

My head rears up, the pounding in my heart, alive and painful in my chest. Dawn is still a long way off. Getting to my taloned feet, I glance through the opening of the wall and see Dyēus's units, looking slightly disheveled and suddenly alert. Several are gearing up, preparing to test the wall again.

The wind rushes and I know a force is approaching me with great speed. I pull away from the wall in time to see a black-scaled dragon approach—Ozias. His amber eyes pin me and something within says I've betrayed him. I smother the sensation, and regard him as he regards me. He's first to look away, to the regiment outside the walls, then up towards the sky.

My talons curl into the hard-packed floor beneath me, imagining taking off, flying in the sky, unbound and un-caring, destination unknown—simply, away. I'm in deep of something greater than anything I've ever known, and I don't know how to swim in these new waters.

*What happened?* he asks.

I clench my jaw tight. Whatever this is with Zhoric, I'm certain I can't let Ozias know. His trust in me is already tentative. Telling him I'm having conversations with the enemy, that there's this feeling inside me that wants to know where Zhoric is coming from, is a betrayal I can't let grow.

I will conceal this one thing. I need to figure out on my own how to stop going to Zhoric.

As I'm about to tell Ozias that there's nothing to worry about, a blast pierces my ears and rubble rains down.

# Chapter Sixteen

Ozias leaps into the air and I follow without a second thought, going higher than even Ozias, well above the wall. It's the first time I've had the wind beneath my wings, but that's not what steals my breath. Out in the wide open Sere, the ground is alive with the movements of hundreds of Dyēus's men, both in their human forms and dragon. Every one of them are heading right for the Realm.

Ozias lets out a low, warning rumble.

*What is this?* I question, slowly drawing closer and closer to the edge of the outside wall, until a sensation of moving through water coasts over the scales of my face.

*Kaisa!* Ozias warns, but I realize my mistake too late.

A snarl rips from me as something latches around my long neck and pulls hard.

Ozias roars as I hurtle outside barrier. I beat my wings,

but I'm unused to them, and whatever force has its grip around my throat has no intention of letting go.

From behind, Ozias wraps his body around mine. It slows us, but he doesn't have enough strength to pull me back. Another hard jerk and together, we tumble and hit the ground on the outside.

My body wraps tight around Ozias, and my scales suddenly feel wrong, bristled and spiked. My mouth opens wide, teeth aching. I'm trembling with the effort to focus, to hold onto my mind, to stop it from going savage. I try to detach myself from Ozias and unfurl my body from his. I need to get as far away as possible. I can't hurt him, and if I stay close, I will. The thin tether I have on my mind is slipping through my hold. The power around my neck jerks me hard and I stumble.

*No,* Ozias's voice comes to my mind and he wraps himself around me tighter, pinning me to him, back onto the ground.

*You have to go back,* I bark. *You'll turn, too.*

*I won't go without you.* I give a warning snap of my teeth near his face and indignation swarms me when he huffs, his laugh deep and rasping in my mind. I snap again, my body trembling with the effort of maintaining my mind. I thrash my head, trying to loosen whatever power Dyēus has holding me.

*Ozias,* I think, loud and incessant. *Let go.*

He coils around me tighter and my muscles begin to twitch, rib cage billowing out erratic, misty breaths.

*No.*

I roar again, my anger swelling like a tide washing high up on shore, and no matter how much I want to fall back, to be absorbed into the waves, it keeps coming and that's when I know I'm going to lose my hold. My vision grows hazy. Ozias stands. I'm draped over his neck.

He crouches, straining against my weight and the force of the curse pressing in. An impact from the side rocks us.

Ribbons of blood ripple past my face in the wind. Ozias tips his head back in a pained roar. Wheeling around, he rips out the throat of his attacker. The dragon falls into my line of sight. In its mouth is an arm—Ozias's arm—talons dangling limp and lifeless.

Horror and rage churn my gut. I whip my head around, but no other dragons are in range of us. Yet.

Thick swaths of crimson red streak and speckle the ground, dripping from Ozias's wound. A snarl slides along my teeth.

*Hold on,* Ozias says.

But I can't. My mind slips. My body thrashes. I am half there, and half not, my mind of reason watching, screaming as my dragon body thrashes and claws at Ozias. I need to stop, but it's like shouting across the plains only to have my words ripped away on the wind, dampened by the siss of the dry grass.

Ozias wrangles my body, pins my thrashing limbs. A sharp pain here and there not registering in my dragon's mindless state, but I can feel it. I'm so close, but too afraid to draw nearer to the beast itself. So I cower while she thrashes and keens. I weep while she pulls apart my seams and I catch the moment Ozias's eyes glaze over, his lips peeling back into a fluttering snarl.

Out of the corner of my eye, the advance of Dyēus's troops draws nearer. They'll kill us. Or take us and use us. Probably both. If I let the beast they've created loose, I will lose everything. I can't let that happen. Not when I know what it's like to have it in my grasp. I sense something inside me break and it's like opening up a door to the outside to let fresh air tunnel through. I let that air flow through me, taking every last bit into myself. The very ground beneath me vibrates. The troops advancing on us stand completely still.

I cast a glance around, but don't see anything stopping them. It's almost as if they're afraid.

*Kaisa,* a voice grits out in my mind, strained and strange. Almost unfamiliar. *I can't...hold much longer.*

Long lines of drool fall from Ozias's mouth, pooling onto the parched earth below, and I'm amazed he can even form a thought with how far gone he looks.

I don't spend another moment wondering why Ozias is losing it, but I'm somehow suddenly holding myself together. I dare a look back out into the Sere. Some of them are in motion now, but most stay at a complete standstill. I need to get Ozias and myself back on the other side, but the openings in the wall are too narrow for a dragon's body. I'll have to go up and over.

Mounting him, I wrap myself around his body, dodging his sharp teeth as he twists to snap at me. My claws dig into his scales and I pump my wings hard and fast. The ache is unbearable and I keen out a long, strangled sound as I muster every ounce of power I have to propel us upwards. Ozias's claws, frantic and wild in his attempt to free himself, slashing clean through the scales on my leg. I ignore the sharp pain. I push harder and harder. We lift but not enough.

*Go,* I hear in my mind, and then I'm rising with Ozias tight in my grip, him fighting with all his might to break free of my hold. My flight is not gentle or graceful. It's a hurried, haphazard dash. We slam onto the wall and across the barrier, and right as we begin to tip over the edge of the wall into the Realm, the sun rises. My body twists hard and fast back into my human form, but Ozias doesn't. Another energy blast expels from one of the dragons of Dyēus, aimed right for us and I give one last shove with my legs against Ozias's body.

Together, we fall.

My breath is stolen from my lungs as we plummet to the ground and all I can do is cling to his mane and shut my eyes tight as we crash into the Realm.

The dust hasn't even settled before I scramble off of

him and to his side.

"Ozias?"

He groans, and with a sluggish curl of vapor, he shifts slowly, so slowly that as he draws back into his human size, I see the slip of his scales back into his skin, revealing the places he's bare and the places he's clothed.

He doesn't move. My hands hover over his form. "Ozias?" I say again. Still he doesn't move, doesn't answer. Leaning down, I put my ear near his mouth, listening for his breath.

Then I feel the brush of his nose against my cheek as his head lolls towards me. I pull back enough to see the grin on his face revealing his perfectly white teeth. "You held it together pretty well out there."

I shove him and he hisses. Lacerations crisscross the lower half of his face and neck, and, without his shirt on, I see they continue down along his chest. Wincing, I curl my hands into fists. "What were you thinking coming after me? You knew what would happen."

"Clearly, I didn't. I wasn't expecting you would be the one to save us."

Shaking my head, I sit back on my heels and cast a glance over my shoulder towards the wall, my mind wandering to the soldiers who stood stock still while I felt like I was drinking in the world. "I'm not sure what happened."

Grunting, Ozias rolls onto his side and pushes himself up with one arm. My hand flies to my mouth, stifling my outcry as my gaze locks onto his left arm, or what would have been his arm. It's gone from above his elbow down, a mess of flesh and blood, though it appears as if it's no longer actively bleeding.

My eyes catch his. My memories already muddled, I can't exactly remember what happened, who did what. I swallow. "Did I—"

Ozias shakes his head. "Not the arm. That wasn't you."

Gashes pepper his skin, some much deeper than others.

"Those, though. That was me."

He lowers his head to catch my gaze. "It's nothing."

I squeeze my eyes shut, a headache thrumming to life behind them. "I'm so sorry."

"It's nothing," he says again. "I've had and will have worse."

"But your arm," I say. "It's—it's because of *me*. You were distracted and I couldn't—"

"It will grow back."

Shock rocks me, making my head spin. "It—it what?"

"Draconem regenerate. I'll have it back in two days," he says, a hint of a smile creeping on his face at my dubious expression, no doubt.

I deflate, unable to truly process what turns out to be a minuscule inconvenience to him, but would have been a life changing event for any human. "Right. Of course."

I push myself up to stand, but as soon as weight goes onto my right leg, I gasp and nearly collapse back onto the ground. Ozias uses his hand and the shoulder of his injured arm to catch me at my waist, his nose nearly pressing into my navel from where he's kneeling on the ground.

"You're concerned over me and have yet to notice yourself." His brows pinch together, a frown drawing the corners of his mouth down. "Don't dole out your apologies so easily until you realize what I've done to you."

I step back, but his hand remains firmly against my hip as I look down. My bare stomach is crossed with cuts just as bad as Ozias's, and on my thigh, a dark red stain blossoms across my linen pants. With trembling fingers I touch the edge of the stain. The pain is so acute that my head hurls back as I bellow out a grunt.

Breathing in through my teeth, I hiss, "Guess we can consider it even, then."

Ozias squeezes my hip. "If you like. I still feel like I let you down," he says, his frown deepening.

Lowering my head, I find his eyes. "You kept me out

of their reach."

His mouth draws into a thin line. "You were only in danger because I'm asking something great of you."

"Not exactly." I shrug my shoulder until it kisses my ear. "I'm in danger because I want the world to change."

A slow, sensual smile curls his lips. "I can relate to that." Hand still braced on my hip, he stands with such fluidity and grace, I feel unsteady simply watching him.

"Let's go take care of that wound." His hand that was on my waist snakes around my back to support me, and I hook my arm around his shoulders to brace myself, then he's moving us into the thicket of trees.

Rustling comes from ahead of us and a moment later Atlanta appears, followed by four others. Her eyes fly across our bodies, hovering on the arm Ozias has wrapped around my middle and the one that he's now missing.

When she looks up, her voice is low and dangerous. "What happened?"

"It seems Dyēus has a nice addition to their team." Ozias kicks his head back behind us. "Get on the wall and see what's happening. We're headed for the infirmary."

At first, Atlanta doesn't move, even when everyone who came with her does. "Ozias..."

"We need your eyes on this," he tells her.

After another moment, Atlanta gives a stiff nod and brushes past us. I can't quite make out the significance of their exchanges. They're close, yet somehow distant. It reminds me of how Kalixta and I behaved with one another after she was chosen and I was not. When mother wanted nothing to do with me, but would bend to the wind to give Kalixta the world. Back then, I resented my sister. Now I understand that Kalixta resented me, too—for abandoning her. For getting the choice to do as I pleased, when I pleased.

Ozias steers us towards a nearby hut, small but clean. Inside, the walls are lined with jars, neatly folded gauzes and linens tucked into baskets. Two long, narrow beds line the center of the room with clean, white linens draped across each. Like his private office, the only windows are small ovals spread out across the upper walls near the ceiling. It's free of people and blissfully quiet.

Without a word, Ozias hikes me up against his side and swings me onto the first table. He passes me a wad of gauze, which I take and apply with pressure to my wound. Then he goes to work, walking over to a sink to pump fresh water into a basin. Even with the one arm, he tackles the tasks with ease. He quickly cleans his wound, unflinching when he applies ointments and dresses it. Then he's rinsing the basin, sanitizing it, and filling it once more.

When he turns to me, washbowl in hand, I nod to his missing arm. "Has this happened before?"

Ozias looks up from the basin, then notices I'm looking at his bandaged appendage. "Once, but on the other side." He grimaces as he sets the bowl down on a table near the bed. "It's more of an annoyance than a pain to grow back."

I suck in my lips and bite them, thinking of how that might look, bones and sinew coming to mind before forming the skin. "I expect that's something you might want to do in privacy."

Towel in hand, Ozias dunks it into the water. He waits for me to move the gauze and then squeezes the towel directly over my pants where the blood stain is. "It's not gruesome. It will steadily reform in segments, each section appearing as it's finished regenerating. Keeps it from getting damaged during the reformation process."

That sounds less horrific than I imagined. He douses my leg again, and the cool water sends a shiver through me. "To get the linen unstuck," he explains.

"I know. I can do this myself."

Ozias looks at me from under his brow. "I know." A pause, then, "Pants off."

My breath hitches, his words a heady reminder of what

we did before the night began. I steady myself and breathe. I don't need to make this awkward, or anything other than what it is. So I lie back on the bed, hook my thumbs into the waist of my pants, and arch up as I draw them down over my hips and backside to the top of my thighs. Ozias watches every moment, pupils dilating at the sight of me curving my body against the bed. I sit up and try to ignore the rising flush of my skin, the rush of desire between my legs. My undergarment is damp from the water he doused me with. I shimmy the waist of my pants down farther, carefully peeling it from my wound, a hiss leaving me, until I free my injured leg entirely.

Ozias's eyes follow the curve of my hips to the wound at the top of my thigh, the length of it twisting around to the inside. He takes his finger and hovers it over the wound, running along the length of it to the inner part of my thigh, then stills. "There's a superficial nick to an important artery. If this cut had gone any further, you wouldn't be here right now."

The heat of his hand radiates against my chilled leg, pebbles of flesh rising. "It's a good thing you didn't, then."

"Mm," he muses, then slips his fingers between my thighs and nudges them farther apart.

I exhale sharply and open for him. He stares at the space between my legs for a beat, before blinking and turning away, the rise of his chest telling me he's taking a deep, deep breath. He hands me a fresh pad of gauze. "Press this against the wound." He gathers a few more supplies, gauze and ointments, and to my dismay, needle and thread.

My throat closes up. "No."

His jaw works for a second. "I don't want to, but it's deep, Kaisa. I can't leave it like that and we don't have time for anything else. When you learn to shift willingly, something like this can heal on its own, but you're still too mortal."

My breath comes fast and tight. I shake my head again, teeth clenching. "It's fine."

Ozias looks at the wound again, then gives me a pointed look. "It's not."

I'm silent, trying to work out an argument that will win me this.

His head tilts. "Have you had stitches before?"

I give him a hard look. "Plenty of times."

"You have piercings."

"So you've noticed."

His smile is placating. "So it's not a fear of needles."

"It's a fear of having a needle put in my flesh over and over while a tiny slip of cotton slides in and out of *that* wound, across a wound that already fucking hurts." My eyes flash, hot and wild. "But I guess you've never had to go through this particular torture." And then I think I shouldn't have had to, either.

He's silent, not biting at my argument, or even rising to the bait.

"Can't you heal this with magic?" I implore.

"Minor wounds we can. This, unfortunately, is no minor thing."

A silent scowl remains perched on my mouth.

"I'll dull the pain," he promises.

I shake my head, looking away at the rows of jars along the wall, a sneer wrinkling my nose. "Just do it."

Ozias waits a beat, then comes in close, settling himself between my knees. I snap my attention back to him. "What are you doing?"

Face close to mine, Ozias leans in, his smell all cedar and sun and mist. "Distraction." He holds up a strip of leather to my lips. "Bite."

I open my mouth and he slides it between my teeth, thumb brushing against my lips before he moves on to the other supplies he's spread around me. He uses a clean towel and basin of water to wash and wipe the wound, then spreads an astringent ointment on the cut that stings, the wound pulsing to life. I'm beginning to think he put the leather between my teeth so I couldn't curse him during this bit, even as I gratefully bite down on the strip. Another ointment goes next, his hand hovering over the wound, heat radiating from his hand to my skin and within moments, the area is numb.

Then he picks up the needle and thread and my skin prickles with the beginnings of sweat.

"Breathe," he reminds me, looking up at me from the wound. "Maybe you can try meditating through this."

"Maybe you can try fucking off," I say, the crass words coming out mumbled and warbled, but his deep, throaty laugh tells me he understood well enough.

"Ready?"

"No." Again, the word is muffled.

"Me either." Then he's going to work, the needle slipping into my skin, the sting muted from the numbing ointment and his magic, but the pressure is still there and it still hurts. I'm glad I have the leather to bite on, even if it's only to ease my anxiety. I try meditating as he suggested, even as my jaw locks down tight on the leather between my teeth. Ozias makes quick work of the stitches, neat and tidy, even with one hand doing the job. I help him tie the thread off at the end, though my hands are quaking. When it's done, I drop the leather out of my mouth, licking my lips to bring them back to life.

Ozias catches the motion, eyes darting across my mouth, before trailing down my torso to my thigh. "Done."

I sigh, the sound shaky and rough edged. I reach for the bandages to wrap it, though my hands are still unsteady.

"I'll do it," Ozias says, and with my body feeling utterly depleted, I don't have the sense to argue. But I should have. I really should have, because next thing I know, Ozias is sinking to his knees between my legs and the sight of him there makes me weak and wanting. He carefully scoops up my injured leg, hooking my knee over the shoulder of his injured arm and I have to lean back on my hands to maintain my balance. His eyes don't leave mine as he takes the bandage and begins winding it around my leg with his one hand. It's loose at first, but he manages to tighten it as he goes around and around my thigh, the backs of his knuckles brushing my skin, each pass like a flame to dry grass.

When it's fully wrapped, he leans in, lips skimming the inside of my thigh, and takes one piece of the fabric between his teeth while his hand holds the other end of the bandage. He looks up at me from beneath the fan of his dark lashes as he pulls the fabric tight with fingers and teeth. His exhale is warm across my skin, skimming up my legs, all the way to my center. His eyes go molten, and I have the same sensation I did when he flew me away from Dyēus.

Ozias leans back, but my leg is still hooked over his shoulder. "How do you feel?"

*Aroused*, my mind says, but I try to stop the thought and the echo of that word from pulsing through my body. We're injured, we're tired, and he's not made a move or mention. What we did before had a clear purpose. If I asked for something now, it would be pure indulgence and completely selfish. He may be draconem, but he can still feel pain, and I can't imagine the agony he must be in right now. I clear my throat, voice coming out an octave too low. "Fine."

There's a lengthy pause where I wonder if he'll go further after all and take this where I desperately want it to go. His mouth is achingly close to my skin. A twist of his face would have his lips coming in contact with the delicate, sensitive skin of my center. Instead, he skates his hand up my knee, unhooking my leg from his shoulder and carefully puts it down as he rises.

I sigh, clasp my hands together, and get a hold of myself. "Thank you. I really could have done it myself, though."

Ozias studies me again, quiet, assessing. "I know," he repeats, "but that doesn't mean you have to." He holds out his hand for me and I take it.

# Chapter Seventeen

Ozias's words ring in my ears and I don't sleep. I *can't* sleep. I sit awake outside of Ninon's enclosure, waiting for her to rouse from her ever deep sleep when morning finally comes.

Sitting up, she rubs her eyes with the heel of her hand, catching sight of me instantly. "I thought you'd be with Ozias or Atlanta by now."

"I'm not supposed to meet them until the afternoon," I say, pushing myself off the stone wall I'd been leaning against, the cool dampness lingering on my skin.

"Then you should be resting," she chastises, getting up slowly. Too slowly.

I frown. "I'm restless."

"I'm unsurprised." She comes to my side and falls into step with me.

"And you? Going to Issa or have you found some kind of library to busy yourself with."

A half smile quirks her lips. "Of course I found the library."

Relief floods me at the same moment excitement courses through my veins. "I should have known. Will you show me?" I say it as casually as I can, but it doesn't matter. Ninon narrows her gaze at me.

"What use do you have for the library?"

"I like to know where you are at all times."

"Some people would find that concerning."

"I consider it being overprotective and overprepared. I might need you. You might need me."

"So needy."

I laugh. "It comes naturally."

Ninon shakes her head, a softness in her eyes telling me she's amused with my antics. "This way."

I follow her to the Alcazar, but instead of climbing up, we descend a set of stairs I'd never noticed before. The Alcazar itself is lined with books, but Ninon told me most of those are from the rest of the outside world, divided into sections based on the language the books are written in. Everything in our language is in the underground library.

A shudder wracks my body as the coolness of the cavern seeps into my skin, reminding me of home. A feeling of being split in two overcomes me—one that says *you do not belong*, and another that says *this is who you are*. An unexpected homesickness twists my heart.

"Strange, isn't it?" she says. Ninon's perceptiveness means, if I require her assistance, I need to prepare myself to divulge everything if it comes to it. If she feels inclined to pry.

"I miss it and yet...I don't."

She nods.

The rock surrounding us is identical to Nevoba's caverns, except where Nevoba is alive with the echo of life, the library resounds with a silence that muffles the ears.

"So what kind of books have you found here," I whisper, not wanting to disturb the quiet.

Ninon's voice is soft, seamlessly fitting into the hush. "Some are accounts of their lives before; some are fictional stories. Others are historical events, or texts about different elahi or unique draconem traits."

"Anything about bonding?" I inquire. If I'm not direct, even my roundabout questions may be lost on Ninon.

Ninon pauses and regards me. "Tell me what's on your mind."

"I just want to be prepared." She doesn't speak while I squirm with the words fighting to fly off my tongue. "I need to do my best."

"Let me help you."

A smile spreads wide across my face. "I was hoping you would." Ninon is smiling too, but she turns away from me before I can relish in it.

We spend a long while combing through the stacks. Ninon pulls out anything she can about bonding from personal accounts of draconem here in the Realm, to more educational texts and historical accounts and events—including one from the time right before Zhoric took power. There's not much else here that's quite that old. While she assembles a pile for me on a large slab of rock that acts as a low table, I scan the shelves for anything on mind walking. I'm not having any luck until a name stops me in my tracks.

*Atlanta of Nevoba, b.y. 15 od, s. Thera et. ~~Voxil~~.*It takes me a moment to register this is the Atlanta I know. Born in the year 15 Of Dyēus, sired by Thera and Voxil. Thera must have been her mother and the other…whoever sired her. Crossed out as it is, either she or someone else didn't want him as an official part of her lineage. Knowing what I do of Atlanta, and my own history, it fits.

I open the book and my chest constricts at the title:
*The Nuance and Practice of Mind Walking Between*

*Bonds – The Close and the Many*

Atlanta wrote a whole book on mind walking? I turn the book in my hands, daunted by the size.

"What did you find?"

"Something on bonds written by Atlanta," I answer with a shrug, then raise my chin towards the books in her stack. "What about you?"

"I can't seem to stop finding them. Clearly it's an important subject."

"Any you care to read and relate to me?"

"The thought of you reading one, let alone ten of these, was too good a dream to be true."

I laugh. "I'm only half teasing. I'll read them."

She picks up more than half the stack she collected. "I'll handle these." The books look heavy and cumbersome in her arms and in the dim light I finally notice the dark circles under her eyes.

"Go sleep."

"You've set me up with a week's worth of reading. I'm not sleeping."

I fix her with a hard stare. "You will sleep or I will take those books from you. You can't fight me."

She blinks at me. "You need me. *Don't* fight me."

"I'll be the death of you." If only if she knew how true I fear my words are.

She shakes her head with a tired smile, passing by me to plant a light kiss on my cheek. "You give me life."

Ozias told me I didn't have to do this alone, but the guilt of asking Ninon when it's clear she's already overexerting herself on my account claws its way up my chest and into my throat. When I don't follow her, she calls down to me from part way up the stairs. "Are you coming?"

I swallow hard. "I'm going to stay and keep looking."

"Don't strain your eyes," she replies, the sound of her steps echo until I'm left in silence.

Once she's gone, I skim Atlanta's words. I begin reading, getting the basics of mind walking and how and why it happens within the first few pages:

*Mind walking occurs when our dragon forms send a metaphysical human form to our bonds or potential bonds. When we mind walk, we allow the other half of ourselves to journey along predetermined paths to our bonds. Those with the strongest potential are easy to see and follow, like a well-trodden trail. Others are more difficult and need crafting, while some are impossible. No matter the strength or validity, they all take work to maintain. However, even the most comfortable path may not be the right one as far as creating an everlasting bond.*

Reading on, I learn that mind walking is a trait that all bonded pairs use to stay connected with one another. There's information on why that is, and references to other books that explain more on those subjects that I'm certain Ninon must have found.

My vision is already burning as I flip through the pages until something catches my eyes:

*For strong potential bonds, it's rather easy, if not impossible to avoid, mind walking, especially if there is already some deep emotion seeded for the other within one or both of the partners.*

I frown. I'm inclined to presume that's my position with Zhoric, but the only emotion I hold for him is seething rage, and I'm fairly certain the closest emotion he feels for me is mild annoyance. Then again, he did stop me from incidentally ending my own life.

I skim through again, taking note of this line: *Physical sensations are possible in mind walking if unbonded, though rare or often fleeting. Once bonded, physical sensations between the pair is possible.* I click my tongue with the side of my teeth. No wonder my hand passes through nearly everything I've touched.

I flip back to the index and skim the topics until I find what I'm looking for: *Unwanted or unintentional mind walking.* When I find the page, I find the section that directly relates to unintentional mind walking.

*Sometimes, particularly with strong potential bonds, one or both parties may unintentionally mind walk. Typically, these unintentional sessions occur when one or both parties are slumbering.*

That explains enough, but I want to know how to stop from going to him. I continue reading through the page, but one thing becomes clear; I won't stop going to him until whatever emotion that's tying me to him stops. Does that mean I have to feel nothing towards him? I don't know how I'm going to let go of my anger.

I groan in frustation and give the next few pages a cursory scan before I notice a line about enacting a bond:

*Bonds are easier to enact once each partner feels emotionally connected to the another. Often, potential pairs will attempt mind walking prior to enacting a bond to ensure they are thoroughly connected to produce an easy bonding experience. For more on enacting bonds, see Vierna lo Draconem, b.y. 3648 pd, m. Sosia*

None of the books in my pile are the one referenced. It must be one Ninon took with her. My pulse ticks in my veins with the sudden desire to know how to bond, to know what to expect.

I read the next few passages, but dread seizes my lungs as one thing becomes plainly clear—a bond is rooted in love. Familial, friend, and most often, romantic love. It makes sense. Ozias did say bonds were secondarily for reproducing and wouldn't creating and raising a child together be easier with someone you were connected with? Which means, the more emotionally connected Zhoric is to me, the more easily I can bond with him. I let the book lower to my lap, my mind churning. Ozias and Atlanta are hoping I'm strong enough to force the bond on Zhoric, but figuring out my strength—my elahi—has been slow. I wonder if it would be possible to make Zhoric feel something for me sooner than we can figure out my power. I wonder if I can seduce him, trick him, into bonding with me.

Intent on testing my theory, I go into the night to try my hand at being friendly with him, or at least, not entirely antagonistic. Only he's not there. There's a feeling of his nearness, but wherever he is, I can't seem to access him.

Two more nights pass, and I wait for him, but he never shows.

I've gone through an unnecessary array of emotions regarding this matter. On edge, at first, wondering when he'd waltz in. Glad, because maybe it's best if I don't see him after all. Annoyed, because if he were around, then maybe I'd be able to do something.

I would have spent my time flying, exploring more of my dragon form, but Ninon is still too weak to stay awake when she shifts at night. Ozias wants me to take to the skies, explaining it will help me further connect to my dragon form, but I can't bear to leave her side. He told me Atlanta gets like that sometimes where she'll go through phases where the nights are hard and all she can do is sleep. I could tell his concern ran deep when he told me, which only made me worry all the more for Ninon.

Ninon is frustrated that I won't leave her side. It's not often that she's truly upset with me, but I explained it has nothing to do with her. That it's something I'm waiting for us to do together, because that's what I want. I don't mention that it's also because I'm terrified for her. Afraid that one morning she might not wake up.

During the day, Ozias and Atlanta have been taking turns helping me meditate. Our goal is to get me to a place where I can shift at will. I fall into a rhythm with my meditations, more determined than ever.

Now, three days after the incident and as many nights

with no meetings with Zhoric, Ozias walks onto his terrace where I wait for him.

"No more scars," I say, looking at the sleek skin of his lower arm and hand. Not a single mark mars his skin, though it is several shades paler than his usual sun-kissed tone.

He fans his hands elegantly before curling them into a fist, studying the new appendage. On the edge of his palm is a smudge of black ink. "Delighted that you've been looking so closely at me."

I raise a brow, though a thrill runs through me. "I always look for scars. Tells a lot about someones weaknesses."

Ozias moves towards me then, stepping so close that I have to tilt my head back to maintain eye contact. "My lack of scars says more about my weakness than my scars ever did, I think."

The meaning behind his words is like a gentle caress and I suppress a shiver. "Care to elaborate on that?"

"A dragon gets scars as easily as our human forms, and with our line of work, scars are an inevitability. The only way our scars disappear is if we've needed to regenerate something new after it was torn away," he says, nodding down to his arm. "If a draconem is lacking scars been broken in ways you can't imagine. The question you'll want to ask then, is *why*."

The conversation Thrace and I had back in Dyēus comes rushing back to me, his words filling my brain, his admission of falling in love with my sister. I wanted to deny it then. Dragons don't love. But I read Atlanta's words. I know my own affection and the way I feel towards those I love—and I am a dragon. So what I once thought was impossible is now a stark reality. And I can either face it and accept it—or run from it.

"What are you thinking?" Ozias asks, eyes scanning my face as if he could read me as easily as one of his books.

My pulse jumps and I answer with the nearest truth I care to share. "Thrace."

His eyes shutter, a slight tic of his facial muscles making the freckle under his left eye flex. "Ah, yes. Exactly what every man wants to hear; another's name on the lips of the woman he's desperately attracted to."

My pulse flies into a full gallop at his candor. "I meant, I was thinking about him and my sister," I clarify. "He said he loved her, but what would he do for her? Does he love her enough to keep her from harm?"

The back of Ozias's fingers brush my cheek, light and tender. "You needn't worry. He would do anything for her."

"You can't possibly know that," I say, the heat of my anger scorching my skin. "He couldn't even get word to her after the birth of her children, after he took her son. He told me so himself. That doesn't sound like a man who would do anything for someone he claims to love."

"It's complicated in Dyēus. The draconem there aren't supposed to choose a carremai they could bond with. It would complicate things for Dyēus because the men there would be compelled to bond with them, which in turn would unleash her dragon. Most of the elites agree with this situation, but a few are not. Some believe that by not choosing the best possible mate, we're not only weakening future generations, but setting something else in motion, too."

I try to focus on what he's saying, but I'm hooked on his words: *those they could bond with*. "Are you saying my sister and Thrace are compatible? That they could bond?"

"I am saying," he says, dropping his hand, "they have bonded."

I rear back, brows drawing together as I struggle to understand. "They—what?"

"I saw their threads once before when I was visiting Dyēus not long ago. They were intertwined in a bond."

"So what does this mean? Can she shift? Is she safe?

Will the Sar Dyēus end her life for this?" The words come out rushed and I clutch my stomach as my insides churn with panic.

"Yes, she can shift, controlled, and as any draconem could." Shock and a hint of betrayal twists sour and sharp in my nose. Ozias goes on. "Zhoric will do nothing. He needs Thrace, and before anyone or anything else, Thrace will keep your sister safe. That's what bonded pairs do."

He's implying my sister comes even before the Sar Dyēus when it comes to Thrace. It makes sense now: Zhoric's reaction the other night when I begged him not to harm my sister. It's not that he *won't*. It's that he *can't*. Which raises the question of what will happen to me when I bond with Zhoric.

I step back, and turn towards the open sky. Big, fluffy clouds drift lazily across the wide, pale blue, all the while a storm swells inside me. I want to kill him, but will I be able to? I toss the thought from my mind. Focus. I need to maintain focus. I can't do anything for Ninon, for my sister, for *anyone*, until I find my elahi and master shifting. And until I do that, I won't be able to get face to face with the Sar Dyēus and bond him to me, one way or another. I look over my shoulder. "Should we get started?"

Ozias splays his hand, new and unmarred, gesturing to the ground. I lie down, the same way I've meditated day in and day out. Only this time a new resolve fills me. A part of me has been afraid to allow this beast to take over my body, to become one with me. I've hated versions of this creature my whole life, but I'm beginning to understand it now. The depth of who and what I am. Maybe if I can tap into this place inside me, I can allow this bud of feeling for Ozias to take root—another thing to hold me here if my bond with the Sar Dyēus threatens to consume me. As my thoughts ready to spiral out of control, I tamp them down and collect them against my chest. Then I imagine lifting my hands and letting them go, giving them away to the gentle breeze.

I fall into myself. Here, I know I'm in control, of my destiny, of my life. It's me against an ever changing world, and I will change with it. I will mold myself into an unrestricted being, one that can harness great power.

I'm so deep within myself that I almost don't recognize Ozias's turning figure. He may as well be the sun or the moon or the stars hovering above, wheeling across this vast plane of existence. Inside, I wander, looking around corners of my mind that I once thought were empty spaces, down tunnels and over mountains, crossing the rivers of my mind until, finally, finally, I find her.

She sleeps. Her breath bellows her ribs—no, not *her* breath—*mine*, in the same rhythm with the rise and fall of my hands upon my stomach.

Dappled sunlight glistens across my scales, pale silvery gray. My head is nestled in the crook of my long tail. My mane swaying on a phantom breeze is a forest green so dark that it looks almost black, like moss in the shade. The beauty of her, of me, strikes so violently, that a sob wracks my body. She blinks, her eyes opening, the same, honey brown color I know so well boring into me. Hot tears bubble and fall down my cheeks in heavy rivulets.

*You found me.*

*Yes.*

She—no *I*—stand, curving my back in a luxurious stretch before ambling towards me, eyes focused, at once predatory and serene.

*This must be what people see before we take their souls*, I think, the thought coming to me unbidden.

*Yes*, she answers, I answer, like I've always known in my marrow who I was and what I was meant for. Only now I realize that knowledge slumbered with her.

Seeing myself in this way, as the dragon, sends a deep longing through me. Like I'm seeing someone I've missed for a long time, but couldn't quite remember who.

My dragon stands so close to me that when she drops her head, she rests her great forehead against mine.

*Home*, I think.

I can't stop the tide of tears that cascade down my face. This gesture, so familiar and comfortable, is what seals everything for me. That it's true. I am draconem. That Ozias and everyone else here isn't trying to shove me into a body or being that doesn't belong.

*This is me.*

*I am you.*

Something stirs in my peripheral, but when I look, nothing is there. It's then I remember my physical body. Ozias has stepped close, only this time, near my wounded thigh. My dragon looks at me, as if to ask, *What will we do?*

But it's already done.

I blink a few times, shaking out of my inner self, only to realize I've moved my body. Unlike before when I took Ozias down for stepping too close, when I reacted blindly, this is different, like moving before I even knew my limbs were a part of my body. He's pinned beneath me, my forearm pressing into his throat, his eyes wide, full of shock and awe. A drop of water lands on his cheek, on the freckle under his left eye. Not water—my tear. My physical body must have been crying, too.

*I found her*, I say, but my mouth doesn't move.

Ozias's eyes soften, like he heard me. A slow smile spreads wide across his mouth, exposing teeth white and straight and a touch dangerous. He pushes himself up, and I ease the pressure on his throat until my arm falls away. One of his hands cups my jaw, thumb swiping away a tear falling down my cheek, the other hand snaking around my waist, holding me close.

I swallow past a lump in my throat. "I told you if you stepped that close to me again I would choke you out."

"I believed you. I just thought that I would see your

attack coming again." His chin dips, eyes darkening. "I didn't."

My gaze flits across his. "Why?"

"Because you were with your dragon. You accessed her and she responded. You're one step closer to shifting at will, Kaisa. We're one step closer to ending Dyēus's reign." He scans my face, his hold on me tightening a fraction. A flood of desire heats my blood.

My hand presses against his chest and his heartbeat pounds beneath my fingertips. "Should I try?"

"There is nothing else you can do but try."

Nodding, and a little wary, I pull away from him, giving enough space for my dragon to exist. I see her in my mind, just as she was—as she is. I reach out my hand to her.

I slip into her scales and take up her space. Slide my tongue across my teeth, sharp and long. Toss my head, and let my mane shake, luxuriating as my whiskers float on the breeze. I drum my talons on the hard floor beneath my feet.

I allow her to take her place. I imagine the bright vaporous energy that always comes from the draconem when they shift, and instead of my dragon ripping and clawing her way out, she simply sighs into existence. I feel like I've climbed a mountain, only to have reached the top and finally caught my breath.

With my wide, wandering dragon vision I look up at the blue sky, dazzling me with colors of the world's energy. Strands of this power flow as if caught in a rushing river, passing me by. I catch them between my teeth and swallow them whole. The gods eyes, usually visible only at night, is a beacon, pulsing steady and frantic, calling to me.

"You are a marvel," Ozias says, something like affection warming his tone.

Seeing him there like that, I want to be with him, fully human. I want him to trust me. I want the possibility of something...more. I want to have something, someone, as mine, of my own choosing, and who will choose me back in equal measures. I realize now it's up to me to take that first step. I won't run away from this.

I slip back into my human skin, letting myself be drawn into his golden gaze, alight and burning. "Do you believe in me? Do you think I'm capable of doing what needs to be done?"

Ozias looks at me, long and deep, and it stirs a ravenous desire within. "I want to. So I do."

It's as simple as that, and sometimes, that's the way things are. "I need to tell you something."

Ozias shores himself up with an inhale.

My stomach flips at his hesitation, but I charge forward. "About what's happening to me at night."

Ozias lets out a breath, then he nods. "You can tell me anything."

I worry what Atlanta will think and say when she learns about this, but we have to trust each other if this is going to work—and it *has* to work. Still, it's a long beat before my mouth will cooperate enough to speak the words. "I'm seeing the Sar Dyēus —Zhoric—at night. In my dreams. At least, I thought that's what it was. Then I did some research and now I know a little more about mind walking, thanks to Atlanta's lovely, yet lengthy, text on the subject."

The muscles around his eyes tense. "She is a savant of sorts on the matter."

Ozias is silent, contemplative. I let him think, but panic sets in. Could this be the moment where I made a mistake? Did I let him get too close and now I've ruined everything and it will take years, decades, centuries, to do what no one else has been able to do before me, all because I didn't want to do it alone? All because I was afraid if I let my heart open to Zhoric, the bond would pull not only him, but me, too? Finally, Ozias sighs, his expression open, giving my anxiety a brief respite. "I'm wondering...I'm wondering if this is something we bring to Atlanta."

Flicking my gaze down, I worry my bottom lip with my

teeth. After a moment, I meet his stare again from under the fan of my lashes. "I overheard you two the other night. It sounded as if she's worried about the strength of my potential bond with him. I can't…" I stop and try to get my emotions under control, but tears are already stinging my eyes and nose. "I can't not try. I can't let this drag on any longer. Ninon…" I shut my eyes and wait for the emotion to pass.

Ozias doesn't say anything and I fall once again into thinking I've made a grave mistake when a warm, steady pressure caresses the side of my face. I open my eyes, and lean my cheek into Ozias's hand.

"I understand and I'm with you." He nods, reassuring and patient. "Let's keep this between us."

Tremendous relief floods me. It's not that I want to keep it from Atlanta, but she sounded so unsure days ago, and I'm glad to keep it between us for now. "I want to use it, Ozias. I know you think my elahi will be enough and I know that I have strength in me…but what if it fails? What if you're wrong and I can't force anything onto him?"

"So what are you suggesting?"

"I seduce him. I make him fall for me so that when the time comes, I can bond with him," I shake my head, "no question, no ifs."

A slow smile spreads across his mouth. "Your mind is as marvelous as your spirit. If you're not careful, you might make me fall for you, too."

I return his smile, excitement thrumming through me. "I don't know if that sounds like such a bad thing."

The expanse of his answering grin is all I need.

# Chapter Eighteen

After that, and all the next day, Ozias and I work on my shifts. I get close, then feel like I don't have enough to force it, and it fades. Sometimes I will it, hard and fast, and I'll shift for a few moments only to snap back into my human form, nauseating me. I shift once more, the feel of transition closer to pulling teeth. After, my limbs are sluggish, my mind hazy.

"Let's pause here for now," Ozias says. "I'm going to check on the borders to see if we can determine new openings for a supply run. Stay here to rest. Meditate if you can't sleep."

"Is everything all right?"

"You know how it went the other night," he murmurs before making his leave.

A shiver rushes down my spine. The night Ozias and I

used my energy to cause a distraction, and the attack that ensued, meant that those who were out to procure food didn't have as much time as they needed for a completely successful run. We didn't account for Dyēus launching a full-on attack because of my burst of energy. Despite where our conversation about seduction ended yesterday, I haven't even dared bringing up to Ozias the prospect of finishing what he started that night for fear of what might happen as a result.

My mind whirls with worry, wondering what I can do to help the supply runs, knowing I'm just another mouth to feed that they didn't account for. I need to control my energy output, keep it smooth and even to create a true diversion for Ozias's efforts elsewhere along the wall. All the while learn to shift at will, explore my possible elahi, and figure out how to seduce Zhoric, especially since he still hasn't shown his face to me in all these nights since the attack.

I try meditating again. I sit inside my mind with my dragon while she slumbers. Quietly, I attempt to shift, but nothing happens. When I try harder and still nothing happens, I grunt my frustration away as I sit up. I should probably be resting anyway.

I move inside Ozias's suites but stop short by the large table, scattered with parchments. Over and over, the same words are written on different parchments, the same scrawl penning the words:

*You are woman and you are power.*
*You have many gifts.*
*But something has been stolen from you.*
*Something you will reclaim.*
*It will shock you.*
*It may frighten you.*
*But you are stronger than you know.*
*You have more in you than you have ever been allowed to understand.*

*When the time comes, be ready.*
*You contain multitudes —*
*It's time for you to live with them all.*

I recall the smudge of black on the side of Ozias's hand I saw yesterday. He must have spent hours writing all these.

His words don't place blame on Dyēus or try to pit the Nevobans against them. I scowl a little. With how fiercely Dyēus attacked the Realm days ago, I fear the Nevobans who would take up arms with them instead of with us. Ozias and Atlanta haven't hidden the fact that there will be some fallout after I take down the Sar Dyēus and it's not an if, but an inevitability. They want to keep their power and we want to strip them of it. I wonder if Ozias should try to entreat the Nevobans to our side. Instead, all he does with this missive is tell them of their worth and their right to it. Then again, I know as well as anyone that ill words against the kingdom would ring deaf on the ears of people like my mother, proud of their carremai title and their own self-importance. This missive would pique even my mother's interest. My face softens as I realize what he's doing. He's taking the risk of them siding with Dyēus in favor of ensuring their transition is smooth and welcome. He's not calling them to arms. He's offering them freedom.

My fingers brush against my faded mark, hoping my people are ready for what's to come. I hope this will be enough.

"Any luck?" Atlanta's voice jars me from my thoughts. I turn to find her standing in the doorway. For a moment, I wonder if she means with Zhoric—that Ozias told her after all. "With shifting," she clarifies at seeing my blank expression.

I huff, shaking my head as I turn away from the papers and lean back against the table. "No. I don't understand what I'm doing wrong."

"Don't be too hard on yourself," Atlanta soothes as she comes in to stand by my side and scans the parchments on the table. "Most of us not born inside the Realm who can shift during the day have spent years to get to this point. The fact that you have at all is an immense accomplishment you should be proud of."

I slide my hands over my face. Impressive as it might be, it's still not enough. "How are things progressing with getting notice to Nevoba?"

Her mouth twists as she takes one of the parchments in her hands and rolls it into a thin tube. "The farmhands are on edge. Word is, Dyēus is keeping a stricter eye on their movements."

"Is that unusual?"

Atlanta shrugs, plucking a bit of twine from a pile and wrapping it around the parchment several times before tying it off. "They go through phases. Usually when there's some shift in power among the elites."

I watch her do another and by the third time watching, I select a parchment and roll one up. She holds out a hand and when I give it to her, she wraps and ties it off.

"Do you know what's changed?"

"Alixor's death, for one thing. But that's the least of what we know. Selnor can't have been happy and he holds a lot of sway among the elites. We assume they know about the dragonsbane by now. Our best guess is they think it came from the farmhands and are trying to determine who provided it."

My hands stop mid roll. "Have they blamed anyone?"

Atlanta shakes her head, holding out her hand. I finish rolling and pass it on to her. "We're not sure. We're working on finding that out."

The soft rasp of our work is too quiet for my ears right now. She doesn't mention me in her ideas on what has changed with Dyēus, but she doesn't need to. "Do you think they will?"

"I wouldn't put it past them, but they need the farmhands to be cooperative. They won't do anything without evidence."

"Do they have anything that could put them at risk?"

"Plenty, but dragonsbane isn't one of them. For everything else they have plans in place to keep anything damning hidden."

I breathe a sigh of relief.

She stops my hand before I reach for another parchment. "Those need drying still. Do you need to rest?"

I shake my head. I couldn't fall asleep even if I tried. "Can we check on Ninon?"

"Of course." Atlanta finishes tying off the last of the dried missives and sets them in a basket she procures from under the table before leading us out.

As we walk, I'm buzzing with a need to pick her brain about mind walking. I can only read so much before my mind goes off somewhere else. Ninon hasn't had much time to read, and I told her not to worry about it. She needs all the rest she can get and I answered most of the questions I had with Atlanta's book.

"How do you think Zhoric would feel about a bond if he knew of one out there? If he knew of me?"

Atlanta tips her head from side to side and eyes me as if she can glean my secrets. "I didn't know Zhoric. I know stories, we've exchanged words, even, but I don't know his heart. Though, I can imagine...I can imagine his loneliness. I think that alone would make him yearn for a bond."

Her words make it sound like she's speaking from experience. "I can't imagine a man with so much power being lonely."

"Loneliness is sometimes a choice."

I decide to ask a question that I hope won't haunt me later. "Did you write your text on mind walking at a time when you were lonely?"

"Ah. Found that, did you?" she says, swinging her arms in sync with one another for a moment.

I shrug and offer a modicum of the truth. "I was looking for information on bonding, to help prepare myself.

Ozias says you're sort of savant on the subject."

She huffs out a laugh and rolls her eyes. "He amuses himself too much calling that."

"But are you?" I ask, tilting my head in question.

Her shoulders inch up in a humble shrug. "More accomplished than most. I've taught myself how to mind walk toward any potential bond I have—here in the Realm or elsewhere."

My eyes widen. "That seems...incredible." I can't leave Zhoric to get back to my own mind, let alone try and get to someone else's.

She offers me a sad smile. "It was more out of necessity than desire. When I first came here, Ozias saved me. I told you before that tactics to get women pregnant were... *different* when I was in Nevoba. I was forced to do things I didn't want to do. I was tortured and abused and when all of that didn't work, they tied me to the end of a rope and flew me near the Realm to threaten me into agreeing to breed. Back then we didn't even have the legends that you'd turn into a monster when you entered—it was known only as a place of certain, terrible death."

My mouth falls open, but I have to close it quickly when my stomach turns and threatens to upend the contents. I swallow hard. "That's horrifying."

She casts her eyes down to the ground. "By that point...I didn't care. I was ready to die. But they got too close and I went across the border. Ozias grabbed me and took me in. He saved me that day, but I wasn't...I wasn't myself anymore. I couldn't touch anyone. I didn't speak. Making eye contact was painful. But I was lonely. So, so lonely."

*No wonder she can imagine Zhoric's loneliness,* I think.

"And so eventually my draconem mind led me to a close connection. Without my physical body present, I was able to start speaking again. Eventually, I sought out other connections and slowly I began to believe in myself again."

"Have you bonded with any of these connections?"

Another sad smile. "No. Many have now met their end and most others I don't speak with that way anymore. Their minds need space to make a bond elsewhere, if they so choose."

"Do you not want to bond with anyone?" I ask, stopping as we reach the top of the wall where Ninon has been spending most of her days.

She opens her mouth, then closes it before giving me another one of those long, sad smiles. "It's complicated."

Before I can probe further, she nods toward the watch-chamber. "There they are now."

I look inside and see Ninon bent over some parchment, pen in hand frantically writing or drawing out something while Issa looks over her shoulder, nodding thoughtfully.

Issa sees us first. "Well, well, if it isn't trouble."

Ninon looks up, her face brightening. "Kaisa, come. I have something to show you."

With one firm squeeze on my shoulder, Atlanta turns and leaves. I watch her move away, my heart heavy for her and the burden she carries. Maybe she's stronger for it, but I can't help wondering how strong and exceptional she would be if she didn't have to fight so hard for every ounce she has now. I wonder how strong *I* would be.

I settle down beside Ninon and she shows me all that she's been working on with Issa. Most of it goes over my head, but from what I glean, Ninon has been able to track a series of patterns Dyēus uses that follow the stars, dependent on the type of clouds visible in the sky that day. According to Issa, if they can accurately place where Dyēus will be on any given night, they can calculate the furthest distance from those posts to create entry and exit points in the barrier.

"She's a genius, this one," Issa tells me, clapping a hand on Ninon's shoulder. Ninon comes as close to blushing as I've ever seen, the light inside her practically beaming.

After that, Issa sends us off to prepare for sundown.

As Ninon and I walk towards the enclosures for the night, I wait for her to tell me to stop following her, to go and explore my draconem abilities as she's done every night since we've both gotten through the savagery. And maybe I should. If Zhoric doesn't ever show again, I might only have my strength to rely on when the time comes.

"No pushback tonight?" I inquire when we make it to the enclosures without her saying a word.

"Hm?" She seems surprised to hear my voice, a bleariness in her eyes. "Oh...right. Of course you should fly."

I bend to catch her eye, my concern an arrow piercing my heart. "Are you all right?"

"I'm tired. I've been working hard with Issa."

I hum, rubbing my mark, far more faded than hers, my brows pinched with worry. "Make sure you're resting during the day, too. Maybe it would help you in the nighttime?"

She reaches up and drags her thumb between my wrinkled brow. "You sound like Issa." When I rear back to give her look of mock offense, a weary smile tips up her lips. She drops her hand. "Your meaning, not how you say it. She uses much more colorful language than you," she says, though it's with fondness that lights up her eyes.

"Issa seems to like you, an amazing feat of accomplishment since she doesn't seem to like *anyone*," I joke.

Ninon's smile unfurls, slow and gentle. "She's a hard one, but I like her."

"She seems like a hard worker, too. I can appreciate that."

Ninon nods, joy lingering on her face.

She *is* tired, but happy, too—happier than she's ever been at home these last few years. I wrap one arm around her upper back and give her a solid squeeze.

"I haven't been able to read much," she says with a yawn.

"I told you not to worry about it."

She goes on, pretending she doesn't hear me. "But I did read something fascinating. Apparently, if your bond dies before you, you keep any magic or elahi they had in life."

That *is* interesting. "Oh, so after I bond with Zhoric, then kill him, I'll get to keep his power?"

"Oh, no. If you're the one to kill them, you lose it all."

*Oh.* The air in my lungs all but leaves me.

"So, probably best not to go killing him," she says.

I wonder why Ozias didn't tell me that when I mentioned killing Zhoric when I first agreed to all this. I want to ask her for more, but her blinks are long and her steps are short. I hope tonight is the last time exhaustion takes her so deeply. I hope that tomorrow she will be awake and alert and we can take to the skies together.

As we say our goodnights, and night falls and my body slips into its scales, I drift off to sleep, wondering if Zhoric will show himself.

I don't wonder for long.

I hear the sound of running water before I even realize I'm asleep.

I stand still as I finally come face to face with Zhoric, watching him cross the room. He stops the moment he sets eyes on me, then his gaze drifts away before he continues on his way. For all I can tell, I may as well be a phantom rather than a manifestation of myself he can actually see. But I know better than that now. "Good of you to show your face tonight," I say.

He ignores me as he heads into another part of his suite that's fully open with no doors. The bathing room. In the very center, the basin, large enough for two, is filling with water from a long, curved faucet. Zhoric shrugs off his robe and it pools to the ground behind him. I spin away as fast as I can, but not before I notice the whole of his back. Like his front, the skin is flawless. No scars cross his arms or body, save for three brutal lines running in jagged ridges across his back, right behind where his heart lies.

"A few nights without seeing me doesn't mean I cease to exist." I think back to those first few days manifesting before him where he couldn't see me, but those days are far behind us now.

"Be gone, Kaisa," he says, but he doesn't push me out.

I sigh. "Clearly, I would if I could." Even I'm tired of saying the same words. I'm certain he's sick of it.

When he says nothing to that, I try for a more conversational approach. Endearing. Welcoming. "What are you doing?"

"Bathing. Clearly." His reply is curt and to the point.

I clench my teeth and whip my head back toward him at the exact moment his pants fall to the ground, revealing the curve of his backside. Also lacking scars. Also very nice, which I could have gone my life without knowing.

"Gods beyond," I say, flustered and exasperated, spinning back around. "A warning next time would be nice."

"As far as I'm concerned, you are not here."

I pin my gaze to the ceiling. *I will stay calm.* "Why not shove me out again, then?"

"I've decided that ridding myself of your presence isn't worth my effort."

I hear the slosh of water. A half sigh, half groan slips from him as he sinks down into it and my low belly responds instinctively at the indulgent sound. Once I'm certain he's settled, I turn back around. His head is tilted back with his throat exposed. I'm reminded of the images of him I saw when I was still savage right after entering the Realm.

"If you're intending to pretend I'm not here, then why speak at all? Or do you perhaps talk to yourself often?" I bite my tongue. Antagonizing him is certainly not going to help, but I can't seem to stop myself. Then again, maybe any response from him other than apathy is progress.

His arms dangle outside of the tub on either side, and I see his fingers twitch. "Endlessly."

I purse my lips to keep from smiling. Still studying the

column of his throat, I walk closer to the bathing chamber, but stop at the door frame and lean against it. From the top of his head to his mid-abdomen he is completely, utterly smooth. An errant thought crosses my mind, an image of me raking my fingernails down his chest, across his back to mark him. That reaction can't be natural. I make a note to ask Ozias or look into Atlanta's book to see if the bond affects physical desire. I swallow thickly, needing a distraction.

"Who did that to you?" I nod to the smooth expanse of his skin. It's not a question I meant to ask, but it's taking up residence in my brain. I can't stop noticing it. I can't stop thinking of it. Not after what Ozias said about scars. I hadn't even remembered he didn't have scars before seeing him again.

There's a beat of silence, then, in a whisper, "Someone tried to tear out my heart."

Everything in me goes deadly still, but a wave of dizziness blurs my vision. It takes me a moment to regain my composure to clarify my question. "I meant who took the scars *away*." I stare him down. He opens his eyes and holds my gaze for so long I don't think he's going to answer.

"Alixor's aggression had nothing on the one who chose me. But that is long since passed and matters no more." His head falls back again, unbothered, as if he didn't reveal something deep and intrinsic about his past—about himself.

I asked, but I didn't expect him to answer. I didn't expect to feel a pang of sympathy strike me to the core. He's saying that his bonded partner did that to him? Or someone very near to it did? I push off the wall and enter the bathing chamber, not stopping until I'm at the edge of the tub by his feet. I thank the gods that the water is cloudy so I don't have to fight a blush. I squat down, the slits of my skirt parting to fall between my thighs—one near flawless, the other torn through with the new, nasty scar from Ozias, still sore and healing. I fold my hands over the lip of the tub and rest my chin on them.

"Then I'm surprised you aren't taking the effort to push me out. I know what me coming here means now. Does that not make you afraid of me?"

His head tips back up so that his dark, forest eyes are on mine. I'd never seen another color like it until I entered the Realm. "Is that why you are here, then? To attempt to seduce me into bonding with you so you can have someone powerful at your side?"

My blood cools in my veins. I try very hard not to let my gaze track down to the god scale pinned to his chest. I ignore the pressing feeling inside me, pushing me towards him. The aggravation of feeling anything but hatred for him seeps out with my next words. "There's nothing that could make me want you."

His pinky twitches, the muscles in his shoulders going supernaturally still.

Cleary, seduction isn't my strong suit. Still, this is not a man who will easily be caught off guard. How can I possibly endear myself to him, then? If I pretend to feel or be something I'm not, there's no doubt in my mind he'll find out. If I fail, I fail Ninon. I fail Ozias, Atlanta, and Issa. I fail my people.

After a pause, he sits up and leans over so that our faces are inches apart, his hands braced on the edge of the tub, his elbows jutting out on either side like a grand pair of alabaster wings. "Perhaps it is *you* who should be afraid. Perhaps, if you keep coming here, I'll enter the Realm and steal you away to claim you as mine. I know what great power you hold. It could be of use to me."

My breath stills in my lungs. His eyes drag down my form, snagging on my injured thigh, a muscle in his jaw pulsing.

I could let him, but then who's to say when he'd come? Tonight? Tomorrow? Never? That's not enough time to get all of Nevoba ready. His grip on the edge of the bath tightens and I realize…he's bluffing. He has no intention of tying himself to me without a real reason. I huff out a laugh, low and tinged with menace. His eyes widen a fraction as my chin lifts from my hands, bringing our faces a hair's breadth from one another, all the while a small smile is pinned to my mouth. "Liar."

His gaze cuts back to mine, cold and glaring. After a beat he says, "You are a nightmare."

"How can I be a nightmare when you don't sleep? Or rather you do, but only after you're done whatever it is you're doing over there in front of the gods eyes every few nights."

Zhoric stills, holding this piece of him that I discovered in his piercing gaze, tension drifting off of him in waves. He doesn't like that I've seen it. Or perhaps he doesn't like that I know something more is happening when he sits out there. It makes me wonder how many others know.

"Insomnia is no serious offense for a king," he finally says.

"I've been watching you for days. You're not suffering from insomnia alone."

"No, I seem to be suffering it with you lurking over my shoulder." His face is perfectly blank as he says this and I have to swallow the urge to laugh. I force a frown on my lips, which I'm certain is not at all convincing given how hard he's staring at my mouth.

All these years with Ninon has made me good at reading people who rein in their expressions and even with what little of his face has changed at my reaction, I can tell he's quite pleased with himself.

A possibility then, a small, infinitesimal possibility that I can enamor him. But I need more reassurance than that. I need something that has him wanting to keep me close instead of pushing me away. Perhaps his loneliness is enough, but I can't know that for sure. There's one thing I do know though: he once craved power enough to steal it from the gods. I know that he's vulnerable on those nights he sits before the gods eyes and I know the elites have pull over him that he can't possibly want.

"Do your elites know how exhausted you are on those nights? It doesn't take a sage to figure out your hold on the balance of power here in Dyēus is contrived at best and tenuous at worst."

There's a long beat of silence as he stares me down. Then, through clenched teeth, he hisses, each word punctuated, "What do you want from me?"

I blink. I wasn't intending to extort him, I only wanted him to stop trying to push me away. "Wouldn't you *want* to bond with me then?" I ask quiet, but stern. "Wouldn't you let me help you?"

"You want to help me." A statement, not a question.

"No," I breathe and give him what I have: the truth. "I want to be with my sister again. I want to be free of the Realm. Of the curse."

"Free is a relative term. Bonded, your dragon would need to remain unleashed, but it's not as if I could ever let you be seen in that form or else the women of Nevoba might wonder."

I swallow down the discomfort. "As if hiding who I am isn't what I've done my whole life."

His eyes narrow. His pulse ticks along the column of his throat in a strong, steady rhythm. "The elites won't like it."

Blood rushes through my veins, dizzying me. He's considering it. He's *actually* considering it. "I hear bonded pairs are powerful. They don't have to like it."

A satisfied expression crosses his face for a moment before he wipes it clean. After a beat he says, "I'll think about it."

I'm so shocked I jolt up, putting our faces nearly nose to nose. I recover enough to say, "Good." I wait before sitting back so it doesn't seem like our nearness intimidated me. "So, what *are* you doing at night in front of the gods eyes?"

He holds my gaze, but doesn't answer my question. "When I said I would think about it, I meant *let* me think about it. As in, go away and leave me to my thoughts."

"Zho—" I start to say his name, mortification thrumming through me as the first syllables roll off my tongue, but before I can finish it, he cuts me off.

"Be content that I'm thinking of what you proposed. Do not speak any more on it and make me regret even that."

I wet my lips and he tracks the movement. I let myself indulge in the attention. It can't hurt.

His eyes are dark as they find mine again.

At least, I hope it can't hurt.

# Chapter Nineteen

Now that Ozias knows about Zhoric, he comes to my room the next morning and I tell him all about my night. It's a relief to finally divulge this strange little secret I've been keeping and Ozias is fully enraptured by my story of last night's encounter.

"Kaisa, you do realize your mission is to seduce him, not threaten him," Ozias drawls, his easy smile telling me he's teasing.

"It's what came naturally." I scowl. "I didn't mean to coerce him."

Ozias shakes his head, reining in a delighted smile. "Either way, using his desire against him will help you when the time comes. You'll still need him to like you for your plan to work, so maybe less threats and more charm."

My frown deepens. "I'm perfectly charming to those I

like."

Ozias bends close to my ear as he moves behind me. "Then maybe you need to pretend to like him."

"I *am* trying you know." After Zhoric told me to leave him be, we didn't speak the rest of the night, and I ended up sitting up against one of his many walls until morning came. I think at some point I fell asleep. At least when he wasn't showing himself at all I was able to help myself to his bed.

"I know, but for this to work he needs to fall for you. That's the only way you'll be in a position of power. I fear he could be leading you."

"To what end?" I ask, crossing my arms.

"He'd be a fool not to want your power," he says, folding himself down on my bed.

I shake my head and turn until I'm standing in front of him. "What does it matter? You said I can break the bond."

"There's a little more nuance to it than that," Ozias says, a slight grimace turning his mouth.

"Ah, of course there is. I'll try to feign surprise—that should go as well as me pretending to like the Sar Dyēus," I quip.

Ozias pats the space next to him on my bed, and I try not to think of all the things that one could do on a bed with someone like him as I take up his invitation.

"It used to be when we'd bond, it was completely reciprocal. Then, things began to change. Power shifts created new practices, evolving until whoever initiated a bond first was the one who held the power to break it."

"You mean someone could get stuck in a bond they didn't want?" My hand goes to my throat and a sudden, sickening realization comes to me. "Is that what happened to Zhoric?"

Ozias's brows inch together. "He told you that?"

"I'm inferring," I correct. "He mentioned someone who chose him being worse than Alixor."

Ozias hums, then mumbles, "I'm surprised he told you that much."

Horror swirls through me, fast and thick. "Did you know?" I ask. How could someone know what was happening to Zhoric and not do anything?

Ozias's eyes go distant. "His bonded was very powerful. There wasn't much anyone could do for Zhoric once she chose him, under the blessing of their parents, no less. And those who could wouldn't have dared for fear of her ire."

The shake of my head is almost imperceptible. "That's… awful. You're saying not a single person helped him?" As much as I hate to admit, if I'd known how terrible Alixor was, and those who loved me did, too and chose silence, I might have wanted to let the world burn, too.

"Thrace did what he could. His elahi is a shield, and so that helped ease some of what I suspect was the worst of it, but even he was forced to keep his distance after a time."

My throat is clogged full of emotion. I have to try several times to swallow it down before I can speak. "What will happen to Zhoric when I take his power?"

"He'll return to his state prior to stealing the god scale."

I cast my eyes down. "But people will come for him?"

Ozias lowers his head near mine, tucking his knuckle gently beneath my chin until I look at him. "Do I need to remind you what he's done to your people?"

"Of course not."

His finger trails up my jaw, tucking my hair behind my ear. "Then beyond you taking his power, and knowing he'll live, there's nothing else you need to concern yourself with in regard to him."

I'm silent as unease runs rampant through my body, coiling my muscles tight.

Ozias catches my eyes again, concern and resolve settling in the lines of his face. "You'll need to enact the bond first. His agreeing to bond means he believes he can control you. You've opened up another opportunity, but put yourself at much greater risk in doing so."

I stand, to give myself some distance from the feel of Ozias's hand clouding my mind. I meander over to the lone window, looking out into the thick forest that leads from here to the border. "So I've complicated things."

"In a manner of speaking," Ozias agrees solemnly.

Heaving a long, heavy sigh, I twist to face him. "I can work better with this," I say with all the confidence I can muster. With this error, I'm reminded of how young I am compared to him, to Zhoric. They've lived years like this, scheming and planning, plotting new ways to escape, and then I come here like a young, wild horse, tearing up order and causing more problems than I'm likely worth. "I just need to make sure I'm the one to enact the bond and I'll be fine." I don't miss the minute waver of my voice. I'm not at all surprised when Ozias moves to my side.

"You initiate the bond, you control when it ends." He slips his fingers into my palm and smooths his thumb along the back of my hand. "Regardless, it would be a good idea for you to make him fall for you. If he does, he might be less likely to force you into a bond first."

I look back out the window, barely feeling his hand in mine. "It seems unfair. Is this how it is? One always at the behest of the other?"

"A true bonded pair who trust one another implicitly would enact the bond the traditional way, with both giving and taking it in the same moment and in equal measure." He says all of this so wistfully, with such reverence that a thought that hadn't occurred to me before comes rushing forth.

"Have you bonded before?"

His head lowers and his hand squeezes mine. "I have."

"One like you've just described," I guess.

He's quiet for a moment. "She was killed after Zhoric took power." I don't have the words to convey my sympathies, but even if I did, he moves on quickly. "Not many in our day bonded the way we did. It used to be the only way to bond, until around four centuries ago."

My brows furrow. "What changed?"

"The human world."

"What do they have to do with this?" I turn back to Ozias. He's so close now, I can see the lines of grief carving down the smooth planes of his face.

"Everything," he murmurs.

"How?"

He looks down at our hands, still twined together. "The mortal world shapes the way we are. Every change they make reflects on us. We are, in essence, a manifestation of how they are evolving. The adaptations to our elahi are a direct result of needs we've had when collecting souls to protect us or help us do our duty. When the mortals change, so do we. When they no longer believed we could fly on our magic alone, they gave our forms wings. When men started warring and pillaging from others, turning away from peace and divinity, we too started to become more gluttonous with our greed and power. It's all connected. Even the gods are affected."

I think of Zhoric's choices, of Dyēus and the way women have been manipulated and made to do as they say. "It sounds like the humans have caused us more harm than good."

"Some of us think that way. Some have no interest in carrying out our divine duty to ferry souls to the gods once we end this."

I'm not certain I disagree with them. My brows pinch together. "So what will change when I take Zhoric's power? What can we do to keep from coming right back here again?"

"We need to remind the mortals that there is more to them than what they're told. The idea of sealing a woman's dragon didn't come from nowhere, Kaisa. It came from the human world. From men who wanted to be revered like the mothers. So they stole from them. They told them they were weak, only good for a set of hips to carry a child."

I shake my head. "But how? How did they believe them?" I find it hard to imagine that people living with peace would do anything to alter it.

"They burned the world. The books and the knowledge keepers. The women who were leaders of thought and peace, calling them wicked things. The men of greed hid behind the gods and gave them different names. After a time, the only women that were left didn't know how to speak peace, or were too afraid to do it. Then, when they moved on to the next life, those after them didn't have the books or teachings to guide them. It was all lost. All it took was a faction of men who thought they could do better and were willing to burn the world to get what they wanted."

My stomach churns and my skin is cool, though I can feel sweat prickle along the back of my neck.

I don't realize I'm still shaking my head until Ozias clasps both hands on either side to stop me. "We will do more than adapt to their ways this time, Kaisa. We will help change them."

"How? *How*? You said yourself it's been this way for centuries. How can it possibly change after all that time?"

"It was once peaceful before the men. Peace will come again. Like you have opened your eyes to your true power, so will the mortals who've been oppressed by those who were perverse enough to think power was a thing to claim."

Like Zhoric. Zhoric is exactly like those men Ozias speaks of. I feel sick over the sympathy I felt for him last night. An awful thing happened to Zhoric, but it does not forgive what he chose to do after.

Ozias places his forehead against mine. "I know I'm asking a great and terrible task of you. But do not lose yourself in it, Kaisa, or you'll doom us all."

I nod and lick my lips. "I won't fail us." I say the words

and hope they're true.

His gaze falls to my mouth. "I know."

We stay there, breathing in one another's air, his hands still caging in my face, not letting go.

My breaths come fast. "Tell me more about bonds. The more I know, the better I can protect myself from him doing it to me first."

"They're difficult to explain."

"You've been bonded before. Tell me what it was like for you."

Ozias presses his forehead a touch firmer against mine, tipping it gently from side to side. "A bond...a true bond built on trust and...love." Ozias's words fade, his eyes falling closed. "There's no better feeling. It's never having to leave a warm bed on a cold morning. It's knowing you'll be taken care of, and feeling true joy when you do the same in return." His eyes open again, locking with mine. "I can't lie, Kaisa. The bond will feel good."

I swallow hard. "Is there any chance," I start to ask, my voice wispy, "that those feelings might happen prior to enacting the bond?"

Ozias wets his lips, his nod slow. "Without a doubt."

I close my eyes. I tell myself it's a good thing. If I can remember that, then I know it's the bond pushing me, not my true desires. I do not want Zhoric. He's done horrible things to my people, to me, and does not deserve an ounce of my sympathy or forgiveness.

"But the bond doesn't control the way you think or feel about him."

My eyes snap open. "What?"

"The bond may prey upon your sexual desires, it is secondarily for reproducing after all, but it doesn't alter how you feel about someone. That's why you need to be careful. Zhoric is cunning—he hasn't gotten to where he is without reason."

So my sympathy is true, but the physical pull I feel towards him I can blame on the bond. At least that's something.

"I would feel more comfortable with this brilliant new plan of yours if we knew what exactly your elahi was."

The laugh that puffs out of me sounds exhausted. "Why does it sound like that's what we'll be working on today?"

Ozias leans back and brings my hand up to his mouth, kissing the back of it. "Because that's exactly what we'll be working on today."

My hope collapses. A kiss on the hand isn't enough for me. Ozias doesn't let me go and moves towards my door, but I hold still and he stops short, looking over his shoulder at me. I'm determined to tell him what I want. To ask for more of him—but I don't have to. I can tell the moment he sees my desire, his eyes tracking a slow path down my body than back up.

He swallows, a muscle in his jaw pulsing. A beat of hesitation. "You said he'd consider it?"

I drop my gaze and fill my lungs. I understand what he's implying and it takes a gargantuan feat not to mimic him and take my time looking my fill, letting him know that my preparation can wait a few minutes. An hour. More. I nod jerkily. "I did."

His mouth is a thin line. "Then there's not a moment to lose."

All afternoon I attempt throwing up shields and manifesting energy into weapons. I try reading energy, seeing more than what's beyond my dragon's vision. I try replicating Ozias's manifestations. I try destroying them. I try multiplying them. Nothing happens.

"Your elahi just *is*," he explains for what I believe to be the tenth time. "You think it, and it happens." Earlier he explained that the first signs of an elahi manifest when a draconem is ten and continues to mature until the age of twenty or so. As I'm already twenty-and-five, there's no reason it shouldn't come to me easily now.

"How do I know what to *think* if I don't know what it *is*?" By this point I'm frustrated and I'm snapping like a brittle twig. I swipe my hand down my face, taking with it the light coating of sweat on my skin.

Ozias places his hands out in front of him like he's pleading for me to give him something I don't have. "We've tried every elahi I can think of. You're certain you're thinking of these things strongly enough?"

I fold my arms over my chest. "You tell me." He sighs. He knows how hard I'm working. How hard I'm concentrating. "Maybe there are more elahi than you know?"

Ozias's head drops to his chest. "I'll do some research tonight. For now though, can we please, *please*, go eat?"

I grin. I haven't let him leave until we tried everything he could think of twice. And then thrice for the elahi that felt promising the first time or that I liked the sound of. The sun is dangerously low. We don't have much time. And I'm not entirely merciless, though maybe, perhaps, some of this is a small aggression against his clear signal earlier that we don't have time to lean into our desires.

"Let's go. You whine worse than I do when I want something."

He darts forward, catching me around the waist, leaning me back just a bit so I have to angle my head to look at him. "I think I'd enjoy hearing you whine when you want something."

Liquid heat pools in my core. I cup my hand around the back of his neck and lean in close. At that exact moment, my stomach growls, and right on the heels of mine, so does his. "You're most unfair."

His head kicks back, letting out a boisterous laugh. "I see. I'll have to remember what a vindictive little thing you are." He stands upright, pulling me along with him, our torsos flush. There's another beat, another moment of hesitation, then he gives me a lingering squeeze, lets me go, and turns towards the stairs.

I need to get a hold of myself and regain my composure. I trail behind him, refocusing my thoughts on elahi and what mine could be. My thoughts lead to my sister, wondering if she has one as well. Then, I remember what Ozias said, about Thrace being a shield.

"Ozias." I move faster and catch up to him, walking quickly to match his stride. "Does Thrace act as a shield for Zhoric now?"

"From what I can tell," he says. "Why do you ask?"

"I threatened Zhoric by telling him I would reveal his weakness after whatever meditations he does at night. That seemed to concern him, but if Thrace is his shield...why would it?"

Ozias furrows his brows and in the next instant, his face lights up. "The babies. Your sister."

My eyes widen with his. "Thrace's power is pulled too thin?"

Ozias nods, a smile lighting his face. "Exactly."

"Which means my threat isn't empty. He might actually be considering bonding with me after all."

"Which means," he says stopping me on the stairs, "that you have power to control the situation."

He's right. Whether to keep me silent or to use me, if he wants to bond with me to have my power, that means he'll be open and accepting of it when the time comes. I feel like I could sweep up the moons with my own hands to bring the night. My smile is untouchable; I couldn't contain it if I tried.

Ozias's face softens as he looks at me with so much tenderness it almost feels sad. "Is it possible, I wonder?"

"What?" I ask, getting lost in the intensity of his golden eyes.

"If there will ever be a time or place when you and I

make sense."

I reach out, hand touching his elbow to trail down his arm. I want him. I enjoy his company. I don't know if I believe in love like Thrace says he and Kalixta have. Like the delicate thing blossoming between Ninon and Issa. But I know desire. I know friendship and companionship. I don't know what Ozias's reservations are, but it's clear he has them. "It doesn't need to be anything more than what it is."

"Attraction? Certainly," he agrees. "And, perhaps, a potential?"

"For?"

"Bonding."

My breath is stolen from my lungs. "Between us?"

Ozias lowers his head, catching me off guard with how seriously he's looking at me. "There's much work that will need to be done when this thing with Dyēus ends. The world will need to be brought into balance. We'll need bonded pairs."

I drop my chin and silence falls between us, the birds seeming to quiet as we stand before one another. All that exists now is me and Ozias. In a place I once thought brought death and danger, but is now possibly my only salvation. "I like the idea of that potential," my heart twisting as I answer.

"Then let's keep that possibility between us." He takes my hand and kisses the back of it again, and this time, it feels like enough.

# Chapter Twenty

When I manifest in Zhoric's chambers, he's already on the balcony. He's shirtless, his pants, looser than usual, sit low on his waist. I realize this is how I saw him that first night I came to him. I approach with slow steps and when I reach the threshold, his head falls forward, the long line of the back of his neck exposed. I shore myself up for night, ready to be open and winsome. Ready to let him feel something for me.

"Tonight would be a fine night for you to show yourself out," he murmurs wearily.

"You sound as tired of those words as I am," I remark, crossing my arms and leaning my shoulder against the threshold.

Zhoric rolls his head over his shoulder until he's looking at me. "You could at least give me some space."

"I'm waiting for an answer," I say, raising a brow.

He holds my gaze, but then his shoulders bristle and his eyelids flutter closed. A small line burrows between his brows, like he's in pain.

A lump lodges in my throat. "Are you unwell?"

He scoffs in response and turns his head to once again face the open sky.

I blow out a breath as I push myself off the threshold and out onto the balcony.

"Don't stand in front of me," he grits out, eyes squinting open, looking at me from his peripheral.

I stop in my tracks. The last time he warned me against something, it turned out to be true, so I'm in no hurry to test him. Still, I ask, "Why?"

"I—I don't know what would happen if you did. No one has ever been here while I've done this."

"And what is this?" I ask, and as I expect to be met with silence, I'm not disappointed. Instead, I sit beside him, a smirk planting itself on my lips. He hasn't agreed to bond with me, and in the event he refuses, the plan is to at least make some kind of positive emotional connection. "Am I mistaken, or are you concerned for my well-being?"

He holds the tension in his body for another few moments, eyes squeezed tight, fists clenched. My pulse hammers in my throat as I wait for him to answer. I'm about to open my mouth to ask him again if he's all right when he sighs, his head falling back. My skin prickles as my eyes wander the length of his throat.

Zhoric breathes in and out a few times before his eyes slit open, dark and glassy. "It doesn't matter what I feel. I desire to feel nothing at all."

His answer surprises me a little. I would think someone whose aim is to have ultimate control and power would want feel something as equally all encompassing. "Is that what you truly wish? To feel nothing at all?"

Zhoric ignores my pointed question. "Did you know

the gods do not feel? Not in their realm, at least. If they ever stepped foot in this one, though, feelings would consume them and make them want it all without remorse or care of whom it hurt. They would love until it suffocated the life out of you. They would eat grief like ripe fruit and get drunk on pain." He swallows, the apple of his throat bobbing slowly. "When you feel so much, you sometimes wish to not feel it at all for fear of what it can do."

"Or for what it has already done?" The words come unbidden, but with everything Ozias and Atlanta have told me, from what I overhead, and what Zhoric has told me himself, this is a man who carries at least a modicum of guilt for his actions. For what exactly, or to what degree I don't know. It shouldn't matter, but I'll pretend that it does for the sake of endearing myself to him. All while I quietly convince myself that it doesn't.

When he doesn't answer, I sigh and resolve to give him a little of myself. "I'm sitting here, pretending I don't know what you mean. When you marked me undesirable, and I wasn't chosen, my mother's ire ran deep. I couldn't think around my desire to change her attitude towards me, and yet my relief and jealousy were at war with each other. All those feelings, all those desires, it tore me apart. So I can understand. In those days, I often wished I didn't feel any of it." I lower my gaze. I expect to feel unsettled after sharing a truth of mine, but I don't. Instead, I feel free, a gentle weight lifting from my shoulders. "Sometimes, I think I feel too much, too deeply," I admit. It's why I love Ninon so much. Her quiet calm to my riotous mind soothes me. When I feel like I'm drifting too far, she's my rein. I sometimes feel like I could destroy more than I'd help if left untethered.

When I meet Zhoric's gaze, his eyes shine like moss in the sunlight. As he looks at me, it reminds me of the way Ninon sees me when she looks at me. It reminds me of the empathy my sister carries. There's something more, too. Something I can't name, or am afraid to. He shuts his eyes, stealing the green away. His breathing picks up again, rapid, shallow puffs of air moving his chest. "I don't know what to do with you," he admits, teeth clenching tight. "Back then, I had no design for you, other than to keep you away. Then Alixor—" His words cut off, his body going rigid.

Confusion and concern whip through me as quick as a dust storm. "Why did you let him choose me, then? If you didn't want me near, why not refuse him?"

After another moment, he sighs, tension slipping from his muscles. "I didn't have any reason I could give to refuse."

"You marked me as undesirable," I remind him, not that he needs it. It's me who needs to understand.

"It doesn't matter. Alixor saw your power through the haze I put over you at your selection ceremony when others couldn't. He could have outed me for concealing you from them, but Alixor was ambitious. He didn't want another claiming you when he could simply have you himself. He made the connection I'd done it to others before you and he held that information over my head. If the elites knew I was concealing the strongest of you..." he trails off and blinks, as if he finally realized he'd been speaking aloud.

Breath sticking in my chest, I have to work to get the words out. "You're saying you were concealing the more powerful of us?"

He lowers his head in a singular nod.

My hope is a running mare, swift and fast and sure. "Ninon?" If she's strong, if she has an elahi that hasn't yet manifestested, then perhaps...

"No. Not her. Not all of them."

Losing that hope is an arrow to my chest. "Why?"

"For some, like Ninon, a match would never work. Her heart isn't made to love a man and so breeding wouldn't have come to fruition. To keep her and others with similar hearts safe from the entitlement of the draconem, I mark them undesirable. That's what the draconem believe the distinction means. For the others, like you, it's to ensure the elites powers didn't get too out of hand. So they wouldn't think to use you in more ways they already were."

How much worse could it be? "In what way?"

He's silent for a time, but when he answers, his response is barely a whisper. "Forcing bonds on you." The very thing I'm tempting him with.

I swallow hard and search for a lie written on his stoic features, but I don't find it. "If Alixor was a threat, that means…killing him did you a favor?"

"In some regards." A hiss escapes from between his teeth as his fingers dig more tightly into his palms. "And not in others." His ribs expand and contract and a light sheen of sweat coats his skin. The dark scale glistens like the night reflecting on the sea. He draws in a ragged breath.

"Is there anything…" I stop, unsure of what to offer. "Can I help?"

His head jerks. "Go. Please."

I clench my teeth and shake my head. "No."

"Kaisa…" he breathes, and the anguish in my name as he says it breaks something inside me. Then his body bows forward and his broad hands slap the stone floor to brace himself. I jolt upright, hands hovering over his shoulders as if they could do something. With immense effort, he lifts his head, his eyes blazing black as he focuses on the dim light of gods eyes out in the obsidian sky. His shoulders heave. Sweat rolls down his temples, dripping off his jaw.

It reminds me of Kalixta giving birth. There is pain here, a sense of some great power happening in front of my eyes. I wished I could lend Kalixta my strength during her struggle and I find myself wanting to lend him strength, too. It's the bond, the thing connecting us, speaking to me. It must be. Even if right now, in this moment, I can't sense the truth of my feelings beneath it. But here, the lie of the bond will help me in my task. And so I lean into it. I feel moisture on my cheek before I even register the prick of my tears. I lay a hand on his shoulder, though I know he cannot feel it.

With great effort, he looks at my hand, then his eyes sweep up to my face. He says nothing, but there is a fathomless depth to his gaze that strikes my core. I lift my chin and nod. I won't bother him further, but I won't leave him either. He closes his eyes and turns back to the sky.

The struggle, as I've decided to call this event, goes on for another hour. Two. I stay by his side while he breathes and grunts, gasps and curses. Watching this in full, I don't know if this is something that's happening to him, or something that he's doing. Despite the question burning on my tongue, I stay quiet. I don't think it would do me any good to ask in his current state, in any case. I'm enraptured by the power flowing around us. I track the energy, feel the way it moves until I see it; the scale on his chest, pulsing like a heartbeat, fast as a bird's. The power is so delicate, yet so immense it frightens me. That's the thing I'm supposed to steal once we bond. I can't imagine holding something like that in my hands. I recoil at the want of holding it to my own chest.

Finally, the scale's power dims and Zhoric's body sags. He's folded forward, his forearms resting on the ground, his head sagging between his shoulders. The moons are high and bright enough that it makes the smooth skin of his back gleam white like bleached bone against the deep night. The gods eyes are brilliant, glistening orbs now, their colors reflecting and shimmering in the smooth stone floor of the balcony. My hand has slipped to the blades of his shoulders, my tawny skin a brand just below the scars that strike the space over his heart.

Only when he starts to rise do I let my hand slip from him. He doesn't sit up straight, though, his spine curled with fatigue.

"What is this, Zhoric?" I ask. I don't have to fake the concern lacing my words.

When he swivels his head to look at me, his body sways, his eyes unfocused and dull. His brow crinkles and a frown tugs at his lips. The great, powerful king of the sky is doing or experiencing a struggle that weakens him. Even I, with the little experience I have, can sense his weakened state. All this power he holds is leaving him and going somewhere else. Either taken or given.

"Could you...stop asking questions..." he murmurs, the words nearly slurring together. Then he sags against my side. I stiffen, but don't attempt to push him off.

"Why?" I ask, peering down at him, the cloud white of his hair, damp with sweat, sticks to my shoulder.

He huffs—a laugh, if the delicate upturn of his mouth is any indication. "I feel compelled to answer."

I let my body relax. I can feel the pressure of him against me, but not the slick sweat of his skin, or the strands of his hair on my arm. "Then perhaps you should let yourself answer."

"If I let myself, I might consume you whole like one of our gods."

My eyes slide down to the god scale. "Maybe you should. Maybe I would like a bond like that."

His breath hitches, holds, then sighs out from him, drawing him more deeply against my side. "Is that the bond speaking, or you?"

I don't answer immediately, but that's because only one answer comes to me and I don't have the strength to invent a lie. His heavy eyelids fall shut, and his breathing evens out. He must have fallen asleep. "It can be both," I admit in the quiet.

Zhoric tilts his head back, and my breath stills in my lungs. Had he heard me? I imagine the feel of his hair tickling my neck. "Were you..." he murmurs, takes a breath, "were you crying for me, or for yourself?"

"It can be both," I whisper, echoing my last answer, the truth resounding loud and incessant in my chest.

He doesn't answer and after a time, his breathing steadies into gentle rhythm. His dark lashes fan out against his alabaster cheeks, slightly chapped lips parted with sleep. I let the tips of my fingers skate across his cheekbone and I imagine the feel of smooth skin beneath my touch. I pull my hand away and frown at myself.

I twist my body towards him until his head is against my chest, then, bracing one hand on his head and neck and the other against his shoulder, I scoot back and lower him down to the ground. Dragging him to bed is out of the question, so instead I stand and go to his bed and grab a pillow from it. I'm halfway back to Zhoric when I realize what I've done. I've picked up an object in my hand. I expect the shock of it to pull this ability from me, but the pillow stays in my grip. The weight of it, but not the feel.

Lifting Zhoric's head, I slide the pillow under him.

When I stand, I look out beyond the balcony and below, I notice movement. Not just a dragon flying by, or a couple walking leisurely together in the night, but a commotion. Squatting down, I look through the railings. It's a dragon, twisting and thrashing, chained and held between two other dragons while someone in their human form leads them down an unmarked path between dense foliage. Faint wisps of dark vapor trail off the chained dragon, drifting away on the breeze as they move. Behind them, someone erases the path, righting branches and mending the way with a touch of magic. Zhoric's admission of Alixor's elahi pounds through my mind, twisting with Atlanta's theory. Could Alixor see my power, or something else?

Standing, I spare a glance at Zhoric and the pillow I brought him. If I can touch that now, then maybe…I rush to the door and my hand falters over the handle. If I can hold a pillow, I can open a door. I press down and the latch clicks.

A thrill goes through me as I push the door open. I stride down the hall and when I don't see them from the nursery windows panic steals my breath. There's a desperation in me to see what's happening and I don't know if it's because of the conversation I had with Ozias today about how we change in accordance to the mortals' actions, or if this is another bond, some other link pulling me to it. I need to get closer. No sooner than I have the thought, the manifestation of myself surges through space, taking me like it did that first night Zhoric shoved me out.

I hit the ground outside running, passing through leaves and foliage like a spirit, untouchable and endless. When I finally get close, shock stops me in my tracks. Selnor and the elite Alixor was speaking to the night of our banquet are there, leading a chained dragon into the depths of a cave. It thrashes wildly, tail sweeping from side to side. The tail goes through me, but I feel reverberations of its power, of its pain and sorrow.

"Stop!" I scream, but my voice is muffled, like I'm screaming under water.

I hear Selnor's voice, distant and dim, but I can't make out his words. They finally wrangle the beast through the cavern's opening, and the dragon kicks its head back, its cloudy white eye locks on me for a long moment. This is one of the ravaged. I'm scarcely sure I've made the right connection when the creature is jerked forward down the long corridor.

I follow, everything sounding and looking waterier the farther we go. It's several long moments before the cavern widens, opening up to reveal more dragons, lined up and chained to rocks. Some are slumped against walls, others breathing raggedly on the floor, while the rest rage against their restraints.

Selnor's mouth moves as they yank the chains off the draconem in their hold and affix them to the wall. I walk the perimeter and pass five more tunnels. Down each, I get the sense of great, resting power within. A power I recognize now. *Draconem*. There must be more draconem concealed down each tunnel.

Atlanta was afraid of this. She suspected this was happening and now I know. I know for sure, and where to find them again. I put my hand against the nearest chain and it ghosts through as if it were nothing. I move closer to Selnor to see if I can make any sense of his words, but it's too muffled. Whatever power got me here isn't strong enough to manifest the details. One of the draconem that was in their dragon form shifts, and he affixes one of the subdued ravaged to the remaining dragon, and they all but drag the ravaged down one of the tunnels. I want to follow, but I'm forcibly stopped short. Something is keeping me here, in this room. Unease rakes its sharp claws down my back.

The elite with Selnor produces a bottle from a satchel. Selnor raises a hand the the ravaged opens its mouth and the elite pours the contents of the bottle down the dragon's throat. Selnor releases the ravaged and the creature's breathing slows, their body swaying, until they settles themselves down on the ground with a heavy thump.

Whatever brought me here loosens its hold, and as soon as it does, I feel the tight jerk to move back the way I came. It's so relentless that fighting it isn't a possibility. Reluctantly, I leave the cavern and mark the place by the stars overhead and the distance and orientation from the castle.

As I settle to make my way back, my body surges even faster through space until I stop outside the nursery. My hands tremble as I run my fingers through my hair. What did I just witness? I wish I could have heard what Selnor was saying, even a word or two. I'll get back to Zhoric and collect my thoughts and figure out the next course of action. Then, the murmur of voices stops me in my tracks.

I take a few steps back until the voices sound clearer and I notice where the wall is unaligned. A concealed entrance. I recognize my sister's voice before I see her through the crack of the door.

She's nursing one of her babies at her breast while Thrace, sitting across from her, holds the other in his arms. My hand goes to my mouth. The room is small and completely enclosed, not a single window looking to the outside along any of the walls.

"Tiring, my love?" Kalixta asks. "I can take her if you need."

"It's nothing I can't handle with you here," Thrace says, swaying his body gently from side to side, but I see what she means. Dark circles rest beneath his eyes, his skin a touch sallow.

"I think me being here is causing you trouble," Kalixta admonishes, her tone harsh, but her finger gently traces the curve of her baby boy's cheek.

Thrace raises a brow, a smile bringing light to his eyes. "What I *know* is that I would be causing trouble if you weren't."

Kalixta leans back. "How long can you keep this up?"

"Eternity. For you—eternity."

My heart twists. Kalixta works to keep her expression stern, but I can see as well as Thrace the pleased smile attempting to break across her lips.

He sweeps forward, his free hand sliding down the side of her face, his thumb caressing her mouth. "Don't you dare keep that from me. I earned that one."

Her mouth blooms into a grin, and he takes it with his lips. A deep longing pulls at my soul. Their exchange is like nothing I've ever seen and it at once breaks my heart and fills it.

When my niece, Anila, whines and squirms, Thrace sits back and bounces her.

Kalixta's smile falls. "Zhoric is worsening."

She says it like a statement, a gut punch that leaves me breathless.

"It's what I thought, but...tonight he didn't seem to

fair as poorly." Thrace looks over his shoulder, as if he can see through the wall to Zhoric's rooms.

Kalixta switches the boy to her other breast. She looks down at him, murmuring, "Sorry Breamus, my love, your sister took her fill." I press a hand to my chest, hearing my nephew's name for the first time.

"We can call for a nursemaid," Thrace offers, dipping his thumb into a container on the table beside him, then reaching forward to swipe a salve to her freed nipple before gliding the back of his index finger down the slope of her breast.

She sighs, giving him an appreciative smile, but shakes her head. "He'll get enough. I'll keep him here all night if I must." Once she has the baby settled, she asks, "Do you think it's because last time was so bad?"

Thrace closes the jar of salve with a free hand. "I don't know. One thing I do know is he's keeping something from me."

"It always seems he's keeping something from you," Kalixta says, shifting from side to side until she's comfortable.

Thrace smirks. "I know how he seems. This time though...it feels like the past. In the days when he wouldn't tell me what she was doing to him. He was protecting me."

My pulse jumps as I realize Thrace is talking about *her*. Zhoric's Alixor.

"I don't like the sound of that."

"It's not exactly the same though. He's keeping something from me, yes, but there's also a sort of...lightness to him."

Kalixta hums. "Will you ask him?"

"I should be able to catch him tomorrow before he fully rouses."

"You mean you'll ambush him?" Kalixta asks with a half-smile.

"He'll be delighted to see me." Thrace grins.

"I wonder...could it be a lover?"

Thrace blows air from his mouth. "I've not seen him speak with anyone. Unless, of course, there's some bond. You remember what it was like when I was able to come to you..."

Kalixta blushes at his words. "No. He can't have bonded with anyone. He wouldn't ever put someone in that sort of danger."

"You're right. Though this thing with Alixor and your sister has changed much around here. If Zhoric found a way to strengthen himself with a bond, he might just do it."

I'm on the edge of panic taking over—celestial manifestation of my form or no, I can't seem to be able to tell the difference right now. What danger does my sister speak of? Does it have something to do with what happened to Zhoric tonight? Or is there something else with the elites?

Kalixta's posture straightens and she looks around. "Your wards are strong?"

"As strong as ever. Why?"

She shakes her head. "I don't know...I'm getting a feeling. Almost like someone is near and watching."

I draw back, nostrils flaring as alarm spears me. Kalixta is my sister, she could be a potential bond. Does that mean she can see me? And if she could, what would she say? What would she do? If I'm here in this form, they'll put together that I'm the one Zhoric can bond with. I can't have them finding out and putting a stop to it.

Thrace stands and gently places the girl down in the bassinet off to the side, then he leans down. "I'll check, but first, kiss me. For energy to strengthen my wards."

She smiles and tips her chin up to capture his lips with hers. "Did it work?"

I sense a surge of power.

"I think we can do better than that." He claims her lips again and deepens the kiss, taking her head in his hands to angle her how he likes. She hums, contented.

I step back until the sight of them is blocked by the wall once more. The words exchanged between Thrace and Kalixta churn over and over in my mind like an oncoming storm. Zhoric is behaving differently. Thrace thinks the king would bond with someone who could give him strength. And whatever it is that happens to Zhoric on these nights is worsening. At least, until I was by his side. The only one who can truly answer any of this is asleep on the floor in the other room.

Back in Zhoric's chambers, I stand over his form, so still in sleep that if I didn't know in my soul that he was alive, I'd think him dead.

"What are you doing to me?" I whisper, my eyes tracing the angles and planes of his face, his shoulders and back, landing on the gnarled scars across his heart.

Dawn is still a long way off and an exhaustion like I haven't felt before in this form sweeps me. I pad away from him and land on his bed, letting the soft pillows envelop me and swallow me whole.

# Chapter Twenty-One

A pair of deep green eyes bore into mine as I open them. Zhoric tenses, his form frozen with his head propped on his fist as he lies in bed beside me, his face awash in the early morning rays of dawn. *Dawn?* That can't be right.

"You're awake," he says, voice low and gravelly, a hint of surprise buried in his words. I flit my gaze down, noting the smooth plane of his chest and torso, the black god scale glittering in the light. I shoot upright. He rises slowly, as if a sudden movement from him might startle me further.

I chance a look out the windows, the morning's early light is no mistake, no trick of my eye. If I'm here in this form, then I'm still a dragon back in the Realm. Though I don't need to wipe sleep from my face in this form, I press my fingers deep into my eye sockets all the same.

"Why haven't you shifted and left?" he asks.

I drop my hands heavily into my lap and tilt my head, annoyed instantly at his question.

A smile threatens the lines of his mouth. "Not much of a morning person?"

"For someone who hates having questions asked of him, you're certainly the curious one in the morning."

He ignores that. "You must be more powerful than I thought to have overcome this aspect of the curse so quickly."

Immediately the conversation I heard between Kalixta and Thrace comes rushing back to me. They feared that Zhoric might bond with someone strong if he thought it would help him keep the upper hand against the elites. Even though it's precisely what I offered him, it didn't seem to truly interest him. Until now. "Does that help in your consideration of my offer?" I hedge.

Zhoric lowers head, like he's about to let me in on a secret. "Of course it does."

I clench my teeth and slowly swivel my head away from him so he doesn't see the panic etched on my face.

"Regretting your little proposal now?" he asks.

"Not if it means I get to be with my sister again."

His brows twitch together. "You do know you're risking your life by entering such a bargain. What if I don't uphold my end of the deal? What if I bond with you, use your power, lock you up, and let you waste away?"

The gallop in my chest begins again and I swallow past it. "You won't."

"How do you know?"

I said what I did to throw him off, but deep down, there's a quiet truth inside that slips out as a whisper. "I know my heart. In this world or any other, it wouldn't reach out to someone like that."

Zhoric swallows hard. "I once thought that, too."

As soon as the words leave his lips, I know what I've said to wound him and I regret it immediately. "Zhoric, I didn't mean—"

He lifts a hand to cut me off and I let him, before any more damning words can leave my mouth, before any more emotions can churn around him and this bond between us. "For all I did after her, I've shown the kind of person I truly am."

I open my mouth to say more, but then I'm lurching backwards, as if pulled on an invisible thread knotted around my middle, and I'm gasping and sputtering water from my mouth, blinking my eyes open.

Sunlight blinds me and I squint and turn away, rolling on the ground, grit sticking to my skin. I lift my head and find Ozias, Atlanta, and Ninon all hovering over me, an empty pail dripping water held loosely in Ninon's hands.

"What was that for?" I demand.

Ozias kneels in front of me and grasps my arms to help me up. "You weren't shifting *or* waking up."

"You weren't responding at all," Atlanta elaborates. "What happened?"

I exchange a quick glance with Ozias. He shakes his head almost imperceptibly. What I learned last night comes barreling back to me. Ozias wants me to keep mind walking to Zhoric from Atlanta, but I don't know if that's an option anymore.

I sigh, push myself up, and run my hands up my face and into my hair. "I need a minute."

Stalking past them, I leave the enclosure and head for my room in the Alcazar. I hear steps behind me, soft and distant, the speed matching mine. When we reach my door, I spin around to face Ninon.

"Was the water your idea?"

She stops, standing as still as a tree. "Less so an idea than an impulse. When they couldn't wake you, I panicked."

I purse my lips and she walks past me into my room without further acknowledgement or explanation.

"You haven't done much in here," Ninon murmurs,

meandering around my space. We haven't had time to visit each other's rooms. Something we used to do daily, usually multiple times, at home in Nevoba.

"You've decorated yours?"

Ninon runs her fingers along the edge of my bedside table, clear of anything save a candle in its holder. "With a few things."

I look around, seeing what she does. A room set up exactly the same as the day Atlanta brought me to it. Ninon on the other hand sounds like she's started to make this her home. I walk over to the dressing table and sit, considering my reflection in the looking glass.

Weariness shadows my eyes, but that familiar spark of outrage is etched everywhere that the shadows don't touch. Every choice, from the moment I ran that pin through Alixor's chest, to agreeing to work with Ozias, to attempting to con the dragon king into bonding with me, makes me feel like I've been stuffed into a cave, like a tiny lizard avoiding the scorching sun. I run my fingers through my hair, long, straight, and unbound, black as the ocean at night. I grip a lock of it firmly by my collarbone and rummage through the vanity before finding what I seek.

Without another thought, I grab a set of shears and poise it over my throat. From Ninon's position, it looks as if I'm ready to slice into my skin.

"Kaisa?" she says my name tentatively, standing utterly still as she takes me in.

Keeping my eyes on her, I slice off a chunk of hair above my shoulder. The freshly cut hair falls to the ground in a tangled heap at my feet. I grab another section, and cut again, repeating the process until my hair is a jagged, uneven mess. All the while Ninon watches. My reflection is feral and feverish. I lower the shears, tears welling in my eyes.

She huffs out a breath and comes to my side. "Let me help you clean it up."

Ninon does her best to even out the ends. Every so often, she gently runs her fingers down the lengths, soothing my mind with every stroke of her hand.

When she's done, I shake my head, feeling lighter and, somehow, much more in control.

"Needed a change?" she finally asks.

Frowning I catch her eyes with mine in the looking glass. "I needed to make a decision that doesn't have my life or the life of those I love hanging in the balance."

Ninon sets down the shears and feathers off the cut hair from my clothes. "Your burden is a heavy one."

She knows as well as I do that when I've committed to something, I will see it through to the end. So, she doesn't make excuses for me. She doesn't tell me to bow out. She doesn't say anything at all, instead she lets me sit with this feeling, allowing it to consume me, with her there as my support. I lean back against her torso and her arms drape over my shoulders, crossed over my chest.

"Do you think I'll succeed?" I ask, looking up at her from under the fan of my dark lashes in the mirror's reflection.

"I know you can do anything. You always have, and you always will."

"This isn't like anything I've faced before." I twist in my seat and she loosens her hold on me. "We hardly know the interworking of this world."

"You feel it though, don't you?"

I don't have to ask her to clarify—I know what she means. I feel the rightness of this world in my very essence. I nod until my head falls and I'm staring down into my lap, the tiny black hairs from the cut sprinkled across the back of my hands. "I've been seeing Zhoric—the Sar Dyēus—at night," I admit to her. Telling Ozias has been helpful, but it hasn't felt like a weight has truly lifted from my shoulders.

"Mind walking." She says it like a statement and I feel her gaze hot on the back of my neck.

I nod.

"Are you planning to tell anyone else?" she asks.

"Ozias knows. But otherwise, no." I life my head, meeting her gaze again. "I offered Zhoric to bond with me. I was afraid of trying to force the bond on him and it not working."

She's silent at first, analyzing the risk I've put myself in. "And what did he say? To your offer?"

"He's still considering. But I think if he does…it's because he plans to use me."

Ninon is quiet. Not because she has nothing to say, but because she is thinking so deeply for the words to express what she wants, in exactly the right way. "Does that bother you?"

I tip my head until it rests against her. I close my eyes. "I'm afraid, Ninon. I'm so afraid that all of this will go wrong and that he will have me in his grasp to use my power how he wishes and make everything worse. I'm frightened that he'll…" I swallow down the emotion clawing its way up my throat "…that he'll take being draconem away again and I'll be imprisoned in the sky kingdom forever."

Ninon bends at the waist and wraps her arms tight around me, tucking her face next to mine. "You have the strength of the Realm behind you. You have the power of our people lying in wait for you to call upon. Don't let go of that, even if it comes to this. Even if he seals your draconem, she's still inside you and a part of you. He cannot take from you what you already know."

I squeeze her arms and hold on until the tension drops from my shoulders and the panic that wound its way around my nerves loosens thread by thread.

"How are *you* feeling?" I ask her.

Ninon stands and lets her hands slide to my shoulders where she gives me a pat. "Good. I'm going to rest today so we can try flying tonight."

My face breaks into an earsplitting grin. This is exactly what I needed to hear. This is what I need to do—to let go of my task for a moment and be with her. To feel what it is to be this beast I once slayed on sight, but now know, beyond any reasonable doubt, is mine. "Then I'd better find Ozias to practice shifting so I can stretch my wings."

Ninon gives my shoulders one final squeeze. "That's the woman I know."

After I've cleaned up and pulled myself together, Ninon walks me through the halls and up the many stairs that lead to the grand circular chamber at the top of the Alcazar to find Ozias. As we climb, the loose pants I wear swish pleasantly across my legs. The deep V-shape at the waist leaves my midriff bare all the way to the simple bandeau top that covers my breasts. With my freeing haircut, I feel ready to take on the world.

"The short hair really does suit you," Ninon remarks as we reach the final landing.

I shake my head, the ends of my hair brushing along my shoulders as I give her a full smile. "Does it make me look more approachable?"

A low rumbling reaches my ears, and, with the smile still plastered on my face, Ozias stands waiting, his amber eyes like liquid fire.

"*Dangerous*," he says. "That's how it makes you look."

My skin pebbles at the deep timbre of his voice, at the way he drinks me in.

Ninon touches the back of her hand against mine, shooting me a gentle, knowing smile before she turns and disappears back the way we came. I know she's going to rest so we can fly together tonight, but without her presence, my confidence turns to resilience under Ozias's solitary gaze.

He steps closer, fingers reaching up to dance around the ends of my hair, his fingertips brushing the top of my shoulder, sending chills down my spine. "I like it. I have half a mind not to let anyone else see you like this until I've had my fill."

My breath comes in shallow bursts, dizzying me. The

sheer possessiveness in those words is at once alarming and arousing. "That sounds impractical," I manage.

"It is, considering Atlanta is waiting in my suite for us," he says, dropping his hand, eyes shuttering ever so slightly.

I flick my hair back and move past him. "Then we best not keep her waiting," I say as I glance at him over my shoulder. His gaze darkens and he stalks after me all the way into his private suite.

Atlanta straightens from her seat at the central table, her mouth opening. "Kaisa, your hair. You look…you look incredible." Her gaze flits over to Ozias for a second before landing back on me.

I incline my head. "With so much changing, I felt the need to change with it." Meeting her at the table, I lean my hands against it, scanning the cluttered workspace before giving her my attention. "I suppose we ought to talk about what happened this morning."

She tucks her mass of curls behind her shoulders and clears her throat. "You were able to stay a dragon after sunrise. That's an astonishing level of progress in such a short time." She sounds hopeful, yet tentative. The same feeling buds in me as she casts her gaze to Ozias, almost as if waiting for him to divulge something. Telling Ninon about mind walking to Zhoric suddenly has me wanting to tell everyone—to hold me accountable, to hold me here.

Ozias leans back against the table between us, his wide hand landing overtop mine. I startle and when I glance at him, I'm rewarded with a winsome smile, casual and confident. "I think it means you're getting closer to tapping into your elahi."

My brows inch together. Is Ozias still trying to get me to keep my secret from Atlanta?

Her eyes flit between the two of us, then busies her hands with the parchments, separating them into tidy piles. "That's one possibility."

Ozias lifts my hand and turns it in his, his thumb gliding

up and down my wrist. "With a sure way to find out."

"More training?" My efforts with Ozias and Atlanta haven't yet produced results I'm content with.

Ozias's smile is rampant.

"I see my torment pleases you."

He shrugs, raising my hand to ghost his lips across the back of it. "More so I like seeing how far I can push you."

Atlanta pushes away from the table. "I'll finish preparing the missives for the farmhands and fisherman to plant out in the Sere."

"I'll take them tomorrow," Ozias says without looking away from me.

Atlanta pauses on her way out. "Why the rush?"

He lowers my hand down to my side and slides his hands into his pockets. "The sooner the Nevobans know to expect something, the better. I have a feeling it won't be too long before Kaisa finally reveals this hidden elahi of hers."

"You truly think we're that close?" Her eyes dart to me, assessing.

"We're coming to the end. I know it."

Atlanta opens her mouth, then bites her lower lip, keeping whatever it is she was about to say inside. She nods, then leaves the room, Ozias and I watching her until she's well out of sight, until the sound of her steps are long gone.

I can't stop looking at the doorway, wondering what she was going to say.

"Come with me tomorrow," Ozias says, drawing my attention.

"What?" I ask, my mind running to catch up to his meaning.

"To disseminate the missives. Come with me."

My mouth opens in understanding. "Out there? Beyond the Realm?" The last time I was over the Realm's border springs to mind; being forced to the ground, Dyēus's forces closing in on us.

"Do you trust me?" he asks.

Tilting my head, I give him a long, lingering perusal. The sharp ends of my hair graze my shoulders, reminding me of change. Reminding me I have a choice. Reminding me that I have power.

"Yes," I say. Even though I'm afraid. Even though things can go horribly, tragically wrong. It doesn't mean I shouldn't try.

# Chapter Twenty-Two

Ninon and I stand together as night comes. Where my muscles and mind are sore from my training with Ozias earlier today, the pain fades into the recess of my consciousness as we slip into our scales and spread our wings wide. Out by the fields where we first met in the Realm, we're surrounded by dozens of other draconem who shift with the change in the sky. Several vault straight up the second their body's shift. Others linger, their bodies swaying with their elegant gaits alongside others—either friends, family, or bonded pairs. I've never asked how many bonded pairs there are here. I know having them is key once I take Zhoric's power over Dyēus, but I haven't asked how prepared we are for this supposed divine duty we must take on. Ozias say some will refuse to take up the call, and I can understand why. Though I think I'd like to know what it is to fulfill my purpose.

I think back to when Kalixta was having her babies, how the nursemaid told her this is what her body was made for. I remember thinking that giving birth wasn't all of it. And as I beat my wings and push off the ground with Ninon at my side, I know. I know I was right.

The wind rushes past me, threading into my mane and twisting the long whiskers on my snout. Ninon and I fall into a rhythm, banking and diving into the airwaves, keeping our wings out to let us soar, tucking them in and using our clawed feet to push off the air, only to snap our wings out again to beat against the wind, giving us greater lift.

We do not need to learn this.

It's intuitive. No, *intrinsic*. These motions are in our very essence and for once, for once, something in this process, is easy, effortless. It makes sense.

Ninon and I catch each other's eyes. I feel approval rolling off of her and into me.

All too soon, we've made our way around the circumference of the Realm's borders. I haven't noticed it in my human form, but now I see the net of Ozias's power, a thin barrier like a layer of oil over water in all the colors of a rainbow, blending and swirling against one another.

We make another circle and then another. It quickly becomes monotonous. It reminds me of when the farmhands bring fish to Nevoba. As a little girl, I'd watch the fish swim around and around. I felt sad for them, then, knowing they had nowhere to go—their space too small, too cramped. They came from that great wide ocean I'd heard of—then later saw with my own eyes—only to end up in a barrel.

The first time I saw the ocean, I realized just how great their loss was.

Ozias has lived a life like that. Knowing what once was, only to come to this.

Ninon heads back towards the open fields and I follow her lead. She inclines her head towards one of the dragons hovering in the sky, and in my mind, I hear one singular word from Ninon, *Issa*.

Yellow scales catch the light of the twin moons and a mane of light blue hair clouds around her head. Her antlers sweep back towards her spine, ridged with a sharp, lethal fan of spikes. Two long whiskers dance lazily on the breeze, framing her wide mouth—an echo of her savage smiles I've seen before.

Hovering in the sky with her, we watch as the draconem organize some sort of dodging game that reminds me of a lot of one we played as children. We'd run towards someone as fast as we could, and whoever got out of dodge first, lost. I suffered many injuries by being last to back away. This is similar in that only one dragon stays stationary in the air, while another hurtles towards it. The difference, of course, is where the draconem can choose to dodge. I watch them go left, right, down, and up.

*Point system based on how you dodge*, I hear a voice in my head explain. *Left or right is one, up is two, and down is three. Your points zero out if you move sooner than your last dodge.* Issa.

Issa doesn't seem to hear my inner thoughts and so I try my hand at communicating with her directly, as I've done with Ninon, Ozias, and Atlanta. I focus on the idea of speaking aloud, then aim the words I speak in my mind in her direction. *Do you play?* I ask.

She shows me her teeth. *Reigning champion for five moon cycles straight*, she answers.

*A challenge, if I've ever heard one*, I counter.

*Are you joining in?* Issa asks Ninon.

I snort in the same moment Ninon says, *Certainly not.*

*Then you get the pleasure of watching me win*, Issa says to her, a gleam in her eyes.

I cast a glance over my shoulder to Ninon as I follow Issa down onto the field. Draconem are limited in how much expression they can show, but if I'm not mistaken, Ninon looks concerned for my well-being or rather, I *feel* her concern. I shake my head to dissipate the low buzz of nerves. Ozias doesn't intimidate me. Atlanta doesn't intimidate me, though she does confuse me. Zhoric is complicated, but I can hold my own against him. Issa though…Issa scares the life out of me.

As we face off, I know the moment I'm in over my head—her speed is incredible, I hardly have time to brace myself when she slams into me full force.

Again and again it happens. By the fourth go, I've managed to dodge out of the way to the left. On the fifth I go to the right. On the sixth, I feel bold enough to try dodging down, which ends up being a mistake, her scaled foot knocking into my cheek and sending me careening down onto the ground.

Ninon lands by my side. *Please tell me you've had enough.*

I'm rolling up on my haunches, ready to have another go when Issa lands on my other side. *I'm done tormenting her. For tonight at least.*

My tongue, long and serpentine, reaches out to lick my wounded cheek as I grumble. I know when not to argue. *That's less of a game and more battle training,* I tell Issa.

*Ah, she finally gets it,* Issa teases.

I let out an indignant humph.

*The skies are crowded now and it's getting late. You two should turn in,* she says, her eyes tracking over to Ninon.

Panic grips me. I want to protest, stay awake a little longer, stay away from *him* a little longer, but I see what Issa sees. Ninon is spent, and after my training today and what Issa put me through tonight, I'm not faring much better.

*Issa came at me like she had something to prove,* I say once we make it back to the enclosure and get settled down for the night. We no longer need chaining, so coming here was more force of habit than anything else.

Ninon hums, the sound coming out like a soft growl. *Perhaps she does.*

*What do you mean?*

Ninon waits a beat, then says, *I think she likes me.*

*I think you're right,* I respond. *So beating me up is proving something to you, is it?*

Ninon huffs. *Maybe more to herself. You're my closest friend. I think it's safe to assume you and I could bond.*

Ozias with his ability to see bonds hasn't mentioned that it's possible with Ninon. Then again, I never asked. Now that I think of it, everything I've read of Atlanta's work and the few other texts I've read about the bond would lead to this conclusion. The thought makes me incredibly happy. I've been so entrenched with the concept of bonding with Zhoric and wrapped up with Ozias and the potential between us, that the possibility of others hasn't crossed my mind. The idea that I could pair with Ninon makes sense and with it comes an immense sense of calm.

*Not that we will,* Ninon says.

My hope drains like a water skein gone dry. I lift my head. *Why not?*

*From what I've been told, enacting a bond makes everything you feel stronger. And I love you and we work well together but...I want to have every aspect of every feeling heightened with my bonded. I think Issa and I share more common feelings for one another.*

It doesn't take me long to figure it out. She's talking of something more than platonic affection like we have for one another. She's talking of romantic love. I lay my head down and try to dampen my disappointment. *I see.*

*I'm sorry,* she says.

*You've nothing to apologize for,* I say earnestly despite my own disappointment. *I understand.*

*Do you?*

I think of my sister and Thrace. I think of a bond with someone that's all-encompassing: mind, body, and soul. The idea sends a tingle down my spine—is that out there for me? I don't know, but I'm glad my sister has it. I'm over the moons that Ninon, who deserves the world, wants that for herself, too. *I do*, I say. *And you deserve it.*

The gentle scuffles of Ninon lying down soothe my ears and calm my mind. I hear her quiet, *Thank you,* as my eyes drift shut. I listen to the whisper of the wind, the buffeting air from the wings of creatures all around me. Black blends with white, colors swirl, and I fall into my mind, all the way into Zhoric's chambers.

He's pacing the floor in front of his suite's doors when I fully manifest by the opening to the balcony, where I assumed he'd be, which is perhaps why my mind placed me here. I watch him go back and forth across the floor, eyes darting to the door every so often.

"Expecting someone?" I finally ask.

He stops dead in his tracks and raises his gaze to me, eyes roving all over my face, catching on the ends of my hair, on my cheek where Issa hit me.

His stillness deepens, turning him to stone, his voice lowers to a deadly octave. "Who struck you?"

My fingers ghost over my cheeks. "It was a game. I lost, if you couldn't gather."

Zhoric's answer is a soft rolling growl. He goes to his desk, lifts his quill, and begins penning something onto parchment.

I move to his dressing table to look for the beginning of a bruise, but when I try to catch my reflection, I see nothing.

"You're not really here," he reminds me without looking up from his papers. "You're but a mere projection of yourself, here through the power of our minds and the bond."

I rise from where I'd leaned over to study myself in the mirror, and slowly look from him to the door, realization dawning. "You were waiting for me."

Zhoric's fingers twitch against the stem of the quill. "No." His reply is curt and, very clearly, a lie.

"Ah." I try not to smile. "I see why you're usually so tight lipped."

He sets down his pen, folds his hands over each other, and focuses on me. "And why is that?"

"You're a terrible liar when you speak," I say with a pleased smile.

He twists his face away towards the window, but his eyes slide back over to me. "You changed your hair."

"You noticed," I say, touching the ends, which feel like nothing but a suggestion in this form.

"I notice a great number of things about you."

My breath catches in my throat and I get the phantom sensation of my body flushing. Such alluring words for such a vile creature. I recall when he first spoke to me here, of the spider web he destroyed when explaining mind walking. He reminds me of a spider now, spinning a beautiful, glittering web to pull me in and trap me.

"You left rather suddenly this morning," he says, the comment casual, meant to be unassuming as he rises to fix himself a cup of tea, abandoning whatever he was writing. It seems almost as if he doesn't know what to do with himself.

All his indecision is putting me on edge, so I stride further into the room and sit on the end of his bed and lean back on my hands. "Rather bold for you to bring that up when you were the one watching me sleep." He says nothing in response. I think back on the nights I came here and he wasn't present. Eventually, I would settle down somewhere in his room, usually on his bed, until my mind drifted away into some vague concept of sleep. I hadn't really thought of what happens to my manifestation during those times. I'm wondering now if, at some point, he'd returned to his rooms to find me asleep. "Do you do that often?" I ask, my muscles tensing as I await his answer.

"Does it frighten you if I admit that I do?" he responds.

If my stare were acid it would bore holes into his back. "No."

Zhoric turns and raises a brow. "You shouldn't cast judgment over the quality of my lies when yours are equally lacking."

The only response I have for that is an amused grin, which he turns from swiftly before I can catch his reaction.

"You *were* waiting for me," I goad. "Who else would it be? No one ever comes here."

"You've been here a matter of weeks. That tells you nothing."

"Tell me who was coming, then."

"Perhaps it was a mistress," he says.

At his words, it's as if the very soul inside me goes still. "Perhaps?"

There's a knock at the door. Zhoric straightens, and my shoulders tense up towards my ears.

"You were waiting for someone," I whisper. The sensation of a lip prying up in a snarl dances through me.

As Zhoric moves towards the door, I hear it escape on a breath, almost as if he didn't mean for the word to pass his lips. "No."

Two thoughts cross my mind at once. He *was* waiting for me, and: I hope he wasn't being serious when he mentioned a mistress. I stand and cross the room as he sweeps open one side of the door.

"Thrace," Zhoric says. I lean against the second door Zhoric didn't open. "Trouble to report?"

"Zhoric, you haven't let me in in weeks," Thrace says. "What's going on?"

"You're with your bonded and children. You should be glad I haven't called on you."

My nerves prickle, dancing on edge—Zhoric knows about Kalixta and Thrace. I step closer to try to catch a glimpse of Thrace, to see if there's any panic in him at the mention of my sister and his children from the great ruler's lips. Zhoric doesn't move aside to give me space to see. And so, I settle my face as near to him as I dare. I catch the subtle flare of his nostrils.

"I can handle both, Zhoric. My family and you."

"I never said you couldn't." Zhoric remains unmovable.

"Let me in." Thrace demands, sounding more like a petulant brother than the draconem in charge of the Sar Dyēus's safety.

"No."

"You have to tell me what's going on. How can I protect you when you don't give me the information I need to do it?"

"Thrace," Zhoric begins and even I can hear the warning in his tone.

"No. Zhoric, no. We've been down that road before and look where we ended up. Look at you."

Zhoric remains silent, the set of his brow deepening. "It's not like the last time," he says and my hope leaps to catch the words, even as I realize it means he doesn't see me as a threat. Good. He shouldn't. If he did, then my plans would be as dead as me if he ever found out what I was trying to do.

"Is it what I think it is, then?" Thrace asks, voice dropping to a whisper.

"Forget it, Thrace. It's of no concern to you."

"It is, Zhoric. *You* are my concern. You always will be."

"You have a family now," Zhoric says, placing his hand on the door I'm pressed against, his forearm a hair's breadth away from skimming my throat and clavicle. "Make them your concern."

"Keeping you safe is keeping them safe. You know that."

Zhoric's fingers dig into the wood. "Speaking of keeping them safe, any trouble with the elites after what her sister did?" I have to stop myself from pressing in closer.

"You'd have known long before now if there was."

"Good. So, Kalixta and the babies are safe."

"You know they are," Thrace answers, but the tone is threaded with mild suspicion.

Zhoric's eyes narrow at the subtle cunning gleam in

Thrace's expression as he moves in a little closer, but Zhoric holds his ground. "Speaking of Kaisa…" Thrace pauses, as if waiting for a reaction. "Has Ozias come pestering you since he took her?"

I wasn't sure what Zhoric thought of my escaping to the Realm, but it seems that he and Thrace have discussed it before.

"Blissful silence from him." Zhoric lifts his free hand to look at his nails.

"It turned out to be rather lucky he was there here still. What a mess that would have been for you if I'd had to intervene instead."

Was that why Thrace came that night? To stop Alixor? I wait for Zhoric to admonish him for it, but he doesn't. My insides swirl with unease. When Zhoric says nothing, Thrace goes on. "I wonder what would have happened if you'd let me go—"

Zhoric interrupts him before he can finish his sentence. "Thrace." His tone is deep and cutting. Thrace's mouth twitches against the threat of a smile. I chew on my cheek, wishing I could have heard what Thrace was about to say. "The elites have been keeping the hoard along the border busy. Any news there?"

"I heard they almost got their hands on two rogues recently. Some reports say one of them of was Ozias himself."

Zhoric's shoulders relax, his hand on the door slipping a fraction, putting his forearm closer to my chest. "They do love to spin a tale."

"The other was gray. Accounts say the draconem's mane was the same shade of green as your eyes."

I scowl. That particular detail bothers me, like even my dragon form wants to find any sort of connection to Zhoric.

"How fanciful of them," Zhoric answers, unbothered. "Perhaps if they spent less time crafting pretty reports, they'd make more headway on the front."

"As if that's what you want," Thrace counters, his

words laced with sarcasm.

My mind is spinning. Isn't that what Zhoric wants?

Zhoric changes the topic again. "Aside from begging an invitation into my suite, have you any other reason for being away from your bonded and children?"

"Are you annoyed?" Thrace asks with a wry grin.

"Thoroughly," Zhoric answers.

"Then I've done all I can." Thrace turns on his heel and walks down the long hall, throwing up a hand after a few steps. "Let me know when you're ready to divulge that secret you're keeping."

Zhoric's mouth draws into a thin line as he shuts the door. "Insufferable brute," he says, dropping his forehead with a thud against the wood. The words, though harsh, are said with reticent affection.

"What was that?" I ask, crossing my arms.

Zhoric twists his neck in my direction, not bothering to lift his head from the door as he pins me with his eyes, staring so long I wonder if he even heard me. Long enough to make me not want to ask the question again for fear of hearing his answer.

"Follow me," he says, lifting his head and opening the door. I blink after him as he strides down the silent corridor.

I hurry my steps to catch up to him as we make our way out of his private suite and into the castle's main halls. I was never around the castle this late at night. Alixor kept our meetings lively, choosing activities over romantic strolls at twilight, though he occasionally mixed in a few. After dark, myself and all the women who were not yet ready to reproduce were locked into our rooms. It had felt respectful. Though not safe. I knew what the dragons were capable of and a solid wood door and an iron lock meant nothing.

The castle, glittering white and splendid in the daylight, feels hollow and devoid of life at this hour, save for the sentinels lining the halls. Those we pass bow low in his presence, eyes to the ground—but as we move down a new corridor,

I notice the sentinels here turn their heads to keep an eye on him. I frown, unsure what to make of that.

Zhoric pauses outside a set of large doors, inset with gold ornamentation among the carved patterns.The sentinels standing guard outside hesitate before opening them to allow us—or rather, Zhoric—into the suite. The smell hits me first. Strong, exotic florals that I remember well, and immediately I know who's room we're in. The setup is nearly identical to Zhoric's, but dressed lavishly in garnet colored drapes and gold accents. Every surface is adorned with glass trinkets and an assortment of glittering treasures, as if he were hoarding the beauties of the world.

As we make our way deeper into the suite, the space opens up to the bathing chamber, the air thick with steam and that thick floral scent. The rear wall is entirely made up of looking glass so that everything in the room is reflected back at us. Zhoric stands alone, not a whisper of me at his side. In a bath partially sunken into the floor and twice the size of Zhoric's, Selnor is spread out with water up to his chest, his muscular arms resting wide along the lip of the tub, his gold blonde hair slicked back from his forehead. On either side of him in the bath are two women, and outside sitting on either side of his head are two more, all naked, faces devoid of expression except for a gentle tilt of their lips. One woman holds a decanter of wine and the other has an assortment of fruits and cheeses on a tray in front of her. All four of the women are eerily still, but most unnerving of all are their ears. Smooth and round on the tops, instead of gently pointed like ours. A shudder wracks my body, realization punching me hard in the gut. Are these...humans?

"I was beginning to think you'd never show your face." Selnor's voice seeps out, dull and listless on the thick steam.

"Selnor. It's been a while," Zhoric drawls. Nerves tickle along my spine. This is the way I remember the Sar Dyēus sounding and I realize that when he speaks to me in private, when I'm in his rooms, he doesn't sound this way.

"Yes, seeing as how you've made yourself scarce since my son was murdered by that harridan."

A muscle tenses in Zhoric's jaw. "I was under the impression as king it was *your* duty to be at my beck and call, not the other way around."

A slippery smile glides onto Selnor's face. "You and I have never had that kind of relationship." The women at his side giggle and draw nearer to him, their hands moving across his shoulders.

Zhoric's gaze narrows. "I've told you before that humans are not your playthings to manipulate."

"I needed your attention. I've had these nearly a week and you've only just come. What has you so occupied these days?"

Zhoric doesn't deign to answer him. "Return them to their homes."

"Their homes? You mean the haunted towns I've plucked them from? They're much happier here."

The women sigh and nod. One of them looks to us, her eyes seeming to find mine. They're vacant, as lost as a hare shot clean through. My breath hitches and my hand clutches Zhoric's wrist. His other hand comes across his body to clasp mine.

"I requested you contact that heathen Ozias. Have you done so?" Selnor asks, holding out a hand to one of the women outside the tub. She dutifully places a glass of wine into his grasp.

"You know I haven't."

Selnor takes a slow, careful sip, then hands the glass back to the woman. "I want her."

I furrow my brow and look down, a lump forming in my throat. Zhoric's fingers haven't tightened around my hand—and though it must be my imagination, I feel it.

"You can't have her." Zhoric's words ring through the chamber and the silence in the aftermath of is deafening. My pulse pounds under my skin. "She's the rogue's problem now."

Quick as an asp, Selnor slams his fist down, cracking the stone surrounding the bath. "I want her *head*!" I jump, but the women around Selnor remain still, doing as they were without any disturbance. Zhoric doesn't react at all.

"You want her power. Let's not pretend we both don't know of her potential."

"That you *hid*," Selnor spits.

Zhoric only stares. "Clearly, I did so for a reason."

Selnor takes the wine glass, swirls the contents around, but instead of sipping on it, he sets it down on the edge of the tub. "Ozias's presence here the night of Alixor's breeding ceremony was rather convenient. One might think it was a highly orchestrated ordeal." Selnor spins the glass, the scrape of it against stone grating against my ears.

"If it were, it would have been the greatest mistake I've made thus far. Perhaps save for putting my trust in you."

My mind whirls and I'm unsure where it will land after this. What is Zhoric doing? Why is he letting me hear this?

Selnor tuts, a look of weary disappointment pulling at his mouth. "Your melodrama is an ever-tedious endeavor. I thought we were past all that."

"And yet you're the one sneaking around taking things he shouldn't, like a child begging for attention." Zhoric leans forward a fraction. "I give you silence and you operate within the guidelines I've set."

"And that has worked until it got my son murdered."

"You chose to forget the power women have. I may have buried it within them, but there are still those who will dig it from the very cavity of their chests when pinned in a corner. She is dangerous and yet he chose her. *That* is what got your son murdered. Kaisa was never supposed to be an option. For anyone." I can't help flinching at the harshness of his words. It reminds me of my mother's biting comments, condemning me to a life alone after bearing offspring for Alixor. I move to pull my hand away, but Zhoric only holds on tighter.

"You should have just killed her then," Selnor hisses.

"If I killed everyone who was an inconvenience to me, you wouldn't be breathing."

"Luckily for me, you can't." Selnor gives a satisfied smirk and lets the woman with the tray of food feed him a bright red berry.

I angle my head to look at Zhoric, wondering at what Selnor means, but he pays me no heed.

"I'm all too aware." Zhoric lets go of my hand then, tucking his arms behind his back. "Never the less, your request has been denied. I'm taking no steps to retrieve Kaisa from the Realm, nor do I ever intend to."

"You're giving them a powerful weapon against us, Zhoric."

"The better to keep you occupied. It seems it worked well the other day. Almost had her then, did you?"

"Until *someone* stopped my forces in their tracks. Our agreement includes no interference on your part."

Is Selnor suggesting that Zhoric stopped Dyēus's forces that day Ozias and I went over the wall? I'd heard a voice in my head, one I assumed was Ozias. My eyes widen. Could it have been Zhoric?

Zhoric touches the center of his chest, where the god scale resides. "Well, we can't know for certain what happened out there. She is powerful."

Selnors scowl deepens. "What we *do* know for certain is we need more rogues. We can't keep using our own to make into collectors. Having her there will only hinder our efforts and our numbers will suffer because of it. The women will mourn the loss of their sons in their lifetimes when they were meant to live forever. What will we do to placate the women when that happens?"

Zhoric's chest hitches, like Selnor's words struck him deep, but he covers it well enough with a pointed sniff. "Let the draconem bond and relieve some of the plight, then."

"And you speak of me acting like a child," Selnor guffaws. "Where are these old refrains coming from? With another elite dead you feel bold enough to test me?"

Zhoric considers Selnor for a long, pefuntory moment, his eyes cold. Then, he turns on his heel. "Take those humans back where they belong. Forget about Kaisa. Mourn your son. There's nothing else left to do."

Selnor's glower could light a dry bush as he watches Zhoric walk away. I stay in the room as long as I can stand before the line connecting me to Zhoric pulls hard and I'm forced to walk away, too.

# Chapter Twenty-Three

My jaw aches from how tightly my teeth are clenched as I stalk after Zhoric down the cavernous halls of the castle. The sentinels have all risen by the time I walk by them, and Zhoric doesn't need to look over his shoulder to be sure I'm with him. He waits by his open door until I'm through, then closes it behind me.

Striding past him, I walk across the wide room until I'm outside on the balcony. I know my body isn't here, but it feels like it. I can't catch my breath, my heart thrums in my chest, reverberating like a drumbeat across the ground. My emotions rest on the surface, riding a rising wave that will crash in on itself and cause destruction to anything in its wake.

Zhoric sets his elbows onto the railing beside me. I can't feel the coolness of the stone under my arms, but I feel like I can sense the heat of his body radiating off of him. I track the clouds drifting across the sky, luminous as they cross the moons. We stay like that for a time in silence, taking in the night.

"What are you thinking?" he asks, gently breaking the quiet with the soft timbre of his voice.

I shake my head as slowly and softly as his question before turning to him. "What are you doing? Mocking me? Confusing me?"

"I'm trying to get you to stay away, Kaisa." The air stills around me as he locks me in his gaze—one filled with desperation. "I want you to keep coming."

My fingers tighten on the railing so hard my knuckles turn white. "What does that mean?" I've never much enjoyed puzzles or riddles in the way Ninon does, but something about the mystery of him feels like it's beginning to consume my every thought. I remember the bond and I grow frustrated—these can't be my own feelings, and yet, from everything I know of the connection, it's only supposed to heighten that which I already feel. It's impossible.

"The other night you stayed with me while I..." He trails off, unwilling or unable to say what it is he does on the balcony every few nights.

"While you what?" I prompt.

"While I was *tending*," he says, enunciating the word, "to what I need to do. No one has ever seen me like that before. Not even Thrace. I've always been alone. With you there, though, feeling my pain, seeing what I do on those nights, it made me feel..." His words leave him again, and I see the struggle to get them out with every swallow he takes to drum up the courage or conviction to say more.

"Feel what?" I know I should brush him off and tell him it was nothing, that I would have done it for anyone. That must be true. If I can stay at someone's side in their pain, knowing they're a monster, it must be true that I would do it for anyone. But I wouldn't. Not for Selnor.

Not for Alixor. And a horrible, spiteful part of me thinks I might not even do it for my own mother for all that she's put me through—all that she neglected.

Zhoric's jaw works as he looks down and away from me. "Like I wasn't so alone."

I don't know what to say. Zhoric isn't the man I supposed he was, and I don't know what to make of it. I don't believe the moment with Thrace or Selnor was an act. I think he was showing me more of himself. Is it so he can lead me like I'm meant to lead him? Or, is it because he's developing feelings for me? I need to get the upper hand, but I'm unmoored, an uprooted stalk taken by the gale. I need him to feel comfortable around me, but I'll have to take care to guard my own heart.

"I'm not much accustomed to loneliness," I say in an attempt to turn the tide of the conversation away from dangerous waters. "Wherever I go, I'm surrounded by those who care for me. My village. My people."

"It was once something I was not accustomed to, either," he admits on a sigh.

He's opening up. As much as I want to ask about the interaction with Selnor and why he can't kill him even though he seems to be the source of much trouble, I won't miss this opportunity to strengthen Zhoric's feelings for me. I take in a fortifying breath, the scent of the sun warmed earth long gone this deep in the night. "I heard you had a sister."

"My twin. In my era of birth, twins were rare, precious things. We were always together. I think after all that I've done, Erenmaag took pleasure in showing me what I lost with every birth I helped fabricate since then. Yours included."

My gaze flicks down to his chest where the god scale lies. Did he steal that from Erenmaag, the god of fate and agency? Or was it another, and Erenmaag was only happy to enact some cruelty upon Zhoric for what he'd done. I remember Ozias mentioning a sister, but I didn't realize it was his twin. His loss hits me harder knowing this, imagining losing Kalixta in the same way.

"Did she not do anything to help you with your Alixor?" I ask.

Zhoric leans further down, resting his cheek against his folded hands atop the balcony to look at me. "She was gone with her bonded much of the time, performing their duty for the gods across the seas." His gaze flicks towards the stars, to the sky that's beginning to take on a purplish hue, signifying that morning isn't too far off and that our time is almost done. "They were marvelous together."

His reverence for their relationship strikes me deep, the longing and want has my fingers itching to sweep back the lock of hair that's fallen across his forehead. Our time is short, and it ramps up the need I have to understand, to know.

"Why did you bond with her? Why not anyone else?"

"No one else would have me."

"Why not?" I straighten and turn to fully face him, giving him the entirety of my attention, pretending the sun has much longer to go before it crests the horizon.

"Solan was cruel, a trait born from her father—he was ruthless. He'd wanted a son, so she did everything she could to show him what she was made of, including pinning me in her sights. My father and mother approved of the match, knowing we'd make a strong pair that would please the gods. With the four of them willing to fight off any of my other connections, and my sister gone, blissfully unaware with a happy, powerful bonded match of her own, no one was willing to rise to the challenge."

"I would have." The words fly out of my mouth, twined with quiet determination. Immediately I want to take them back.

Zhoric rises, his jaw clenched tight, and he storms back into his rooms.

I follow him and reach out, but don't touch him.

"Zhoric—"

"No." He spins to face me, raising a finger. "*No*. You do not get to come to me now when I am *this*." He turns his finger onto himself, pressing deeply where the god scale rests on his abdomen.

The emotion in his words are so powerful I have to devour a ragged breath of air to steady myself. "And what are you, exactly?"

"A despicable creature who's unleashed unspeakable pain and suffering upon the world all so he could end his own." His shoulders heave as he stares at me, eyes wild and desperate.

I'm nodding. I need to hear that. It's something I know and I shouldn't soon forget.

"Yes," I say. "I cannot and will not convince you or myself otherwise. That what you've done: whatever part you played to make me and the women what we are, is despicable." My tongue is pressed tight to the roof of my mouth, desperately trying to keep in my next question, but I have to know. I need to know if there's more to him. What does it say about me if my strongest bond, my strongest potential, lies with *him*. "What I'm asking is what are you now?"

His nostrils flare, eyes still wild. "The thing that's keeping this broken world from falling into the depths of complete darkness and ruin—and I will not take you there with me."

My breath leaves me completely. This is no act. Zhoric truly feels something for me; or, I'm the greatest fool to have ever lived. I fear it may be both. A man who's willing to let go of this bond to spare me isn't the wretched creature he claims to be. I want to tell him that, but instead, the dawn comes blindingly bright, reflecting in the white stone walls of his room and washing out the image of him, and then I'm gone.

Sharp rocks dig into my knees. I blink my eyes open in

the Realm, brushing dampness from my cheek. I drop my face into my hands and inhale slow and steady. Too close. I got too close to him and it's ripping me apart. Atlanta's words warned me. Ozias shared how it feels to bond with someone—but nothing could have prepared me for this. It's like a knot is tied around my heart, and with every admission Zhoric made, the rope has tightened to the point where I'm not certain I can undo it without severing something vital.

I have to get a hold of myself.

I blow out all the air from my lungs and shake my hands. Steadying myself with a few more lungfuls of air, I stand. I can't bring myself to face Ninon yet. She'll see every seed of panic planted on my face.

"Kaisa?" I hear her call. I spin towards the rock wall of the enclosure and count the stacked stones from bottom to top until my breathing slows and the muscles in my face and shoulders relax.

She says my name again, this time louder as she rounds the corner into my enclosure. Turning to her, I smile. "Hey, you're awake."

Ninon's eyes move across my face at a rapid pace. Before she can ask, I stride toward her. "I can't believe how sore I am still after going up against Issa," I say, rolling my shoulder. "How does my face look?"

Angling her head, Ninon inspects my injury. "Almost healed."

I grin, rubbing my cheek. We walk down the pathway into the bustling energy of the Realm's center square. There was always a sense of community in Nevoba, but this... this feels like how it should be: women and men standing side by side, living and working together in tandem. Equal parts thriving together, not one greater than the other. The children seem freer, too, less reserved and quiet than back home.

"How are you feeling?" I ask once we're past the noisiest section.

"Great, actually," she says. "I suppose I may have been pushing myself working with Issa."

"I'm not surprised." My words are light and I let the easy conversation with Ninon soothe me. This is what I know to be true. Ninon's presence at my side. Knowing how, when she's on to something new, nothing else in the world exists. "Do you have plans today?"

"Back on the wall with Issa. She's bringing some journals from the Realm's early days for me to read."

"Exciting," I tease.

She elbows me, but a hint of a smile tugs at her mouth. "It's important to know what happened in those days."

My next inhale is shaky as it enters my lungs. "I don't disagree. You'll have to give me the abbreviated version when you've read them."

"I always do."

We part ways at the Alcazar, my nerves vibrating close to the surface with each step that brings me closer to Ozias. I don't know what to tell him. He didn't believe Atlanta's theory about Dyēus harboring the ravaged to unleash on us. I wonder if he will now that I have proof, or, perhaps this is something I should go to Atlanta with? If I do, I'll have to tell her everything. The dread consuming me at the idea of explaining myself to Atlanta when she's been nothing but kind and welcoming has me dragging my feet.

I meet Ozias where we usually do, on the adjacent balcony just outside of the expansive meeting room.

When Ozias catches sight of me, his face drops its easy grin. "Bad night?" he guesses.

"That's one way to put it," I say, raking a hand down my face.

"Do you want to rest?" he asks, meeting me halfway across the balcony and placing a mug of black tea in my hand, which I accept with a grateful smile.

"No." I cover my expression by bringing the mug to

my lips, taking a moment to gather my thoughts as the hot liquid slides across my tongue, bitter and grounding. "The sooner I can shift into my human form at night, the better."

"What happened?" Ozias asks. He always asks, and I generally give him the highlights, but only in brief. When I told him of the night Zhoric sat before the gods eyes, Ozias guessed he was calling more energy from the gods to his scale, or else shoring up all the threads of magic he has spilled out across the world. I didn't tell him how I stayed by his side, or how his pain twisted the bond deeper into my skin.

"We took a walk."

"Sounds romantic."

I roll my eyes. "We went to Selnor's rooms. He had women, human women."

"What did Zhoric do?" Ozias crosses his arms, fingers pressing hard into his biceps. He doesn't like the sound of it as much I didn't like witnessing it.

"Told him to send them home," I sigh and grasp the back of my neck, tugging and pinching to work out the tension. "Apparently he does things like that to get Zhoric's attention. Zhoric hadn't been to see him since before the night Alixor died."

Ozias hums. "Anything else?"

I debate how much to say about Thrace. I don't want anything I say to hurt my sister, but I don't see how Ozias could do anything that would put her in danger. "Thrace came by. He seems worried for Zhoric."

"He's always worried for Zhoric. Ever since they were kids."

That has me standing straighter. "You knew them both in your youth?"

"Quite well, actually. Our circles weren't too close, but close enough."

The urge to ask more about Zhoric and his past threatens to part my lips so I press my mouth closed tight and nod.

Ozias remains silent for a time, then he gently removes the cup from my hands and sets it down on the nearby table. "I'm asking too much from you," he says.

Shaking my head, I say, "No. I'm fine. I want to keep pushing."

"Your tenacity is something I admire about you." Ozias tips his head to one side, studying me carefully. "But even the most tenacious need to rest and recover."

My hands fist. If I show how panicked I am, he'll know. He'll know I've gone too far with Zhoric. I need some time away from him. I need to shift. My fingers uncurl and curl again. "I don't want to sleep. I can't rest right now."

Ozias cups my cheek in the palm of his hand—warm, secure, anchored. "I know. That's not what I'm suggesting. We have another job to do, remember?"

I search his golden eyes, trying to see if he knows the full extent and reason for my anxiety, then I remember what he asked me to do today. "We're going over the border?"

He smiles, dropping his hand and making his way over to a far wall lined with shelves. He takes down a basket of missives, checks the contents, then ties the lid down tight. "As long as you don't mind hitching a ride on my shoulders."

The flight I took with Ninon last night was incredible—my own wings, my own power—but it wasn't enough. I need more space, more sky. And now Ozias is offering me that. This is exactly what I need. I shrug and grin. "There are worse places I could be."

He comes close to me and presses the basket low against my torso. "And far better, I assure you," he murmurs.

Grasping the basket, I look away, but let him see my smile.

Ozias huffs and shakes his head.

"What?" I ask, my brow quirking.

"You're going to ruin that poor bastard."

I frown. I hope he's right.

# Chapter Twenty-Four

With the basket of missives secured behind me, I grip a handful of Ozias's mane at the base of his neck like a pommel on a horse's saddle. A throaty vibration rolls through him as he rumbles his approval, and I squirm as the sensation makes its way between my thighs. He puffs up with a series of quick grunts that I easily read as amusement. As we prepared to leave, I fretted about him leaving the safety of the Realm after what happened last time. Apparently though, Ozias replicated Thrace's magic years ago and during the day has no trouble wielding a shield. Without further warning, Ozias launches straight up into the sky. We clear the trees, and then we're in the thick mists shrouding the Realm. The moisture clings to my face and suffuses my tongue and nose with its lichen and floral scent.

Then we're above and beyond the mists, into the clear,

dry morning. The sky is a crisp cerulean and below the Sere expands far to the south until the landscape shifts with the yellow-green grass of the Nevoban plains, all the way to the valleys and crevices that look like a wasteland of nothing but rocks, belying the truth hidden below the ground—the vast system of tunnels and caves that house my people. People who know nothing of their truth, who are living their lives as easily as they can, ignoring that longing lodged in their heart, or calling it something else. Here in the sky, in the Realm, I know what it is. I finally know what it is that's been missing from me. And soon they will, too.

Ozias banks towards the mountains, keeping us out of eyesight of Dyēus's troops on the ground. He takes his time, picking up speed gradually and smoothly, his dragon eyes seeing more than mine through this mist. We're heading towards the northern shore, keeping Dyēus far off to our east. I may not be on my own wings, but I can't deny the fullness in my chest at being high in the sky with the wind teasing my hair and filling my lungs.

There's nowhere else I'd rather be.

I squeeze my knees a little tighter on either side of Ozias and drop his mane, spreading my arms out to the side. I always wanted to do this when I rode Alixor to the sky kingdom, but with him I couldn't quite bring myself to let go. With Ozias and no one else watching, I do it. Once we're well past Dyēus's encampments, Ozias veers towards the east, and I hold on with my knees, leaning into the turn, my grin wide and unrestrained. Ahead, I make out the first signs of the glittering ocean. The closer we get, the more clearly I see the white caps crashing beneath tall waves, the water a deep, fathomless blue.

Ozias increases his speed, and plunges low so we're coasting a mere eight hands over dry, cracked earth, careening towards the precipice of a cliff face. As we crest over the edge, my breath leaves me at the sudden drop visible below us, the wide white sand beach meeting the boundless blue of the ocean. Ozias dives and then evens out over the sand, the sound of waves mingling with the wind, the scent of salt on the air a balm to my excitement and as he glides his belly close to the rippling water, a sense of contentment washes over me. The undulation of Ozias's flight lulls me further, my fingers loose in his mane, my muscles like liquid.

At some point after the sun has dipped past the apex in the sky, Ozias jerks, and I grip him a little harder to maintain my balance. He does so again a moment later, and then, after a longer time, shoots skyward. I cast glances around me, searching for danger, but all around us the sky is free of anything save the occasional cloud.

"Are you playing with me?" I ask, leaning down to his ear. His answer is to drop then raise swiftly so that my chest flattens against him. I laugh and sit up, engaging my body, feeling how he moves. I close my eyes and reach down to my dragon, eager to entice her out, hoping that perhaps I could fly on the power of my own wings. When I find her, tucked tight inside me, I ask, *Do you feel this? Do you know what this is? Come see, come see.* She ignores me, a grumbling, sleeping giant that has no interest in paltry air tricks. I imagine sitting myself next to her, leaning my back against her neck. I'm filled with tentative fascination as I mentally coexist with this part of myself that, not long ago, I didn't even know existed. My fingers flex on Ozias's spine and my eyes start to sting with the beginning of tears. For so long I didn't understand why I didn't feel like I belonged, like my sense of yearning was unfounded and ungracious. Inside, I feel the dragon shift against my human self, drawing closer, comforting me. *I've been here all along,* she seems to say. *I am with you always.*

Ozias jerks again, this time more violently, as if he hit something. Or something hit *him.* My eyes spring open, teardrops sprinkling down my cheeks. A snarl raises his lip. The wind whips his mane as he swivels his head slowly left, then right. I scan the skies, above and below. I note that the sun has dropped closer to the horizon, the late afternoon turning swiftly towards evening. A shadow catches in my peripheral vision, but then it's gone.

"What was that?" I ask, my tone taking on the form of a huntress, firm and cautious.

*One of the ravaged,* Ozias answers.

On full alert, my muscles tense. The sudden disappearance of the dragon chafes along my spine. "So where did he go?"

*That's what I'm trying to—*

Before he can finish speaking, the glistening surface of the water below us breaks and a wide open jaw with teeth sharp as blades vaults directly towards us. Ozias rears back, thrusting us up, then tumbles through the air, evading the attack. I hold on tight, even as Ozias twists upside down for the barest of moments, before seamlessly turning us upright.

*Are you all right?*

My blood is sharp as it courses through me, prickling my skin. "Good." I feel behind me, thankful that the basket is still secure. "How can I help?" Since I have no weapons and no way to transform, I know there's not much I can do.

*Hold on tight. I'll get to shore and drop you. Keep low.*

Ozias hurtles us through the air, back towards the distant beach. Glancing over my shoulder I see the dragon, droplets of water flicking off its body as it swims through the sky, eyes wholly white and unfocused like a dead fish. Strangest of all is the vaporous black mist drifting off its form and out into the breeze, as if the beast were on fire.

"It's gaining on us," I say, keeping my voice steady. "Are you using Thrace's elahi?"

Ozias bares his teeth. *It's not coming as easily as it should.* My fingers tighten into his mane.

Ozias pushes, but he's been flying for hours now, indulging me in the air, trying to give me the break I so desperately need. Before we can get to the beach, the ravaged is on Ozias's heels and lunges for us at the exact moment Ozias lowers towards the ground so close it kicks up a gust of fine sand.

*Jump,* he says and without hesitation, I leap from his back.

I land hard, rolling through the sand, the granules catching in my hair and sticking to my skin. I stop myself and look up in time to see Ozias knock his antlers into the side of the ravaged dragon before spiraling back towards the ocean, his body twisting and straightening like a lock of hair caught on a turbulent wind. He's trying to draw the ravaged away from me, but the dragon has me pinned in its sights and ignores his jab, instead coming straight for me.

Ozias roars, lunging to catch them, but the ravaged slips past and Ozias's teeth graze along the dragon's back hip.

Panic surges hard and fast in my chest, and inside my dragon rears up her head. I hear her tell me she needs more energy and something in my gut pulls hard. In a burst of mist I transform, right before the ravaged careens into me, teeth sinking into my shoulder. My head slams against the cliffside and my vision goes dark.

Gasping, I open my eyes to a blinding whiteness—but it's not the white of the beach. It's the white of Dyēus's castle floors. I snap my head up, my wide eyes meeting Zhoric's.

Zhoric goes preternaturally still. He's sitting on his throne and I sense a crowd behind me, though I don't know how great. I'm on my hands and knees, heaving, shaking my head. Zhoric's fingers seize around the throne's armrests. In my mind, he asks, *Where* are *you?*

I can't answer. Elsewhere, beyond this room, I'm thrown to the side, and it causes me to jerk here, a scream grappling its way out of my throat, and I squeeze my eyes shut.

When I open them again, I'm back on the beach,

breathing hard, lying on my side in my human form. My shoulder is on fire, but I push myself up and scuttle back until I'm nestled into the short, scraggly grasses and reeds that cling to life on the huge white rocks pockmarking the land. I settle near a crevice, but it's not deep enough to conceal myself from the ravaged.

Over the ocean, Ozias and the ravaged tussle, though it looks more like a dance. Ozias ducks and weaves, his movements calculated and graceful while the ravaged collector lunges and swipes, jaws snapping and chasing in a relentless drum. The miasma comes and goes, wisps of it coming off the dragon's body and drifting away on the wind, but never clearing, merely getting carried away like a passing cloud.

Ozias is wearing the ravaged down, his careful movements reserving his energy while the ravaged expends all of theirs. A part of me wishes he would just put an end to the creature, but I know he can't. Not when it will mean one of our own will die. I wish I knew what his plan was for the ravaged. The fight serves to remind me of what I learned last night. I want to reach out Ozias and tell him that if he can subdue the creature, maybe we can somehow bring it to the Realm with us and we can figure out a way to save him – to save them all. I try to speak to him, mind to mind, but there's only silence.

They've moved to the swell of the surf. The ravaged's chest puffs in and out, its roar like a tormented prey seeking an end to its misery. As Ozias twists to slam his tail against the ravaged, the beast twists back towards me, coming fast. I press myself deep into the rock, but before the ravaged can make it past where the surf crashes against the sand an enormous white figure slams down onto the beach from out of the sky. In an instant almost too fast to track, Zhoric snatches the ravaged's neck into his great maw. A spray of red arcs into the air, the ocean waves reaching to catch the drops of blood and pull them into its fold.

My chest heaves. Zhoric looms over the body of the ravaged, its blood-soaked head tumbling down the shoreline. He pulls back a clawed hand and dives it into the beast, yanking out a black mass before tossing it into the water—*the ravaged's heart.*

Zhoric lumbers over to me, crimson staining the white of his mane, speckling his shining scales. His breath comes in pants as he pins me with his gaze.

In a billow of clouds, he shifts. The red of the ravaged's blood stains his mouth and crimson flecks mar his otherwise pristine white attire that I was once most accustomed to seeing him wear. He stands before me, too close and yet too far, watching me, saying nothing.

I'm thrumming with the need to stand and go to him, but instead I keep myself rooted between the rocks, blood trickling down my arm.

Ozias hurtles towards us. He transforms a hair's breadth from Zhoric and uses the momentum from his speed to swerve to my side, kicking up a cloud of sand in his wake.

Ozias's gaze is hard as he holds Zhoric in his sights, but the king's eyes are fixed on me. None of Ozias's casual grace from when he was with Zhoric in Dyēus is here now. I buzz in anticipation, waiting for someone to strike, with words or blows. When Ozias seems satisfied Zhoric won't move, he half turns to me, placing a palm on the side of my face. The anchor of his hand feels like a restraint. One I fear I'm in desperate need of. "Are you okay?"

I don't take my eyes off of Zhoric. "Bleeding, but fine."

Zhoric tracks the path the pad of Ozias's thumb makes down my cheek towards my mouth. The muscles around his eyes tighten.

Ozias looks between the two of us, but his discerning eyes land on me.

"You're not usually in the habit of traveling beyond Dyēus's islands or its provinces," Ozias comments before finally giving the Sar Dyēus his attention. "To what do we owe this pleasure?"

Zhoric continues to look at me for a long moment, then turns his head to the side, his profile awash in the golden evening light. "I wished to see the view."

Ozias hums.

"Sunsets are quite beautiful from the ground," Zhoric adds.

"Ozias," I gasp, my hand seizing his forearm as I realize just how low sun has travelled.

Zhoric follows the movement, but his expression remains neutral.

"We'll make it," Ozias reassures. "Enjoy the view, then, your majesty."

"Ozias?" Zhoric says, casual as a lizard bathing in the sun.

"Yes?"

"If you let another drop of blood fall from her veins again, I will ensure yours runs dry." Then he shifts, pushes off the ground in a spray of sand, and joins the clouds.

Ozias watches him go, a frown pulling at his lips.

My heart is a riot in my chest. I swallow hard, but my mouth is dry and sand coats my tongue. "I might need to speak with Atlanta about the nuances of mind walking after all."

Ozias softens then sinks down in front of me to lay his forehead against mine. "I've got you. I won't let you fly too far."

The last of the air in my lungs seeps out of me. His gaze flicks back towards the horizon, a curse parting his lips, but he says nothing more as he shifts and lowers down for me to climb on. I scramble onto his neck, wincing as my shoulder protests, my head dizzy, my vision dotted.

As we fly, our shadow stretches across the white sand, dark and dangerous in its length. The trip here was long, Ozias is exhausted, and I fear for my ability to remain conscious enough to hold on. It was a mistake for me to leave the Realm, but Ozias wanted me to come and I didn't have the self-restraint to say no. I wanted to do whatever else I could to free my people. *My people. The missives.* I gasp, checking behind us.

The basket is long gone; all the work he poured into those notices lost to the tide. I only hope there's time to warn Nevoba still—after today, I'm not sure how much longer I can hold back the aching need to bond myself to Zhoric.

# Chapter Twenty-Five

The Realm comes into view the moment the sun is severed in half by the line where sky meets land. Above, the sky is turning the deep blue of night, the first stars glinting into their glory to announce that evening is nigh. Unconsciously, my body tightens its hold on Ozias. Somewhere along our flight home, the tension of Ozias's muscles eased, but the stiffness is back again as we draw closer to the Realm, yet still too far.

*We'll make it,* he vows, but I know it's a lie meant to soothe me. As he spurs himself on faster, grunting with the effort, I offer what comfort I can, drawing slow, delicate circles on the side of his neck.

I glance over the Sere, the ground dark with long shadows dragging behind each rock monument, signifying the end of our time beyond the Realm. Movement catches my attention. My hand on the side of Ozias's neck stills. He cants his head, a snarl ripping from his throat as he sees what I do.

Dozens of dragons moving in tandem—straight towards us.

Ozias beats his wings faster, snorting as he pushes himself, his ribcage expanding and contracting with his efforts. I hold on tighter, but I'm weak from the attack and the long hours I've spent clinging to Ozias today. The sun is a deep red, like an angry watchful eye telling us we're out of time.

From the mountainside, another pack of draconem appear. An ambush. Ozias leaves the Realm often and as far as I understand, this has never happened before. The only difference this time is me. Perhaps if Ozias hadn't expended so much energy he could drum up what he needs to use Thrace's power. Perhaps, if I could shift and use my power, I could help him hold them off. But he did, and I can't. I brace myself for whatever happens next.

The Realm is within our reach, the last slice of the sun barely visible beyond the horizon, its final glow a brilliant warning. Then we're nearing the concealing haze of the Realm. A tingle races up my spine. My skin coats with a sheen of light sweat that mingles with the mists.

As Ozias adjusts to begin his descent into the Realm. The dragons behind us close in, the ones on our right from the mountains not far behind. From the corner of my left eye a movement steals my breath. I open my mouth to shout a warning, but it's too late. A dragon collides hard with Ozias's back end, knocking my grip on him loose. I scramble to recover, but the impact sends Ozias spinning, and then I'm falling, twisting in the air as Ozias plummets, wings wrapping around his feet. We were up so high that the damage he'll inflict—upon himself and whatever stands in his wake—will be immense. The Realm below is a riot of frantic movement. From the lookout wall, Isaa and another draconem I don't recognize leap off and dart for Ozias and grasp his tail and an arm between them to slow his fall. Another dragon slices through the air under me and catches me hard on her back behind a set of powerful wings.

*Are you all right?* Atlanta's voice. Adrenaline settles into my system at the same moment a shiver wracks my body. My bones crack and I feel the transformation jolting through me. My mind and body are so out of sorts that falling into it smoothly is well beyond my reach.

*Kaisa?*

My fingers press into her red-orange scales, my breathing labored. In her effort to catch me, Atlanta's trajectory is facing up, toward the open sky, instead of down into the safety of the Realm.

*Kaisa, answer me,* she pleads, worry etched into her voice and I swallow, drumming up the will to respond.

Atlanta roars and her body jerks hard mid-flight. I dig my fingers into her tough scales, splintering my nails. Blood fans across the open air. Atlanta wheels around and plunges her sharp talons into her attackers face again and again until he releases her wing. As we tip sideways, Issa shoots as fast as an arrow towards our opponent and gouges him with her antlered head. Atlanta plummets and we cross into the Realm's border, one wing flapping hopelessly while the other hangs limp at her side. Our fall turns into a full spiral, then another. My mind whirls. Another twist and I'll be pinned beneath her. I let my transformation take over. I curl my talons under her and pump my wings, slowing her as well as I can, my injured shoulder screaming at me to give up.

With a frustrated growl, I implore my body to do as I say, and will every ounce of power to come to me. From all around, wisps of energy stream towards me. It comes from the sky. It comes from the magical barrier around the Realm. The energy travels to me in cascading ribbons from every dragon within my line of sight. In that moment, Atlanta feels as light as air, my lungs breathe easy, and the pain in my shoulder dissipates as if carried away on a wind.

I lower her gently to the ground on her uninjured side, and Ozias meets us, running, in his human form. Without meaning to, without even thinking, I melt back into my human skin.

Atlanta stays in her draconem, and I can't make out the difference between her scales and the blood that runs in rivulets down her side from the apex of her wing. Ozias yells for water and healers, kneeling beside me to examine her wing with frantic yet practiced movements. The healers come at once, cleaning her wound. I inch my way towards her head, laying a hand on her brow.

"Thank you," I whisper.

Atlanta tips her head further into my hand, a soft whine wheezing out of her.

Ozias joins me at her head. "Atlanta, can you hear me?" he murmurs.

She whines again. The line along his jaw tenses. He cranes his head back towards the healers, checking out the wound. His jaw tightens. "It's deep. You're in pain. But you'll heal from this. You'll be fine."

Atlanta sighs and lets her eyes drift shut. Her breathing begins to even out as the healers finish cleaning the wound, draping it with a damp cloth suffused with the deeply astringent scent of herbal antiseptics.

Ozias lets his forehead fall onto the side of her neck, his own eyes closing, his breaths flaring his nostrils. He cares for her in a way that goes beyond loyalty.

Looking at them twists some emotion inside me I can't name, and I rise, giving them space, and make my way to the infirmary to get cleaned up. I feel my dragon battling with me to come out again, but I take the calm, cool air of the night into my lungs and will her to do the same.

The single healer left in the infirmary wastes no time helping get the blood cleared from my face and shoulder. It doesn't sting like it ought to, and when the blood is gone, there are only tiny, nearly healed indentations from where the ravaged punctured my skin.

The healer's brows twitch together. "That happen tonight?"

"Earlier this evening," I admit.

She hums. "We heal fast, but that's unheard of." She sniffs around me. "Smells like your blood, otherwise I'd ask if you were sure if the wound was that deep."

"Could faster healing be my elahi?" I ask, wondering if that's why Ozias and I haven't been able to figure it out. Then I remember my wounds from the time we were taken out of the Realm. I healed at a pace on par with Ozias then.

The healer shrugs. "Only one way to find out." And before I can open my mouth, she slices the back of my forearm with a knife.

My mouth snaps open in surprise. "Brutal," I hiss, as she places an herbal cloth over the new wound. She pulls it away, and still it bleeds.

"If it's as healed as the wound on your shoulder in a few hours, then you'll know for sure."

"Thanks, I guess," I mumble, then turn and leave before she has a chance to open me up again. Her hearty chuckle follows me out the door.

When I step outside, the dark of night obscuring my vision save for the reach of a few lamps along the pathways, I remember again I'm still in my human form. Beneath my skin, I feel her itching to come out. *No. Not tonight.* The pull I felt towards Zhoric on the beach rocked me to the very depths of my core. I can't afford to be weak.

Somewhere along the way, I've gone deeper with him than I intended, and I fear the tide of my feelings if I go to him tonight. He saved me. I appeared before him, distraught and hurt, and he removed himself from whatever he was doing to save me. To kill a ravaged for me. I stop short. A ravaged died tonight. Which means...*Ninon.*

My feet move on instinct and I sprint, running full tilt

towards the enclosures. One after the other after the other empty. Doubling back, I tear through the pathways, the wild beginning of the night still in the air as people clean up debris from Ozias and Atlanta's falls into the Realm. I ignore all of that. I run for the fields, my eyes jumping from draconem to draconem, a hoard of them grounded for now, a scant few in the sky. I see Issa's bright scales and head for her, the twine wrapped around my heart finally releasing when, right over Issa's shoulder, I see the familiar form of Ninon's dragon.

Ninon spots me at once. She bounds over to me and presses her large forehead to mine, her mane tickling against my temples.

*I heard you were fine, but it's good to see with my own eyes,* I hear her in my mind.

I'm nodding, but my breaths come ragged and erratic as the evening's events catch up to my mind. Tears fall, and my chest is unbearably tight.

*Breathe,* I hear her say. *Breathe.*

Her breathing comes deeper and longer and I struggle for a few beats to match hers before mine evens out.

I feel my dragon nudge me and I squeeze my eyes tight. "Kaisa."

I twist my head. Ozias is standing there, a short distance behind me. He holds out his hand. With great effort I lift my brow from Ninon's to hold her gaze. After a time, she nudges me with her nose, the touch conveying that we're both fine. She's right. I'm okay. *She's* okay.

I briefly lay my hand on the side of her face. Then I turn and take Ozias's hand, grounding myself in his touch. I will stay here in this form. Nothing will take me out of it, despite the incessant press I feel in my bones, begging me to shift. The itch of my skin, enticing me to transition to my smooth, armored scales, pulses like a drumbeat in my ears.

Ozias pulls me along the pathways towards the Alcazar. I remain silent, knowing we have much to discuss, but not having the energy to bring it up or explain myself.

When we make it to the top of the Alcazar, Ozias releases my hand and walks out onto the terrace overlooking the Sere all the way to Dyēus. I join him, the bracing wind sweeping my hair away from my face.

"You saved Atlanta tonight," he murmurs.

"She saved me first."

Ozias turns to me then, his gaze flitting down my figure and back up before returning to Dyēus. "Zhoric doesn't leave Dyēus unless he must. You've done it, Kaisa. He cares for you."

I look away, out across the Sere, catching on the northernmost and largest island. The castle. I pin the place where Zhoric's chambers are before answering. "Impossible. There's been such little time between us. He doesn't even know me."

"It doesn't matter."

A frown pulls tight on my lips. I don't know why that bothers me.

Ozias holds his posture, his breath, before releasing a sigh that seems to melt his form, and in a liquid motion he turns, hooking his thick, muscled arms around me, burying his face into the top of my sea-salt-washed hair. He breathes in deep and slow, and I turn into a puddle at his touch. The anxious energy buzzing under my skin, shouting at me to shift, ebbs away until all I can focus on is the scent of him, the warmth of him, the taste of salt as my lips press lightly to the center of his chest.

Ozias lowers his mouth to my ear. "Are you falling for him?"

I recoil, but he doesn't let me go as I pin him with a fierce, hard look. "No."

Zhoric could have killed Ninon tonight with his recklessness. He's harmed me and countless women from the time he took the power of a god to the moment he sealed my baby niece. Despite all I know of his past, of what he's shown me of his character, I grasp tightly to my hate. I push down the twisting desire to turn into my dragon so I can see him again.

"Does he think you are?" Ozias questions.

I draw in my lips, considering. "Possibly."

"He showed up for you today, Kaisa. That is no small feat. But then again," Ozias searches the planes of my face, a tenderness almost like sadness smoothing the hard angles of his brow, "you are easy to love, Kaisa. It's no wonder he's already fallen for you."

My eyes are hot and my tongue thick with a tide of tears I manage to hold back. I've not felt easy to love in my life, but hearing Ozias say it fills me with an unimaginable hope I hadn't realized I'd been holding onto.

"Kiss me," I murmur.

He sweeps his eyes up and down my face, holding himself rigid, hesitating. I think he'll rebuff me again, but then, he lowers to press his lips to mine, soft, gentle and cautious.

It's not enough, though. I need more. "Touch me, Ozias."

His breath hitches, like he's surprised at my boldness. I may have kept things from him, but I've never been shy. My hands trail the length of his arms and slip over the backs of his shoulders. I press myself closer to him, until my chest meets his.

With our faces close, the knowing whisper of his question ghosts across my mouth. "What do you want, Kaisa?" It's a question he knows the answer to, one he teased me with not long ago, and one I have no qualms answering.

"You once offered to show me your bed. Does that offer still stand?"

Ozias presses his face into the crook of my neck. He stays like that for a long moment. "There are reasons why we shouldn't," he admits.

The beat of his heart is frantic against my own. "Please," I say, grasping the muscles along his back. "Stay with me. I don't want to go to him tonight and I'm afraid if I'm not with you, I'll transform. I don't know how to stop myself from going."

Ozias squeezes me so hard I can't draw a single breath of air into my lungs. We stay like that for a long time until finally he agrees. "Okay…Okay."

When it's not a resounding, uproarious yes, I doubt his desire for me. I suddenly want to take it back. "We don't—"

"No," he says, stopping me. "I want to. First though, I need to show you something."

"Are you…" my gaze flicks down between us, "well?"

Ozias growls deep in his throat, pressing his hardening length against my lower stomach. "It's perfectly fine, I assure you. What I'm going to show you has to do with bonding."

I open my mouth. "Oh. I see."

"You're close with Zhoric, which means another event like today could happen."

My brows furrow for a brief moment while I try to figure out where he's going when my mind alights with a thought. "An opportunity to get close to him again. To force the bond with him."

"It's less forcing and more like slicing through butter with all the feelings he must have for you by now."

"We don't know that for sure."

"He has enough feelings for you that he came to your aid in a time of need. That is more than enough."

I lick my lips and squirm against his body. I clear my throat. "All right. Show me."

Our eyes are soft on each other, his words softer. "Come to my bed chamber." He doesn't need to ask me twice, and so I follow him in the dark of night through the place I've only seen in daylight. We go through the entrance I've never set foot past before, and into an untidy room with a collection of things on nearly every surface. It's not a neat display like Ninon's would be, but it's about the amount of things she'd have in her own room.

Ozias settles me down next to him on the bed, angling us so that our knees touch. I get more comfortable, sliding one of my legs up onto the plush mattress. He lights a lantern on the bedside table, the soft glow stark against harsh edges of the night.

"The bond is a soul connection." He takes my hands and tucks them against his chest where I can feel the steady rhythm of his heart. "Our bodies house our souls, and the closest physical connection we have with our souls is our blood. It's the only thing fluid enough that a soul can tether to. That's why when something stops the heart, whose duty it is to keep the blood flowing, we die, because our souls can no longer hold onto us."

Ozias turns my hands so my wrists are facing up. "A few arteries carry blood directly to and from the heart—our strongest soul points. The first is in your wrists, at the spot you can feel your pulse. The next you already know about…" He runs a finger along the inside of my thigh and I shiver at his touch, longing to feel the drag of his finger coast higher between my legs. "And the third and strongest is here, alongside our necks." He points to the spot along the column of his neck and the pulse of the powerful artery that lies beneath. "This is where you connect our souls—this is where you make the bond."

I look between his neck and his face. He told me where and what these points mean, but my mind isn't lining up with the execution. "How?"

"You drink from me," he says, tapping the side of his neck. "Right here."

My face screws up in disgust. "Your blood?"

"You eat meat, I presume."

"Yes, but—"

"And drink mares' blood?"

"For *ceremonies*, and it's mixed with the milk, but—"

"And is this not the same?"

I open my mouth. Because in a way, it is a ceremony. In a way, it is the same. I narrow my gaze. "I hate the taste."

"Someone as bloodthirsty as you?" My narrow gaze sharpens and he smiles. "I promise mine's sweeter than a mare's blood."

"You can't possibly know that," I say. "Actually, I imagine you've had your fair share of split lips and bloody mouths."

"It's like you know me."

I know what he's allowed me to, but even with the charismatic, open way he speaks, I don't truly know Ozias. I know what he's doing, what he stands for, and that he's attracted to me as I am to him. But he's had years of living. So much life that, even if we had eternity, I'm not sure I'd learn about every moment of it. I'm not sure that he'd want to share that with me. I tackle my mind back to our conversation. "So what do I do? Make a cut, take a cup, and tip you over like a teapot?"

Ozias barks out a laugh, his smile genuine and beautiful. "As much as I'm sure there are several people in this world who would like to see just that, it's more straightforward. If you could conjure your teeth alone, you could bite me and drink directly from the vein. But seeing as that's a bit advanced for your current skill set..." He opens his hand and lets a talon come forth from his index finger, then he hovers the sharp claw just over his jugular. "Whenever you're ready."

My insides are twisting, both in anticipation of the action, and at having to actually drink his blood. "Wait. I'm...bonding with you?"

"No. I'll stop you before it locks into place."

My chest is sore from how hard my heart has thrummed today. I feel exhausted, but I also realize he's putting a lot of faith in me. I know that if I were to follow through and bond him to me, I'd be in control. And here he is, letting me do that. Putting his trust into me. I place a gentle hand on his wrist.

"You're a good man," I whisper. Ozias's mouth draws tight.

"I'm not sure about that."

"I think...maybe that's how we're all taught to feel. That we're not good enough. Maybe it's time to say, whoever we are, however we come...that in itself is good enough."

His smile is tenuous. "I like that, Kaisa."

My low belly tightens, a delicious, dangerous heat spreading through me. The possibility of us, like he once proposed, churns and tugs in the back of my mind. "I like you, Ozias," I admit.

"I like you, too," he says, his golden gaze piercing me straight through. "Are you ready then?"

I steel myself and nod. My insides vibrate, even if my body is motionless, even if the rise and fall of my chest is barely a whisper against my clothes. "All right. I'm ready." The words come out surer than I feel.

"Come closer."

My breath is a soft breeze as I rise up on my knees and lean over, bracing my hands on his shoulders, face close to the hand above his neck. Without further ceremony or words, Ozias slices into his skin, his rich crimson blood welling up to the surface. I'm stunned for a second, watching it flow.

"Kaisa." Ozias's hushed voice brings me back.

I open my mouth and place it against his skin. The initial tang of his blood on my tongue is a mix of revulsion and ecstasy. I lock my teeth over the wound to keep it open, lips flared out on his smooth skin. Ozias hisses, hands coming up to grip my sides, just below my ribcage. I suck in a deep draught of blood, and I hum. He was right. The taste isn't the problem. The problem will be stopping the tide of feelings rushing through me. The problem will be stopping when he tells me to.

My hand on his other shoulder slides up and around the back of his head, angling it away to grant me better access. I hear Ozias suppress a moan, making it sound throatier. Without meaning to, I press in closer at the third swallow, my chest pushing against his as my knee slides over one of his thighs, then the other, so that I'm straddling him. He wraps his arms around me on my fourth swallow. I grind into him on my fifth, and I feel him stiff beneath me. On my sixth swallow he rocks me against him and my moan muffles into his neck. He whispers my name into my ear, hot and rasping.

He presses his own mouth against my throat. "And if we were doing this, really doing this, I'd take from you here at the exact. Same. Time." His words send a thrilling rush down my spine.

On the seventh drink, I feel it at the same time Ozias says, "There it is. Stop."

The bond dances across my tongue, but I find the power to let it go and I feel it fizzle out in my veins. I pull away, his blood welling for a few seconds more before the wound closes up. I lick up the column of his neck, taking the last vestiges of his blood into me.

A shiver wracks his body and then he's on me, one hand bracing the back of my neck, the other under my thigh, flipping me onto my back, pelvis grinding into mine before he stills. He's shaking as he hovers over me, breath billowing his chest.

"I'm trying very hard," he says through his teeth, voice gravelly, "not to come undone and bury myself in you."

Heat and desire pool between my thighs.

"Do it."

# Chapter Twenty-Six

Saying the words is like unfurling a sail on a torrent of wind—wild and untethered. His mouth descends upon mine, his hands pulling my body more firmly to his. The sweep of Ozias's dancing tongue along the roof of my mouth blissfully erases all thoughts from my mind. The pressure of his body dampens the feel of my dragon scratching at my seams. His fingers press into my thighs, enticing me to part my legs further for him to nestle in more deeply.

I'm not shy with my want as I rake my fingernails down into the neck of his robe, pushing the fabric off his back. Ozias trails hot, open mouthed kisses down my neck and unbinds the tie holding my top together until my breasts spill free. He stops, pressing his forehead against my breastbone, gathering his breath.

I whimper, needing him to move, to keep me here. My

dragon pulls and tugs—as if to tell me he's waiting for me on the other side. To tell me she wants me to go. I squeeze my eyes shut tight, wrap my legs around Ozias, grasp him by the jaw and lead him up to kiss me again, pressing my bare chest to his.

He moans into my mouth and I take it. I need to fill myself up, and keep my mind and body heavy with this want and desire.

When Ozias lifts his head, breaking our kiss, his eyes are a dark ochre. "What are you doing to me?" he asks, genuine confusion pinching his brow.

"What?" I ask, breathing heavy. I hazily recall asking Zhoric the same thing days ago.

"It feels…sometimes around you, I feel weak."

I frown, which has him shaking his head.

"I'm explaining it wrong. I don't know how to describe it."

Squirming beneath his scrutiny, I pull back, feeling myself fade. As swiftly as I pull back, that pull from my dragon rises.

"And now it's gone," he says, dragging his hand up along the side of my ribcage, passing all too briefly along the side of my breast until he cups my neck.

"I'm sorry," I whisper.

"What did you do? To make it stop?"

"I—" I hesitate on the words, trying to decipher what was happening. "I pulled back."

"Don't."

"What?"

"Whatever you were doing before—do it again."

I shake my head as if to say I don't know what he's talking about, but his mouth is on mine again and I try doing what I was before—I take. I imagine filling myself up with Ozias—his power, and I move desperately against his large, hard frame.

His mouth trails down my throat and over my breastbone again. Only thankfully, this time he doesn't stop.

"Yes, Kaisa." His tongue finds the peak of my nipple. He swirls it around his tongue. "This is it."

"What?" I ask again, breathless, the question thick.

"Your elahi. You're taking power from me."

I tighten my hold around him and go completely still.

Ozias's hands move to replace his mouth on my nipples, rolling and pinching them between his thumb and forefinger as he tips his head up to look at me. "Don't stop. Take from me, Kaisa. Whatever you need, take it."

I need him too much right now to deny him, and so I do. I arch up and let his mouth trail down my belly towards the band of my pants. His mouth and movements become languid, almost as if he were intoxicated. He pulls my pants down over my hips, my thighs, all the way until he tosses them aside.

Now that he's mentioned it, I notice it; his energy is a waterfall, sliding off his shoulders and into me. I feel heavy and on edge with his power. I recognize this now. I've done this before. From the very air around me, from the dragons of Dyēus when Ozias and I were dragged over the border, tonight from the rogues, and anytime I've maintained a shift during the daylight.

This is what I can do.

*I can take.*

Ozias's hand trails down from my breast all the way to the top of my mound, his thumb slipping between my legs to brush along the seam of my sex.

"Gods," he curses. "You're already so wet." He slips his thumb inside of me and I arch, my inner walls pulsing with need around the single digit.

I wiggle my hips from side to side, seeking more friction, just, *more.*

"Ozias," I whine. Annoyed at the sound of my voice, I groan.

He pumps his thumb in and out of me once, then twice,

before placing his thumb into his mouth, tasting me, and he rumbles with approval.

"Stop teasing," I order. "You've done enough of that."

Ozias's chuckle is low as he slides up my body. Somewhere in the time he'd been down there, he'd taken off his own pants, and now nothing separates us. "Why don't you make me?"

I rise to his challenge, drawing so much of his power into me, he visibly loses his breath. I take the opportunity to flip him onto his back so that now I'm astride him. He runs his hands up my thighs, my hips, to the curve of my waist, all the way to my ribcage. I reach down between us and take him in my hands, heavy and hot.

Ozias is breathing hard again, so I loosen up my hold on his power.

"Don't," he says. "Keep it."

I pause to make sure he means it, then slowly bring it back, as slowly as I stroke the length of him. He hisses, watching my hand glide over him. Watching as I poise him at my center. Watching as I sink down onto him, taking him into me little by little, rising and lowering until I'm fully seated on him.

I want to hold here. To make him wait. To feel the delicious lick of desire pulse within me. But I can't. I rock my hips and the relief is immediate. I move again, seeking my pleasure. Ozias moves with me, almost like he's a vessel for my release.

"Take, Kaisa."

I don't stop moving, I don't stop chasing that twisting sensation pulling taut, low in my core. I stay with it, driving that sensation higher. Last time Ozias stopped me before I could tumble. This time, I won't let him. My body bows over as my release grips me tight, coiling hard around Ozias before fluttering into bliss.

My undoing loosens my hold on Ozias's power and he grunts as he thrusts into me. He lifts me off of him, rotating us so that I'm lying flat on my stomach on the mattress. I move to raise my hips as I've done before with farmhands once I'm done with them and need them to release their spend, but he pushes me back down, his chest on my back, his hard length lined up to enter me again while I'm flat on the bed.

"You made a mistake letting go of my power," he says into my ear, taking my dominant hand and guiding it down between my body and the mattress, ensuring my fingers are pressed exactly on the bundle of nerves at the apex of my thighs. "I'm going to have you come for me again and again. I won't hold back."

All I can do is whimper and press myself back against him.

Then he thrusts into me fast and deep, only to pull out slowly and slide into me again. His movements, the feel of him filling me up combined with my fingers pressing on myself, bring me swiftly back to the edge. And Ozias makes true on his promise. He makes me come undone again and again.

When I don't think I can handle a single orgasm more, he moves fast and wild and I crest with another wave of pleasure, taking Ozias with me. He growls and huffs as he pumps into me, eking out his own pleasure as I lay sated with mine.

Ozias kisses the side of my face, tender and sweet, nuzzling into me for a long moment before he rolls off to lie by my side.

We stare at one another for a long time. He looks beautiful. He also looks like a stranger. I shore myself up with a deep breath and turn my head towards the ceiling. My mind already spinning, already on the thousands of thoughts constantly vying for my attention in my head. I hold onto the one that brings me most relief. The one that's mine and mine alone.

"So I have an elahi," I say.

Ozias grumbles, though the words are good natured. "No 'That was amazing, Ozias.' Or 'Thank you for your time.'"

I turn to him again to see him smiling. I smile back. "That was amazing, Ozias. Thank you for your time."

"Was that so hard?"

My gaze flicks down between us. "Could have been harder."

His nose wrinkles in a faux growl, and he snatches me around the waist to draw me into him. "You're a menace."

"One that has the ability to take power from others."

"A nightmare, then."

My heart skips a beat. Zhoric said the same and now I'm thinking about him. I can't. I *can't*. I tug on Ozias's power to tether me here. I have to stay here tonight. Bile creeps up my throat at the thought of seeing Zhoric now after being with Ozias like this.

Ozias seems to sense my mind unease and he presses a kiss to my mouth. One that's gentle, but that I quickly turn fevered. He doesn't question it. He doesn't stop me. He simply lets me take.

And so I do.

Dawns early tendrils seep into Ozias's room. He's asleep, laid out on his back, chest bare. As beautiful as he is, and as wonderful as our night together was, there's a sour twist in my stomach. I move slowly, trying not to rouse him from sleep as I slip out from between the sheets, dress silently, and pad across the room. Once in the receiving hall, I breathe easier and move swifter. It's the way I always end my night with someone I've been intimate with. My mind shuts off during the act, but once my partner has fallen asleep, it resumes running, putting off rest until my body can't stand being awake another moment.

Down the stairs, I stop short.

"Atlanta," I say, startling at seeing her up and about so soon after her injury.

She looks at me, a quick up and down. "Ozias—" I wait for her to continue, but that's all she says.

"He's asleep," I say. She turns her head.

"I'll come back another time." She pivots and bounds down the steps.

"Atlanta," I call after her, but she doesn't stop.

"*Atlanta*," I call again, moving faster to catch up with her, placing my hand on her shoulder. "Are you well?"

"I am. Thank you."

She isn't, but I can't guess why she won't say. "Your wounds?"

"Nearly healed already," she says, barely turning her head to answer over her shoulder.

"Are you…certain?"

She sighs and nods emphatically. "Yes. I'm sorry. I was hoping to see Ozias. I didn't realize how early it was."

I cast a glance out the nearest window, noting the dim light of dawn. "Of course."

I feel her take in a steady breath, then she faces me fully. "And you? Are you all right?"

"Fine. Thank you, for yesterday. You put yourself at risk saving me."

"It was nothing."

"It wasn't," I argue. "I owe you." There's a pregnant pause between us where I want to say more—I want to tell Atlanta about my omission. Even though Ozias has his reservations, he respects her a great deal. I wonder if now is the time, but she still seems shaken from last night and the words die on my tongue. "I'll see you later?"

She holds my gaze for a moment, a flicker of disappointment crossing her features. "Of course. Get some rest."

Suddenly I realize she must know, or at least have

guessed. She knows more than anyone about the power of mind walking. At some point in her own journey, she hid this very thing from others, too. She's just waiting for me to tell her. "Atlanta?" I call after her.

She stops again and turns.

"I have something I need to tell you."

To my relief, she doesn't look surprised. Instead, she heaves a sigh, sits on the step, and waves me over to join her.

I start with a piece of the truth. "I told you I read your work," I begin. "On mind walking."

She nods, laces her fingers together and waits for me to speak.

"I wish I was a faster reader. Or rather...I wish I had come to you sooner." The words I need to say stick to my tongue.

"You've been seeing Zhoric." A statement, not a question.

My mouth draws into a thin line and I lower my head in an approximation of admission.

Her sigh is heavy and it pains me to feel her displeasure, reminding me of all the times I let down my mother.

"I wish you'd come to me, too. Does Ozias know?"

Relief soothes some of the tension pinching along my shoulders. At least he kept his word. "He does."

She's silent for a long while. "How are you doing with it all?"

"The potential we have...it's strong." I meet her eyes, showing her every ounce of my strength and determination with the lift of my chin. "But I know my loyalty."

"Why didn't you come to me?" she inquires.

"I couldn't risk you questioning whose side I was on," I admit. "Not even for a moment. I think...I think Ninon is at risk. I couldn't have you pulling me from the task because you feared I'd choose him."

Atlanta's quiet again for a long moment. "Has it been

every night?"

I nod.

"Did you happen to find out anything useful?"

My brows pinch together. I've learned so much, but there's one thing that I learned she would hae most interest in. "You were right."

Atlanta angles her body towards me more fully. "About?"

"The ravaged. They're hoarding them. Selnor is keeping them. Dozens of them at least, if not more."

She grips my wrist. "Do you know where?"

I nod and explain how I followed them from Zhoric's chambers, the pathway they covered, and the cavern they were sealed in.

She considers this for a long moment. "Did you tell Ozias?"

I shake my head. "It never came up. We've been so busy trying to find my elahi – which we did. Finally."

"What is it?" she asks

"I can...take energy from others."

"It makes you stronger?"

After my night with Ozias, I know it does something more, too. "And them weaker."

She blows out a breath. "That's good. With an elahi like that and such a strong potential...I guess that means you can bond with him at any time?"

"Ozias seems to think so," I admit. And realization dawns on me as surely as it does on Atlanta. We can end this anytime we like. I can't imagine how surreal that must be for her, who's been trapped here for so long.

Her thumb runs along the heel of her hand, but after a while, her head drops. "He needs to know. About the ravaged hoard."

I nod. Of course he does. Shame whirls in me at having forgotten to mention it to him. I've been so wrapped up in Zhoric, in Ozias's attentions, that it slipped from my mind.

"Can I tell him?" she asks. Her face is so open and raw, that even if I had a reason to deny her, I wouldn't. I've already taken up so much of Ozias's time these days, and it's clear that they care deeply for one another. It reminds me of how I feel with Ninon spending so much time with Issa. Atlanta has been trying to convince Ozias of her theory on the ravaged a long time, and I don't want to take this moment away from her.

"Of course you can," I say, then after a beat, I ask, "Are you angry at me? For keeping this from you?"

Atlanta sighs, pushing her hair back from her shoulders. "I understand where you're coming from, but I could have helped you. You could have been in real danger if Zhoric—"

"Wanted me dead?" I finish for her.

"To put it mildly." She's quiet again. The early morning air is so cool it makes the hair along my body stand on end. "This isn't going to be easy," she murmurs, almost as if she didn't mean to say the words out loud.

"What?"

"The end."

While I contemplate that, Atlanta rises, pats me on the shoulder, and descends the stairs. "Get some rest," she calls over her shoulder.

I sit there long after she's gone, until my body feels numb. Then I stand and go back to perch on the receiving room's terrace to watch the sun rise. The light washes Dyēus in gold, chasing away the blue of the night. I didn't sleep at all. I wonder if Zhoric did.

Laying my forehead down on my bent knees I close my eyes and try not to think of him alone in his rooms, but I can't help but wonder if last night he suffered on his lone balcony again.

When I open my eyes, it's because I feel the heavy weight of a hand on my shoulder. I gasp, raising my head, and find Ozias sitting beside me. A small flicker of disappointment rushes through me, but I push it away.

"Do I snore?" he asks.

"What?"

"You're sleeping here. I wondered if it was because of me."

I blink my bleary eyes and note the sun has tracked higher in the sky. "I'm sorry. I couldn't sleep."

Ozias hums and takes my hand in his. I let my legs stretch on the ground, wincing as my muscles protest.

"We can take things more slowly," he offers.

"No," I say, thinking back on my conversation with Atlanta, remembering the reason why I hid all the things I did. For Ninon. "There's no time to waste. I want to end this thing with Dyēus as soon as we can."

Ozias dips his head to catch my eye. "I meant this thing between us."

My heart flutters. "Oh." I avert my gaze to our entwined hands. "And what is this thing between us?"

"Potential. I hope."

"To bond?"

He inclines his head. I fall silent and close my eyes.

"It's your choice, Kaisa. You don't have to answer our kind's calling. There are other options."

I shake my head. "To go against our nature? I don't think I want to fight that anymore."

Glancing up, I see him offer a small smile.

"Are you afraid?" I ask.

"Of what?"

"Of doing this with someone else?"

Ozias draws in a long breath. "I am. But I know she would want me to go on." He leans in. "I know she would like you."

I smile at that. I let my gaze roam over his face. He's kind and genuine. He's helping my people. He would be a good partner. I can see it, that path that would lead me to him. There are places my heart would never be able to touch his, where it still belongs to her. I think that would be okay. "Slowly, then?"

Ozias brings my hand up to his mouth and places a soft, lingering kiss on the back of it. "As slow as you like."

As I smile, a crack splinters somewhere deep in my chest.

# Chapter Twenty-Seven

"Would you like me to distract you again to-night?" Ozias whispers in my ear as he thumbs away tension in my shoulders. I spent the entire day with Ozias practicing drawing his power into me, and exhaustion has settled deep into my veins.

"I don't think I could stay awake and stop the transformation even if I tried," I admit.

Ozias hums and continues to massage my shoulders as the sun lowers. "You can stay on the balcony and sleep there."

I glance at Dyēus hovering outside the open-air window. Its visage is hazy in the impending dusk after a recent dust storm out in the Sere. Even the thought of trekking all the way down to the enclosures with any haste is outside my capacity. "All right."

Ozias hands slide down my back until they reach my waist, then he slowly spins me towards him until we're chest to chest. We've done a lot of touching throughout the day, and I've needed it. To feel grounded. To feel here. I needed to avoid Zhoric last night, but today, after so much progress with my power, with this tentative possibility of a future with Ozias, I feel ready to face the Sar Dyēus again.

"Are you ready to go back to him?" Ozias asks, his tone threaded with tension, his fingers tight on my hips.

My shoulders heave with a sigh. "As I'll ever be."

"Do not forget your strength. Your elahi." He leans his head close to mine and presses a kiss to my forward. "Get some rest tonight?"

I promise that I will and he leaves just before the sun sinks down below the horizon. I step out onto the terrace as the transformation sweeps over me as sweetly as a cloud drifting by on a clear day. I unfurl my wings in a long, luxurious stretch then fold myself down onto the floor.

With heavy eyes and slow blinks, I attempt to stave off my weariness, but the battle is lost and I feel content as I slip into sleep. Blissful and dark, not a thought or a dream in my mind for a long while.

By the time I'm conscious again, the stars are bright beacons in the ink black sky, marking the deepest part of the night.

"You didn't come."

Zhoric's voice is a quiet timbre in the room. It's dark in here too, but my eyes immediately lock in on him standing at the precipice of the balcony, facing the gods eyes. It's luminous tonight, the light undulating within the oval rings.

I stand where I arrived in the middle of the room, taking him in and burning with the desire to go to him. To lay my forehead against his back and hear his heartbeat in the silence. I want desperately to feel regret for keeping him a secret from Ozias and Atlanta, but it won't come and it makes me feel like crying. "Were you worried?" My voice barely breaks the quiet, but he hears me all the same.

"And if I was?" he asks, twisting his head and shoulder to finally look at me. The moonlight lands perfectly on his face, highlighting every agonizingly beautiful feature, and I hate him for it.

"You shouldn't be," I whisper. Suddenly, my rage is the violent sea during a storm. "You shouldn't be feeling anything for me, for anyone. Not after all you've done."

Zhoric quirks a brow, a flicker of some emotion gleaming in his eye that makes my heart twist unpleasantly. "Making me your villain again?"

"Are you not?" I demand.

"I saved you. So am I?"

"You may have saved me, but you doomed someone else."

"He wouldn't have made it another week. Nothing would have changed."

"Why not put him with the others you have stowed away, then?" I lash, fierce and biting.

Nearly imperceptible, he stiffens. In slow motion, he fully turns to face me. "What did you say?"

His surprise hits me like a punch to the gut. *He doesn't know.* How could he not know? I don't say any more. If he isn't ordering the ravaged to be imprisoned, does that mean Selnor is doing it on his own? Now that I think of it, the conversation I overheard between them indicated Selnor often acts on his own. Something as big as this, though? I have a hard time believing it. My eyes narrow.

"Kaisa," Zhoric warns, stepping towards me.

"Fine. Keep it to yourself," I seethe and spin on my heel, moving away from him. I'm trying hard to be angry and I know it. I think he does too.

I come to a sudden stop as something warm and firm wraps around my wrist. I spin, shock zipping down my spine. His hand. I can feel it, as surely as if it were real. I snap my gaze up to meet his eyes.

"Can you feel that?" I ask, breathless.

His jaw is tense, his eyes burning into me. "I can."

Stunned, I rear back a bit. Still, he doesn't let go. "So when...when I choked you? Did you feel that too?"

He doesn't answer for a long moment, his nostrils flaring as he regards me. "I did."

"You couldn't breathe?" He didn't react at all then to my touch. It would be impossible that he didn't breathe for all that time I clenched his throat in my fists.

Zhoric doesn't let me go. He pulls and I let myself be tugged closer. "I haven't taken a single breath in your presence since I saw you at your selection ceremony."

A rush of angry heat burns my chest at his admission. "You don't deserve to lose your breath over me, and even if you didn't, you wouldn't be fit to share the same air."

Zhoric doesn't look away. He stares longer, deeper, seeing me, and in his eyes I recognize his utter anguish at feeling anything for me. "I know it. And yet, I cannot stop it."

"Why?" I demand, my own anguish reflecting back at him—sharing this feeling. A feeling that isn't fabricated, because the bond can't do that. It can only bring to the surface what already exists. "Why me?"

Finally, Zhoric lets go of my hand, only to step closer into my space. "You think I know? I can tell you that your unique mix of attributes draws me to you. I can tell you that your beauty keeps me ensnared. But it's beyond that. Others have had the same before you and more will after, but there has never been anyone I was certain of the way I am certain of you. It's not a thought or even a feeling. It is the very essence of my heart that speaks to yours, even if you cannot, will not, or wish not to hear it."

I stare into his eyes, realizing how lost I feel. I've discovered this intrinsic part of myself, one that he took away, and my heart wants to give itself over to him. What is wrong with me? How can this be where my heart wants to go?

"When I came to the beach, I thought I'd finally scared

you off for good."

I'm shaking. I don't know when it began, but I can't stop it now. "It did. It scared me."

His smile is sad. The kind resigned to some fact that I don't want to hear. "I was afraid of that."

"Why?" I step closer, and the distance between us is paper thin, ready to rip given the right pressure and angle.

"Because if you're scared, you're feeling what I'm feeling. And I cannot promise to keep your heart safe."

The heart that he speaks of beats wildly and even though I'm not physically here, I feel it as sure as if I were. I try to swallow down the words creeping up my thoat. Try I as might to keep my tongue pressed to the roof of my mouth, a question tumbles out. "Would it be loved?"

His answer comes without hesistation. "Entirely."

My heart flutters and my eyes close. They're hot and ready to shed tears that I desperately don't want him to see.

"Leave, Kaisa," he tells me again, gently this time. I cannot count the number of times he's said this to me. "Don't return. I'll find some way for you to visit with your sister, but you will not bind yourself to me to do so."

I'm already shaking my head in protest. "I—"

"You can," he says, cutting me off. "You did stay away and now you will continue to do so."

I'm losing him and that means I'm losing my chance to bond with him and end this. I've ruined everything. "Zhoric, please—" I start to beg, I don't know what for though.

He holds up his hand and the pressure of his power pushes against me, but I'm too weak to take it from him. Or maybe I can't in this form. Or maybe, I don't have the willpower to resist him any further. "I have work to do."

With the gods eyes looking so bright, I know that's not the work he means, but a moment later, my eyes widen. "The ravaged."

His mouth turns down, eyes so sad and forlorn that I can't make out what he means to do, with me or the infor-

mation I've inadvertently given him.
   "Leave, and never return."
   Then, he pushes me out.

# Chapter Twenty-Eight

I lie on my back in human form, my fists clenching as I stare up at the starry night. I can't stop the flow of tears. I've failed. I have no chance of getting near Zhoric now. No chance of stopping him. And what's worse, I don't know what he's going to do with the ravaged. I have to get up, but my body feels heavy and burdensome.

Inside, my dragon paces. I could let her out if I wanted. She's close to the surface and it would be so simple to unleash her and let her take her place in my skin. Somehow, though, that feels like hiding. If I were to armor myself with her scales and get close to the divinity she represents, all these feelings inside me would dim and change. I would feel restless in a different way and for now...for now I don't want that.

"Kaisa?" Ozias's voice rings across the receiving room

to the landing I'm still laying on. Footsteps hurry to my side.

His firm hands grip my shoulders and pull me up.

My glazed eyes catch in his golden stare. "I'm sorry."

"Sorry? For what?" he asks. I look away and he gives me a gentle shake. "What happened?"

I shut my eyes. "I've ruined everything."

"How?" Ozias implores. I can sense his face close to mine, and when I open my eyes all I see are his, full of concern.

"He told me to stay away. For good this time. It's over."

"No. No, Kaisa." Ozias doesn't let me look away, holding my gaze, holding my face. "You did it. You can bond with him now, no force necessary."

My brows pinch together. "I don't understand."

"He's pushing you away. To protect you. You've done something we didn't even consider possible."

My breathing is shallow. "Oh." It hadn't occurred to me that's why he'd do what he did. But now that I think of it, of course it is. Why am I putting myself in danger and at risk? For the love I have for Ninon. For my people. Why do we do anything in this life if not for that? Of course, there's still a good chance Zhoric is lying. Pretending to love me so that when the time comes, he can enact the bond first. It would be safer for me to believe that.

I swallow the lump in my throat. "It's all well if he... *feels* something for me, but how will I ever get close to him now that he wants me to stay away?" It doesn't matter that our bond is strong and ready to enact if I can't get near him to do anything with it.

Ozias considers this, both of us looking out over the Sere. The dawn is arriving and with it another dust storm rises from the deep Sere. I remember each storm season well, and with it a gnawing hunger. Ninon's mother passed during a storm. The hunger along with our grief brought Ninon and I closer than before. I cannot lose her.

"There will be no more deaths," I say. He turns to me, waiting, expectant. "The storms are coming for the season. Prepare everything you need. I'll master shifting at will and during the day, under the cover of a storm, I'll go to his rooms and wait for him."

"And Thrace and Zhoric's wards?"

"If he wants to protect me like you believe, They'll let me in. Or else I'll pull enough power into me to tear it down." When Ozias doesn't protest, I know he believes it would work.

"You are strong and wise. It's a good idea, but it won't be possible for you in so short a time."

My frown is deep, unpleasant, and I'm about to tell him he doesn't know what I'm capable of when he stops me.

"You won't have to shift at will," Ozias says. "I'll go with you, and you can pull my power to maintain your form. I won't let you put yourself unnecessarily at risk."

"And you shouldn't leave the Realm when it will be most at risk."

"This is my burden as well as yours, Kaisa. I can replicate Thrace's shield. I'll make sure we arrive safely."

I'm shaking my head. "You can't though. Not with me. Not when I'm taking your power. Otherwise you would have done it when we were coming back from the beach."

A flick of hesitation before his expression turns calculating. "Then that's what we'll practice. You holding your form while I maintain the shield. That, at least, we can accomplish."

My features soften on a sigh. I'm so used to being the one caring for others, that to have it given to me so freely is a welcome relief. I shouldn't take it for granted.

"I'll gather our people this afternoon, and we'll officially announce our plan. During the next big storm, we'll have volunteers ready to send to Nevoba to warn them of the coming change and evacuate them from the caves while you and I go to Dyēus."

I nod. "It's so soon and yet so far."

"It's been long enough. It's time this era ended," Ozias says, taking my hands in his. "You'll lead us into a new one, and together, all of us, will find our place in this new world and set it to rights."

Both he and Atlanta have mentioned the end. But I can see it for what it really is. "It's only the beginning."

When Ozias looks at me, full of beautiful, endless hope, I grasp onto it and I don't let go. I won't fail.

After he leaves me, I can't sleep, but I do eat and bathe. I take my time readying myself. Ozias is going to share our grand plan with the people of the Realm. He will tell them they will finally be free to transform and fly over this wide world and let the final piece of ourselves fall into place. We will rejoin the world as conduits between this plane and the next, cleansing and carrying souls to the afterlife to be reborn again. Once I'm ready, I leave my room, clad in a dusk purple skirt, each linen panel swaying easily on the breeze, revealing my tanned legs. My shirt twists up around my neck to secure my breasts, showing the last faded trace of my mark at the bottom of my sternum.

I've transformed into this new creature, and yet I have never felt more myself. As I stare at my reflection in the looking glass, my stomach clenches at the task that lies before me. The betrayal I will perform on Zhoric. He showed me his heart. He told me he'd love mine. And now I will rip his from his chest.

Ozias told me it wouldn't kill him, but he cannot know that. What Zhoric did hadn't ever before been done. Taking the god scale might unravel him. It will certainly expose him to his enemies—the elites who've been lying in wait for the moment his power dims enough to strike. I turn away from myself and swallow hard. Zhoric made his bed long ago. There's nothing that can save him now.

It's early evening by the time I leave my room and I fall

into step with others on their way to the central square. Excitement thrums through the streets directly into my veins. I make my way towards where Ozias stands, with Issa and Ninon off to the side. I don't see Atlanta anywhere. I stand next to Ninon, and with a nod to me, Issa moves over to an older man and woman, and a younger, astonishingly tall man, who looks similar to her, though he has piercing blue eyes and a tanned complexion.

"Her parents and her brother," Ninon whispers.

"Have you met them?"

Ninon's smile is reserved as she gently waves in their direction. "I've been taking my meals with them. They're very kind. Issa's mom reminds me..." Ninon swallows as her words catch in her throat.

I hold her hand and squeeze. She doesn't need to say more.

"Thank you all for joining me here." Ozias's voice thunders across the square. His eyes squint, searching the crowd. "Most of us have gathered, and so I'll not delay any further."

"Not unless you want to scream your announcement to the skies," shouts someone from the crowd, drawing a healthy ration of laughter.

Ozias smirks good-naturedly. "I would rather save my voice for the moment we can all rejoice together."

His words bring a palpable tension to the air, as restless as a bee's beating wings.

"For those of you who have not yet met Kaisa, our newest addition to the Realm, she came to us with a unique ability. For her safety, and all of ours, I will keep the details of her mission a secret for now, but know this; in the next few days, the sky will be yours."

Murmurs rise like the tide, sudden and close, then receding just as quickly as they came as Ozias goes on. "All of you know that breaking our curse does not end our fight. When Dyēus falls, and it will, we will fight. We will scrape and claw our way to victory with all of our combined power, all of our combined strength, all of the love and community and respect we've built together over these many long years to stand as one. We know Dyēus is divided. We will use that against them and we will take back the skies, even if it means shackling them down to the very land they entrapped us."

Eager shouts roar in my ears and I'm swept up in the fervor, wanting what Ozias is calling for all while wondering if this is the only way. But it must be. If there were any other means, Ozias and all those trapped here would have found their escape decades ago.

"I'm requesting an assembly of volunteers who will ride out to Nevoba when the time comes—already our allies among the farmhands and fisherman have disseminated information to those willing to hear the truth. There are many who won't or can't, but in the coming days they will know, just as we all do, who they are really meant to be."

The crowd erupts in celebration. Smiling, joyful faces all around, and I'm smiling along with them, feeling their elation reverberate inside my very being as if we were one. We're so close. The people who have been here since the beginning or those trapped for years will finally know freedom. It's what we've all hoped for.

Among the roar of elation, people start screaming. Among the sea of men and women, sections scramble and hunch, bowing down like a wave. A heavy weight slams into my shoulder and slides down my side.

For a moment I don't understand where it's coming from, because the truth is impossible. My arms react automatically. I catch her. I lower us to the ground. My mind's not comprehending what's happening, but my body knows, my blood freezing in my veins.

Ninon's body lies heavy in my arms, still warm, but the weight of her...I'm familiar with this kind of weight. I know the stillness of a chest that's had its last breath.

I blink hard, rapidly, hoping that each moment my eyes see nothing but dark, the light will return in hers. But it doesn't. She remains as she is, staring up at me, vacant and unblinking. "Ninon?" Her name leaves my lips as a whisper. My ears feel filled with linen, the sound of the crowd a ringing bell from some far off distance.

I stare, my eyes wide. Each blink lets loose a tear that falls upon her cheek. This wasn't supposed to happen. I can't be too late. I gasp and clutch her to me and squeeze my eyes shut. Where I should hear the beat of her heart, there's hollow silence. I heave on the sob I've been holding back, the force of it threatening to choke the life out of me, and I'm tempted to let it. To let this darkness that took Ninon take me too.

A hand comes to Ninon's cheek and I snag their wrist in my grip, stopping them.

"Kaisa." Issa says my name, her voice hoarse, like she's been screaming. I snap my head up, my face split with gritted teeth, somewhere between agony and anger. She's shaking her head, her mouth pulled in a deep frown.

I twist my head around; more people kneel around others. Ozias is shouting, pointing, a panicked rage in his eyes. I hear him call Atlanta's name, over and over.

I pull in my lips, tucking in the scream clawing its way up my throat.

Zhoric. I told him. I told him about the ravaged. He said there was work for him to do. I never imagined he would annihilate them...for what? And now...and now... now I know exactly what I must do.

I look down at Ninon's face one more time. I squeeze Issa's wrist harder; she doesn't so much as flinch. I meet her gaze, but she's unclear, my vision veiled by unshed tears.

Carefully, so carefully, I give Ninon to Issa. Another sob gasps out of me as I pass my trembling hands down the length of her arms and hold her cooling hands in mine. I lean down and press my forehead hers, long and hard, before placing a kiss of equal force upon her head. I breathe in the scent of her, sealing it into my memory.

I'm caving in on myself, heavy and buried under the weight of my growing grief. I don't know how I'm going to muster up the courage I need to leave her. To do what I'm about to do. I lift my head, taking a long time to meet Issa's eyes. In them, I see the love that was blooming for my friend shed like petals down her cheeks.

"When I take the Sar Dyēus's power," I say to Issa, my voice shaking with each word, "and you can leave the Realm, find Haven or Antir. Tell them I sent you. They'll help you."

Understanding dawns on Issa, determination in her expression. She grabs the back of my neck hard and pushes her forehead against mine. "Go bring down that motherfucker."

I nod jerkily. Still, I don't move.

"*Now*, or he'll stop you."

I know who she means.

But I know, too, that I cannot be stopped. Not in this. Not now.

Issa pushes me and I stand. I walk backwards for as long as I can, searing the image of Ninon, dead on the ground in the arms of another, into my mind. People run in front of me, taking my view of her. Issa has curled her body down and around Ninon. Ozias comes her to side and I'm out of time.

I turn and run for the wall.

# Chapter Twenty-Nine

The Sere is blanket of dust as the storm building from earlier rolls through. I'm standing on the precipice of the wall. If I want to make it to Dyēus before the sun sets, I need to shift now. All around me energy flows, a dance of ribbons on the surface of wind. I capture them and take them into myself, as easy as pulling rocks from the sand. Every bit I bring into me, draws my dragon closer to the surface. A force behind me approaches. Ozias.

I take the last bit of energy I need, and jump from the wall.

My transformation takes hold.

My wings catch the wind and then I'm barreling through the storm with no heed to the dust and debris pummeling my scales. I bank around where I last knew Dyēus's troops were, though I know even they will not be out in this mess.

If Ozias followed me, I can't feel his energy signature. I hope he stays away. I hope I can maintain this form.

The moment the thought crosses my mind, my body grows heavier and I plummet a few feet. I beat my wings harder; I draw more energy from the storm into me.

I fly, shrouded in dust, the world before me blurred out. I'm alone, stuck in this void. Inside me, the woman is weeping. It feels fitting for her to be lost in this storm, lost as she is without Ninon. It wouldn't matter to her right now if we never made it out.

But it does matter. *I* matter. And even if she can't see it right now, I won't let the years Ninon lived be for nothing. We will free the others, as I have been freed. It's all I have. The woman in me agrees. She wipes her face, and we fly.

I break out of the storm and the distance I still have to fly to Dyēus is staggering. The mass of lands that make up Dyēus still remain far outside my reach. My resolve flags. My efforts feel more like running through the grassy plains on my own feet instead of racing across them on Aspa's back.

It's too far. It's too far and I'm not prepared. I should have stayed, and I curse my anger. I chance a look over my shoulder. My grip on flight falters, and I drop before catching myself on the wind again, heart racing as I hold onto my form.

I can do this. I can get to Dyēus, and if I can can get close the Sar Dyēus's chambers, he'll let me in. He has to.

A blast of wind catches my side, pushing my body off course. I manage to right myself, only to see a dragon speeding towards me, coming from Dyēus. One I don't recognize.

I dodge to the side at the last moment, like in the game I played with Issa days ago, narrowly missing the dragon catching me in the wing with its teeth. I fly harder and faster towards Dyēus, but the dragon chasing after me twists in the air and is back on my trail. A screech rends the air.

From high above, a white dragon dives into the one pursuing me. They tussle in the sky below, teeth and scales flashing. There's a burst of green-blue energy and the dragon that had been after me stiffens. Its form hovers in the sky, then sinks to the ground, landing in a cloud of dust.

With my attention unfocused, the power in me slips and I drop to the side before righting myself. I'm panting hard, trying to hold onto the power I've collected. It's too much and not enough. I free fall again. I can't hold it and I lose the shift.

A scream tears out of my human throat, my wide eyes lost in the endless sky above, then a blinding moment as I fall down into the depths of the storm. This wasn't how I expected to die. At least it will be swift. There's nothing but air and lightness. The burden of having the weight of my people's truth on my shoulders flies up and away. I tell the wind to let Ninon know I'm coming. That we'll be together. This was truly the end, after all.

Then, much too soon, I'm landing painfully, only to lurch upward again. I open my eyes and find myself not on the ground, but on the back of a pure white dragon.

*Zhoric.*

I close my eyes with relief, and yet a fresh wave of anger swallows me up. I want to scream at him, rage, but none of it will bring Ninon back. None of it would do any good save releasing this churning anguish inside. There will be places to use that once this is through. After all the torment I felt at having to do this to him, Ninon's death is what I needed to see clearly. I'll let him lead me to his downfall, and now, I'll do it gladly.

The buffeting wind alerts me to our impending landing. Slowly, I open my eyes. Zhoric transforms and I'm cradled in the warmth of his arms. He stares down at me, his bare chest rising and falling much more rapidly than I would expect, the slightest tremor coursing through him into me, electric and wild. Still, he says nothing. He simply looks at me like there's nothing else in the world to see. With the gentlest movement, he lowers his arms to let my legs slide down his body to the ground. His other arm doesn't release me. The deep green of his eyes doesn't leave mine. The heat and texture of his skin is nothing like the feel of him while mind walking, but there's a familiarity that feels like home. Like I'm exactly where I'm supposed to be.

My gaze falls to his mouth and I catch the surge of alarm in his eyes. He doesn't push me away though. He doesn't draw me in, either. He stays still, as if at any moment I might vanish.

Outside, the sky is turning a deep blood red. In the corner of my vision, the gods eyes flash bright and forbidding in the rays of the setting sun. Zhoric won't be swayed though. His eyes are only for me. I tip my head back a fraction. Zhoric holds his breath. I rise up on my toes, moving closer and closer to his face. My teeth tingle and I know I have the strength to draw my sharp teeth to my mouth, that my dragon wants to let me do it. I mean to strike, to sink my teeth into his neck, but when I get to it, I push myself the rest of the way up until my mouth collides with his.

Zhoric remains still for the barest second before his breath rushes out of him and his hands scoop behind my head and into my hair to hold me to him. He kiss is fierce and tormented. I can feel how much he wishes he could stop, but he doesn't. And I know in this moment, he would do anything for me.

So I kiss him back like I mean it, and I do. I kiss him for all he could have been, for all he could be, if he hadn't killed Ninon with his decision. I sweep my tongue into his mouth and he groans and pulls me hard to him, like he doesn't want me to escape. And that's when I pull too, taking a thread of his power into me.

Zhoric sways, like he's light headed. His kiss hesitates. I pull again and I know he cannot stop me, because I have exactly what he would need to stop me. His power. *My* power. I take more into me and Zhoric physically rears back, but doesn't make it far.

"Stop." His word ghosts across my mouth and I wish that I could. I desperately wish that I could. But I can't. I take more power into me and his forearms land on my shoulders. He struggles again, but it's in vain. This has to happen. "Kaisa." It's a plea. Fear swarms his features.

His eyes lock with mine. I cannot care.

I drag his power into me again. I take another step until he's flush against me, chest to chest, hip to hip. I raise my chin, mouth opening towards his neck. Realization dawns bright on his face as the last vestiges of daylight illuminate us, setting us aflame. His hands, still in my hair, grip harder at the base of my neck, pulling enough to hold me back but not hurt me. He puts an inch between his skin and my mouth. I take in more of his power, feel my muscles contract as I snake a hand up the back of his neck, drawing him towards me so that my lips skim across the fluttering pulse at his neck.

"Stop," he says again.

It's too late for that now.

My teeth sink into his flesh. His blood wells and coats my teeth, my lips, my tongue. I pull and swallow, and as fast as a strike of lighting, as quickly as I've taken a small part of his essence in me—he's mine. The bond slams into place, fizzing and zipping down my spine. Feeling a bond connect us is like falling into bed after a long, tiresome day. It's pure comfort, the promise of warmth and respite.

Zhoric draws me close as the bond settles, but then he tears his neck from my mouth, blood pouring from the wound, pooling in the crevice of his collarbone, running in rivulets down his chest and splitting over the deep black of the god scale. The deed is done. He still holds me against him, his ribs billowing in and out, every bit of contact between us pure, undiluted energy.

"What have you done?" His voice is an echo in my

ears, the bond a vibration in my soul, his power a thrum through my veins.

Finally his arms slacken, or I've taken so much of his power that they fall to his sides of their own accord. I slowly step back, and trail my hand around to his chest, pressing my palm into the god scale. It's cold, like the sea. Cold, like the feel of lifeless flesh. I dig my fingers into his skin and he grimaces. His hand comes up, leaden, to grasp my wrist. But the attempt is feeble. I'm too full of his power. I peel the god scale from his chest as easy as pulling skin off ripe fruit. Where there was once the shiny black parcel of a god, now there's nothing but faint, pale streaks webbing out like lightning that struck the ground and left a starburst behind in the force of its wake.

I lean close and whisper, "Taking back what's mine."

Zhoric wobbles, his breaths short and fast. His eyes roll back and he collapses into my arms as the sky rumbles and cracks.

# Chapter Thirty

A tremble rocks the world as I ease Zhoric to the ground. There's a static to the air, an energy that feels heavy and oppressive. Peering east, far across the Sere, and above the dispersing mists of the Realm, I see draconem rise. My fingertips slide along the smooth, empty skin of my sternum. My mark is gone.

It's done.

I offer Zhoric one last fleeting glance. My elahi pulled his energy into me. I don't know enough about draconem magic and energy to know if it will stay with me, never to return to him, or if it's something that he's able to regenerate, like a cut limb.

I don't stay to find out. I can't.

Once, not long ago, I imagined taking a dagger to his heart after this moment. But now that I'm here, after I've seen him night after night, after he's offered small pieces of himself that feel as real as any piece Ninon or my sister ever gave to me, I can't bring myself to do it. I can leave him though.

I head into his rooms, intending to find Kalixta, but as I do, there's a twisting, snarling voice inside me demanding I go back. The trembling of the world intensifies so much that what little items Zhoric has around the room rattle. Inside, my draconem roars at me, a knowing instinct thrashing, warning that danger is near and I need to protect what's mine. *No. Not mine.* It doesn't matter what I tell myself, though. I'm ripping myself apart the farther I am from Zhoric. I grit my teeth and squeeze my eyes shut. I can't imagine how Zhoric's bonded was able to hurt him. How was she able to fight against this tearing sensation within herself to do what she did to him?

Booms and cracks split my ears and I drag my feet towards the arched openings on the far side of Zhoric's bed. All around Dyēus, as far as I can see, draconem take to the skies, flitting back and forth, sensing the impending doom as well as I. The sun is a half orb on the horizon behind a heavy haze, casting a red-orange glow on the craggy land below and blanketing the sky above in gold.

The battle between the Realm and Dyēus is inevitable. The women of Nevoba are free to choose their sides. I look down at the god scale in my hand, cold and heavy. Why then, do I feel like I've unleashed another sort of curse upon the world?

My gaze tracks to the place in the sky where the gods eyes are meant to be…and they're gone. Dread sucks the air from my lungs.

With a violent lurch, the world tilts, taking the ground from my feet. I stagger, barely catching my balance. Furniture scrapes and screeches as it slides on the marbled floor. The tea set hits the ground and shatters, piercing the air with its sharp cry. Zhoric's wide bed groans as it slides towards the balcony—towards Zhoric. I move before I have chance to think. I race back across the room, hurtling over the fallen bedside table, and in the next instant, I'm transforming and gripping Zhoric in my talons, vaulting out the balcony window and up into the open sky.

The view of Dyēus is so baffling that at first, I don't realize what I'm seeing. The islands tilt heavily to one side. I stay in place in the sky, but the land drifts down and away. Clarity rocks straight through me, bile collecting in my throat.

Dyēus is falling.

With Zhoric between my talons, my first thought is of Kalixta, her babies. *The nursery.*

I jolt myself out of my stupor and hurl through the air, following the steadily gaining trajectory of Dyēus's downward spiral. I'm dizzied as the land moves in one direction beneath me and I in another. Anything unsecured flutters up and fills the sky with debris, joining the draconem escaping the impending fall. I dodge both as I speed towards the nursery.

I grasp onto one of ledges leading into the nursery with my forelegs, my rear still holding Zhoric. Tucking my wings in tight, I scrabble to get through the window and when I land ungracefully on the other side, there are four dragons already there, turned to me, teeth bared. I recognize Thrace first.

Next to him is another dragon. It's not the identical gray scales to mine or the color of her eyes, or the unfamiliar lavendar silk of her mane that I recognize. I know her on instinct alone. *Kalixta.*

*Kaisa. Help.*

I don't waste another moment. Leaving Zhoric's prone form by the window, I move through the space and scoop as many children into my claws as I can.

*What happened?* Thrace growls, wrestling some of the older tots in his arms, his gaze set on Zhoric.

I don't answer. I can't. I don't know what I've done.

Dyēus lurches again, in time with the sickening crack of a collision somewhere far off. It knocks all of us except Thrace to our bellies.

*We need to go,* he roars.

I take Zhoric in my taloned foot and we all vault out of the window, rising up as Dyēus falls.

I watch the land plummet. It races away, yet it seems as if it's sliding through sand instead of through thin air. Thrace guides us away from Dyēus, moment's away from crashing to the ground, and behind the safety of a wide expanse of rock monuments. As gently as I can, I put the three children I carried down on the ground, their cries washed out as the first of Dyēus's islands smashes to the earth, thundering in my ears.

*Oh gods.* Bile fills my mouth. So many people. So many women who didn't know they could shift. Kalixta did though. And whoever helped us with the babies. Maybe they made it. Maybe—

My gaze locks onto Kalixta's. She looks at me in horror. *What did you do?*

My nostrils release a steam of air. *I freed us.*

Kalixta turns to Thrace, her bonded.

His eyes bore into me.

*Go to Nevoba,* I plead him. *Help them. Please.*

*Where will you go?* Thrace asks.

*Back to the Realm,* I answer.

*With him?* He looks at Zhoric.

*If I go with you, the elites will follow. It's safer if I take him with me.*

Thrace growls. He doesn't like it. Why would he? He's spent years protecting Zhoric and I'm the one who just put him at the greatest risk.

*I've got him,* I promise. I couldn't let harm come to him right now even if I tried. Not until I remove the bond.

Thrace seems to know this, to sense the change in

Zhoric, if not myself. *Then we'll separate. For now.*

I swivel to catch sight of Kalixta. She says nothing, but I know it's because she has too much she wishes to say. I have too much to answer for. *I'll see you again.*

She huffs hot air from her nostrils and bows her head.

Then I surge upwards, Zhoric still in my grip. I tear through the air, but stay low to the ground, under cover of the dust kicked up from Dyēus's fall and from the recent storm. I can't stop the tide of panic at the chaos I've unleashed. *What have I done? What have I done?* I don't notice the draconem until it barrels into my side. I grunt, hitting the ground, spraying more dust into the air. I tuck Zhoric close to my body and launch back into the sky. It's easier now, since I don't have to fight to remain in this form, but I need more energy. If they keep coming for me like this, I need more. And, just as Ozias said, the moment I will it, I feel it happen. I suck energy from the passing storm into me. From the draconem flying too close. From the power of Dyēus's fall. Anywhere and everywhere, I take. I wonder how much more I can fit inside me, but I don't stop.

I'm so consumed with calling energy into me that I miss when another draconem manages to get close enough to sideswipe me. I lose my hold on Zhoric. I roar and twist, my teeth catching a draconem's throat. I jerk my head and rip it out. The draconem's body twists and plummets into the swirling dust below.

Then, like a rope tied around my soul, I feel a tug towards Zhoric and dive for his falling form. I pitch my body at a sharper angle and dart under him, and he lands on my back, cradled in the soft waves of my mane moments before hitting the ground.

I growl as I sense more dragons from Dyēus joining the hunt for me. Or for Zhoric. Perhaps both of us. I could steal their power and take it into me. But I don't want it. I simply want them gone. I release my hold on the power I gathered and stole from the world around me. I let it blow out of me like a raging tempest, and the dragons of Dyēus closest on my tail shoot backwards, tumbling through the sky, tangling with others following our trajectory.

Behind me, the sky is a riot of draconem. A swarm of angry bees against a red backdrop. They know as well as the Realm what's happened and they will fight with all their teeth to take back what I've reclaimed. But they're too far behind to catch me now.

I loosen Zhoric's power from the depths of my well. I feel movement as it leeches out of me back into him. His head lulls side to side, groaning.

The sun hasn't moved any farther down the horizon, like we're stuck in a permanent twilight, and the haze has grown thicker. I tell myself I'm imagining it—that the sun has moved, and everything else that's happened since I bonded with Zhoric and released the god scale took no time at all. It's a pretty lie that covers a brutal reality—something is happening. Something I can't begin to understand, and can only hope someone else does.

Zhoric's moving more now, his body adjusting against my back, maneuvering around until he's fully seated across my neck. His chest lays heavy against the back of my head. His hold on my mane is tight, reminiscent of when he held me back from his neck. My ribcage heaves to catch my breath. So much energy. In and out so quickly. I feel dizzied and drained.

Zhoric leans forward, close to my ear so the roaring wind doesn't take a single word from his lips. "What have you done?" His voice is low, deadly. My stomach churns, unease taking root.

*What I had to.*

His anger, his anguish, rolls off him in waves, drenching me, pulling me down. "Ozias is a gods damned fool to have used you like this."

Again, my insides twist and I'm half afraid I'm going to lose the hold on my shift.

Zhoric is still leaning forward, speaking into my high-pointed ear, though he could have whispered the words from a mile away and I still would have heard. "And because of it, you've doomed us."

My heart stutters and I bank, losing my focus, my gaze going back to the sun that still hasn't moved. *What do you mean?*

Zhoric is silent. The grip he has on my mane tightens.

*Zhoric,* I snarl. *What have I done?* The words are a toll in my head, but I'm sure he hears them ringing in his as surely as my own.

"All those years...I was holding back the gods. And now they'll come to kill us all."

I lose hold of my shift.

Back in my human body, Zhoric and I tangle together. He wraps one arm around my shoulders, the other scooping me up behind the knees. "Hold on," he says into my ear, and then he's shifting, soaring towards the Realm.

Somewhere in the shift, I end up sitting astride his neck in the soft folds of his cloud-wisp mane. My fists grip his mane so tight they ache. I have nothing to say. I know of Zhoric's nightly struggles and it's easy now to imagine that's what he was doing in front of the gods eyes. I saw for myself how it changed each night he tended to it. And somehow, through the bond, or my draconem instincts, I know what he says is true. I can feel it as sure as I can feel my dragon waiting inside me or some ancient connection to the gods stirring to life within me. My jaw clenches, staving off the urge to scream. I keep my focus trained on the horizon, on the sun that has refused to move, letting it burn my eyes. The haze has grown thicker, making the sky look on fire, making the cardinal moon a wide, unseeing eye in the distance. An omen. Or worse.

As we near the Realm, the mists that normally shroud the towering forest kingdom are gone, and the full glory of the Realm is visible, from the tallest-reaching tree of the

Alcazar, to the village that sprawls across the deep brown earth. Surrounded by the dusty Sere, on and on until the mountains beyond. It's impossible, like a mirage on a brutally hot day.

Zhoric glides into the main atrium of the Alcazar, at the same time a painfully familiar dragon slips in from the other direction. Zhoric shifts just before he lands and I'm in his arms again, and Ozias is standing in front of us, hands curled at his sides, waiting.

Zhoric doesn't put me down. I'm not entirely sure I can hold myself up yet.

Ozias's eyes flit between us, before landing firmly on me. "You did it."

My muscles tense and anger rips through me, shaking me from root to tip. Zhoric's hold on me tightens a fraction before loosening and I slip out of his hold. I take a few steps forward until I'm standing between them. I'm at the point of anger where I'm not sure if I'll cry or start stabbing something. Teeth bared, I say, "And just what, exactly, have I done?"

"Freed us all," he answers.

"And the cost, Ozias?" I snarl. "What was the cost?"

"The fall out of Dyēus was worth it." He's calm, in control. My temper, by comparison, makes me feel small and naïve, but I can't contain it. I won't.

"Did you know that would happen?" I ask, whipping my arm back to point to where Dyēus used to hang in the sky.

"I knew it was a possibility."

"There were people there, Ozias. Good people." I say, a sob catching in my words.

"There are good people here and in Nevoba and look at how we were treated all these years," he says, gold eyes blazing. I understand his anger, his frustration. I do. But that doesn't make it right.

"And the gods?" I demand.

Ozias's gaze flicks to Zhoric. "What of them?"

"They are afflicted, Ozias," Zhoric answers. "They are not the same creatures they once were."

Ozias narrows his eyes, disbelief fanning his features, his eyes glancing down to take in the striations on Zhoric's chest where the god scale used to live. "What are they now?"

"Worse than the ravaged," Zhoric answers.

A muscle tics in Ozias's jaw. "What will they do?"

"Unleash themselves upon the earth and devour us all," Zhoric says, calm. Factual.

Ozias's chest heaves with his breath. And then finally, finally, Ozias appears as enraged as I am. He seethes through his teeth, "Why didn't you tell me?"

"There wasn't a reason. Things had changed and there was no going back. No fixing it."

"*You* could have fixed it. You could have given the gods their power back all those years ago and ended this."

Zhoric's eyes flash. "You think I didn't try?"

"Then you could have made the dragons bond! You didn't have to let it come to this."

"It was too late. The gods' vengeance began the moment I took that," he says, pointing to the scale still in my hands.

"You can't blame me for this. I may have orchestrated this scheme to free my people, *our* people," Ozias growls, throwing a hand out toward me, "but exactly whose fault is it that the gods have gotten so vengeful?"

"*Mine*," Zhoric all but shouts, a small crack splintering his voice, making my heart ache. "You think I didn't try? Everything? After my sister?"

"My bonded," Ozias rages.

Shock twists my nerves into a tight knot. Zhoric's sister. Ozias's bonded. They are one in the same.

"I know. I know," Zhoric says, breathing heavily. "The elites were strong. The god's were weakening me. One slip and all that was bad with this world I'd created would become so much worse. So I bore the burden. Alone. And everything was fine."

That's exactly what I used to say, used to feel. *Fine*. But then I wanted more than fine, better than fine, but not like this. Not when it means the end to everything and everyone we love.

"But it wasn't," I say to Zhoric, finding my voice. "We were dying, slowly, painfully. And you," I turn on Ozias, and take a steadying breath, "and I have just thrown us all into the fire." I flick my gaze between the two of them, tension straining my muscles, adrenaline pouring through my veins, making my head swim.

Ozias's breaths are ragged. Zhoric turns his face away, staring out to the burning sky.

"What's done is done," Ozias says. "What can we do to stop it now?"

He's waiting for Zhoric to answer, but my mind races to find the solution. I look down at the god scale in my hand. I close my eyes. I search for my dragon, but she's already there, waiting. She presses her forehead to mine.

Whispers cascade through my mind, sissing like the grasses banking the plains of Nevoba. In my mind I see hazy images, two-faced figures, warring with one another, with themselves. I see them clawing at gates, jaws gaping. A figure, no two, small and meek, stand before them. Swirls of black, smoky mist race out of the two-faced gods and into one of the figures before channeling into the other, cycling again and again. Then a new mist, clear and effervescent, rises from the figures and settles over the two-faced creatures. They fold themselves down and become something new. A hand reaches. The god scale pulses in my grip.

*Oh. I see.*

I open my eyes. Both Ozias and Zhoric have their eyes trained on me.

"My elahi..." I meet their gazes. "I can't just take energy. I am a fathomless well that can hold it." I focus on Zhoric. "I can take all the god's power into me. We can cleanse it. Together."

His nostrils flare. "No."

"It's the only way."

"They will *consume you*," he snarls. A wave of protectiveness surges off of him into me.

I hold his gaze. I will not bow. I will not break. I will not bend.

Then, his face crumbles, defeated. Unbearable sorrow in his expression grates against my soul, his suffering a tangible thing, like the weight of his choices has brought this down on all of us. And though in part that's true, the other truth is that a million other choices followed his, and I know, better than most, that our decisions aren't always what they seem when viewed from the outside. A drifting thought crosses my mind: *If I could steal the sky, I can make the sun move—I will mend the gods.*

The thought vibrates out of me, an energy all its own. My breath rises in my chest, steeling my spine.

"You will take me to the gates of the gods." My words are hard and resolute. Zhoric's eyes narrow, cautious, but he doesn't refuse me. He doesn't push me away, or placate me with soft words or hopeful musings, or warn me against the dangers and the odds we're up against. "Together, we'll end what you started."

# *Acknowledgements*

I've dreamed of writing this portion of my book for ten years, and though the road has been long, it has been filled with support, encouragement, and love. *This* is for all of you.

A heaping dose of gratitude goes out to my editor, Charlotte Hayes-Clemmons, for pointing out the places my vision could shine and kindly flagging all the areas that weren't. Your gentle hand, incredible knowledge, and excitement for my story and characters helped make this book the very best it could be.

To Helena, who read the very first, messiest, all over the place version of Steal The Sky back when it was a baby YA book and still thinking it was worth it, even through all that.

Love and thanks to Fiona who has read a few iterations of several of my manuscripts now; your encouragement and kindness helped me keep going through the tough times.

I might just owe my life to Holly Rose for all that she's helped me, guided me, and been through me with, both with this book and on this indie journey. For the times we bemoaned this route to the ones we've been overjoyed for, I'm glad to have you by my side throughout it all.

For all my panic and worry, my thanks goes out to Olivia for pulling me back from the edge of insanity. A special thanks to Shay for loving Ozias and his slutty little robes in the earlier revisions of this novel and to all my HQties who have been there to support each other, cheer one another on, and for general shenanigans and nonsense (affectionate).

To all the wonderful people I found who made this book into an actual *real* book that can be held, admired, and adored (if only by me); the folks at Illustration Zone, Maria for coordinating and guiding me through the process, Danlin Zhang who illustrated this absolutely gorgeous cover that I still have to pinch myself over every time I look at it, and Jay Vollmar for making it as pretty on the inside as it is on the out. A big thanks to Tomasz Madej for the chapter header and page break illustrations and expertly executing my vision in a 2D format.

To Amy and Mike and all the wonderful staff at Wyrd Bookstore for keeping me caffeinated and hyped. You've truly created a special place for our community to gather and take part in one another around a shared love of books and human connection.

Knowing what true friendship is wouldn't be possible without my core group; Jennifer, Erica, Molly, and Shannon — only one out of the four of you actually even *like* fantasy books, and to have your excitement and love surround me while I pursued my dreams is everything a girl could want out of her bestfriends.

Nothing says feminine power more than having two

fierce sisters by my side, Brittany and Hayley, I always knew how strong women were thanks to you two. To my brothers Jon and Victor, my stepmom Mary, and all my extended family — thank you for believing me and never once making me feel silly for pursuing my dreams. And, most especially, to my dad for showing me the best example of what a good man should be and what unconditional love truly looks like.

To my daughter, Ferrah. I hope that you see the hard work mommy is doing; that I'm doing it for something I love. I wish that one day you can find a path that makes you feel like you never have to work a day in your life. Being an author comes second only to being your mama. I love you with all my heart, all the time.

And most ardently, to my husband, Fran. Not only did you have no reservations, no restrictions, on how I published my novel, you encouraged me to put out the best book I could and that I would be most proud of. Because of that, I didn't take the easy road, but you and I know more than most that the best things in life never are. Thank you for always choosing "yes." I love you.

Lastly, I want to thank you, reader, for taking a chance, picking up this book, going into worlds unknown, and I hope you left here feeling a little braver, a little stronger, and knowing you have more in you than you ever thought possible.

# *About Marina Massino*

As with most authors, Marina has a love of words and stories. She loves capturing human emotions, both the basic and the chaotic, and wrestling them into a fictional, fantastical existence. Marina writes adult fantasy romance that feature mature, feminist women who own their emotions and discover their power within, all the while finding worthy men to love along the way. Marina is PARSEC Ink's 2020 Short Story Contest Winner and was a finalist in F(r)iction's Literary Spring 2020 Flash Fiction Contest.

Marina has a background in marketing and public relations, but she left the 9-5 life for one of chasing around her very active daughter and writing during those precious little moments she's otherwise occupied. When Marina is not writing or dreaming of new worlds, her and her family love to travel and experience living in the great wide world. When they're not carting themselves off to their next destination, Marina and her family live in Annapolis, MD their big, gray tabby-cat Scout who's ungodly howls the moment the lights go out could wake the dead, but never seems to wake their daughter.

*For more on Marina Massino
and her books:*

Find her Online!

Join her Newsletter!

www.marinamassino.com

Goodreads: www.goodreads.com/author/show/53582319.
Marina_Massino

Instagram: www.instagram.com/marinamassinoauthor

Facebook: www.facebook.com/MarinaMassinoAuthor/

TikTok: www.tiktok.com/@marinamassinoauthor